Skies of Ash

ALSO BY RACHEL HOWZELL HALL

Land of Shadows

SKIES OF ASH

Rachel Howzell Hall

A TOM DOHERTY ASSOCIATES BOOK

NEW YORK

SKIES OF ASH

Copyright © 2015 by Rachel Howzell Hall

A Forge Book
Published by Tom Doherty Associates, LLC
175 Fifth Avenue
New York, NY 10010

www.tor-forge.com

Forge® is a registered trademark of Tom Doherty Associates, LLC.

The Library of Congress Cataloging-in-Publication Data is available upon request.

ISBN 978-0-7653-3636-1 (hardcover)
ISBN 978-1-4668-2882-7 (e-book)

Forge books may be purchased for educational, business, or promotional use. For information on bulk purchases, please contact the Macmillan Corporate and Premium Sales Department at 1-800-221-7945, extension 5442, or write to specialmarkets@macmillan.com.

First Edition: May 2015

Printed in the United States of America

0 9 8 7 6 5 4 3 2 1

For Maya, my blue-sky girl

Acknowledgments

Jill, you got me, and hugs and hugs for that. Kristin, you get me and Lou, and much love to you for that. Forge Books and Tom Doherty, you all are amazing, and I'm so happy to be a part of the family. And to Titan, my publishing family across the pond, thanks for bringing this Yankee to the UK! To the best publicists ever, Alexis at Forge and Ella at Titan, thanks so much for introducing me to so many great people and wonderful experiences. You both have helped make dreams come true.

Tyri Williams, thanks for giving me a glimpse into the world of firefighting. And not thinking twice when I asked, "If I wanted to burn down a house, how would I do it?"

Anthony Saunders, we've known each other since forever. Never thought I'd be coming to you with video-game questions when we were in choir together so very long ago. Thanks for the help—and for helping to make kick-ass games in real life. Gaming: it's my getaway drug.

Louvenia Williams Howzell, thanks for all things insurance. I had no clue and you guided me there, and with your help, I created one of my favorite characters!

Mom and Dad, Gretchen, Jason, and Terry, I remain grateful and thankful for all your love and support. I'm also thrilled to share this coolness with you. Cuz it is pretty cool, huh?

David, no words for all you've helped me achieve. I'm crazy and I'm driven, and all too often I never take enough time to enjoy it all. Thanks for forcing me to relax and breathe when I won't do it on my own. I need help now—another trip to Kauai in case you wanted suggestions.

And Maya Grace, thank you for writing Tori's poem. It's magic. And also, thanks for helping to edit with highlighters. You probably shouldn't be reading crime fiction at your age, but you don't know how to twerk and you don't eat a lot of candy and you brush your teeth every night and you pray before every meal, so it's all good. Carry on. I love you so very much, and I can't wait to cowrite one of these stories with you!

I'm all done with hating you. It's all washed out of me. I hate people hard, but I don't hate them very long.

—RAYMOND CHANDLER, *The Lady in the Lake*

Tuesday, December 11

1

I took Greg back the first time because he said he loved me.

I took Greg back the second time because my heart still ring-a-dinged every time he touched me.

I took Greg back the last time because my sister's bones had been discovered after twenty-five years and my heart and head had become tangled messes and I needed him to fix me.

And so, on this Tuesday morning, with my blood racing and my heart pounding, I was ready to take him back in *every* way.

Maybe I shouldn't have pulled out that rubber.

Copper-colored sunlight crawled across our bed as my beloved of eleven years gawked at me. His pecan-colored eyes, the color of that copper sunlight in happy times, now darkened into skies of tornado and flash-flood warnings. He went stiff with my touch (and not the good stiff) and gaped at the silver-foil square between my fingers. "It's been six months, Lou. You *still* don't . . . ?" His voice softened like the rest of him.

I flinched and opened my mouth to say, "Hell no, I don't trust you. You just ended your fling with what's-her-face six months ago, so are you *kidding* me with that question?"

But I didn't say that. Instead, I waggled the condom as playfully as a woman could waggle a condom at her husband. "Yes or no?" Then, I kissed his lips. "Yes?"

His jaw clenched.

So . . . not a yes.

The telephone rang from the nightstand. Caller ID droned, "Rodriguez, Zak Rodriguez." Another man was calling me.

"Lou," Greg barked, "ignore it."

"Can't," I choked. "I'm back on call."

Greg rolled away from me and clenched his body into a tight bronze ball.

I sat up in bed. "We spent all Sunday and yesterday together. No dead bodies. No zombies. Nobody but us for two days. That's a record, right?"

No response from him—which *was* a response.

The phone rang.

And Greg pouted.

And whatever murder my boss had chosen for me kept going unsolved.

I slung the condom toward the bathroom, then grabbed the receiver. "Morning, L.T."

Greg climbed out of bed with his wide shoulders hunched high and his bare ass tight as a clam. He muttered, "Fuck this," then stomped to the bathroom and slammed the door.

"Am I interrupting anything?" Lieutenant Rodriguez cracked.

I tugged at my earlobe. "Same as it ever was."

"So," he said, "there's been a house fire in Baldwin Hills."

"Been a lot of house fires in Baldwin Hills."

"This one has bodies."

"Oh dear."

"Strange circumstances surrounding those bodies," he added. "In the 911 call, a female occupant's heard saying, '*Something, something* kill me.' And then, there's a cough. And then, there's nothin'."

I cocked an eyebrow. "Kill me? You win. Strange circumstances. Hence your call to me on this beautiful Tuesday morning."

"And with all the fires in the neighborhood lately," he said, "and budget cuts, Arson is happy to throw us a bone."

Just moments ago, I'd had a bone in my possession but had gambled it away because of my silly fear of herpes.

As soon as I hung up with my boss, the phone rang again.

Caller ID said, "Taggert, Colin Taggert."

Another man calling.

"So you startin' fires just to see me again?" Colin said.

"Yep. I'm hoping a beam drops on your head. Maybe then I'll get a good partner."

"Brought you coffee," he said, "but you need to bust your ass."

I threw off the comforter and hopped out of bed. "Getting dressed now."

As my partner talked about a woman he had picked up in the coffee shop, I pushed aside the gauzy window curtain and peeked out.

The wet asphalt twinkled with sunlight. The silver collar on the beagle in the yard across the street twinkled with sunlight. The chrome on the neighbor's VW Bug twinkled with sunlight. Everything and its mother twinkled with sunlight except for the crap in my frigid bedroom.

Maybe I shouldn't have pulled out that rubber.

The bathroom door opened.

Greg stepped out wearing black boxer briefs. Even in his midthirties, he still rocked hard abs, that firm ass, and those eyes—how I loved those eyes.

". . . thinks possible murder, with the arson to cover it up," Colin was saying. "You're not talking. Mr. Norton hoverin' and glarin' at me through the phone?"

"Yeah," I said. "See you over there." I tossed the phone on the bed.

Greg, arms crossed, leaned against the dresser. "That Colin?"

I found my nightshirt in the sheets and slipped it over my head.

Greg plucked the rubber from the carpet. "This is crazy, Lou. But I get it. I messed up. Again. And I can't apologize enough for that." He forced himself to meet my eyes. "If it'll make you feel better, I'll go to the doctor and have myself checked out." He dropped the condom on the dresser. "No problem. It's all good."

A kiss, a hug, and ten minutes later I was dressed in heavy work boots, a blue long-sleeved department T-shirt and jeans. And from the closet shelf, I retrieved my Glock from its gun case.

Downstairs, our living room smelled of forest—we had purchased a Christmas tree on Sunday, but the seven-foot noble pine still sat there, naked.

"Maybe we can decorate the tree tonight," I suggested.

"Probably have to work late," Greg said. "You can start, though."

I froze—*who decorates a tree alone?*—then grabbed my bag from the couch.

On the way to the garage, we walked past his home office, a grotto filled with video-game boxes piled atop art books perched against tubs of markers, pencils, and empty Gatorade bottles. I noticed on his drawing table a charcoal sketch of a busty, brown-skinned female with long, windswept hair, a badge on her giant left boob, and a big-ass cannon on her ultracurvy hip.

"Look familiar?" Greg asked, standing behind me. "Pretty good, huh?"

My skin flushed—I was staring at me, reimagined and hypersexualized for teenage boys and their gamer dads. The complexity of Lou had been rendered to boobs, hair, and gun. "New character?" I asked as my inner June Jordan wept.

He gave me a lopsided smile. "Maybe."

This drawing of Sexy Cop would soon join drawings of Sexy She-Elf and Sexy Marine on our walls. *Yay?*

My favorite LAPD unmarked Crown Vic, a light blue beauty that reeked of sweat, Drakkar Noir cologne, and dill pickles, awaited my arrival. It was parked next to Greg's red and black motorbike and my silver Porsche Cayenne SUV, the automotive equivalent of a decathlon-competing supermodel who built rockets in her spare time.

Greg hit the switch on the wall and the garage door rumbled up and away.

The sky was bright blue and the sun was as high and white as a crank head in San Bernardino. Little clouds puffed from my mouth as my skin tightened. No breeze wafted from the west—no salty, decaying smells from the Ballona Wetlands at the end of our block or from the Pacific Ocean just a mile away.

"What are you doing today?" I asked, watching him amble to the driveway. My mind ran that query again to ensure that it didn't sound as suspicious as I had meant.

He grabbed the newspaper from the pavement. "A stand-up at ten to see where we are on *Last Days* and then over to the mall for surveillance."

Even though he was now vice president of creative development for M80 Games, Greg still enjoyed watching customers play the titles he had designed. He had spent a month in Tokyo working on the art for his new "zombies meet the Book of Revelation" series. Between meetings, he had also worked on a purse designer named Michiko Yurikami. Greg was a master multitasker, an unfortunate result of my soft-gloved management style.

For this last transgression, I had won a "baby, I'm sorry, maybe I have an addiction" diamond-platinum cross pendant. Even though I'm not religious enough to buy or wear a cross. I wore it, though, and ignored the frothy anger in my stomach, just like I drove the "please, baby, please" Porsche with whitened knuckles.

"This you?" Greg held out his phone to show the *Times*'s Web site and its picture of a two-story, Spanish-style house engulfed in flames. The headline screamed, FIERY BLAZE IN THE HILLS.

I startled seeing that house on fire, knowing that someone had died in one of its rooms. "Think so." I stopped reading—I needed to see the mess firsthand to make my own calls.

"How does Rodriguez know this is a homicide and not an accident?" Greg asked. "People die in house fires all the time."

I shrugged. "There was this strange 911 call. Guess I'll soon find out."

He slipped his arms around my waist. This time, he melted against me, and we kissed slowly . . . deeply . . . "And you will solve the case," he said. "A winner is you."

"Totally."

"Your ass looks great in those jeans."

"Not intentional."

"Never is. Where's your jacket? It's cold out here."

"In the car," I said, certain he didn't want me covered up cuz of the *weather*, not *really*.

After one last kiss, I slipped behind the Crown Vic's steering wheel. After a whinny and a cough, the giant Ford rattled to life.

Greg smiled and waved at me as I backed the beast out of the garage. Strange (but not infrequent) rigidity filled me again.

Because of his smile . . .

What was he hiding?

2

The chatter and bursts of static from the Crown Vic's police radio pulled me from lingering unease about Greg's smile, and I loosened my grip on the steering wheel.

". . . requires additional units . . ."

". . . still in the house, one may be a Hispanic male . . ."

". . . 4893 Crenshaw . . . Stand by . . . Shots fired . . ."

All of this as the city sipped its first cup of coffee.

I raced toward the sun, toward Baldwin Hills, a neighborhood just three miles east of mine. Stark columns of black-and-white smoke hung over upper-middle-class homes, waiting for me to see them before they smeared like paint and pencil across the sky. I passed La Brea Avenue, where I should've turned right but didn't. I kept east and passed the McDonald's, the ghetto Ralphs supermarket, and the KFC that always forgot to put in your biscuits. I glanced to my right at the perimeters of the Jungle, my childhood home.

Moldy, cramped apartments surrounded by prison-yard wire. *Check.*

Red spray-painted tags of BPS JUNGLES and BFL dripping like blood on walls. *Check.*

Plaster and glass and telephone poles shot to shit by bullets and poverty. Stumbling crackheads. Gangbanging drug dealers. Storefront payday check-advance scams. *Still too early for that, but "check" in advance.*

I worked this part of Los Angeles and visited here more than my own home. Twenty-five years ago, a man named Max Crase had murdered my big sister, Victoria, at a liquor store right down that street. Crase had later helped build fancy condominiums on that street over there. Six months ago, he murdered another seventeen-year-old girl as well as her sister, a case—my case—that still haunted me. And as I passed Crase Parc and Promenade (*Units Still Available!*), I lifted my middle finger and then controlled the urge to ram the car into the condo's terra-cotta lobby. *Later, Lou. Not today.*

Memorial tour complete, I busted a U-turn and headed back to La Brea. As I sped up the hill, gray powder swirled and flecked on my windshield. Los Angeles's version of snow. The snowstorm intensified, and the smell of smoke and melted plastic wafted through the air vents. I hated the smell of toxic chemicals and burned dining room tables in the morning. Smelled like . . . job security. Unfortunately.

Fires kicked our asses. First of all, murder is hard to nearly impossible to prove. And then, most times, homicide detectives reached the scene hours after the fire's start. By then, witnesses had wandered back home. Crucial evidence had been destroyed by flame, water, and heroes wearing galoshes. And the victims—they rarely survived swelling and blistering so severe and complete that no one, not even their mothers, recognized them, and so the coroner had to study porcelain uppers to call them officially by name.

My Motorola radio blipped from the passenger seat. "What's taking you so long?" Colin asked.

"Dude. I can't fly there."

"It's a tragedy, Lou. Guess there were some kids in the house."

My fingers went cold. "I hate this case already."

"You need to get here, though."

"The fire all the way out?"

"No. Still some hot spots here and there."

"Those bodies getting more dead?"

"C'mon, Lou—"

"Stop wringing your hands, Taggert," I snapped. "I'll be there, all right?"

Last year this time, Colin had been working homicide in a Colorado Springs suburb. But he had shared the D with a chick who was *not* his fiancée. The fiancée's dad, who was also the city's police chief, took Colin's betrayal of his daughter personally, forcing the young detective immediately to serve and protect a city with no bounty on his head.

On my best days, Colin merely annoyed me—like the constant beeping of a truck backing up. To be fair, I didn't know many (okay, *any*) twenty-eight-year-old, white-boy detectives from the Rocky Mountains. And he didn't know any thirty-seven-year-old black female detectives from Los Angeles. So there was a cultural rift between my partner and me. A rift that was three galaxies wide.

Before I pulled onto the street that would shoot me up to the fire site, I parked near an elementary school closed for winter break. I grabbed my iPhone from my bag and held my breath as I tapped the Bust-a-Cheat icon.

Should I

1. Turn on Greg's cell-phone mic and use it as a bug to listen to his conversations?
2. Use the GPS tracking system to pinpoint the whereabouts of his phone and him?
3. Or, simply check the phone's RECENT CALLS log?

But then what would I do if a Japanese country code—Tokyo's was 011 + 81 + 3—showed up in RECENT CALLS?

I bought Bust-a-Cheat two weeks after I had forgiven him.

I bought Bust-a-Cheat because he had never let his iPhone out of his sight.

"You bought Bust-a-Cheat cuz you know you's a *sucka*." That's what my girl Lena had blurted on my deck, where we had been guzzling tall glasses of absinthe and cranberry juice. "And if you gotta do this," she had continued, "gotta buy spyware—which, by the way, why didn't they have that when Chauncey was diddlin' homeboy in the back of my Range Rover—then you don't trust him, and *à quoi bon?*"

Six months later, here I sat. Not trusting him.

I tapped RECENT CALLS.

The phone's screen blinked, blanked, then filled.

NO CALLS ON 12/11.

"Thank you, Lord," I whispered, sounding small, sounding like a woman not packing a semiautomatic in her bra and a .22 Magnum Pug mini-revolver in her ponytail.

Personal drama handled, my heart found its regular pace, and I shoved the phone back into my bag. I muttered another "thank you," then jammed up the hill, following a dank river of water and ashes that would end in blood.

3

Don Mateo Drive resembled a neighborhood in a Norman Rockwell painting. A baby grand piano sparkled in the living room window of an army-green bungalow. The Cape Cod's hedges had been shaped into snow-men, squirrels, and rabbits. Christmas lights glowed on the eaves of the ranch-style, and fire-hose water shimmered on its roof. Sludge gathered at the base of every window frame at every house.

Except for 6381 Don Mateo Drive, the former Spanish-style house I'd glimpsed on the *Times*'s Web site. There was no sludge on those windows. Barely any windows. Hell, there was barely any house.

Crews from every local news station had set up at the sawhorses. And as I rolled past, reporters shouted, "Detective, detective!" One brave soul knocked on my passenger-side window. A flash from a camera blinded me. I bared my teeth and growled, "Back the hell off."

I grabbed the Motorola from the passenger seat and toggled the switch. "I'm here," I told Colin. "Have one of the guys move the press back some more."

"Crazy, right?" Colin asked.

Just glimpsing the destruction, the *angriness* of this fire made me shiver. "I don't like it here."

"Hell, Lou, you don't like a whole lotta things. But on this: yeah, I don't like it, either."

A patrol cop lifted the yellow tape, and I drove through, parking near a Frank Sinatra–style house, all weird, cool angles and *bop-bop-bum*. I wrapped my Windbreaker around my hip and clipped my silver badge to my belt loop, then grabbed the small digital camera from the glove compart-ment. I climbed out of the car and took pictures of a smoking, charred heap now boasting crime-scene tape and broken ceramic roof tiles. Every house, except this house, had its trio of trash cans—blue, green, black—sitting out at the curb. I snapped pictures of that, and then I photographed the crowd: a bald black man holding a toddler, an elderly Asian couple wearing matching jogging suits, a dark-skinned weight lifter with headphones around his thick neck, and the heroines of *Waiting to Exhale* wearing yoga pants and fruit-colored tank tops.

Did one of you do this?

The *tchick-tchick-tchick* of lawn sprinklers and *terp-terp-terp* of birds had been drowned out by the growl of fire trucks and the roar of chain saws cutting holes in walls.

A sky of poison loomed over the neighborhood—we shouldn't have been breathing this crap or walking through muddy ashes flecked with half-melted police tape, warped household plastics, and shards of charred wood, some pieces slick with paint and varnish. Even with no visible flame, the ground still burned beneath the thick soles of my boots.

Colin, coffee cup in hand, and the fire marshal, Denton Quigley, who clutched a walkie-talkie, stood in the house's driveway next to an ash-covered Mercedes Benz SUV and a garage door now hacked to pieces. Sweat had darkened and flattened Colin's blond hair. Ashes had landed on his LAPD Windbreaker. But his brown cowboy boots looked right at home. In that strange morning sun, my partner looked golden, bizarrely handsome, Steve McQueen in *The Towering Inferno*.

Dixie Shipman, her nougat-colored skin also sweaty and ashy, stood on the lawn with a digital camera and a jumbo tape measure.

"Hunh," I muttered. "She's already here?"

In her former life, Dixie had worked the LAPD's Arson Squad, but two years ago she had been caught in a big, fat lie. Which is why she now wore a blue and white Windbreaker with the logo of MG Standard Insurance on the sleeve.

Her ex-coworkers, men in black jackets, ARSON in white letters on their backs, were also taking pictures.

I trudged toward the wreck, its death scent assaulting my nostrils.

Colin met me halfway with the coffee cup extended.

I took the drink and glanced at his crisp blue jeans. The creases were as sharp as thousand-year-old cheddar. "You just take the dry cleaner's plastic off?" I asked.

He held up a leg. "Can you tell?"

"Not at all."

"Bodies are still in the house," he said, "and the firefighters need to get some debris out of the way so we can see 'em. They're thinkin' we can go in, in about an hour."

I checked my watch—that would take us to eleven.

"So the next-door neighbor," Colin said, "an old lady named Virginia Oliver." He pivoted and pointed at the house with the animal-shaped hedges. "She lives right there. She called it in around three-forty this mornin'. Mrs. Oliver says she started *not* to call cuz the smoke detectors in that house were always goin' off. Seemed like the Chatmans—"

"That the family name?" I asked.

He nodded. "The son was always settin' shit on fire. So the old lady thought nothin' of it 'til she *heard* the fire. She said, and I quote, 'Sounded like God was frying bacon.' According to *another* neighbor, Eli Moss"—he pointed to the green bungalow with the baby grand piano—"a patrol unit got here before the fire trucks. I'm guessin' because of the 'kill me' part of Mrs. Chatman's 911 call."

"You talk to the R/O?"

Colin nodded. "His name is Bridges. He says when he got here, the fire was mostly in the center of the house, second story. He tried to get in, but that"—he pointed to the wrought-iron security door propped against the house's side—"kept him out. The fire trucks got here a few minutes later. The neighbor says that once the trucks got here, it took them some time to find the hydrant, which is at the end of the block and too far for the one-hundred-foot hose."

I shook my head. "Ticktock."

"Almost an hour into the fire—that would be close to five o'clock—the man of the house, Christopher Chatman, pulled up in his car." He pointed to the dark blue Jaguar sedan now covered in LA snow and abandoned near a sawhorse.

I frowned. "It's five in the morning and Christopher Chatman ain't home?"

Colin smirked. "Yep."

"Why the wonky hours? He a doctor or an astronaut or something?"

"He's a commodities broker. Don't know what the hell *that* is, but there you go. Anyway, he pulls up, runs to the house, makes it a few feet away from the front porch, where he's tackled by a few of the heroes. Seems he was tryin' to save his wife and kids. Her name is Juliet and the kids are Chloe and Cody."

"Are all three dead?"

"Yeah."

Lieutenant Rodriguez had warned me that there would be blood, but I still wanted to make him a liar.

"And where the hell was Mr. Chatman?" I asked.

Colin peered at me. "Pissed already?"

"No time like the present. Where was he?"

"At work."

I jammed my lips together and said nothing. A chill ran up my back, split at my collarbone, and numbed my neck and scalp. "And where is Mr. Chatman now?"

"At the hospital," Colin said. "Concussion, minor burns, scratches, and shock."

I forced out a breath and said, "Okay." Then, I strolled over to the Jag and pulled a small flashlight from my jacket pocket. I aimed its beam at the Jag's thick tires, the chrome, and its tan interior.

"What are you lookin' for?" Colin asked.

"*That.*" A dark drop of dried liquid on the back of the driver's seat. "And *that.*" Another drop, this one on the driver's-side passenger door.

Colin checked out the cabin. "Looks old. Could be ketchup."

"Does this car look like it sees a lot of Happy Meals, ketchup squirts, and milk shake spills? Cuz other than these two strange drops of dried, reddish shit, there ain't a crumb, a crumpled straw paper, not one crushed piece of nothing in this car."

Colin stared at the drops. "Warrant?"

"Yep. And is that Benz SUV her car?"

"I'm guessin'."

We walked to the truck. I clicked on the flashlight again and took a look inside.

"Definitely a mom car," I said.

Scattered about the cabin: an open bag of gummy worms, phone charger, broken pencil, lip balm, school bulletin, paperback novel, and an empty McDonald's cup.

The back windows were tinted, but I still hit them with light. "Interesting. When you call Luke, tell him to get a warrant for the Benzo, too."

Colin peered inside. "I see . . . one, two, three suitcases. What's crazy about that?"

"Suitcases combined with that 911 call of 'something, something kill me.' What if they were trying to escape? We need to figure out what happened yesterday when they were packing these suitcases. Before shit got real. What's in this truck may help us figure out what happened in that house."

"Got it." Colin brought the radio to his mouth and called Luke Gomez back at the station.

I turned away from him and watched big men in yellow field jackets remove a charred . . . *thing* out onto the porch. My shoulders drooped as I gazed at the Chatman house, as I held my breath, as the cold that came with death pinched my heart.

4

Five minutes after eleven o'clock, Colin and I moved up the walkway, glass and wood crunching beneath our shoes. Every third step, I stopped and sniffed the heavy air: smelled burned wood, as well as the fabrics and synthetics that filled every home. But there was something else, too. Something toxic and harsh.

Colin sniffed. "Turpentine, maybe?"

On the porch, past banks of drifting white smoke, I saw a used-to-be couch left next to an end table and footstool. The house's decorative security door sat against the fence. But as we moved into the house's foyer, that smell continued to hold my attention. And just like the scent of the dead, this odor would cling to me long after I had left this house and showered.

The spongy, sopping-wet carpet bubbled with each step or gave way to the crack of broken glass. Books, plates, and cushions had been knocked down and trampled, then marred with black boot prints or scorch marks.

A firefighter with bloodshot eyes and brilliant white teeth handed me a disposable respirator that would cover half of my face. "To keep you alive a little longer," he said, handing Colin his own mask.

"LAPD's finest is finally here." The fire marshal, Denton Quigley, had lumbered straight out of central casting and into this damp foyer. Ashes flecked his ruddy Irish skin and chocolate handlebar mustache. "How's it goin', Detective Norton?" He towered over me with a clipboard in one hand and the radio handset in the other.

"Depends on what you're about to tell me, Quig."

"So the fire started up there, on the second level." Quigley pointed above us, to where parts of the ceiling had been pulled down.

I followed his finger to see blue sky and the exposed second story.

"You'll have to climb up a ladder to see the heaviest damage and the three vics," Quigley was saying. "A boy, in a smaller bedroom. And then the mom and daughter in the master suite. Wanna see them before we talk?"

"Please." I glanced one last time at the blackened rafters, at the flaking and peeling plaster, at the pool of water glistening on the dining room table.

"Hold up," Quigley shouted to the heavens.

The banging and sawing stopped. Eerie silence swept through the house.

Joined by the squad's videographer, a thick white woman named Sue, we ignored the burned, frosted-looking staircase and climbed up the silver ladder. We reached the hallway, and five careful steps brought us to the master bedroom.

My heart punched against my chest—there they were. The bodies of a woman and a school-aged girl, huddled in the corner farthest from the door. Their brown skin was blistered, and their noses and mouths were crusted black from breathing poison. The woman wore a sweatshirt and leggings, and the girl wore a nightgown.

In the woman's left hand, she clutched a pink rosary, its cross lost somewhere in her daughter's hair. And in the right hand . . . silver barrel, black grip.

The video camera whirred—Sue was zooming in.

Colin stooped and said, "Smith and Wesson .22."

Guns—I knew guns. Fire was Tasmania to me. But guns and the people who used them? Just another day in Southern California.

Colin snapped pictures of the rosary and the revolver. "Why was she packin'?"

"*Something, something* kill me," I said. "Don't forget that." Eyes still on the gun, I asked, "You see a phone? The one she used to call 911?"

Colin regarded the room. "I don't see shit. Everything's wet and Cajun-style."

The woman's fingernails didn't appear splintered or ripped—no indication that she was trying to escape the fire by clawing her way out. Nor were there defensive wounds on her palms or wrists to suggest a struggle.

"On our next trip up," I told Colin, "after the ME takes custody, we'll tag and bag the gun, and hopefully we'll find the phone."

The bedroom walls were shades of gray and brown. The pictures and mirrors that had remained on the wall were blackened, but the wall behind them had remained white.

To reach the second bedroom, we tiptoed past charred paint cans, twisted nails, and heaps of splintered, charred wood. Here, the walls were almost completely black with soot. The thick bedroom door and heavy plaster had shielded the room from open flames, but it had not been enough protection.

The adolescent boy in bed wore a Lakers jersey and shorts. His skin had also blistered, and there was soot around his nostrils and lips, though not as much as his mother's and sister's. He clutched a melted Nintendo Gameboy to his chest.

We took video, still pictures, and measurements of our three victims, of the darkened bedroom walls, of burned posters, of wood window frames where varnish had bubbled and hardened. We took more measurements, stared out broken windows, stared at the dead. For several minutes, we studied what had been a bathroom just a day ago and gaped at the surviving porcelain bathtub now clogged with water, wood, and ashes. Crisped, black paint cans lay around the small room. The faceplate around the bathroom's electrical outlet had blackened completely. Colin and Sue captured that image more than any others.

Then, down the ladder we climbed. As we joined Quigley at the base of the porch, the growls of chain saws and the hacks of axes resumed.

My hands trembled as I pulled off the mask.

"One of your guys was telling me," Colin shouted, "that the house went up pretty quick. Why's that?"

"Cuz most of it was made of *wood*," Quigley snarked.

Colin cocked his head. "But houses just don't . . . *combust*, even if they're wood, right? And your guy used that word. *Combust.* Houses don't do that normally. Right?"

"No, they don't normally *combust*."

"So the cause?" Colin asked.

"Don't know. Looks like that outlet in the upstairs bath has the heaviest char pattern."

"Has the power company been out?" I asked.

"Yep," he said. "Them and the gas company."

"So no natural gas?" I asked.

"Nope."

"Electrical?"

"Possibly. There's that bathroom outlet to consider."

"Deliberately set?" Colin asked.

Quigley frowned. "You mean arson?"

Colin smirked. "That's what a fire's called when it's deliberately set."

"Anything's a possibility," Quigley said. "It's possible that a meteor came hurtling out of space and crashed into the Chatman's attic, thus starting the conflagration."

"A meteor," I said. "That would be one for the ages." I waited for his smile, but Quigley's grimace only hardened. Onward, then. I sniffed the air.

There it was again: sharp, chemical, brief.

"Hey, Quig," I said, "would I be smelling whatever it is I'm smelling if the house had caught because of faulty wiring or kerosene?"

Quigley waggled his mustache. "I would say yes if the structure had been a paint store. Cuz that's what you smell." He dropped his chin to his chest. "It appears that the Chatmans were redecoratin' and . . . none of this is official yet, understand? So the Chatmans were painting that upstairs bathroom, and for whatever reason the socket in there shorted. There were paint cans and thinners and drop cloths on the ground—"

"And the spark from the outlet hit the thinner and rags," I said.

"Then, ka-*boom*," Colin added.

"Is 'ka-boom' my guy's word or yours?" Quigley asked. "Anyway, the hallway goes up cuz thinner's everywhere. And it burned like it did cuz the whole neighborhood was asleep." He sighed. "We warn folks all the time about properly storing paint cans and rags."

Colin dumped Tic Tacs into his mouth, then said, "When I was a kid, the lightbulb in my pet iguana's tank caught fire." He chewed and chewed, then chuckled. "I thought my mother had set the fire. She hated Iggy."

Quigley and I waited for Colin to finish his stroll down memory lane.

But the faraway look in Colin's eyes meant that he was now lingering in its gift shop.

"We're starting at the least-damaged area," Quigley said, "which is right where we're standing, to the most damaged. And that's the bathroom."

"So if this is arson," I said, "who should I look for?"

"Nowadays?" He shrugged. "Anybody. The boy was an aspiring firebug, but this . . . This ain't the work of a kid. And in this neighborhood, you won't find your typical suspect: white male, midteens to thirty, undereducated, troubled, angry at the world."

I scribbled into my notepad. "A white male. What the hell would *he* be angry about?"

Colin glanced at the exposed rafters. "How about a black woman gettin' to carry a gun and a badge? What kind of world allows *that* shit?"

I stuck my tongue out at him.

"This fire ain't like the other ones Burning Man's been setting around here," Quigley noted. "Those fires occurred outdoors, with leaves piled next to the side of the house and kerosene used as an accelerant. This one, the MO is different. *This* fire started inside, not with leaves, not with kerosene, I don't think."

"So you don't think this is a serial pyro?" I asked.

"Nope."

"Anything missing inside the house that shouldn't be?" I asked. "Photo albums, wall safes, jewelry? Stuff folks wanna save before they burn down their house?"

"Can't say right now."

"Any signs of forced entry?" I asked. "Someone leave a window open or open the doors for ventilation to help the fire spread?"

"Nope, but we did find PVC pipe in the window sliders. Guess to keep out intruders."

I cocked my head. "You'd have to pluck out the pipes to open the windows, right?"

As Quigley started to respond, two blue and white medical examiner's vans eased past the yellow tape. They would ferry the three bodies to the coroner's office near downtown.

My stomach twisted as we watched the vans maneuver past trucks and police cars and roll closer to the house.

"We lookin' at a total loss?" I asked.

"Except for the converted garage," Quigley said. "That'll only need minor repairs."

"So," I said to Colin, "we need—"

"Yep." He reached into his Windbreaker and pulled out a folded sheet of paper. "Already got the warrant to search the house."

Dixie Shipman joined our little group. "If I was a betting man—"

"You *are* a betting man," Quigley quipped.

"Which is why Winston is divorcing you," I added.

"If I was a betting man," Dixie said, not missing a beat, "I'd say the butler did it in the library with a candlestick." Then, she laughed. *Huh-huh-huh.*

Quigley rolled his eyes, then tapped my shoulder. "I'll get you something more official first thing tomorrow morning." Off he went, radio to mouth, eyes on the worrisome piece of drywall sagging near the living room.

After introducing Colin to Dixie, I flicked a gaze at her jacket. "Fleece. Very official. Very *la-di-da*."

She sighed. "Here we go."

"You can always come back to the force," I said. "A mea culpa, a sword in your gut, and it's all good."

"I don't miss the force's bullshit," Dixie said. "And I *like* having a personal life."

"Stop frontin', Dix," I joked. "It won't become true even if you say it a million times."

She glared at me, then said, "Did you hear back about your interview with HSS?"

My face burned, and I forced myself to smile. "Touché, Dixie Shipman."

Homicide Special Section, a part of the famed Robbery-Homicide Division of the LAPD, handled high-profile murders like the O. J. Simpson case. I wanted a spot that had become available after a squad dick's retirement, and I had applied with Lieutenant Rodriguez's very reluctant blessing.

"They told me I was *this close* to being selected." I pinched my finger and thumb together. "But see: Southwest needs good detectives like me in the division, and Rodriguez really didn't want me to go. But I was *this close*, Dix," I said, pinching my fingers together again.

A smile crept to the edges of Dixie's lips. "It ain't horseshoes, boo. You lost." She pulled from her bag an expandable folder already thick with papers and photographs. "So Christopher Chatman's parents, Henry and Ava, purchased this place back in the fifties for ninety thousand dollars. Twenty years later, they bought their first hundred-thousand-dollar policy from MG Standard. About thirteen years ago, Christopher Chatman and his wife moved in.

"In 2009, the house was burglarized while the Chatmans were out. Homie stole five computers, three cameras, and the Blu-ray disc player. We paid the fifty-thousand-dollar claim. Then, last year, the Chatmans raised their policy from four hundred thousand to five hundred and fifty thousand. Since then, they've been remodeling, and up until early this morning, the house had five bedrooms, two full baths, a half bath, formal dining room, home office, den, laundry, and the studio apartment out back."

"So why are you here?" I asked the ex-cop.

"'MG Standard: we live to improve life.' And I'm here cuz my ass was on call." Her gaze wandered to a black Jaguar sedan pulling into the driveway of the weird-shrubbed house.

A man with skin the color of French-roasted coffee climbed from behind the Jag's steering wheel. He wore a blue pinstripe suit and a steel-blue dress shirt, no tie. A silver watch flashed from beneath the shirt's left cuff.

"Who's Oscar de la Renta?" I asked.

"Girl, that's Ben Oliver," she said, gaze trained on the man now striding up the house's walkway. "Ummmhmmm."

"Stop purring, Dix," I said, even though the same feline rumbling vibrated in my belly.

"You gon' have your work cut out for you. Mr. Oliver is a big-time insurance attorney. We been on opposite sides of the table many times. He's the one who called us on behalf of Mr. Chatman, and he's also Chatman's best friend."

Ben Oliver glanced over to Dixie and me as though we were crushed pylons. Then, his eyes shifted to his friend's house. A frown flashed across his face—the same pissy-sexy look Abercrombie & Fitch had been hustling since the eighties.

"He's an asshole," Dixie said, "but he's a fine-assed asshole. He got that pimp juice, Lou. Watch ya back and your panties." And then she laughed. *Huh-huh-huh.*

5

Even as the noonday sun worked across a sky crowded with soft, killer clouds of smoke, no one rushed through the on-site investigation. And no one rushed through the slow extraction of three bodies.

The press hunkered at the yellow tape as LAPD spokeswoman Val Xiomara offered our official statement—*three fatalities, no suspect, no comment, a tragedy.* Print reporters, their heads down, scribbled furiously onto pads or tapped words into tablets. The talking bobbleheads with don't-get-too-close-to-an-open-flame hair held mics to their plumped lips and flicked sound bites to viewers at home like birdseed.

Early this morning, firefighters were called . . .

. . . pronounced dead at the scene . . .

. . . investigate the origins of the blaze . . .

Silence came to Don Mateo Drive as one blue body bag, followed by another and then another, was gurney-rolled to the coroner's vans by men in LACCO Windbreakers.

My muscles tightened as I watched that somber recessional.

Cameras clicked. Neighbors gasped and sobbed into their hands. A woman in the crowd whispered a prayer for the dead. "May their souls and the souls of all the faithful departed . . ."

And then the vans drove away.

The smoke continued to drift to unsuspecting galaxies, but the fire's lingering heat still baked away my juicy motivation. Gangsta heat had parched my throat, already scratchy from nibbling ashes all morning. Cinders, dried drops of sweat, and observations from arson experts peppered the pages of my notepad. Now, though, I needed to talk with the other experts: the folks who saw the Chatmans every day.

At the army-green bungalow across the street, the one with the piano in the window, a slender, brown-haired white lady sat on the porch. She was the type of woman you ignored until it was time for her to do your taxes. Women like that made for great observers.

She told me her name was Delia Moss and that she'd seen Juliet and the kids on Monday. "It's unbelievable," she said, blowing her nose into a tissue. "They're gone. They're really gone. And what are we supposed to do now?"

"Well," I said, "you can answer a few questions that I have."

"'The bad end unhappily, the good unluckily. That is what tragedy means.'" She clutched her neck. "I didn't write that. Tom Stoppard did and it's rather fitting in this situation, yes?"

"Yes." I blinked, then asked, "How was the family yesterday? Anything happen out of the ordinary? Any strange visits or strange people hanging around?"

"I hate that house," Delia Moss said—she hadn't heard a word I'd just asked. "You all must knock it down—that house does not deserve to remain standing. Not after it trapped Jules and the babies. That house must go. You all must put it out of its misery. Haunted piece of shit."

"About the Chatman family," I said. "Who—?"

"They were a wonderful family," she said. "A truly special group of people. Their inner light affected everyone they met. Their auras were . . . indescribable."

"They sound perfect," I said, eyebrow cocked.

"I wouldn't want to live if my family were gone. Really: How could I go on after losing *three* loved ones? How many pills would I have to take to dull that kind of pain? What would I do once my friends returned to their own lives? Would I survive the After? Would I eat the end of a gun? What would I do?" She looked up at me with waiting, cried-out eyes.

"What do you do for a living, Ms. Moss?" I asked.

"I'm a playwright."

I gave Delia Moss my card and turned to leave. "I'll call you once the shock wears off."

"The cops in the uniforms," she called after me. "They told me to pay attention. To report anyone who looks suspicious, who doesn't fit in. But what does that *mean*, Detective Norton? It's Los *Angeles*. And we live between the ghetto, Hollywood, and the airport. Everyone and no one looks suspicious in this city. Suspicious? What does that mean? It means nothing." And with that, Delia Moss rose from the steps and stumbled into her house.

And the curtain dropped.

End scene.

A middle-aged black woman wearing a silver-sequined sweater and an all-the-way-down-to-there hair weave as glossy as Delia Moss's baby grand lingered near my Crown Vic. Her eyes bit into me like a hungry hound dog nibbling an uncooked Christmas ham. I would let her have a few bites—but she'd be sick of me before the week ended.

"Jules *loved, loved, loved* her Barbra Streisand roses," Nora Galbreath told me, near tears. The air around her was ten degrees warmer—the sequins from her sweater reflected sunlight.

Galbreath lived in the Frank Sinatra bebop house on the other side of the Chatmans. Her home had suffered singed eaves, a broken kitchen window, a trashed side yard, and destroyed security cameras.

"Jules balked when Chloe asked to plant sunflowers beside those roses," she whispered.

My pen had stopped working. No one used "balked" in everyday conversation. Even a dollar-store Bic knew that.

"Jules told Chloe 'no, no, no,'" Galbreath continued, "the sunflowers won't match.'" She dabbed her eyes with tissue. "She promised Chloe that she could plant seeds in the backyard at springtime. But no sunflowers in the spring. No roses in the spring. Just awful, awful, awful."

I looked back at the damage done to the Chatmans' rose beds by fire crews, investigators, and utility guys. Those Streisand roses, especially the bushes that lined the walkway, had been shaken apart, and the mauve petals crushed into ashes and mud.

I scribbled invisible loops on my pad to coax the pen back to life. "I'm told that Mr. Chatman wasn't home when the fire started."

"He wasn't," Nora Galbreath said. "Neither were my husband and I."

"Do you know where he was? Mr. Chatman, I mean."

"I'm told he was at work. My husband, Micah, and I—that's M-I-C-A-H—we were staying at a lovely bed and breakfast over in Playa del Rey. Oh, it was lovely, lovely, lovely. We were celebrating since I had sold three condos—"

"Thanks for your time, Mrs. Galbreath." I handed her my card. "I'll contact you—"

"You don't want to know about the guy?" she asked. "I was just about to tell you about the guy. I've seen him around the neighborhood a few times.

The last time was two days ago, early, when I was walking to the park. Black, midtwenties maybe. Suspicious. He carried a black backpack, and he kept staring at me like *I* didn't belong. *He's* the one who didn't belong."

A suspicious guy? My pen ejaculated all over my hand and the notepad.

"And he was wearing an orange hockey jersey." She handed me a tissue to clean up. "Isn't that suspicious? A black man in a hockey jersey?"

"Maybe," I said. "Would you be able to identify him again?"

She nodded eagerly. "He really looked like he was up to something."

I took down a more specific description of the Guy in the Orange Hockey Jersey: five foot ten, muscular, brown eyes, dreadlocks, neck tat, and another tat of a dragon on his left calf. Dreads could be cut. And that dragon tat could also be removed, but that would leave a helluva scar.

"Wait, wait, wait," Nora Galbreath said. "Before I forget." She opened her hand and selected a slick business card from the small stack. SELLING A HOME? TOP-RATED REALTOR NORA GALBREATH CAN HELP. Beneath the text was a picture of Nora Galbreath, her arms folded, wearing a red-sequined sweater.

I thanked the real estate agent, then wandered over to the brick two-story house, where an impossibly round black woman had climbed out of a red Camry. She carried a giant purse in one hand and a Bible the size of an unabridged dictionary in the other. The car's back bumper was decorated with two Jesus fish and three MY CHILD IS ON THE HONOR ROLL bumper stickers.

Ruby Emmett had lived in this neighborhood for almost twenty years, and she, too, had seen the Guy in the Orange Hockey Jersey. "I was plannin' on callin' the police if I saw him again. Wish I had."

"He could be just a guy," I said. "Don't beat yourself up about it."

Ruby Emmett shook her head. "Can't think that way no more cuz look what happened. I'm never one to question God but . . . Why *this* family? Why *this* house?"

But why *not* this family? Why *not* this house? Bad shit had to happen to *someone*—the "good" someones, too. Children as well. Even the Bible said so.

"I just came from the hospital," she said, hoisting the giant purse onto her sloped shoulder. "That Christopher: he's such a brave man. I told him: the Lord give *strength* to His people; the Lord blesses His people with peace."

"And how is he doing?"

"How you *think* he doin'?" she growled. "He almost killed himself tryna save his family. He was comin' home from work and he saw the fire and tried to run in, but the firemen tackled him. Banged up his head. Nearly broke his arm."

I pointed to the bumper stickers. "You have kids. How are they?"

"Devastated," she said. "They gon' be all right cuz they know: they can do all things through Christ, who strengthens them."

"Still," I said, "it must be so sad and scary for them."

"They grew up over at Uncle Christopher's and Auntie Juliet's. They swam in the pool. Played Ping-Pong in the backyard. They went to all of Chloe and Cody's birthdays and"—she squeezed shut her eyes, took a few deep breaths, then whispered—"Thank you, Jesus. Be with me, Lord."

"Would you mind if I talked to your kids?"

"Why you need to talk to *them*?" she asked, eyes narrowed at the snake in the garden.

"Maybe they heard the Chatmans talking about troubles they were having. Or maybe Cody confided—"

"He ain't set *this* fire," Ruby said, with a shake of her head.

"*This* fire?" I asked. "What do you mean? What other fires did he set?"

Ruby licked her upper lip. "Well, there was the Fourth of July—that was just boys bein' boys. There was firecrackers and leaves in a trash can. And you know, just little . . ." She swallowed. "He just . . . He ain't start *this* fire." Her eyes darted between me and the Chatman house.

"He may not have." I assured her. "He probably didn't. But I need to know that for sure. *You* want to know that for sure."

She closed her eyes again, and her lips worked in silent prayer.

As I waited for her to finish, the noise in my head competed with the noise of demolition.

She dabbed at her wet eyes. "I got some oil on Christopher before the nurse kicked me out of his room. I wanted to stay a little longer, though, and hold him up in prayer. Let him know that he ain't alone. But the Lord will renew his strength. We gon' get through this. *Together.*"

She glanced back over her shoulder to the smoldering heap that had been a family's home just a day ago. "Ain't nothin' ever gonna be the same for any of us again. Lord help us all."

6

No such thing as easy for the the murder police, especially in Los Angeles. So many beaten, stabbed, and shot-up bodies in this city. Even with three hundred homicides last year, a pretty low rate for a city as big as many sovereign nations, that's still three hundred bodies, three hundred families, three hundred accordion file folders with cases that had the potential of going unsolved. Unsolved not because we were inept Keystone Kops. But unsolved partly due to barriers around this town. One hundred—that's how many languages the Department of Motor Vehicles accommodated every year. And those people—the ones whose native tongues included clicks or whose cultures required women silently to accept violence, as well as those homegrown U.S. citizens whose creed was "Fuck the Police from Sea to Shining Sea," well . . .

No such thing as easy for the the murder police.

The Chatman investigation would not be simple—even though I had in hand enough search warrants to gift wrap every item at Walmart.

"No lie: this will be hard," I warned my team, now assembled near the porch of the house. "It's already the hardest scene I've ever processed. Still: we got to do this right." I tried to take a deep breath but failed—felt like village women were doing a grape stomp on my lungs. "Look for any trace evidence like fingerprints and palm prints, especially in those upstairs bedrooms. Look for blood, ripped fingernails, bullet casings, knives, *anything* that will help us figure out what happened to these folks." I nodded at Arturo Zucca, the lead criminalist and one of the smartest men in the world.

"Be extra-careful," Zucca said. "Since everything's wet and mushy, we'll be taking longer than usual. You see something that looks organic, give a holler and get the hell out of the way."

Detective Luke Gomez, stout and beer-bellied, asked, "We're taking normal things, too, right? Important-looking papers, receipts, mail—"

"Photographs, computers?" his partner, Peter "Pepe" Kim, asked as he pushed back hair freed from a Dippity-Do stranglehold.

"Yep," I said. "Be incredibly thorough. With the water damage, mold's a-comin', so we won't have many chances to boomerang. Oh. Look out for a set of car keys and a cell phone. Another 'by the way': a few neighbors saw a suspicious black male wearing an orange hockey jersey hanging around." I rambled off the guy's physical description. "If you see him, detain him, then grab me or Taggert."

With that, we all donned masks and gloves, then stepped into the foyer. Pepe climbed up the ladder to the second level. Luke and the two dicks from Arson headed to the garage. And Colin and I stayed on the first floor.

"Geez." My partner stood beside me with his eyes cast upon those exposed wet rafters.

"Stop worrying," I said, even though worry tightened my arms and legs.

He rubbed his jaw, then sighed. "Just got a feelin' that we won't get much outta here."

"I know. Everything will be soaking wet or charred to a crisp, but we can't *not* look."

He cocked his head, an almost-admission that I was right.

I rolled my eyes. "What now?"

"Say that Chatman burned his house down." He had said each word carefully, testing it to ensure that it would not make me explode. "It's his personal property—he has the right to burn it down. Maybe he thought the house was empty, that the wife had taken the kids to Disneyland, but he didn't know that she'd changed her mind cuz she had cramps or somethin'."

"Cuz ladies always be havin' cramps."

He blushed. "C'mon, Lou."

"It's a . . ." I stopped, then started again. "It *was* a beautiful house. Why burn it down?"

"Folks do strange shit."

"If people died in the course of his, what, artistic statement about, I don't know, the superficiality and the worthlessness of the American dream, his ass is still grass, my friend."

"A lesser charge."

"His ass is grass."

"So sayeth you?"

"So sayeth the California felony murder rule," I said. "Don't know how it is back in Colorado, but here in California, dead is dead, accident or not."

"I wonder if Juliet and the kids were dead before it went up. And I wonder why she was holdin' that gun. Or if any of that matters."

I crept through the debris and toward the dining room. "To a defense attorney? Hell yeah, it all matters. You can't kill somebody who's already dead. As for the gun . . . We'll find out if she fired it, if there's any blood from . . . We'll figure it out."

"Can't kill the dead," Colin said with a sigh. "And how did they get dead?"

"Taggert, please." I stood at the dark-wooded, country-style dining room table. There was a long bench on one side and heavy slatted chairs on the other. To the table's left, out through the full-length patio doors, was the flagstone backyard. "Right now, I can't answer that question, if they were dead or alive. Right now, I need to find stuff, all right?" I pointed to my left without looking. "You start over there."

Colin didn't respond, but his boots crunched to "over there."

The Chatmans' wedding portrait sat on the dining room table, the faces of Juliet and Christopher burned away. There were also soot-covered school pictures of a chubby girl—Chloe—with milk-chocolate skin and sandy eyes and of a boy—Cody—older, less chocolate and more nougat, just as chubby, with doe-big brown eyes. A third picture had also survived: Chloe and Cody standing with Shamu at Sea World. *Cheese* for her. *This is wack* for him.

A few steps brought me into a stainless-steel, white-marble kitchen. The cream paint now looked gray. Smoke wisped the high ceilings. Soot covered the mangoes sitting in a bowl on the center of the island.

A Bubba Gump Shrimp Co. refrigerator magnet clung to the fridge door. Beneath it: a soccer picture of Chloe wearing six ponytails and a pink and black soccer uniform.

"The Cotton Candies," I whispered, reading the magnet. "Fall 2013 AYSO."

Four dinner plates, three pots, and silverware had been left in the dishwasher. Three clean milk shake glasses and a roasting pan sat in the drying rack. There was an empty wine bottle—a Syrah from Santa Barbara—in the otherwise empty waste can.

Dinner last night?

At the breakfast bar, a girl's wet peace-sign fleece jacket hung off the back of a tall chair.

A book of damp paint chips sat on the bar. Yellow sticky notes flagged olive, tan, and brown.

I wandered down the soggy hallway to a home office.

The fire had ignored this room. The giant cherrywood desk did not look any different on this day than it probably had on Sunday. Two flat-screen computer monitors had not toppled over, nor had the VLG company mug been knocked to the ground. The view out the window showed parked fire trucks and my Crown Vic.

I took pictures and measurements of the entire room, pictures of the computer, the desk, and inside the desk drawers. My eyes returned to that view of Don Mateo Drive.

What had Christopher Chatman been thinking about last week this time? What to buy the wife and kids for Christmas? Charitable contributions to make before the year's end? Or . . . ?

"*Something, something* kill me," I said.

What did Juliet mean by that?

The roar of blood rushed through my ears as my mind imagined hearing the panic in Juliet Chatman's voice. It would sound no different than the panicked voices of other women I'd heard pleading for help, begging for mercy, begging for life. That icy finger, the one that had dragged down my spine when I had first arrived, now returned. And with friends.

I pawed through the seven desk drawers and found pens, notepads, a stapler, highlighters, and business cards, including Christopher's.

CHRISTOPHER CHATMAN, M.B.A., VANDERVELDE, LANSING & GRAY, LLP, THOUSAND OAKS, CALIFORNIA.

I took a few of those cards. And I also plucked from the middle drawer a prospectus created for Peggy Tanner. Chatman's name had been the only broker listed on the account. And then, I got greedy—I took the desktop computer, a banker's box found in the closet, a digital camera, miscellaneous papers in the in-box tray, and thumb drives.

After my shopping spree in the den, I toured more fire-damaged rooms in the lower level of the house. My eyes picked through the jumble of things, including broken, expensive-looking vases that had been filled with the discarded orchids and long twigs of faded blooms. My mind worked the three-second rule shrinks used with hoarders.

Sterling silver angel?

Don't need.

A soiled pink ballet slipper. An oboe case. A metronome.

No. No. Don't need.

A signed first edition of *Slaughterhouse Five.*

Wow, but don't need.

I saw everything. And nothing.

"So it goes," I whispered.

I saw a slashed Diego Rivera lithograph, a pair of crystal candleholders, a clay imprint of a child's hand . . .

That hand. So small. So innocent. *For Mommy. I love you. Chloe,* scratched into its back.

"Shit." Panic swirled in my stomach and nausea washed over me. I muttered, "Shit," again and closed my eyes.

A hand touched the small of my back.

"You okay, partner?" Colin was peering at me.

The softness in his tone sounded foreign to me, and if I hadn't been looking at him, I wouldn't have known that the hand on my back had been his.

Colin had aged since arriving on scene: his blond hair had grayed from all the dust, and dirt had lodged in his skin, already weathered from long days skiing on the slopes of the sunlit Rockies.

I inhaled through the mask and slowly let out a breath.

"I grabbed Chatman's keys to open the Jag and the SUV and . . . You okay?"

"Mmhmm."

He squeezed my shoulder and waited.

"I'm good," I croaked.

"Pepe found a cell phone—it had been upstairs hidden beneath the vics in the master suite. We also found a laptop in there—pretty damaged, but maybe we can still get somethin' off of it. Zucca hit those droplets on the Jag's leather with ninhydrin, and they glowed like you thought they would."

"Wonderful," I said. "I'm gonna pull you in a minute so we can chat up some more of the neighbors."

He gave me another shoulder squeeze. "Call me when you're ready."

I stood there, alone in the living room crammed with Dead People's Stuff. No. Not alone. Three ghosts brushed across the back of my neck and pleaded with me in cold, quiet voices to make it right.

7

Colin and I reunited, looking more like chimney sweeps than homicide detectives. At my car, we splashed water on our hands and faces, then dried ourselves with towels that came away as black as midnight in a Louisiana bayou.

After guzzling two bottles of Gatorade, then inhaling a flattened Snickers bar found in the Crown Vic's boot, and after feeling my heart rate slow and my breathing deepen, I turned to Colin. "Ready, guv'nuh?"

Colin chomped the last third of a stale granola bar. "Ready, pidge." He sighed, then pushed up the sleeves of his T-shirt—even the Cracker Jack tattoo on his forearm was slick with sweat.

We hurried past creepy squirrel shrubs and hopped onto the muddy porch of 6385 Don Mateo Drive.

If I hadn't witnessed firsthand Ben Oliver disappearing behind that closed door five hours ago, I would have thought that no one was home. But someone *was* home—his Jag was still parked in the driveway.

I knocked and waited, rang the doorbell and waited some more.

The insurance attorney answered. He was six foot four with lovely chocolate skin, a thin mustache and goatee, *damn damn damn* just . . . everywhere.

Okay, so his hotness made my nerves go boom! and my stomach shimmy. But I didn't throw parades for hotness alone—Los Angeles abounded with gorgeous men, oranges, avocados, and smog.

"Yes?" Ben Oliver asked in a smooth baritone.

Colin introduced himself first.

Then, I introduced myself, flashing my badge just in case my staggering beauty caused the man to disbelieve that, yes, I was a cop.

"We're here to talk to you about the fire," Colin announced.

"*Now?*" Ben Oliver asked, his bloodshot eyes wide, as though Colin had just requested we all go skinny-dipping in a Siberian lake on Christmas Eve.

"You're an insurance attorney," I said, with no room for rebuttal.

Ben Oliver considered me for a moment, then said, "And that seems outré to you?"

"A representative from MG Standard Insurance is here," I pointed out. "Did *you* suggest that Mr. Chatman file an immediate claim? Or did he call them from the hospital's room phone? I'm just trying to figure out the timeline of when best to talk to you about this, especially since the insurance company is already here, which, to me, is outré."

He squinted at me, then stepped back and opened the door wider.

The house smelled of cinnamon, bacon fat, and Vicks VapoRub. In a room somewhere, a television blared and an actress raved about the wonders of Downy fabric softener. Framed pictures hung along the foyer walls. Praying Jesus in the garden of Gethsemane. Hopeful Jesus looking up to heaven. Pensive Dr. Martin Luther King, Jr., staring into space.

"After we talk with you," I said to the attorney, "we plan to head over to the hospital."

"A feckless endeavor," he said. "I just called—Christopher is suffering from a concussion, but they finally let him sleep."

I cocked my head. "I expect that he'll wake?"

"Of course he'll wake."

"Then . . . ?" I shrugged and offered a quizzical, *What's the problem?* smile.

An old black woman in a pair of pink-and-white-checkered Vans shuffled from the living room into the foyer. Her snowy, coarse hair had been pulled into a ponytail. Both pockets of her green housecoat had been stuffed with remote controls. She was my type of granny. She peered at me over the tops of her pearly-pink spectacles. "Who you?"

"Mother," Ben Oliver said, "this is Detective Taggert and Detective Norton. I assume they're handling the investigation. Detectives, this is my grandmother, Virginia Oliver."

The old woman kept her gaze on me. "I already talked to the white boy right there. Tol' him how I heard the fire and called the police." She hurled a look at Colin. "Ain't you remember that?" Before Colin could answer, she turned back to me. "So what *you* want?"

I cleared my throat, tasting peanuts, caramel, and cinders. "We need to further understand the circumstances surrounding the fire, ma'am. And then determine how the . . . *deaths* occurred."

She glanced at her grandson. "Benji, ain't they say it was an accident?"

He shrugged. "I guess the city doesn't mind wasting money on piscine expeditions."

I chuckled. "This is far from a fishing trip, sir."

"Y'all gotta talk to me right *now?*" the old woman asked. "To you, it's three o'clock. To *me*, might as well be midnight."

"May I stop by tomorrow then?" I asked.

She gave Colin the up-and-down. "Boy, don't go trackin' no mud round here with them boots you got on." To her grandson, she said, "Put 'em in the parlor." Then, she pivoted on her sneakered heel and scuffed down the hallway.

Ben Oliver glanced at his watch à la Arthur Fiedler conducting the Boston Pops, all swooping arms and cocked chin. "Detectives, I have a meeting at four o'clock, so you have three minutes." Then, he strode down the hallway, three fingers held up as visual confirmation.

Colin and I rolled our eyes and followed in the maestro's wake.

Sure: in its heyday, this room *would* have been called a parlor. But the glory had faded from this place the moment Nixon had skulked out of the White House and boarded Marine One. There were magenta-taffeta-covered walls and lamps with dusty ruffled shades and shedding tassels. A yellowed songbook sat in the music stand of a spinet piano. The silk flowers in the vases had died. There was more life in King Tut's tomb than Virginia Oliver's parlor.

The attorney flopped onto the purple plastic-covered sofa.

Colin hunkered on the matching plastic-covered armchair across from him.

With no other seating option available, I perched next to Ben Oliver on the couch. "How is Mr. Chatman?" I asked.

"He doesn't know the full extent of what's happened," Ben said as he rubbed his chest. That hand thumped to his side, and he gave a heavy sigh. "And, in a way, that's preferable. He needs to regain his strength. What he's about to endure . . . It won't be easy." His eyebrows gathered and his hand returned to his chest.

"How long have you known Mr. Chatman?" Colin asked.

"All my life. We were born and raised in this neighborhood. Me in this house, him next door. We both attended UCLA as undergraduates. Then, UCLA Law for me and Anderson for an M.B.A. for him."

"I went to UCLA Law," I said.

"Oh?"

"Class of 2000."

"And now you're police."

"I wanted to *save* lives, and lawyers . . . are people, too."

He smiled and rubbed the top of his lip.

"So you and Mr. Chatman are something like best friends, then?" Colin asked.

"The bestest."

"And what firm are you with?" Colin asked.

"Kensington, Scott, and Merrill in Century City."

"And Mr. Chatman," I said. "What now is his métier?"

Ben Oliver cocked an eyebrow with my correct usage of the ten-dollar word. "He's a commodities broker."

"Nice living," Colin said, still uncertain what the hell that was.

Ben Oliver leaned forward. "He's more than a money man, though. He's an *honorable* man. And my heart aches for him. Juliet was a marvelous woman, and the kids . . . Chloe . . . This—the fire, the deaths, talking to police . . . This is just . . . *surreal.*"

"When did you hear about the fire?" I asked.

"Early this morning," he said. "I was on my way home from the airport when my grandmother called and . . ." He jammed his lips together, and his body tightened. He dropped his head and covered his face with his hand. His shoulders shuddered for several seconds. Then, he went still and his breathing slowed. "I apologize," he said.

Head still down, he pulled a handkerchief from his pants pocket and dried his face. He exhaled, then straightened in his seat. "My grandmother called," he said, looking at me, "and at first, I didn't understand what she was saying—she kept screaming, 'They're gone, they're gone!'"

"Do you live nearby?" Colin asked.

"I'm about three miles away," he said, that baritone not so smooth now. "In Westchester."

"Some neighbors mentioned seeing a strange man around," I said. "Black guy, midtwenties, wearing an orange hockey jersey, carrying a backpack. You see him?"

Ben Oliver pinched the bridge of his nose. "Haven't seen anyone fitting that description. But I'm only here for a few hours a week to check on my grandmother."

"Are you aware of the recent arsons in the neighborhood?" Colin asked.

The attorney nodded. "I'm very aware. I'm representing one of the families whose home was torched two weeks ago. Their insurance company, no surprise, is haranguing and deceiving them." He cocked his head, then held out his hand. "Wait a minute. This hockey jersey—did he set—?"

"We don't know anything yet," I said, shaking my head. "Who this man is, who did the arsons, if this case is even related. That's why we're here: to gather as much information as possible."

Ben Oliver pounded a fist against his thigh. "I'm just trying . . . I'm trying to hold it together." He squeezed shut his eyes, then opened them again. "To make sense out of the nonsensical."

"When was the last time you saw the Chatmans?" Colin asked.

He stared at the coffee table as he thought. "Took my daughter Amelia and Chloe to get frozen yogurt on Sunday. I saw Juliet on Monday morning. And I had lunch with Christopher back on Wednesday? Maybe Thursday?"

"How old were the Chatman kids?" Colin asked, writing in his pad.

"Cody was turning thirteen in March, and Chloe . . ." He bit his lip, inhaled, then slowly exhaled. "Nine in July."

"Were Juliet and Christopher fine before the fire?" I asked.

He shook his head. "I don't know where to even begin answering such an open-ended question. I only know what Christopher tells me."

"Okay," I said. "Let me back up. Tell me about your relationship with him."

"Well"—he waved his hand, dismissing what he was about to say—"we compete. More him than me. But that's what men do, right?" He asked this of Colin, who also had a penis.

"Especially lawyers and bankers," I said. "That's a lot of ego in one area code."

He threw me a glare but couldn't refute my observation. "When I bought my wife—"

"You're married?" I asked, just noticing the gold wedding band on his ring finger.

He smirked. "Disappointed?"

"No," I said, unblinking. "We may need to talk to your wife. And what does she do for a living?"

"She's now home with our daughter," he said. "But in a previous life, she also practiced law."

"Insurance?" I asked.

"Mergers and acquisitions."

I nodded. "You were saying about competition . . . ?"

Ben Oliver offered a slow smile. "When I bought *my wife* a new SUV, Christopher—"

"You always call him Christopher?" Colin asked. "Not Chris?"

"He doesn't like his name shortened," Ben said. "Anyway, my wife, Sarah, always asks, Why can't you be more like him? And I always ask her, Do you want me to work twenty-hour days and consume Maalox by the gallon?" He chuckled. "Her answer is always yes."

"She sounds . . . delightful," I said. "So Mr. Chatman works all the time is what you're telling me."

"Which is why he wasn't home when the fire started." Ben tugged at his right ear. "He has to keep unconventional hours. That's just the business, especially in this economy. He has to be aware of everything all the time. Too many typhoons in Indonesia and a drought in Nebraska affects the prices of rice and wheat, which then affects his clients, which ultimately affects his firm's bottom line. But he enjoys trading, and, more than that, he loves providing for his family.

"But I know he despises himself right now. Because he had been working late when . . ." His nostrils flared, and he tapped his fist against his thigh again.

I waited for him to gain control of his emotions, then asked, "Is Mr. Chatman the jealous type? Is he possessive? Quick to anger?"

Ben Oliver gawked at me. "*Christopher?* Absolutely not. He's *far* from possessive. He worships Jules, and he dotes on the children. Gives them everything they need and deserve." He covered his mouth with his hand, then whispered, "Past tense."

"Excuse me?" Colin said. "I didn't hear . . ."

A sad smile overtook the attorney's face, and his eyes brightened with tears. "I'm talking about Juliet and the kids as though they're still . . . here. I don't know what Christopher will do—he has no one now. I don't know what *I'd* do. No. I *do* know—I wouldn't want to live. And I can't see Christopher wanting to live, either. Juliet and the children were his world, and I hate to say this, but I wouldn't be surprised if I found my best friend . . . if I found him dead."

8

Ben Oliver apologized for ending our interview and suggested that next time we make an appointment. "I don't want to be a jerk about it," he said, rushing down the walkway to his car and *totally* being a jerk about it, "but my days are labyrinthine. Next time, call my secretary, Dawn—she'll set up an appropriate time."

"Actually," I shouted after him, "you'll need to come down to the station to give an official statement."

"Certainly. Soon. Promise." Then, he slipped behind the Jag's steering wheel, started that V-8 engine, and roared down Don Mateo Drive like Mario Andretti.

One last brake-light blink from the Jag's ass, and *poof!* Gone.

No cars, trucks, or busses jammed Sepulveda and Wilshire boulevards. A small miracle. It took only forty-five minutes to drive from Baldwin Hills to UCLA Hospital. By then, dark clouds the color of dingy socks and second-day bruises had rolled in from the west. Would it rain or were those just Hollywood clouds? Nice fronts with nothing behind them.

Beneath those stormy skies, the college town looked deserted, as though the rain had already beaten down the city and washed away its people.

No crowds meant better parking, though. And better parking meant less walking. And zippity-do-da, I pulled into a parking space only seventy-six miles away from the hospital.

Colin, driving his own car, did not share my luck and found a spot two rows farther back.

"Preordered your hubby's new game yesterday," Colin said as we marched toward the entrance. "Zombies and big guns and Bible stuff? Sounds kick-ass."

"Good for you. He'll love to hear that," I said, checking my phone for any voice mail left by said husband.

"Ha ha," Colin said with a smirk. "Hashtag Sarcastic Lou."

"That was so sincere, it hurt," I said. "Gregory Norton loves the love and the attention. One fan, a million fans, doesn't matter. As long as he's being adored, he's happy. He's a puppy in that way."

No voice mail messages from the puppy.

I called the puppy's two phone numbers. He didn't answer either, so I left a message on his cell's voice mail. "Hey, still working. Just calling to check in. Talk to you later." Frowning, I disconnected and ignored Colin's, *You okay? What did he do now?* gaze. I tossed my partner a strained smile. *It's all good. Carry on.*

Patients and their families and all of the Westside filled the lobby, occupied every chair, and took up every empty space available. And everyone coughed or sneezed or oozed liquids the colors of infection and/or imminent death.

"I can *feel* the Ebola," Colin said as his eyes darted from the snotty-nosed toddler to the old man who wore a face mask not over his mouth but on his forehead. "Tell my mother I love her."

I didn't speak—I didn't want to open my mouth. But the air that managed to creep through my nostrils and hit my taste buds tasted more like swine flu.

We held our breath as we rode the elevator up to the third floor—and we exhaled as soon as the door opened to a calm, deserted waiting room that smelled of Listerine and soap.

"Where is everybody?" Colin asked. "His people, I mean."

I, too, had expected throngs of well-wishers sitting shivah with Christopher Chatman.

A nurse pointed us thataway to room 303, and a minute later we stood in the doorway.

A middle-aged Lena Horne lookalike sat in the room's visitor chair and peered at the screen of her iPhone. She had a café au lait complexion, and her hair had been captured into a shiny chignon. Her thin, pinched nose, inherited from a European grand-someone, nearly grazed the corkboard ceiling. That nose . . . Until now, I'd never witnessed anyone actually holding her nose in the air. This woman did, and I marveled at that more than I marveled at her plum wrap dress and red-bottomed heels.

Both shoes and dress kicked the repressed fashionista in me, the one that now stank of sweat and firemen.

The woman looked at me, then at Colin, then, nose high, returned her attention to the phone. She was over us already.

Christopher Chatman lay in bed, beneath a light-blue blanket. His big brown eyes were at half-mast. Blood had pebbled and dried on his bottom lip. His left arm was wrapped in a sling, and bandages plastered his face and the back of his skull. Complicated machines flanked him, monitoring his heart rate, blood pressure, and hydration levels.

"May I help you?" A pretty Indian woman dressed in pink floral scrubs touched my elbow. Her name tag said RAMA.

I badged her, introduced Colin, and then asked about Christopher Chatman's injuries.

"Minor fracture to his left arm," she said. "Minor concussion. Cuts and bruises."

"So he'll live?" Colin whispered.

She nodded.

"A few of his friends expressed concerns about his mental health," I said. "They worry that he may attempt to end his life."

Rama frowned. "We'll keep watch for that. He does show signs of distress, which is common in this unfortunate situation, and also common with brain injury. But suicidal?" She shook her head.

"Can we . . . ?" I pointed inside the room.

"You may. The woman sitting with him now is Sarah Oliver, a family friend. I'm sure she won't mind."

Sarah: Ben Oliver' wife, ex-lawyer and driver of the SUV.

"Does Mr. Chatman realize what's happened?" I asked the nurse.

Rama glanced over to her patient. "Not yet."

I stepped across the threshold and into the room.

Sarah Oliver slipped the phone into her purse.

We both watched as Rama tut-tutted over the man in bed. We watched her slip a blood-pressure cuff over his right bicep, then watched her adjust his pillows.

Christopher Chatman stirred and croaked, "Jules?"

Sarah Oliver hopped up from her chair.

Rama moved aside to let the woman come closer.

Sarah Oliver whispered into her friend's ear.

"Wha'?" he mumbled. "Wanna see her."

Sarah Oliver, eyes bright with tears, peered at me, bit her lip, then whispered in his ear again.

My heart jumped. *Crap. Is she telling him they're all dead?*

Christopher Chatman's eyes widened. "I wanna see my wife," he shouted, waving his free arm. "Where's my son? Where's my boy?" He tried to sit up, tried to leave the bed, tried to yank away the tubes. "Where's my boy? Where's my wife? Where's—?"

A male nurse a little bigger than Goliath lumbered past us and joined Rama in restraining their patient. Rama reached into her smock pocket, pulled out a syringe filled with clear liquid, then stuck the needle into the IV feed. Seconds later, Chatman melted back into the pillows. The tension in his face dissipated—mouth slack, eyes dull, oh, the magic of medicine.

I followed Rama out to the hallway. "When will he be released?"

"Tomorrow morning," she said. "He'll be staying with Mr. and Mrs. Oliver."

Before climbing back into my Crown Vic to attack rush-hour traffic, I darted to the bathroom. As I was leaving, though, Sarah Oliver, red-eyed and pink-nosed, was entering.

She gasped seeing me standing at the paper towel dispenser. She was as tall as me, lesser-boobed, and smelled of lilacs and vanilla.

I introduced myself and offered my hand.

She offered her name and took a moment to appraise my hand.

Finally, we shook. And as we shook, her nostrils flared as much as they could. Touching in a bathroom did not thrill her.

"Is Mr. Chatman resting now?" I asked, very couldn't care less about her thrills and mildly hoping that she thought I had skipped soap and water.

"Yes, he is." She sighed, then rubbed her right eyebrow. "I can't understand. What *happened*? Ben told me that some *monster* in a hockey jersey did this. Is that true?"

"We're still trying to figure that out," I said. "It's too soon to say how the fire started."

Her face darkened, and a small teardrop rolled down her cheek. "I called Juliet's parents to let them know since Christopher . . . He's come undone, and I don't know why . . . I don't know why . . ."

I waited for the strings and tinkling piano to fade in, for her to look up to the fluorescent lights and warble, *Don't know why, there's no sun up in the sky* . . . Not that I disbelieved her single teardrop. But the woman who had tossed me That Look back in Chatman's hospital room did not weep in public restrooms like the woman who now stood before me.

She crossed her arms to hug herself. "Any minute now, I'll wake up. I'll wake up and I'll hear Coco laughing with my daughter. That's what I keep telling myself. That this is all . . ." She squeezed her elbows, then whispered, "Because I just *saw* them. Not even twenty-four hours ago."

"Around what time was that?" I asked.

"Six," she said, letting her arms fall to her sides. "I stopped by to see if Juliet wanted to go to Zumba with me. And I dropped off an *Architectural Digest*. They were remodeling."

"Did she go to Zumba?"

Sarah Oliver stared at the badge clipped to my hip. "She didn't feel like it—she had been fighting the flu since the weekend."

"So you went to class alone?"

She nodded. "Before I left, though, I sat and chatted for a few minutes. Then, I kissed the kids good-bye, kissed Juliet good-bye, then left." Her cheeks flushed, and she regarded me with sad, wet eyes. "Juliet was like a sister to me, and Chloe like another daughter. Is there anything I can do to help?"

"Not right now, but I will need to talk to you formally." I gave her my card.

"About?"

"Everything."

She pressed her lips together. "I know some people will take this as a chance to say awful things."

"About?"

Her lip trembled. "Cody. About how he would set fires. Harmless—the fires he'd set . . . He was just . . ." She closed her eyes and dropped her head. "I don't know how I'm going to tell Mimi that Coco . . . Amelia gave her that nickname because she couldn't say Chloe when they were babies. Mimi and Coco wanted to do everything together. Sleepovers, tea parties, vacations. Sometimes, I had to tell her, 'Honey, Coco has her own family. She can't be over here all the time.'"

Another tear slipped down her smooth cheek. "The girls had these shirts that matched and"—she swiped her face and exhaled—"they wanted to be in each other's weddings when they grew up. And for someone to take that away . . . Whoever did this needs to pay." She straightened and lifted her chin. "Juliet and Christopher, Chloe . . . They deserve justice. My *daughter* deserves justice. I'm sure you'll see to that, Detective Norton."

"That's my job," I said. "And I'm sorry for your loss."

"I am, too. Now if you'll excuse me."

I took a step back to the paper towel dispenser.

She glided to the middle stall like a swan across a pond. Before disappearing behind the locked metal door, she tossed me a smile so bright it fed the sun.

9

The hot, diseased breath of the hospital was waiting for Colin and me as we returned to the main lobby. We rushed toward the exit for the parking lot, lips clamped together as the sick lurched and coughed and spat into tissues. Outside, the air smelled of exhaust and cigarette smoke, the regular carcinogenic stink that caused domestic diseases like lung cancer and COPD.

After inhaling a few pounds of poison, Colin said, "So Christopher Chatman."

"What about him?" I opened the Crown Vic's driver's-side door and slipped behind the steering wheel.

"All that ruckus and the waving arms and all that. Really?"

I cocked an eyebrow. "You're such a cynic, Colin."

"You don't get the impression that he's puttin' on?"

"Would you rally back quickly if a beautiful woman was at your bedside and tending to your needs?"

"Hell no." Colin chuckled. "My ass would be an invalid at all the right times, but strong and potent when it mattered."

My fingers tapped across the car's computer keyboard. "Looks like we were never called out to the Chatman house for domestic drama," I said, scrolling through the address's history. "Just the burglary back in 2009."

Colin leaned into the car. "Any priors for him or her?"

I typed in Juliet Chatman's name. "A speeding violation last year." I typed in Christopher Chatman's name. "And he's totally clean. He's even an organ donor."

"The man's a saint."

"I wanna go back to the house," I said. "See if Pepe and Luke found a MacGuffin."

The temperature around the Chatmans' property had cooled some, and heat no longer pulsed from the ground. Melting plastics and paints had hardened into stalactites, opaque orbs, and swamp things.

In the front yard, now lit with halogen lamps, firemen clomped in and out of the house, checking for hotspots, tearing venting holes into walls. On the perimeter, the last news crew reported live from the scene. Pepe was hunched over a crimson-brocaded couch. Luke was snapping pictures of all the items we had collected throughout the day.

"What's up, ladies?" I asked.

Pepe wiped his sweaty brow with the back of his forearm. "People own a lot of shit. That's what's up."

"We need some good food after this," Luke said.

"It's Pepe's turn," Colin said.

Pepe scrunched his eyebrows. "I got food on Friday."

"AM-PM is not food, amigo," Luke said. "I'm talkin' six-pound Hollenbeck burritos with enough cheese and guacamole to constipate a walrus."

"You *are* a walrus," Colin cracked.

Luke flipped Colin the bird and said, smiling, "*Vete y chinga a tu madre.*"

Pepe groaned, then laughed.

"That's illegal, Luke," I said, shaking my head.

"What he say?" Colin asked. "Something about my mother? What was that other stuff?"

"Changing the subject," I said. "Find anything good?"

"Remember the piece Miss Lady was packin'?" Luke asked. "We ran the serial number. It legally belonged to Juliet Chatman. She picked it up last Thursday at a gun store in Duarte."

"*Duarte?*" My eyes narrowed. "That's, like, fifty miles east of here. Why not buy a gun at the store over in Culver City? That's three miles away."

"Did she fire it?" Colin asked.

"Nope," Luke said. "Oh, and we never did find Mrs. Chatman's car keys."

"Think someone took them so she couldn't leave?" I asked.

The men shrugged and nodded and shook their heads.

"Y'all are as sharp as marbles." I swiveled and pointed to the SUV in the driveway. "You search it yet?"

"Not thoroughly," Pepe said. "Zucca sprayed the inside, but he didn't find any blood. Nothing but old soda spills, Skittles, and hard-ass french fries."

"Let's take another look," I said, pulling gloves on as we stepped over to the car.

"We did grab a few things from Chatman's Jag," Pepe said as we walked. "A CVS drugstore receipt from December tenth, which was yesterday. A botanical-gardens ticket from December tenth, which was yesterday. And a charger and cell phone hidden in the compartment beneath the driver's seat."

"Ooh," I said. "Secret cell phone stashed in the secret seat cache."

"We found some pain meds in the Jag's glove compartment," Pepe continued. "Hydrocodone prescribed for Mr. Chatman. And we found an EZ-Mail invoice for personal mailbox service for November. And that's about it."

"That phone gets me hot," I said. "We'll need warrants to pull phone bills, to get voice-mail messages and texts." I popped the truck's rear compartment to see those three suitcases.

"Were they going on a trip?" Pepe asked.

I opened the hard-shelled, hot-pink Hello Kitty suitcase. "Girls' shirts, panties, calf-length Cons, skinny jeans. Chloe, I'm guessing."

Next, I opened the battered black piece covered with shoe prints and skateboard bumper stickers. "Games for a Nintendo DS, checkered skinny jeans, three pairs of clean socks, and . . . a Bic lighter." I pointed at the Bic. "Cody."

"Oh boy," Pepe said, taking pictures of that lighter.

Then, I opened the last suitcase, a newish Louis Vuitton piece with no nicks or scratches. "Obviously Mrs. Chatman's. Designer blue jeans, stiletto boots, two bras, lots of panties, T-shirts, and . . . a box of bullets for the Smith and Wesson."

More pics taken of the bullets.

My eyes combed the rest of the SUV's compartment. "Do y'all see what I don't see?"

Pepe, Luke, and Colin scanned the cabin.

"Two kids and a lady," I pointed out. "Where's *his* bag?"

We searched the SUV again.

No suitcase for a man.

"Anybody see a suitcase in the house?" I asked. "Maybe he hadn't put his in the trunk."

Luke shook his head. "We would've noticed that."

Pepe turned the key in the ignition. "The gas tank is full. Wherever she and the kids were going, she wasn't planning on stopping soon."

"Or for Daddy Bear to come along," I said.

"Oh boy," Luke and Pepe said together.

"Okay, so let's backtrack," I said. " '*Something, something* kill me.' And she died holding a gun."

"She had been scared of something," Colin said.

"Or someone," Pepe added.

"So scared," I said, "that she purchased that gun, filled the car's gas tank, and packed up the kids. But before they could escape, before she had a chance to fire that gun and drive four hundred miles east to wherever, she had been stopped."

"By what?" Luke asked.

"By whom?" Pepe wondered.

"The fire?"

"Her husband?"

My body went cold. "Or both."

10

Beneath the December moon, beneath a sky still smoky from fire and ash, the Chatman house resembled the *War of the Worlds* plane-crash movie set found on the Universal Studios lot—random wood boards strewn across the property, plaster and wallpaper hanging off walls like dead, burned skin, dirty insulation dripping from the eaves like broiled intestines. All of this but without the crashed 747 on the front lawn. Hard to believe that a family had lived here. But as I surveyed the destruction, I found it easy to believe that a family—three-quarters of it anyway—had perished.

As a homicide detective, I regularly entered the homes of slain victims. There, I smelled tobacco caught in the curtains; smelled spilled beer and whiskey fumes in the rugs and wafting from the mountain of empties in the trash can. I noticed walls dented by doorknobs, fists, and skulls; crimson-colored splatters on ceilings and floorboards; teeth stuck in carpet.

With the Chatman house, I saw nothing personal like that. Just groups of big men swinging axes, wielding chain saws, shouting "*Whoa whoa whoa*" over the crackle of radios. Mops, water vacuums, and chamois cluttered the lawns and sidewalks. The business end of death.

"I wanna go back into the main house for a moment," I told Luke and Pepe. "To make sure there ain't a packed suitcase for Mr. Chatman." Then, I pointed to Colin. "Then, we'll check out the back house."

The electricity to the property was still shut off, so we clicked on our flashlights to navigate through the darkness. But we didn't find a suitcase—not in the foyer, den, or home office.

No suitcase in the laundry room, either. "Looks full," Colin said, peering through the window of the swanky dryer. "Maybe he was washing the clothes he planned to pack."

"Maybe."

He opened the dryer door, then pulled out pink shirts, white shirts, jeans, and girls' swimsuits, a few bath and hand towels, and soccer socks—all of it covered in glitter. "Nothin' but girl. What the hell's bells is all *this*?" He brushed glitter from his clothes, but the flecks only multiplied.

"Looks like a stripper threw up all over you," I said, grinning.

"Is that a *thing* now? Putting glitter on clothes?"

I nodded. "But you wash it first, to get off the excess. The rest gets caught in the lint filter. See?" I lifted the filter from its slot.

Clean.

"That's strange," I said with a frown. "Usually . . ."

Colin rubbed his left eye. "Think some of that shit flew in my—"

"Where's the lint from this load?" I wondered. "There should be some of the usual gray stuff along with glitter from Chloe's shirts."

"Does it matter?" Colin blinked to be sure that the glitter had left his eye.

Uncertain if it mattered or not, I stared at the filter. "Just find it strange." I plucked the digital camera from my pocket and snapped pictures of the clothes, the clean filter, and the machine itself.

Flashlights in hand, Colin and I crept out of the service porch door, stepping over boards, debris, and leaves, all soggy from drizzle and fire-hose water. Our beams of light led us to the Chatmans' Away Place. And except for a plywood sheet covering the busted bay window, the converted garage had escaped disaster.

Colin clucked his tongue. "Crazy how some things survive."

I tossed a cone of light up and down the structure. "Take this." I handed him the Mag so that I could snap pictures.

A moment later, flashes of light from the camera popped in the darkness. I took one more picture, then tilted my face to the misty rain, closing my eyes as my skin tingled and tightened.

Colin wiggled the doorknob.

Unlocked.

The darkness hid the room's detail. But it felt close and damp. If the air, the Persian rug, and the sofa didn't dry out soon, mold would come and that would be that—another claim form for Christopher Chatman to submit. The walls were light-colored, and three dark wood beams traversed the ceiling.

"Mice in here?" I whispered.

"Fire probably scared 'em away." Colin chuckled. "You scared of critters?"

"Nope. Scared of vermin."

We wandered around the room in silence.

Something scurried and scratched behind a piece of furniture.

I went rigid and stopped in my step. "Vermin?"

"Big ones, too," Colin kidded.

I swung the light: a bookcase stocked with books, a desk strewn with papers, and a glass mug filled with tea, the tea bag resting on a coaster. A book of stamps sat near that glass of tea. A planning calendar had been opened to January.

"She was sitting here yesterday," I said. "Started doing something—writing a letter, planning that getaway—and the doorbell rang or the kids called her to the front."

"Didn't get to come back and finish her tea," Colin added, his voice tight, his flashlight trained on the mug.

Next to the planning calendar sat a daily planner opened to December 10. In neat print, someone (Juliet?) had written "APPT @IMG @ 2:30," and on December 11, "FUP w/Dr. K @10."

I flipped to the past week: on Thursday, December 6, she'd had an appointment with Dr. Kulkanis at ten o'clock. A business card from the obstetrician-gynecologist had been stuck in the journal's crease. Three appointments, just days apart.

Sarah Oliver had mentioned Juliet being sick. And Juliet was supposed to visit her doctor this morning. A baby doctor.

How many women died each year after visiting baby doctors and then sharing the news with their significant others? Too many.

I took the journal and the calendar and then opened the top drawer—pens, pads, clips. In the large bottom drawer, I found letters bundled together with strands of raffia.

As I browsed through the envelopes, Colin drifted over to the bookcase.

I found nothing obvious in the first couple of letters—notes from friends and from her mother—but I took them all anyway. I stepped over to the coffee table: a *Self* magazine with Heidi Klum on the cover. A pen and two slips of paper. I shone light onto the words of the first note, written in neat cursive.

Vanity of vanities, all is vanity. Our life is a lie. It will be over soon and what we are will no longer be.

Hunh.

Then, I read the second note. "Found something." My stomach clenched as I took pictures of both documents.

Colin stood beside me and read the first note under his breath. "Suicide?"

I shrugged. "Read note number two."

His eyes skipped across the page. "Shit."

"Yeah."

"May not mean anything."

"You just said *may not*."

He gazed at me, glanced at the notes, then pulled two evidence bags from his pocket.

Those notes weren't teeth lost in carpet, banged-in walls, or pools of blood on bathroom linoleum. Nothing hard like that. But the family's pathology—secrets and fear and betrayal—were starting to poke out and stink.

11

The drizzle had stepped up its game, and now, thin rain, the kind that destroyed hair and made driving more dangerous than skydiving, fell from those Hollywood clouds. Colin and I left Juliet Chatman's Away Place as the fire company loaded equipment back onto the engines and as two patrol officers wrapped new stretches of yellow tape across the front yard. Pepe and Luke had beat it back to the station with boxes of evidence crowding their cars' trunks and cabins. At Ruby Emmett's brick bungalow across the street, a group of neighbors huddled on the lawn.

Colin smiled. "Looks like everybody's home. Be a shame to leave right now."

"It would." I winked at him. "Ready, partner?"

"Always, partner."

"No mention of the gun or the suitcases or the 911 call."

"Got it."

Interviews are usually conducted in isolation—you and the witness in a locked room, knee to knee. But after finding that second note on the coffee table, I wanted the women of Don Mateo Drive in one room, clucking like pissed-off hens. A dangerous game? Certainly. But the potential payoff . . .

All group discussion came to a halt as Colin and I approached.

"Evenin'," Colin drawled.

No one responded.

Delia Moss, the playwright, clutched an iPad to her chest. A chubby, balding white guy stood behind her and rubbed her shoulders. Round Ruby put her hands on her hips as Nora the real estate agent readjusted the plastic bonnet that protected her weave from the rain. A hatchet-faced black man and Ben Oliver smirked at me.

"I know it's dinnertime," I said, "but we'd like to talk to anyone who's willing." I smiled and nodded at Ben Oliver.

He didn't smile back.

My face warmed, and my jaw tightened so much it creaked.

"I'm tired of all this pokin' around," Ruby said. "Y'all, the reporters, everybody."

"We don't want to talk about it anymore," Delia Moss added. "You're only interested in placing blame on the victims."

"Not true," I said, shaking my head. "I'm interested in the truth."

"We've told you everything we know," Ben Oliver said.

I forced myself to remain smiling. "The sooner you talk to us, the sooner whoever did this is brought to justice. If you folks won't do this for Juliet and the kids, who will?" I turned to Ruby. "'Let each of you look not only to his own interests, but also to the interests of others.'"

Ruby waddled to the front door. "Come on in, then. I'll talk. Ain't got all night, though."

Those three years of Sunday school memory verses had just paid off.

A minute later, Colin and I found ourselves hunkered on a low love seat with sunken cushions in a stuffy living room crammed with an upright piano, an overdecorated Christmas tree, and brass elephant planters filled with peacock feathers. We were joined by the others who had stood with Ruby on her lawn—including Ben Oliver.

Ruby's kids, thirteen or fourteen years old and just as round as their mother, had been splayed on the carpet in front of the large-screen television, playing *Left 4 Dead* on the Xbox. "Y'all need to take that noise upstairs," Ruby told them.

"But—" both started to say, but stopped once Ruby gave them The Look.

Obedient children, they huffed out of the living room, throwing me sullen gazes as they retreated up the stairs.

"My husband should be back soon," Delia said. The white guy, Eli Moss, had run next door to grab his video camera.

As we waited, my stomach rumbled—Ruby had fried some type of meat for dinner, and I hadn't eaten since that smashed, three-o'-clock Snickers bar.

Ben Oliver sat in the armchair across from Colin and me. He considered me coolly as though I had planned to sell him expired Amway products.

Eli Moss bustled into the living room with his camera. "Thanks for waiting."

The attorney glanced at his watch with irritation. "Another last-minute interrogation, Detective?" he asked me. "Many of us have been up since four o'clock this morning."

I leaned forward and glared at him. *This is my meeting, not yours.*

Usually, men shrank under that glare. Ben Oliver, though, also leaned forward and blossomed under my glare like a sunflower on the first day of summer.

Damn. I would have to consult my witch's spell book for a glower just for him. Something frosty enough to kill sunflowers.

"Let's start with an easy question," I said. "What was Juliet's state of mind, say, last week this time?"

Several confused moments of silence before Delia said, "She was happy."

The room buzzed with murmurs of approval. *Good answer, good answer.*

"She was never sad," Nora added. "Never, ever, ever sad."

"She was a devoted wife," Ruby volunteered as she plopped onto the piano bench. "An excellent wife is the crown of her husband, Solomon wrote, and Juliet was definitely Christopher's crown."

"She adored her children," Delia Moss continued. "She went beyond loving them."

"Are any of you familiar with Melissa Kemper?" I asked.

Blank stares from everyone . . . except from Ben, who had narrowed his eyes.

"No one?" I met the gaze of each person sitting before me.

A breeze suffused with the aroma of fried meat wafted through the room and twisted into my nostrils. Light-headed now, I felt my stomach rumble louder. "Okay. Back to Juliet. And I'll be blunt just to save us some time. Did she ever talk to any of you about wanting to die?"

Ruby shrieked, *"What?"*

Nora clutched her neck. "Jules was probably the most well-adjusted woman on our block. How could you ask something so—?"

"Nora, please," Micah Galbreath said. He was the hatchet-faced black man who had stood with Ben Oliver.

"So intrusive," she complained. "Intrusive and totally disrespectful."

"These questions," Delia Moss said, "it's too soon to be asking these questions."

"I know that this is difficult," I said, "but I'm asking because we found two notes in the back apartment." I flipped through the pages in my pad, then read, "*Vanity of vanities, all is vanity. Our life is a lie. It will be over soon and what we are will no longer be.* We believe this note may have been written by Juliet Chatman."

Ruby cocked her head. "I know the first part of that, about vanity. It's from the book of Ecclesiastes. It basically means everything we do is in vain and is meaningless."

"What about the rest?" I asked. "The part about it being over soon?"

Everyone shrugged.

"The second note we found," I said, "was written by the mysterious Melissa Kemper. *Dear Juliet, you need to know some things. I don't want to bring it up in a letter—you've ignored my other ones so far—so please stop ignoring me and pick up the phone and CALL ME. It's a matter of life and death!!!*"

Ben Oliver cleared his throat. "Melissa is a friend of ours."

"What kind of friend?" Colin asked.

"A good one." Ben glared at Eli and the video camera. "Must you record this?"

Eli kept the camera trained on the attorney.

"Was Christopher cheating on Jules with this Melissa?" Delia asked.

Micah rolled his eyes. "Here we go."

"This is absurd," Ben said, his voice an octave higher, his hands clasped behind his head to negate any anxiety. "What makes you think . . . ? They, *we*, were friends."

"And why would he cheat on Jules?" Micah asked. "She's beautiful. Well, she *was* beautiful before she got sick and started losing all that weight and . . . But she was beautiful."

Eli chuckled. "Show me a beautiful woman. I'll show you a man tired of fucking her."

The men—even Colin—laughed.

Ruby smacked Eli's head. "This is a Christian house, hear? We don't use that word."

The chastised filmmaker rubbed his head, but the frat-boy grin stayed on his lips.

"Detectives," Delia said, "what does Melissa Kemper have to do with the fire?"

Ben Oliver waved his hand. "She has absolutely *nothing* to do with the fire."

"Mr. Oliver may be correct," I agreed. "We just want to make sure we talk with everyone who may help us understand what happened."

"*I* know for sure that she's not involved," Ben Oliver said.

"Okay," I said. "So who is she?"

"Doesn't matter."

"It *does* matter," I retorted, "and it's my job to find out. Wouldn't you want me to talk to *everyone* about this awful situation?"

All eyes turned to Ben. *Well? Wouldn't you?*

The lawyer sighed. "Melissa Kemper is the ex-wife of Ron Kemper, and Ron is also a friend of ours. We all attended UCLA. He's now a partner over at Gibson, Dunn & Crutcher. Before the divorce, Mel worked as a publicist at Paramount Pictures. When they divorced this summer, she moved to Las Vegas with their son. Again: none of this is pertinent to the fire."

"I found her." Delia passed the iPad to me.

And there she was: Melissa Kemper in *Los Angeles Confidential*, a magazine you never knew existed because you weren't important enough to know that it did.

This picture had been taken in April 2013 at the Carousel of Hope Ball benefitting diabetes research. Kemper stood with her now-ex husband, a tall and tan white man with wavy silver hair. She should have been gorgeous—she had bright green eyes, long auburn hair, and gigantic knockers that strained against her emerald cocktail dress. But she wasn't gorgeous or pretty or even cute despite all the nips and tucks and layers of expensive makeup. Her face had been pulled back so much that her smile had become a grimace; her brow stood so high, she would look surprised even after death.

Ruby peeked over my shoulder, grunted, then moved back to her seat on the piano bench. "This the Gila monster Christopher chose?"

"He didn't *choose* her, Ruby," Ben said with exasperation. "You know Christopher is totally devoted to Juliet."

Nora frowned. "I cannot *believe* he'd betray Jules for this . . . this . . . Joker in drag."

"Nora," Ben said, "he didn't—"

"Maybe she has a sparkling personality," Delia quipped.

"*Personality?*" Nora said. "She probably takes it in the—"

"Okay, okay, okay," Ben said, clapping his hands. "That's enough."

"We should move on," I said, not wanting to move on, not *really*. "I'm not asking about Melissa Kemper to accuse Mr. Chatman of doing anything . . . questionable. I just need—"

"Why are we even going down this road?" Micah asked, arms spread. "His family just died not even twenty-four hours ago."

"Yeah," Eli said, "can the man grieve? Geez."

But the women of Don Mateo Drive weren't done—there was still meat left on the bone.

I elbowed Colin: my evil plan was working.

"Why do men do shit like this?" Nora asked, arms crossed.

Eli pointed at the real estate agent, then gawked at Ruby. "*She* gets to curse, but I don't?"

"My house, my rules," Ruby said. "Now hush up."

"It's never enough," Nora complained, shaking her head and glaring at her husband.

"Cheaters should be castrated," Delia mused. "Slowly, and with a rusty, dull scalpel."

I felt Colin's muscles tighten. "We should move on," he croaked.

Nora gasped. "You think Jules knew?"

Again, the room turned to Ben Oliver. *Well? Did she?*

The attorney rubbed his face, then touched his forehead. "There was nothing for Juliet to know. And Juliet didn't *suspect* anything because there was nothing to suspect. This is a snipe hunt, folks. Can't you see what Detective Norton is doing? She's trying to make it so that she can arrest Christopher for murder. Or maybe even blame poor Cody, just twelve years old. Which also means that the insurance company won't have to pay his claims."

"Again," I said, "*you* bring up insurance issues. Mr. Oliver, this is not about you and what you do for a living. We're here in this room because a fire—"

"Cody ain't had nothin' to do with this fire," Ruby said.

"He was just a *boy*," Nora said, wringing her hands.

"Ma'am," Colin said, "we're not sayin' that Cody—"

"We're here," I said, tamping back anger, "to try and find out who murdered two children—"

"And you're trying to pin it on my best friend," Ben Oliver interrupted. Then, he waved his hands at the people in the room. "*Our* friend. *Our* family."

I nodded. "And I understand—"

"No, you don't understand." He slowly pointed to each person in the room. "Many of you mentioned seeing a suspicious person wearing an orange hockey jersey. Has Detective Norton even *looked* into this? Of course not. She's colluding with MG Standard to cheat our friend of life, liberty, and the money he's entitled to, on the policies he's paid on for thirteen years. This way, she'll get to close the case and get a promotion."

"Again," I said, sensing the room tilt to his side, "I'm not here to argue with you, Mr. Oliver."

"Because you know I'm right," he said, relaxing in his chair. "I know about the insurance investigator that MG Standard sent out this morning. Dixie Shipman: a disgraced arson cop fired two years ago after she was caught receiving kickbacks from insurance companies."

"Three people," I said. "Three people that you all loved died in a fire early this morning. I'm only interested in finding out who is responsible for their deaths. I'm only interested in—"

"Last year," Ben interrupted, "MG Standard Insurance Company and companies like them collected one trillion dollars in premiums." He gazed at me and light beamed in his eyes—it was the satisfaction that came with cornering prey. "One. Trillion. Dollars," he repeated.

The people in the room gasped.

"Incredible."

"Crazy."

"I can't believe that."

The Inner Lou also said, *Holy crap, that's a lot of money.*

"Each day," Colin said, "one in three women are murdered by their partners. And half of the men who abuse their wives also abuse their children."

I elbowed my partner. *Wrong stats, man. Wrong stats.*

"Are you saying that Christopher is a *wife* beater?" Micah cried. "That he beat his *kids*?"

"No," I said. "We're saying that early this morning, a woman and her children died—"

"Have any of you been *fucked* by the insurance industry?" Ben asked.

"I'm not through," I spat.

His eyes narrowed. "How about the police? Any cops fuck you over?"

Colin started to rebut, but I shook my head. *Let the asshole finish.*

The room fell into silence—the only sound was Ruby's daughter singing a Rihanna song.

Finally, Eli said, "Our house got broken into, and some crackhead took every piece of electronics that wasn't nailed down. We only got three hundred dollars for our claim."

"A cop stopped me last week," Micah shared. "Said I looked like a *suspect*. How many *suspects* wear Brooks Brothers suits and drive BMWs?"

"When my mother got cancer," Ruby said, "the insurance company wouldn't pay because she had a preexisting condition."

Mouth dry, I sat on that couch with my soul hunched over until the storm passed.

"She could be lying," Eli suggested as he stared at his pudgy hands.

"Who?" I asked. "*Me?* Lying? About?"

"About all of this," the man said. "Cops say shit to make *you* say shit but *their* shit ain't true. But they use *your* shit to twist the case any way they want. My buddy Ross got stopped by a motorcycle cop over on Wilshire who said he had made a left turn after seven o'clock. But it wasn't seven; it was 6:54. So the cop's lying, right? Ross went to traffic court to fight the ticket. He brought in charts and pictures to prove his innocence, and the cop didn't even show up. Ross found out that the cop had a history of making shit up. *Lying.*"

Ben's smile broadened. "Denying people the help they need: isn't that what the LAPD is about? To serve and protect? Maybe to serve and protect each other, but certainly not the people of *this* city."

Case closed.

Blood and pressure surged at my scalp as though I stood upside down.

"What about Christopher Chatman's mental state?" Colin asked as though the last ten minutes had not happened.

"What about it?" Ben sniped, that smile of his sent back into hibernation.

"Last week this time, was he depressed?" Colin asked. "Sad? Angry? Erratic?"

"No, four times," Ben said.

"Sir," Colin said, "we asked *you* already. I want someone else's opinion."

But the others in the room said nothing.

Colin glanced at Ruby. "No trouble ever at the Chatman house?"

The woman, arms folded tight against her large bosom, shook her head. "Nope."

He found Eli next. "No cops called? Ever?"

Eli said, "Nope."

"So everything was A-OK," Colin said.

Fuck the police from sea to shining sea.

I closed my notebook, aware now that Ben had presented a pretty convincing argument against lying cops and the cheating insurance companies that they protected. "We're only here to help," I said, pulling myself from the couch. "We're only here to find the person or persons who committed this horrendous act. Unfortunately, that means we'll have to keep asking hard questions until we get the truth. And that means you all will be seeing us again." To Ruby Emmett, I said, "I'd like to talk to the kids now, please."

Sighs and groans followed Colin and me up the stairs and down the hallway.

We found the teens in the boy's stuffy bedroom. Posters of baseballs and basketballs—no athletes to worship, just balls in motion—along with maps of the world and Afro-Jesus had been tacked to the walls. The boy, LaTrell, sat on the carpet, game controller in his hands and a bag of Cheetos Crunchy on his thighs. His eyes were glued to the thirty-inch television on the dresser. His sister, LaTanya, lay on the bed, controller in her hands, and a bag of Flamin' Hot Cheetos near her elbow.

Ruby stood in front of the television. "Turn it off. The detectives got some questions."

The girl aimed the remote at the TV, and the boy tapped the swirling green power circle on the Xbox console.

"How old are you guys?" I asked.

"Fourteen," the twins said together.

"You both know what's going on across the street," I said. "We're trying to figure out how it happened. We hear that Cody's set fires before. Do you know about that?"

The boy and girl regarded each other, then looked back at me.

She said, "Yeah, he used to do that."

LaTrell folded his arms and dipped his chin to his chest.

"Boy," Ruby growled, "you better get right, right now."

He reached into his jeans pocket and pulled out a cell phone. He scrolled through his digital photo album, found a picture, tapped it, then handed me the phone. "It's a video."

Cody Chatman had been sitting in a park when he reached into his grungy black backpack. He pulled out a piece of clothing and shook it out: a man's blazer. "This cost, like, one grand," he said, his voice deep and hoarse.

"Nice," LaTrell had wheezed. "Your daddy's a baller."

"My daddy's a *punk*," Cody Chatman had snapped. He pulled an orange Bic from his pack, then held the flame to the jacket's sleeve.

"That's cold," LaTrell had said.

"That's beautiful," the boy said and tossed the lit blazer on the grass. He smiled at the phone's camera, then stuck out his tongue.

"He did that kind of stuff all the time," LaTrell told us now. "He'd take something from his mom or dad—"

"Or from Chloe," LaTanya said. "He'd take, like, her dolls and stuffed animals and everything. And then he'd burn them up."

Colin and I looked at each other. *WTF?*

LaTanya bit her lip, then said, "And he used to bully—"

LaTrell tilted his head back into his sister's chin.

Ruby saw this, and growled, "Boy . . ."

LaTanya gazed down at her brother's head, then sighed. "Cody used to bully his cousin all the time."

I cocked my head. "Cousin? Who—?"

"Mimi," she said. "Guess she's really his play cousin. He hated her, and he'd take her stuff and hide it, and she'd start cryin' and he'd fake cry, and that made her cry harder. One time, he locked Mimi and Coco out of the house. Remember that, Momma?" she asked Ruby.

The woman nodded solemnly. "We were coming home from the store and the girls were sittin' on my porch, just weeping." She pursed her lips. "Cody thought it was funny."

"Did he get in trouble?" Colin asked, spots of color high on his cheeks.

"His dad took away his skateboards," LaTrell said. "That's when he did this." He held up his phone.

LaTanya nodded. "And Mimi was sad cuz her momma wouldn't let her come over anymore by herself."

"Anything else you can tell us?" Colin asked.

LaTrell said, "His best friend's name is Parker McMann. He goes to the same school. He ain't that nice, either."

"Skateboards and fire, too?" I asked.

The twins nodded.

"Thanks for talking to us," I said.

"As you were," Ruby told her children.

Almost immediately, the Xbox fan whirred and the bags of Cheetos crumpled.

Back at the Crown Vic, I took several breaths and waited for the nausea to pass. Then, I opened the trunk and threw in my bag. "I need a drink after that."

"I screwed up a little," Colin admitted. "The abuse thing. Oops."

"Can't show your cards like that," I told him. "Defense attorneys would argue that we went in there suspecting Christopher or Cody Chatman."

He swiped at his mouth, then slowly exhaled.

"It's all BS, this happy, perfect family," I said.

He nodded at the Chatman house. "Happy, perfect families don't buy guns and write cryptic letters. Happy boys don't burn up their sister's Wetty Betty or lock them out of the house. Someone's lying. I *know* it."

"It's Betsy Wetsy, Colin." I yawned. "And it's been a long day."

Colin stretched and his muscles bulged against his tired T-shirt. "Let's grab a beer."

"Can't. So Melissa Kemper."

"What about her?" He ruffled his spiky blond hair.

"We need to figure out how she's connected to this," I said, pulling out my cell phone.

"We need to figure out a whole bunch of things."

Having no voice-mail messages from Greg made my shoulders slump.

"What did you tell me when I caught my first murder in this city?" Colin asked, watching the phone slip back into my jacket pocket.

"You eat an elephant one bite at a time." Lieutenant Rodriguez had told me the same thing on my first murder.

"We're at the tail right now," Colin said.

"The ass is next."

"I don't mind eatin' ass," he said, cracking a bright smile.

I groaned. "TMI, Taggert. TMI."

"All I'm sayin' is, we'll get through it."

"'Vanity of vanities,'" I said. "'All is vanity.'"
Our life is a lie. It will be over soon and what we are will no longer be.
What was vanity?
What was a lie?
And *what* would be over soon?

12

The Princeton University psychologist Julian Jaynes once said, "Civilization is the art of living in towns of such size that everyone does not know everyone else." And this thought stayed with me, like a stone tumbling around my belly, long after leaving that living room klatch with the residents of Don Mateo Drive. Jaynes had been right: Ruby and Nora and the rest didn't know *jack* about the Chatmans. Worse: they didn't *know* that they didn't know jack.

As a rookie detective, I had worked one case in which a gardener for an apartment complex had smelled something dead wafting from unit 4F. The gardener knocked on the door but no one answered. He retreated to the landlord's office, and the landlord used a master key to enter 4F. There, on the brown-stained living room carpet, lay the tenant, Mario Lewis, still clutching a .38, his head blasted open, dried brains and splintered bone splattered on the couch and television.

The gardener and landlord closed the front door, ran back to the office, and called 911.

Twenty minutes later, I stepped past Mario Lewis and crept down the short hallway to the bathroom. There, I found his girlfriend, Lisa Ferguson, dead in the bloody bathtub and the couple's three-year-old daughter, Sasha, lying beside her, just as cold and blue. The trio had been dead for five days. No one had seen the murders or suicide coming—not Mario's family, not Lisa's family, not the couple's neighbors. And over the course of the investigation, each person kept telling me, "Mario woulda never killed his baby. Mario woulda never killed himself. Nuh uh. Not Mario."

Two weeks before the killings, Mario Lewis had been diagnosed with schizophrenia. A month before that, Mario had assaulted a female coworker. And according to Lisa Ferguson's hairdresser, Mario had threatened to kill his girlfriend twice before.

I told all of this to Mario's people.

"Not Mario," his mother had cried. "That ain't the boy I raised. That ain't the boy *I* know."

Well, she didn't know Mario.

Back behind the wheel of the Crown Vic, I zigged and zagged, revved and roared west on Jefferson Boulevard at breakneck speeds, hoping that Greg held a doctor's note in his hand and was tense and eager to do bad, sexy things to me.

But at almost nine o'clock, all the lights were off in the condo.

Still, my lustful heart thumped wildly as I zoomed into my parking space.

His Ducati wasn't parked in its spot.

I rushed through the garage door and into the house.

Quiet. Darkness.

With quickly depleting adrenaline, I wandered from room to room, turning on some lights while leaving others off.

Envelopes and catalogs sat in the mail slot. A parcel sat on the porch—a new novel, probably sent by my buddy Lena Meadows. Morning dishes still sat in the kitchen sink. The tree standing in the middle of the living room still needed gem-colored balls and a few bars of "Deck the Halls" to transform it into a Christmas tree. (If the noble fir had been stolen that afternoon, my living room would have looked just as it did back in May.)

I stood at the base of the stairs, surveying my empty home with tired eyes. "Oh well."

After storing my Glock in its case, I undressed and showered. Ten minutes later, I left the bathroom and called out, "Greg?"

No answer.

I slipped on boxer shorts and a T-shirt, then fell into the bed. I tore the parcel open and pulled out the novel. The cover was true art: a muscular blond, bare-chested man with a giant fin for legs was somehow carrying a cross-eyed brunette into the sea. The title: *The Love of a Merman.* Cheesy romance novels were my getaway, and so Lena sent me a new title each month. I flipped through the pages of *Merman* and landed on, "His tentacles wrapped around me, and one slithered into my slick walls to find my deep, slick pearl. I yelped in pleasure . . ."

"Funny. A merman with tentacles." I grabbed the phone from the night-stand.

Greg answered on the third ring, in midsentence with Patrick, who was one of his level builders and one of the 150 people on his team.

"You're at work," I said, relieved but disappointed.

"Hey, babe. Yeah. Sorry. We hit a snag." Then, he rambled on about Level Three glitches that included a zombie stuck in a bog. He chuckled, then said, "Bored yet?"

I smiled. "Never. Did you get the zombie out of the bog, though?"

"Nope. May have to kill it."

"Head shots are the best shots."

"You would know," he said. "I'll be home in . . . I don't know."

"I called you earlier, left you a few messages."

"I know. Sorry again. Just been jammed up."

"I can bring you food," I offered. "Sushi or—"

"We've already ordered. Thanks, though."

I fluffed a pillow, then said, "I had a long—"

"I gotta go, babe. Sorry. They're waitin' for me. The zombie's waiting, too."

A hitch caught in my throat, but I managed to say, "Okay."

"I promise to be home before midnight." He hung up.

I stared at the receiver and listened to the beeping dial tone that told me that I had voice mail. I scrolled through missed calls and saw my mother's number.

Didn't have the bandwidth to hear her voice live, so I did not call her back. Instead, I hit the button to hear her message.

I guess you're working today. I finally made the decision about Tori. I think you'll be satisfied with it. Call me. I love you. Bye.

Back in June, during the investigation of that murdered high school cheer-leader, Monique Darson, we had found the remains of my sister, Victoria, buried in the storage basement of Crase Liquor Emporium. After more than twenty-five years, my sister was finally home—and Mom kept her ashes in a sapphire-blue urn on the mantel. She and I had talked about holding a small memorial service, but then the discussion took a left turn.

How could you ask me to let her go again? Mom had asked in tears.

You want to keep her on the mantel forever? I had countered.

You don't understand.

No, you *don't understand*.

Not ready to deal with Mom and Tori, I grabbed my iPhone from my bag and considered the Bust-a-Cheat app.

Greg was at work—I had called his office number, and he had picked up his extension. I had heard Patrick talking in the background.

What time had he gone to work?

And how *long* had he been in the office?

Did that Tokyo phone number *really* belong to a coworker?

Or did that phone number belong to *her*?

He lies. Don't forget that he lies.

I could never forget that. Ever. Because each time he lied, that lie built upon the other lies like polyps building coral reefs. And each time I caught him in a lie, I hurt. And he apologized. And I accepted his apology. Then, he lied again. And I hurt again. We were in syndication by now, with story arcs that wrote themselves.

My trembling index finger hovered over the icon.

Rule number 1 for a successful marriage: Trust Your Husband.

Trust him.

Like Lisa Ferguson had trusted Mario Lewis?

I sat the iPhone on the nightstand—I was not Lisa Ferguson, and Greg would never hurt me. Not like *that*. Not in *that* way. Right?

Wednesday, December 12

13

The scent of bacon, burned bread, and fresh-brewed coffee pulled me from sleep. My muscles creaked as I sat up in bed. My eyes adjusted to my surroundings, barely lit by the weak light of a December morning. A pair of cargo shorts had been discarded near the hamper, and soap on steam wafted from the bathroom. My throat felt raspy, and my mouth tasted like I had eaten every cigarette butt in every ashtray in Reno.

Must be Wednesday.

My eyes rolled back in my head.

Juliet.

That name jolted me awake.

Something, something kill me.

Smith & Wesson revolver.

Vanity of vanities.

I glanced at the clock on the dresser.

Almost eight thirty.

"Damn it." I kicked away the comforter and jumped out of bed.

Death had a way of movin' your ass.

Greg had slipped into the house sometime after eleven o'clock to leave those shorts near (not *in*) the hamper. By then, I had been visiting REM dreamland, a place where no one got shot, stabbed, or killed.

Out the window, I saw a heavy gray sky and rustling leaves on trees.

So I dressed for fifty-five-degree weather and a possible trip back to the Chatman house—relaxed jeans, a T-shirt, and a gray V-neck cardigan that I was losing to moths. After retrieving my gun and slipping my feet into a pair of loafers, I popped a few ibuprofen just in case the raspy throat was a true thing.

In the living room, the bare pine tree still held court.

I pointed at the noble fir as I passed. "You're gettin' dressed today."

Greg sat at his drawing table in his office, lit only by two twenty-inch monitors. On the screens: three zombie marines. Discarded paper proofs piled around his chair like wood shavings. Patrick's nasally voice blared from the speakerphone—something about the bog being an important quest location.

"Hey," I whispered from the doorway.

He turned in his chair and waved at me.

I came to stand beside him, and pointed at the newly turned marine on the monitor. "That's good," I whispered, then kissed the top of his head.

Greg patted my ass, gave it a good squeeze, then scribbled on a sticky note, *You were asleep when I got in. Didn't want to wake you.*

I shrugged.

He scribbled on another sticky, *I'll call you later.*

I nodded.

One last note. *Left you a little breakfast.*

Another kiss, another squeeze, and I left the office and entered a kitchen where the stainless steel appliances twinkled like daggers.

On the breakfast bar was a small plate. There, Greg had left a yellow sticky. "EAT ME." Two strips of bacon and a toasted English muffin. The yellow sticky on the half-full cup of coffee said, "DRINK ME." A Target bag also sat on the bar, and one last sticky note had been slapped onto it. "WEAR ME."

I opened the bag. A new pair of massaging-gel shoe inserts. "Awww." I tore open the package, plucked out the insoles, and stuck them in my loafers. I was now ready to do what detectives did all day: stand, walk, and stoop. I shoved bacon into my mouth, took a bite of muffin, gulped the coffee, then grabbed my cell phone from my bag. *Meet you at LACCO,* I texted Colin. The autopsies of the Chatmans were being performed today.

Colin texted back, *Been here since 7. Where you at??? Everything OK?*

Everything OK? Asking but not asking about Greg and me. I winced as I typed, *Running late. Wiped out last night.*

Screwing up already and I hadn't even been awake for an hour.

14

The autopsy chambers located within the redbrick walls of the Los Angeles County Department of Coroner have seen some of the world's most famous celebrities who died questionable deaths. HSS detectives were thrown those cases—Whitney Houston, Michael Jackson, and Natalie Wood. As a homicide detective with a beat in regular Los Angeles, I investigated everybody else's deaths—the fans of the rich and famous. The coroner's office had become another home away from home away from home for me. I had climbed those tall stone steps, sat in the lobby in those bloodred armchairs, and trudged down those hallways, shallow-breathed and fidgety, too many times to count.

By now, dead bodies didn't bother me—the living ones, the violent ones, did.

Dressed in blue scrubs darkened with sweat at the neck and underarms, the deputy medical examiner, Spencer Brooks, M.D., met me in the antechamber of the autopsy suite. I had arrived during a quiet time—no high-pitched squeal of drills. No threatening growls of Stryker saws. No bodies in various states of dead forming an assembly line outside the cutting room. Beyond Brooks and through the observation window, another pathologist quietly soup-ladled blood out of a dead soul's chest cavity. Colin, dressed in blue scrubs and a face mask, stood nearby, arms crossed, legs set wide apart to keep from crumpling to the rust-colored tile.

I had known Spencer Brooks for more than a decade—both professionally and personally. He was a good friend of my girl Syeeda McKay, and that meant Brooks and I had bonded over margaritas, baskets of onion strings, *and* gunshot wounds.

On this morning, though, since neither of us smelled of tequila or grease, and since this building smelled of pine cleaner and formaldehyde, I addressed Brooks by his title—doctor—and he called me by mine—detective.

"Almost ten o'clock," he said to me. "You're late." He clutched a folder in one hand and swiped at his sweaty forehead with the other. "We started at seven this morning."

"Me being late is like Halley's Comet streaking across the sky."

"A rare and precious thing," he admitted. "However, you've missed out."

"Next time." In our line of work, there was always a "next time."

"Colin's finishing up with Chloe right now," Brooks said. "And we'll hold them until the family sends the hearses."

"How did he do today?"

"Better. Kept his mouth shut, and when he opened it, I didn't want to take a saw to him." Brooks shrugged. "I hate him less than I did last week."

"He remember to show you the photos of the crime scene this time?"

"Yep."

"He remember to bring you the preliminary report?"

"Yep."

"Helpful?"

"Finally." He pushed back his silver wire-rimmed glasses and rubbed his eyes.

"So what can you tell me?"

"Sy called."

I twisted my lips, then said, "Already?"

He nodded.

"And you told her . . . ?"

"That I hadn't even started the autopsies yet."

I narrowed my eyes and studied him: Brooks had a crush on Syeeda, and sometimes he fed her tips for stories. "How did she take that?"

He shrugged. "She thinks I'm conspiring with you to keep her in the dark."

I rolled my eyes. "So the Chatmans?"

Brooks opened the folder and flipped to a page. "They ate dinner several hours before they died. Beef, asparagus, potatoes. I smelled dairy, too."

"There were milk shake glasses on the sink."

"That explains the strawberries." He found another sheet. "We did a preliminary tox on all three. Juliet had alcohol in her system. But booze didn't come up in all three screens."

"What did?"

"Large amounts of Valium. But I found no pills—the drug had been fully absorbed before they died."

"No one got up," I said, "because they were all knocked out."

"Perhaps. Usually diazepam won't kill. There have been instances where people take forty pills and suffer nothing more than losing two days to sleep. Sometimes, the body goes into deep coma, and then you need medical intervention, like several doses of flumazenil. For the Chatmans, since there wasn't an antidote around and oxygen became depleted by the fire . . ." He shook his head.

"But Juliet came to," I said. "She grabbed her gun, then made a 911 call saying that something was trying to kill her."

He scrunched his eyebrows. "What time was that?"

"Don't know. I'll find out and get back to you." I scribbled a reminder in my notepad. "So the Valium slowed them down and the carbon monoxide from the fire finished the job."

"Basically."

"Who had the Valium scrip?" I asked.

"Don't know. And you'll need a court order to find out. But it certainly contributed to their unconscious state and, ultimately, to their deaths."

I added another to-do item to my growing list—so many things to do, so many things I didn't know.

"Speaking of CO_2," he said. "I measured levels in their blood."

"And?"

"More in Juliet—she was breathing heavily before she died."

"Panicked, maybe. Or trying to escape."

Brooks shrugged. "Chloe had almost twice the amount of Valium in her blood than Cody, but he died sooner—rigor mortis was more established in him than his sister."

"Cody's bedroom was closer to the point of origin," I said. "Right next to the bathroom."

The door to the chamber opened. Brooks's assistant Big Reuben, a black dude as large as Mount Rushmore, filled the tiny foyer even though he had only poked out his head. "We need you in here, Doc. What's up, Detective Norton?"

"On the hunt," I said.

Colin looked over to us and cocked his head.

I gave him a quick wave.

"You late," Big Reuben said.

I nodded. "I'm aware."

Big Reuben said, "All right, then," and backed out of the door.

"I'll give Taggert the swabs and clippings and all of that once we're finished," Brooks said, handing me the folder he'd been holding. "But this is for you right now. After you read this, you may want to talk to her doctors."

"I found her planner last night," I said. "She had appointments back on Thursday, Monday, and yesterday with an ob-gyn. Was Juliet pregnant?"

"According to my blood tests," Brooks said, "no, she was not."

A necessary question—"killed by their lovers' hands" was the leading cause of death for pregnant women.

I read the words on the report, and all feeling left my face. "Oh crap."

"Yeah. I'll print pictures."

I muttered, "Crap," again.

He opened the door to the chamber. "Kinda changes things."

"Yeah."

"Again, I suggest you talk with her doctors," he said. "You'll probably need a warrant first."

"I'll do that now."

"Let me know about that 911 call," he said.

An administrative assistant let me nest at an available work space that boasted a wobbly chair and a broken ceiling light. As I sat, my phone vibrated.

A text, and then another text, from Syeeda. *Where are you? I officially have questions. Why haven't u called me back???*

I typed one word—*WORKING*—then shoved the phone into my bag.

In less than twenty minutes, I had received from Brooks autopsy photos for the murder book and had prepared warrant requests for Juliet Chatman's medical records along with records for Chloe and Cody. I faxed those requests to Judge Keener for approval.

Minutes later, I slid back behind the wheel of the Crown Vic.

Had Juliet known about her condition?

Is that why she saw her doctor twice in less than a week?

If so, what had been her reaction?

And how had Christopher Chatman reacted?

The suitcases.

My stomach clenched as a horrid thought formed in my mind.

Had she poisoned Cody and Chloe because she knew . . . ?

Or had the fire merely been a coincidence? God's way—or the devil's way—of finalizing her wish to die—and to die with her children.

15

The medical office of obstetrician-gynecologist Maria Kulkanis was located in the seaside town of Santa Monica, just a stone's throw from the Pacific Ocean. I parked on the quiet tree-lined street in front of an Italian restaurant, a block away from the outdoor shops of the Third Street Promenade. The sun had slept in, leaving behind soupy gray skies.

Judge Keener had approved and faxed my search warrant requests while I was en route to Santa Monica. With the expandable case file tucked beneath my arm, I quickly stepped into the building and rode the elevator up to the third floor. A moment later, I entered an empty, softly lit waiting room that smelled of potpourri. The sound track to *Cats* whispered over the sound system.

I approached the reception desk and badged the Latina woman sitting there. "I'm here to talk with Dr. Kulkanis."

"One minute," she said, immediately picking up the phone.

I stepped away, feeling my fingers and toes thaw from the chill.

On one wall hung a poster of a smiling woman in soft focus, childless thanks to the long-sounding pill name she had been taking. On the other walls hung more posters of smiling women as they cradled bellies—swollen and healthy with a little help from Vita-Life and Estro-Natal.

Childless, pregnant—both versions made me sweat. *Technically*, by now, I was supposed to be one of those tummy-clutching mommas to be. Back in the spring, I had planned to go off the Pill—I was thirty-seven years old, my mother wanted grandkids, and I probably wanted her to have them. But women's intuition had whispered in my ear, "*Gurl*. Keep poppin' them pills. Shenanigans are afoot."

Indeed, Greg had been diddling the Japanese skank.

I had immediately refilled my pill prescription, although not smiling as broadly (or at all) as the poster lady passively praising the wonders of that long-sounding contraceptive name.

But I forgave him. (*You took him back. Again, you took him back.*) That meant, in the near future, a baby could still happen.

Dr. Kulkanis was ready to talk to me, and I tripped down the hallway to a large office with a view of the Italian restaurant across the street. I sat across from the older white woman with fresh-scrubbed porcelain skin and a wild silver bob. No posters on these walls. Just Christmas and Hanukkah cards, framed diplomas, and pictures of babies, more babies, and babies with their parents. Even the mug near her hands had a picture of a baby on it.

After banter about her practice, I slipped the faxed court order on her desk.

"On Thursday, Juliet thought she was pregnant," Dr. Kulkanis told me. "She didn't seem happy with that. I've been her doctor for over twenty years, and so I know her. *Knew* her." The doctor's breath caught, and her blue eyes filled with tears. "She kept saying that she couldn't be pregnant, that it was impossible. But she was experiencing drowsiness, lethargy, nausea. The muscles in her arms and legs hurt, and her last period came before Halloween.

"I asked her if she'd had sex with her husband, and the look of revulsion on her face . . ." The doctor shook her head. "One time: that's what she told me. She'd had sex with him once since the summer. And I laughed and asked if she needed a refresher course on how pregnancies occurred."

"She hadn't been on birth control?"

"Seems like you may need one, too," Dr. Kulkanis said. "Yes: Juliet had been on the Pill. Remember, though: there's still a one percent chance that you can get pregnant."

The sound of rushing blood filled my ears. Something (my ovaries) jabbed at my abdomen. Their way of saying, "Damn, Lou. Maybe you should take two pills a day, eh?"

"What about the Valium prescription?" I asked.

"I had prescribed five milligrams twice a day for her anxiety. But she told me she'd stopped taking them back in the summer, once she had started to feel drowsy and fatigued."

"Dr. Brooks found excessive amounts of Valium in her blood," I said.

The ob-gyn lifted the mug to her lips and sipped.

"And he found a lot of Valium in the children's blood, too."

I let my inference hang in the air as she sat the mug back on the desk.

"Juliet had been distressed," Dr. Kulkanis said, "but she wasn't suicidal. Nor was she *homicidal*. She'd never . . ." She swallowed, then met my gaze.

My body went cold as a "best of" list of murderous moms scrolled through my mind.

Susan Smith.

Andrea Yates.

Marybeth Tinning.

"Her visit on Thursday," I said. "Anything strange about it?"

Dr. Kulkanis reached for a tissue box on the corner of her desk. "She, umm . . ." The doctor blew her nose into a sheet, then sighed. "She had lost seventeen pounds since her appointment back in May. Her blood pressure was low—ninety over fifty. I did a blood draw, which—in addition to the urine test—confirmed that she wasn't pregnant."

"Anything else happen on Thursday?" I whispered.

"I examined her and felt a large mass on her right ovary. I told her that it could've been a cyst—she'd had those before. So I performed an ultrasound."

"To look at what you were feeling?"

"Correct. The most typical cysts are usually filled with fluid—she'd had those. But on this visit, the ultrasound didn't show what it typically did. Instead, it showed a large mass on her ovary and black spots just like it all around her uterus."

"Did you tell her that?"

"I told her that I was concerned and wanted better imaging to know what I was seeing, that the tissue could've been benign. Fibroids, for example."

"And Juliet's reaction?"

"Still had pregnancy on the brain. She kept saying, 'I can't have another baby. I don't want another baby.' And then she said—her exact words were—'Another baby would *trap* me.'"

"Trap?"

The doctor nodded. "I scheduled a CT scan at another facility for first thing this past Monday morning, and then a follow-up appointment with me for Tuesday. Yesterday. Both of which she missed."

I cocked my head. "Do you know *why* she missed them? She was alive on Monday."

The woman shrugged. "She didn't call—she just . . . didn't show up."

I wrote a note. *Why did she skip her appts?* What had been more important than those black spots growing inside her?

"When I sent her for imaging, I knew what our conversation would be, and I had planned to tell her in person during our appointment. Not knowing about the fire, I left her a message yesterday afternoon, when it was clear she wasn't coming in. I asked her to call me and . . ." The doctor's voice broke. "At the time, I didn't know she had also missed the CT. I thought that today . . ."

I pulled out three autopsy pictures from the file: Juliet Chatman's abdominal cavity was congested with cancerous tumors that resembled pieces of raw, fatty rump roast. "The medical examiner took tumor samples to analyze, but he thinks ovarian cancer." I handed her the photos.

With a shaky hand, Dr. Kulkanis studied each picture twice, then whispered, "I agree."

Ovarian cancer: a mean disease that will not tell you it had arrived until the hurt became too explosive to ignore. By that time, the cancer had grown past the ovary to contaminate other organs. Doctors throw surgery, chemotherapy, and radiation at the disease. Patients and their loved ones add prayer, lots of prayer. If you are blessed with an early diagnosis, you can make plans past five years: see your daughter married, watch your son march across a stage for his diploma, take that cruise to the Bahamas. Women with advanced disease, though, women like Juliet Chatman . . . Their families would experience those life moments without them.

The doctor's face darkened as she pushed the pictures away. "I'm not an oncologist, but I've been a gynecologist for thirty years, and if what I'm seeing . . . With advanced disease like this . . . This Christmas would have been Juliet's last."

16

Juliet Chatman was dying.

And she had no clue that cancer was killing her.

A house fire, though, would kill her first.

Last Thursday, December 6, out into the world she went. It had been a crisp winter day in Santa Monica. On any other morning, maybe she would have stopped by the spa for a massage or a manicure. Eaten lunch at Shutters, sitting at an outside patio table despite the cold to watch waves crash against the shore. Maybe she would have ordered a Bloody Mary or three. Flirted with the cute waiter. Wandered the aisles of Fred Segal afterward in search of a cute blouse or an interesting hat.

But on that Thursday, she had learned that something inside of her wasn't right.

It was now half past twelve, and even though I'd gobbled two strips of bacon and an English muffin, I was plagued with shaky hands that came from hunger. But I wobbled past the cafés and bakeries of Santa Monica beckoning me from the sidewalks with their clean round tables and bud vases and lazy twists of steam wafting from pots of fresh-brewed coffee.

Twenty-seven hours had passed since I had caught the Chatman case, and I still couldn't answer one question: Who killed a mother and her two kids?

The Crown Vic was as cold as a museum, and stinky. No matter how many times I sprayed "crisp linen" air freshener around the cabin, the stubborn odors of man sweat and pickles hung around like an ex-boyfriend with my house key.

I turned the ignition and pulled away from the curb.

My iPhone rang from my bag. A picture flashed on the screen: a big-eyed, brown-eyed woman with caramel latte skin and a smile as crooked as Lombard Street. Syeeda McKay and I (along with Lena Meadows) had been friends and sorority sisters since college. As a member of the fourth estate, though, Syeeda officially chapped my ass. Talking to her often left me limp—and my insides feeling as though they'd been shredded by a metal hook. All good detectives know, though, that one of the best weapons to have is a reporter. Still: I tasted my own blood whenever Syeeda and I had to push our friendship aside to do our jobs.

"Please tell me this case is a domestic dispute," she said, "and not an arson turned murder."

"I don't know what this case is about yet, and good afternoon to you, too. Interesting that you want my opinion as a police officer *now* even though—"

"But you all *haven't* told the public anything about the arsons. I'm filling a void—"

"With fluff and crap."

"My last article—"

"Was fluff and crap. Well written, however."

"Fine, then. Tell me: Should my mom, who lives a half mile away from the Chatmans, freak out? Should she buy a gun, cuz that's where she is right now? Has the Burning Man upped the ante by killing people—*children*—in their beds now?"

"Sy. Take a knee. And tell your mom to take a knee, too." Then, I told her the bare bones of the case.

"Is that supposed to make me feel better?" she screeched. "Some . . . crunked-up psychopath killed two kids and their mom *on purpose*?"

"Is that a journalistic term? Crunked-up?"

"What about the autopsies?"

"Ongoing."

"Off the record."

"Ongoing, *girlfriend*."

"This isn't funny."

"Yeah, cuz I'm busting up right now."

"Any suspects?" she asked.

"Not right now. We're in the process of interviewing friends, family, and neighbors."

"Your first thoughts?"

I took a deep breath, then exhaled. "Whoever did this is the most disturbed, fucked-up, hell-bound motherfucker outside of an institution, and when I catch him—"

"Or her—"

"I will shove my size seven Cole Haan loafer so far down his throat—"

"Okay, so I only have five hundred words."

"Hey: Do you know the Chatmans by any chance?"

"No."

I inched onto the 10 freeway eastbound. Cars, cars, cars, bumper to bumper like a junkyard. Behind the steering wheels, people texted (illegal), people talked on cell phones using their hands (illegal), people lipsticked-blushed-mascaraed in vanity mirrors (not totally illegal, but bitches, please).

"How about Ben Oliver?" I asked. "He's an insurance attorney—"

"Who's representing one of the families with a burned-down house."

"So you know him?"

"No," she said. "I read. It's fundamental." She paused, then said, "Are you asking me to . . . ?"

"Thank you," I said, smiling. "That is all."

"No, no, wait. Off the record."

I paused, which was her answer. Then, I said, "Call your mom, Sy. Tell her not to worry."

"What am I looking for specifically?"

"Don't know, but whatever you find, I'll need receipts."

"Got it. So I stopped by your house this morning. I wanted some of your busy eggs for breakfast."

"That would've been good," I said. "But I'm out of green onions. And bell pepper. And eggs. Rain check. I'll throw in cinnamon rolls."

She cleared her throat. "So . . ."

"Uh-oh," I said. "What's wrong?"

"I saw your husband a few minutes ago. At the Marina Starbucks with some white girl who was making googly eyes at him."

Pow! Her punch landed in my midsection. My head snapped forward. Bursts of light twinkled before me, and I almost rear-ended the chick in the Honda who needed to replace that mascara wand with a magic wand.

I took a breath, then said, "Starbucks, huh?"

"Mmhmm."

"He see you?"

"Can any man *not* see me?"

"So he saw you. Did he turn to stone?"

She chuckled. "No, but his posture changed."

"Okay," I said.

"Probably nothing."

A thick pause, seconds drowned in cold molasses.

"You okay?" she asked. "Should I have kept that to myself?"

I shook my head. "I wanna know. Thanks."

After ending the call, I exited the freeway and tried to take deep breaths, but I couldn't—a result of the rabbit punches Syeeda had just dealt. Taking guppy breaths (the only kind available), I pulled into a gas station and parked.

I hadn't used Bust-a-Cheat for more than a day. Now, though . . . My clammy hands shook as I tapped the app.

The car felt too hot now. I punched off the heat button and rolled down every window in the car. The roar of traffic overwhelmed me, and I rolled up three of the four windows.

The RECENT CALLS log loaded.

Pinballs clanged from my now-vibrating phone.

Greg's picture—three-day growth, pecan-colored eyes—brightened my screen.

"Hey," I said with forced cheer.

"I'm out on the bike," he said, shouting over the whir of hydraulics and the clank of tools. "Martinez needs to put on new brake pads. I was just thinking about you."

"I was just thinking about you, too," I said, my chest tight.

"Saw Sy this morning."

"Yeah?"

"At Starbucks. I was there with Kelly."

"Who?"

"The girl who wears all those stupid barrettes in her hair? Cosplay Kelly. She wants to move over to Creative, so she bought me a coffee to kiss my ass."

"Did it work?"

"I pointed out that she misspelled 'Revelation' twice on my last press release. Then, I told her that she's lucky she still has a job."

I chuckled. "So I guess that's a no."

"Wanna grab a quick bite later?" he asked. "Tokyo's having QA issues, and I won't be home until late."

"How about dessert?" I asked.

"Dessert. That means you naked on my bike."

"And then, afterwards, a trio of crème brûlée."

"Sounds good. Hit me up when you're home."

We ended the call. Bust-a-Cheat had timed out. Fine. I considered that, and all the other apps I had purchased since buying the device.

An app to stream music.

An app to read books.

An app to bust your unfaithful mate.

Too much information.

Bust-a-Cheat would give me an ulcer by Boxing Day.

I eased back onto the freeway. As cars separated into different lanes—downtown here, San Bernardino there—I pressed Bust-a-Cheat until all the apps wiggled, until an X appeared at the top corners of each square. I tapped one X only, Bust-a-Cheat. The icon blipped away, and then my muscles relaxed, tears of relief welled in my eyes, and all suspicion and doubt became foam that would dry and evaporate—and soon I would forget that I had ever doubted him.

Until the next time.

17

The two-story building that houses the Southwest Division of the Los Angeles Police Department is located on Martin Luther King, Jr., Boulevard, a major valve of South Los Angeles. A major valve with no coffee shops, no ATMs (except for the machine in our lobby), and lots of churches.

Noontime meant *siesta*, and the squad room was unusually quiet. Luke's head drooped over his belly as he caught snatches of sleep. Pepe typed and yawned, typed and yawned some more. The fluorescent lighting tubes buzzed. The soundproof interview rooms where suspects and their mommas came to cry were all empty.

It had been three days since I'd sat at my desk. Three days since I'd smelled stale coffee, Luke's cheap cologne, and the rankness of weed on a perp's jacket. Smelling all of this now made my skin tingle and my mind reel with memories, like Proust and his cookie but six times more fucked up.

My desk almost faced a window, but I wasn't missing much. Kids ditching school. Hookers. Thugs. Homeless. Cops. Traffic. Poverty. Pigeons. No, my view consisted of Colin's cubicle, its walls tacked with so many pictures of him skiing, tanning, and smiling that you thought he had died too young, too soon.

"At least we're not the asshole of LA," Lieutenant Rodriguez always touted. "Seventy-Seventh is a *real* shithole." Zak Rodriguez had been my boss and mentor since I'd stopped flunking the bar exam and chose instead to mete out justice as a sworn officer of the LAPD. At six foot six, he hadn't planned to bust in doors and wrestle Bloods to the ground. He'd dreamed of being paid millions of dollars to tackle other big men in big arenas. He'd been on his way to doing that until cancer took away his mother—and his spirit.

He now towered over my desk, a pack of Camels in one dragon-sized hand and a can of RC Cola in the other. "So the Chatman case is where?"

I had just sat at my desk to scroll through the hundred e-mail messages clogging my in-box. *Reporter, reporter, spam.* "Not sure," I said. "It's all very strange—the people I've talked to so far say the Chatmans were a happy family. But, first: people lie. And, second: happy families don't carry handguns and stow packed suitcases in cars with full tanks of gas. *Normally.*"

My boss shrugged. "Maybe the gun was for protection since they'd been robbed before. And maybe the suitcases were for emergencies, like earthquakes and riots and whatnot."

"Maybe."

"How much longer to turn 'maybe' into 'definitely'?" He paused, then added, "Would be nice to close this out for the year."

Ah. The coveted clearance rate.

"It's solvable." I stretched, and the bones in my shoulders clicked like toppling dominoes. "I should have the arson and coroner's reports in hand sometime soon. Those should answer most of my questions. Then, we'll make an arrest and you'll throw me a parade and—"

"She's here!" Colin sauntered into the squad room holding a foil-covered plate. "Guess who picked up Porto's for lunch? And guess who saved you some?"

My stomach jitterbugged as I took the plate and peeled off the foil.

"What's that she got?" Pepe asked.

"Taggert saved me some potato balls," I said, my mouth full.

"Hey, no fair," Luke whined. "You snooze, you lose."

"Leave her alone," Colin said. "She's got my balls in her mouth."

I shoveled in another lump of potatoes and ground beef, then said, "And they're delicious, too." Eating had energized me, and my body felt buoyant again.

"Let's get an update," Lieutenant Rodriguez said as he settled on top of my desk. "Lou, you can talk in between eating Taggert's balls."

Everyone took a seat as I pulled a small whiteboard from beside my file cabinet. I set that up on a worktable, then cleared my throat. I leaned back in my chair and then told them about my meeting with Dr. Maria Kulkanis, about Juliet Chatman's Valium prescription, about Juliet's use of the word "trapped" when speaking about being pregnant again. "What bothers me the most about this case is that Juliet had as much a motive for killing herself as her husband did."

"What motive does Christopher Chatman have?" Lieutenant Rodriguez asked. "Other than 'nobody wants to kill your wife and kids except you'?"

"Don't know," I admitted, blushing. "I'm just being prejudiced: men suck."

"After the autopsies, after Lou got the warrants in, I went through the family's medical records," Colin said, flipping through his notepad. "As far as drugs, Juliet had the Valium scrip. The kids didn't. Cody had a Ritalin prescription, though, and he'd gone to the emergency room a few times for suspicious burns."

"Kid was a firebug, right?" Pepe asked.

"Yep," Colin said. "But back on Thursday, looks like he'd gone in for a bruised ulna."

"How'd he get it?" I asked.

"Roughhousing," Colin said.

"Busy day on Thursday," I said, looking to Luke.

"I talked to the guy who owns the shop where Mrs. Chatman bought her gun," Luke said, taking my cue. "Sam Duffy's his name. Said she came on Thursday—he doesn't see many black women in Gun Runners. He remembered that when she first came in, he looked at her driver's license and saw that she'd come from LA. She told him that she wanted protection, that she didn't have any experience firing a weapon. This second visit, she seemed nervous, but that didn't strike him as much as her just bein' in the store."

With a black marker, Colin started a timeline on the whiteboard. "It takes ten days to buy a gun. So ten days before last Thursday was Monday, November twenty-sixth." He wrote "JC BUYS GUN."

Then, we filled in other dates we knew: Juliet Chatman's last doctor's appointments, the date of the fire, Juliet at Gun Runners, Cody in the emergency room. Arms crossed or leaning forward, we all stared at the whiteboard in silence.

"Can I hear the 911 call?" I asked.

Pepe tapped a few keys on his computer keyboard, and soon the familiar blurp of an incoming emergency call answered by a female operator filled the squad room.

Operator: *Fire and paramedics. What is the address of the emergency?*
Juliet Chatman: *I need help! Help me! My house is on fire.*
Operator: *Okay, ma'am. What is your address?*
Juliet Chatman: *Oh god . . . Oh no! Wake up, baby! Wake up!*
Operator: *Ma'am, what is your address?*

Juliet Chatman: *[static] trying to kill me![coughing]*

Operator: *Ma'am—*

[Dial tone.]

Operator: *Ma'am?*

The call disconnected.

For another minute, we all sat there, barely breathing, not speaking, soaking up the abject fear in Juliet Chatman's voice.

Wake up, baby!

She was pleading with Chloe.

A flush crept across my face and burrowed beneath my skin. I swallowed hard, then asked, "What time did that call come in?"

Pepe peered at the computer. "Three thirty-one that morning."

"She used her cell to make that call?" I asked.

"Yep," Pepe said. "The R/O got to the house at 3:51 and called it in again—fire trucks were en route already because of Virginia Oliver's call at 3:45."

"Oh yeah," Colin said. "'Sounded like God frying bacon.'"

I handed out assignments:

Luke would handle the Chatmans' phone records.

Pepe would delve into the family's finances.

Colin would liaise with Forensics and handle the murder book.

Lieutenant Rodriguez would manage media inquiries.

I would do all of this and more, while also interviewing family, friends, and the husband.

Just as we were about to break, my e-mail alert chimed.

Quigley had sent over a PDF.

I hit PRINT.

Luke and Pepe read the hard copy of the fire report as Colin, Lieutenant Rodriguez, and I peered at my computer monitor and the nineteen pages of sketches, floor plans, and photographs.

The summary detailed the square footage and number of rooms in the Chatman house. Three pages detailed the on-scene investigation: what had been on fire upon the fire department's arrival and preliminary observations of where the fire had started and had found its victims.

"'Lab analysis shows,'" I read aloud, "'a household petroleum product.'"

"What?" Colin asked. "Like oil or Vaseline?"

I pushed away from my desk and rubbed my bottom lip. "How would a household petroleum product—say, Vaseline—catch fire?"

Lieutenant Rodriguez continued to read the report. "'Point of origin . . . electrical outlet in the upstairs hallway bathroom.'" He cocked his head. "And how would it spill into an electrical outlet to spark and hit those paint cans and rags?"

"He or she used a trailer," I said. "Does the report mention newspaper or dryer sheets? Typical trailer trash?"

The men read in silence until Colin said, "No mention of a trailer, but the investigation ain't over."

Lieutenant Rodriguez's gray eyes had turned the same color as the pewter sky outside. He grunted as he hopped off my desk. "This is bigger than we thought."

"Devil's in the details," I said. "And you know I live and breathe details."

"*El diablo sabe más por viejo que por diablo*," he countered.

The devil knows more for being old than for being the devil.

My muscles tensed—he was right. I hadn't lived on this planet long enough to know everything there was to know about evil. And despite living for the details, I didn't even know what I didn't even know.

18

Spencer Brooks was in the cutting room and couldn't be disturbed. So I left him a voice mail. "Juliet Chatman's emergency call came in at 3:31 A.M., which confirms your finding lots of carbon monoxide in her lungs. She was alive for much of the fire. Hope that helps."

It would: the devil was in the details.

I pulled from my bottom drawer a small white Christmas tree with tiny red and green bulbs and a miniature polar bear clinging to the top. I sat it next to my fuchsia orchid that never saw the sun and was slowly dying on the corner of my desk.

I clicked back to my virtual in-box, and, just like that, its contents had grown by twenty. Brooks had received my voice mail and had e-mailed me his thanks. Another message had been sent by Sam Seward, the assistant district attorney assigned to the Monique Darson murder case. My stomach lurched as I scanned the preview pane of Sam's e-mail: "grand jury summons . . . Max Crase . . . competence trial."

As I read, my eyes burned and my nose twitched.

A forest . . . in the middle of the Pacific Ocean . . .

"Colin," I snapped. "Stop stinking."

My partner now hunkered over me, his eyes twinkling like liquid blue topaz. "Put your panty hose on. We got visitors." He tapped a bulb on my Christmas tree. "You being ironic?"

I sneezed three times. "Maybe if you wore *more* cologne, you'd kill me *all* the way." I plucked tissue from the box on Pepe's desk and blew my nose.

"Ladies love Armani," he said, sauntering toward the interview rooms.

"Ladies love oxygen, too," I said, following in his overscented wake.

A moment later, we sat in interview room 3, the nicest of the three craptoriums used to interrogate suspects and their loved ones. This room had

retained nearly all of its gray soundproof padding and had sufficient ventilation for two people. Across from us sat the short, balding white man from
Don Mateo Drive and his mousy-haired playwright-wife, Delia.

"Eli Moss," he reminded me as he crossed his hairless pink calves. Under-
arm sweat rings darkened his red THING 1 T-shirt. The pockets of his
green cargo shorts had been stuffed with who knows?

Delia wore an eggplant-colored sweater two sizes too big, thick black
leggings, and shearling boots.

They had dressed for two of California's climates.

"So what can we do for you today, Mr. and Mrs. Moss?" Colin asked.

"It's more, what *I* can do for you." Eli thrust out his chin. "I created something of a minidocumentary of the fire." His lungs, filled with self-satisfaction,
expanded beneath his shirt.

All my forward thinking froze and I blinked at him. "Why would you
do that?"

A vein throbbed in the middle of his forehead. "I'm a filmmaker, remember?"

I didn't remember, but I still said, "Ah, yes." Then, I blew my nose.

His nostrils flared, but he swallowed to tamp back his anger. "See, I wasn't
home that night."

"Okay, so where were you?" I asked.

"My other job," he said. "I work at the airport. Anyway, I wasn't home
that night, but everyone else in the neighborhood was. And almost everybody used their phones to record parts of the fire." He nodded as a huge
smile spread across his face. "So I took everybody's snippets of video—"

"I actually used our video camera," Delia interjected.

"And the footage Delia got," Moss continued, "and edited it all together."
He sat back in his chair with a smug smile. "Later, I'm going to make a docu-
mentary about it. Then, I'll enter it in Cannes or Sundance. Win a few awards
and everything. But I'm here today to give you a sneak peek at what I have
so far. For your investigation." He pulled a DVD from his stained khaki
rucksack. "For your eyes only."

"Thanks," I said, taking the disc.

Delia cleared her throat, then said, "I saw Christopher leave the house
on Monday night."

"Yeah?" I said.

She nodded. "I was getting ready for bed and heard his car start around eleven that night. I peeked out the window and watched him back out of the driveway."

I cocked my head. "Was he alone or was Juliet with him?"

"He was alone."

"Was the house dark? Had the others gone to sleep?"

"Guess so."

"You see him leave late like this a lot?" Colin asked.

Delia nodded. "At least twice a week. When the fire . . ." She took a deep breath, then slowly released it. "When the fire started, I thought he had come home by then. It was late or early, or . . . We didn't notice that his car wasn't in the driveway until he showed up."

"How long have you known the Chatmans?" I asked.

Delia and Eli looked at each other the way couples do when they're unsure of the answer.

Eli scratched an angry red splotch on top of his balding head. "Maybe six, seven years?"

"They have any enemies?" I asked.

"Everyone has enemies," Delia said. "We often call them friends. Or lovers. Or—"

"Heh," Eli said, rubbing his jaw. "Didn't think we'd be asked serious questions. We just wanted to drop in and give you the film."

"So you're a documentarian." I pointed to his rucksack. "Are you taping our conversation right now with a hidden camera?"

Eli turned the color of pomegranates. "Is . . . that a problem?"

"No," I said. "When it is, you'll be the first to know. So: enemies?"

"Like in the neighborhood?" Delia asked.

"In the neighborhood," Colin said. "At work, school, wherever. Were they assholes? Sounds like the boy was a Grade A jerk, settin' shit on fire, gettin' into fights, bullying little girls. And his old man: last night, in Mrs. Emmett's living room, we talked about him and that dog-faced redhead he was bangin' on the DL."

I blanched and kicked Colin's foot. *Dude, take it easy.*

The couple considered each other again with bit lips.

"Don't be nervous," Colin continued, not taking it easy. "In this room, you can speak ill of the dead. We want you to. Helps us figure out why they're dead."

"The boy setting fires," Eli said, shaking his head. "A phase. Nothing more. Boys do stuff like that, y'know? I'm sure you played with matches when you were a kid."

Colin said nothing.

"They're actually nice people," Delia said. "They work hard, love their kids, go to Mass every Sunday. No strange visitors at the house. No mysterious comings or goings in the middle of the night. Everyone on the block likes them, but you can easily imagine people being jealous." She tugged at her sweater sleeve. "You don't have to actively *do* anything for people to hate you."

"Think he has Mob connections?" I asked.

Eli's right knee, close to popping out of its socket from all the bouncing, abruptly stopped jiggling. "The *Mob*? Why would he fool around with gangsters?"

I shrugged. "Because even Baby Fat Larry and Johnny No-Thumbs wanna make legit ends off of wheat and silver."

Wide-eyed, Delia held up her trembling hands. "I don't understand, Detectives. Enemies and Mob bosses? There was a *fire*. It was *accidental*. And, *tragically*, Juliet and the kids *died*. The end. It was the most horrific . . ." She lifted her face to the ceiling. "My eyes were burning just . . . *standing* there yesterday. There I was, out in the open, and I couldn't breathe. Desperate, that's how I felt, and . . . and . . . panicky. Numb. Hysterical but unable to do anything about it. If *I* felt that way, how did Juliet and the kids feel? To be trapped in that inferno, in that hell on earth? But then the fear of death, says Publilius Syrus, is more to be dreaded than death itself." Her hands dropped into her lap.

A lump formed in my throat, and I gaped at Delia Moss and wanted to stand, clap, and throw roses at her feet.

Not a fan of the theater, Colin yawned, then said, "Okeydokey. Anything else?"

"The guy in the hockey jersey," Eli said. "You catch him yet?"

"No," I said.

"Is this fire related to the others?" Delia asked.

Colin said, "We can't say right now."

I smiled at Eli and Delia. "Anything else?"

The couple shook their heads.

I picked up the DVD and waggled it. "Thanks for stopping by. And thanks for giving us this. I'm sure it will be a great help in our investigation."

"For your eyes only," Eli reminded me.

"Cross my heart," I said, crossing my heart.

A DVD recording of a fatal house fire.

The devil hadn't planned on me winning *that*, had he?

19

Colin escorted the Mosses down to the lobby.

I ambled to my desk, DVD in hand.

The red light on my phone blinked. Voice mail.

I slipped the disc into my computer's DVD player, then listened to the phone message.

The caller introduced herself as Adeline St. Lawrence. "I'm Juliet's best friend," she had said, and she wanted to talk to me, but today wouldn't be good. "I'll need you to come out to Corona, where I live, cuz my car's on its last leg." Then, she rambled off her address. "Anyway, her parents think I should talk to y'all. Guess I got a lot to say about all this. And I'll talk to the devil himself if that means that hobbit motherfucka won't get one thin dime of Jules's money."

St. Lawrence's last words roared in my ears. Who was the hobbit? And money? What money?

I returned the woman's call.

No one answered.

I left a message. *Tomorrow. Ten in the morning. See you then.*

Colin, back in the squad room, plopped into his chair and placed his boots on the edge of my desk.

"Were you raised in the mountains or something?" I asked, knocking his feet to the floor.

"Yup," he said with a smile. "Were you raised in the ghetto or some-thin'?"

"Yep. And I'll lay it on you straight: if you put yo' kicks on my desk one more time, I'm gon' pop a cap in yo' honkey ass, you dig?" And then, I clicked PLAY in the DVD menu.

By the time Delia Moss started to record, the fire trucks had already arrived. The upstairs bathroom was on fire, and the flames had stretched catlike to reach Cody's bedroom. Chaos reigned as firemen rushed up and down the slick, wet streets of Don Mateo Drive with an unconnected hose. Except for Norah and Micah Galbreath's bungalow, every light in every house on the block shone bright.

Even at my desk, five miles away and two days in the future, that monstrous, fiery glow burned my face.

New shot: Delia, dressed in a black peacoat, standing with Ruby, bundled up in a puffy pink nylon jacket, and the twins, also wearing big coats. LaTrell held his phone in front of him, probably recording.

I glanced at the recording's time stamp in the lower left corner: 4:10 A.M.

New shot: a soot-faced firefighter approached the huddled neighbors. His coat and helmet smoked. "How many people in the house?" he shouted.

"Four!" Ruby shouted back. "Two kids and two—"

Boom!

The windows of the Chatman house blew. Car alarms shrieked. Glass rained from the sky.

LaTrell shouted, "Damn!"

LaTanya shrieked.

Ruby ducked as Delia dropped the video camera and hid her face in her hands.

Ashes danced in the wet air. Black smoke poured like liquid from every crack and window. Wood screeched as the fire howled and roared like a three-headed dragon, as high-pressured jets of water threatened its end.

New shot: at 4:32 A.M., a firefighter climbed out of a broken north-facing window as smoke poured from behind him.

New shot: Delia had recovered and had grabbed the camera from the ground.

Between gasps, Ruby and Delia muttered back and forth—*Where are they? Why can't he find them?*—as the large fireman backed down a ladder.

Someone shouted, "Whoa!"

Pop!

More sirens joined the *thwap-thwap-thwap* of an invisible police helicopter, the shouts of men, the rush of water, the squawking of radios, and the thunder of falling debris. A fireman, lost somewhere in that burning hell, howled in pain. The mean snarls of chain saws and the *hack-hack-hack* of determined axes and pike poles drowned out his anguish.

At 4:40 A.M., Ruby shouted, "He's alive!"

Delia panned left of the burning house.

Christopher Chatman, dressed in a blue tracksuit and running shoes, had parked his Jag at the sawhorse and now stood in the middle of the street, eyes wide in aggravated wonder. He took one step, then another, and charged toward his burning home.

Two firemen tackled him at the foot of the porch.

He fought them.

They all fell to the ground and tussled. The back of his head struck the concrete, and his cries that had carried over the roar of the fire abruptly stopped. His body finally went limp. He had lost consciousness.

The two firemen who had saved Chatman from running into the blaze carried him to a waiting stretcher and ambulance.

"What about Jules and the kids?" Ruby asked.

The fire climbed, attacked, and threw bits and pieces of the house into the black sky.

After recording for five more minutes, Delia stopped taping, and the DVD faded to a black screen.

Colin rubbed his face and groaned.

Mouth dry, I clucked my tongue.

Fortunately, Luke and Pepe barged into the squad room. "Kobe's got a pissy attitude," Luke said, waving his hand.

"Jordan couldn't shoot a three to save his life," Pepe shouted.

I twisted in my chair. "Lucy and Ethel! Come here a minute."

"We're more like Laverne and Shirley," Luke said as he waddled to my desk.

"Yeah, yeah, whatever," I said. "A neighbor recorded the Chatman fire, and I need your opinion on something." I found the frame that captured Christopher Chatman standing at the sawhorse, then clicked PAUSE. "What's the expression on his face?"

"That the grieving husband and father?" Luke asked, peering at the screen.

"The one and only Christopher Chatman," Colin said.

We watched the grieving husband and father run, fight, and collapse. Watched the EMTs load him into the ambulance and whisk him away.

"He doesn't know what's happening," Pepe said.

"That *giete* is smilin'," Luke said. "Sick, fuckin' awe."

Pepe shook his head. "He's in pain—his family's trapped in there."

"He's thinkin'," Luke said, "'my evil plan worked.'"

"No. That's confusion. What's happening? What's going on?"

"Bullshit. He knows *exactly* what's going on."

"Terror. Pure fear."

Luke turned to me. "What do you think?"

"Don't know yet," I said. "I have an assignment for you two." Then, I reminded them of Cody Chatman's fire addiction, which he had shared with his best friend, Parker. "Talk to this kid. Find out what he knows—if Cody talked about burning down the house or anything else strange."

"This Parker kid go to the same school?" Pepe asked.

"Yep." I thanked them again, then watched the duo wander back to their desks, with Luke correctly insisting that Michael Jordan was the greatest b-baller in all NBA history.

Three more times, Colin and I studied the recording, and by then our muscles had hardened into stone. We both saw in our mind's eye every lick of flame, every neighbor's reaction, every twitch in Chatman's face.

Five minutes before three o'clock, I closed the DVD player's application and rotated my stiff shoulders.

Colin stood from his chair. "I need some regular, depressing crap to look at." He slipped on his corduroy blazer. "Goin' across the street for a taco. Want anything?"

"Nope." I riffled through the Chatman case file and found one of Christopher Chatman's business cards.

One ring, and "Vandervelde, Lansing, and Gray, this is Stacy." The receptionist sounded young, Justin-Bieber-fan kind of young. I-just-learned-how-to-use-a-telephone-seven-minutes-before-you-called kind of young.

"Could you connect me to Christopher Chatman's office, please?" I asked.

"Christian Chan?"

"No. Chris-to-pher Chat-man," I said slowly.

"What extension?"

"I don't know. Can you find it and then connect me?"

The young woman paused. "Umm . . . Well . . ." She sighed. "Hold on."

I had been holding for only five seconds when Stacy returned to the line. "Sorry. There's no Christopher Chatman working here. So I guess there's no office?"

Was she asking me?

And was that *Dora the Explorer* theme music playing in her world? Because, if so, Stacy saying, "There's no Christopher Chatman working here," was akin to her saying, "OMG gravity doesn't exist cuz I can't see it, LOL gtg☺."

After ending my call with Stacy, I typed "Christopher Chatman Commodities" into Google's search bar: 1,103 results.

I clicked on the Vandervelde, Lansing & Gray hyperlink and was taken to Christopher Chatman's profile page.

There he was, a decent-looking black man with those big brown eyes, a pleasant smile, good posture, and an impressive list of clients—from studio moguls to large corporations. His résumé listed a name-brand university (UCLA), as well as impressive past employers—Big Name Bank and Highfalutin Financial Services Corporation. He spoke Spanish *and* Mandarin *and* had been rated a National Master by the United States Chess Federation.

And he wore bow ties?

Hell. *I'd* give him money.

20

Used to be the prettiest house on Don Mateo Drive. The terra-cotta walkway, rosebushes on each side leading to the wrought-iron front door. Inside, bamboo floors and lots of windows, agonized-over marble and granite, a large backyard with a fire pit, and interesting art, the kind found not at Cost Plus but at a gallery.

I stared at photographs of the Chatman house taken just a year ago, then gazed at the mess beyond the Crown Vic's windshield.

Yellow tape . . . blackened wood . . . lots of light only because some of the house had burned away or had been torn down by axes and chain saws.

Gawkers stood at the perimeter and took pictures of the house with camera phones.

Fire Marshal Quigley and his team huddled around something in the living room.

Colin stayed in the car to finish a phone call with his ex-fiancée, Dakota. His eyes had squeezed shut two minutes into the call, and his side of the phone conversation had consisted of "but," "no," "we're not . . . we're not."

I left him to his personal business and strode up Virginia Oliver's walkway.

The old woman threw open the front door before I reached the green welcome mat. She clutched a machete, which was rusty, lusterless, and swimming in tetanus.

I jerked as though she had already jabbed me and I reached beneath my blazer for my Glock.

"Oh, it's the lady cop," she said with a chuckle.

"Good afternoon," I croaked, eyes on the giant knife, fingers pinching the butt of my gun.

"Thought you was one of them J'ovas Witness. They keep comin' roun' here even though I tol' 'em to leave me be."

Virginia Oliver wore a curly auburn wig and a bright canary jogging suit with hot-pink Keds. She had applied a pound of makeup on her face with a paintbrush—and in the dark. She had also overplucked her eyebrows and had penciled them in two inches off the mark.

After I stepped into the foyer, she closed the door and locked four dead bolts. Then, she slipped the machete into a hanging sheath the way other grannies stowed coats and umbrellas.

Somewhere, the theme music of *Dr. Phil* blasted from a television.

We settled at the breakfast table in the kitchen, a bright space with a red-squared tablecloth and a faded wall painting of the Last Supper.

"Hope you don't mind if I eat," the old woman said, pointing to a small skillet of white rice, cabbage, and shredded pieces of chicken. No plate. Just skillet. "Ol' ladies like me gots to eat at a certain time a day, else I'll be up with gas and the scoots and . . . You hungry?"

"No, ma'am." I pulled a small notepad and pen from my bag. "Thank you, though."

She stuffed her mouth with cabbage and chewed with an opened mouth. "What you wanna know?" she asked. "I been round here since fifty-two. Back then, me and my husband was the only colored family living on this block."

"I'm gathering all the facts surrounding the deaths," I said. "Facts that will help us determine what happened and who's responsible."

Virginia Oliver peered at me with sharp eyes. "My grandson tol' me not to talk to y'all. He think y'all just tryna start some mess."

"We're actually trying to make sense of the mess," I said. "To be honest, it was probably a mess before we even got the call."

"That's what *I* tol' him. But Benji suspicious of everybody. Just his nature."

"So: Christopher Chat—"

"Them Chatmans," the woman said, spooning her rice. "His people responsible for all this. The fires, the deaths—all of it. They dead, but that don't make no difference."

"What . . . ?" I shook my head. "Do you mean, his *parents* are responsible?"

"You deaf?" she snapped. "Ain't that what I said?"

"I . . . I was just clarifying."

"They moved next door a year or so after me and Willie bought this house. Christopher's daddy—Henry—was a carpenter for the state. Ava took care of the house like womens did back then."

She grabbed the crystal saltshaker and sprinkled sixty tablespoons' worth of salt into the skillet. "Christopher was a peculiar boy. His momma and daddy thought he was the second comin' of Einstein. Everything he did was amazin', never been thought of, never been done before. 'Course he was always winning some kind of award or certificate or what have you . . ."

She wiped her mouth with a crumpled napkin. "His folks always wanted things *just so*. O-per had a show about it a few years ago. OCD, she called it. Them Chatmans had the OCD. Nothin' was ever out of place in that house. No keys layin' about. No shoes in the living room. It was like one of them model homes you visit. No soul. Just shine."

Although Virginia Oliver's house was very neat and smelled of lemon furniture polish, there were slippers in the pantry, a Barbie doll and the pink Barbie Corvette on the dining room side bar. And now, there was a sprinkling of salt on the breakfast table.

"Ain't nobody ever visited them," the old woman continued. "Not that you wanted to. They was always tellin' folks what they was doin' wrong. Couldn't eat nowhere 'cept the dining room. Couldn't eat no chocolate. Couldn't read no books 'cept religious ones. Couldn't watch no TV. They ain't never smiled, even though childrens of God *supposed* to have joy."

"How did all of that—OCD, religion, high expectations—affect Christopher?"

She chuckled. "He was never at rest. Always lookin' to do better. To be *more*. He was a sweaty little thing cuz he had to put on this show that he was perfect. I made the mistake of mentioning to Ava that he needed to play some and just *be*. But she tol' me that relaxin' meant idleness, that good Christians ain't nervous, and that the boy had overactive sweat glands."

I smiled. "In other words: mind your business."

She rolled her eyes, then tore into a piece of chicken. "Couldn't even call the boy Chris," she complained with a full mouth. *"That's not his name.* Ava would always say that. *That's not his name.* And then he brought home a Catholic girl." She cackled, and meat flew from her mouth and onto my notepad.

My stomach clenched. Blood and guts? No problem for me. Chewed-up food? Break out the smelling salts. My hand discreetly swiped across the chicken-filled notepaper.

Virginia Oliver used her pinky nail to dislodge rice from her left molar. "Even when he got grown, he never got upset, even when he had cause to. When he asked Benji for money—"

My pen froze on the page. "What did he need money for?"

"Benji say he was just havin' a little problem. Nothin' to worry 'bout. Probably cuz that girl wanted somethin'. She always needed a new this, a better that."

"And how long ago was this? And how much did Mr. Chatman borrow?"

"Oh . . ." She sucked her teeth as she thought. "He asked about a year or so ago. Don't know how much. Benji was annoyed he was askin' for that money in front of me."

"Did he pay Ben back?" I asked, writing a note to follow up on the status of the warrant requests for the Chatmans' finances.

"You gotta ask Benji that."

"Did you ever hear Christopher and Juliet argue? About the house? About money?"

"They had *uncomfortable conversations*. That's what Christopher called 'em. But they ain't never shouted at each other. And Juliet hated that house. Well, that house was just one thing outta millions of things that girl hated," the old woman said.

"Why didn't they just sell it?"

"It's his house, and he wanted to keep it. Give it to his boy when the time came. Juliet didn't care nothing about no heritage or none of that. And she never stopped scheming to move."

My fingers numbed. "Interesting word you used. *Scheming*."

"I says lots of interestin' words."

I grinned. "So how did she scheme?"

"She'd clog up the pipes on purpose. Sprinkle sawdust around, like they had termites. Silly things like that. She wanted a bigger house is all. A newer house over where Benji and his family live. She always talked about how beautiful the houses were up there.

"But the kids loved their house. The attic and the backyard. That girl . . . She wasn't ever satisfied, no matter how much money Christopher gave her to fix it up. New furniture. New paint . . . Paint: ain't that what killed her?"

I gave a solemn nod, then asked, "Did she ever come to you for advice?"

"Of course she did," the woman said. "I tol' her to take her tail back to work. Tol' her to make her own money and stop nagging Christopher to work more. That poor boy was already puttin' in sixteen-hour days. But she ain't want to work, and so she felt trapped and she hated it."

I stared at my notes: "money," "scheming," "trapped" . . . "Trapped." Juliet seemed to have used that word a lot. "So Cody Chatman—"

"Needed a few good wallops to his behind. He got too much, too soon, and so he was spoiled and bored. And *mean*. That boy was as mean as the days is long."

"We heard that he'd bully Chloe, and when Amelia Oliver was over—"

"He'd mess with her, too," Mrs. Oliver said, nodding. "Sarah hated that boy. And she ain't care if everybody knew how much she hated him." The old lady held up her hands and shrugged. "I ain't like him myself, and I pray 'bout that cuz he just a child. Like I said, he need one good whuppin' to set him straight."

"We're considering the possibility that he set the fire, either accidentally or—"

"No," she said, shaking his head. "He loved his momma. He'd never wanna hurt her like that."

"What kind of child was Chloe?"

Virginia Oliver smiled. "Friendlier than a box of puppies. I called her Angel Baby. Nothin' like her brother. Had her daddy's calm nature, you know. But Juliet was always picking on the girl cuz she was a little plump. Always puttin' the girl on some kind of diet. The baby was only eight years old, but Juliet had her eatin' them Lean *Cuh-zine* TV dinners."

"What did Chloe think about her brother?"

"Loved him. Feared him. But loved him more. When he let her, she'd follow him around and watch him do tricks on that board of his. But then, an hour later, she'd run into the house cuz he said somethin' crazy to her."

"Would he hurt her?" I asked.

The old woman opened her mouth to speak but closed it and remained silent.

I closed the notepad and sighed. That was fine. Virginia Oliver's other statements had already softly beaten me down—like millions of cotton balls falling onto my back, one by one, over a two-week span. "Would you say they were a normal family?" I asked.

The old woman pushed away from the table and carried the empty skillet to the sink. "'Normal' ain't the word I would use."

"Okay," I said, so tired now. "What word *would* you use?"

Virginia Oliver gazed out the kitchen window. "What word . . . ?" Finally, she turned to me and said, "Doomed."

21

Colin had settled behind the Crown Vic's steering wheel.

Revitalized and freed from the onslaught of killer cotton balls, I slipped into the passenger seat. I turned to my partner with a tired grin. "Dude. I almost shot that old lady. She came to the door holding a freakin' machete. Who owns a freakin' *machete*?"

And then I told him about my conversation with Mrs. Oliver.

"Scheming," Colin said. "Never satisfied."

"Hell, sounds like every woman I know. Me included."

"Yeah?" He smirked. "And how, may I ask, will you get some satisfaction?"

I cocked an eyebrow. "I see someone's taken his little blue pill this morning."

"One blue will get you four."

And we grinned at each other like a couple of goofs.

"Juliet Chatman sounds like a shrew," I said. "Just like Christopher's mother was a shrew. And they both henpecked that poor, dear man every day of his life."

"Until early Tuesday morning," Colin pointed out. "But now he'll have you."

"A surrogate shrew?" I asked.

"The best kind."

I fastened my seat belt. "Mrs. Oliver isn't breaking up into pieces over Juliet. Guess she feels that Saint Christopher will finally get some rest for the first time in his life."

Colin plucked his little box of Tic Tacs from his pocket, then dumped hundreds of candies into his mouth. Between crunches, he said, "Dakota's comin' to California. She's planning to"—his fingers formed air quotation marks—" 'visit friends' in San Diego before Christmas. She wanted to 'swing by LA' just to say 'hi.'"

"Girls don't learn."

"If an alpha like you won't . . ."

My ears burned as the car sailed away from the curb. "You excited to see her?"

He grunted.

I tapped his knee. "Maybe you two will reconcile and live happily ever after. Go back to the Springs and make towheaded, bucktoothed babies."

He glanced at me. "Is that what *you're* doing? Reconciling? Living happily ever after?"

Blood filled my head. *Was I doing that?* "Yes. But my babies will have perfect teeth." And then my iPhone rang. I hit the speaker button and said, "Yeah?"

"Are we on for happy hour?" Lena's chirpy voice filled the cabin.

"Forgot about that. Umm . . . Not sure if I can. Oh, and thank you for the novel. And Colin's here. Say hello, Colin."

He said, "Hello, Colin."

I took the phone off speaker and held it to my ear.

"You promised," Lena was shouting. "You flaked on me last week when you went out with what's-his-face instead."

I rolled my eyes. "Please call Greg by his name."

"I hate it when you do this," she said.

"When I do what?"

"Go dumb over dick. You owe me, Elouise."

"Fine. Where should we meet?"

"Kay and Dave's."

"Fine."

"You mad? Don't be mad."

"What time?" I asked.

"Six thirty."

"Happy hour?" Colin said. "Every time I ask you to go out and grab a drink, you tell me no. What's up with that?" He turned left onto Hillcrest Avenue. "You've gone out with Luke and Pepe a million times. We're partners. That's it."

"You're right," I said. "Just don't feel like rockin' the boat right now." As we drove downhill, I threw a glance at my childhood home: mint-green apartments, boarded windows, sad grass. Cracked sidewalks where Dad had taught me to ride a bike . . .

"We're gonna be partners for a long time," Colin said. "He's—"

"Immature like that, yes, I know. Again: not in the mood to teach life lessons to a grown man. It sucks, but we all do what we gotta do."

"Whatever's clever, Lou. Since when are you not in the mood to teach life . . ." Colin's gaze moved past me. "Hey."

I followed his gaze to the dreadlocked muscular black man sauntering down Hillcrest. The man wearing an orange hockey jersey. A battered, bulky backpack was slung over his right shoulder. There was a tattoo on his left calf. "Ain't that the dude . . . ?"

"Yeah." Colin swerved over to the curb.

I rolled down my window. "What's up, partner?"

Dude kept steppin', tossing a surly glance at us, and then he took a longer look—a white guy was driving a Crown Vic in *this* neighborhood. He realized that we were 5.0, and his eyes bugged. He muttered, "Oh *shit*." And, just like that, he raced down the block.

"Motherfuck—" I jumped out of the car and took off after him, glad that I'd worn loafers today instead of heels.

The Crown Vic's tires squealed.

Dude's legs pumped him down to Santa Rosalia.

He'll make a right. They always make a right.

At the intersection, he busted a right.

"Stop! Police!" I yelled, knowing that he wouldn't stop.

He darted across the street and into the abandoned Santa Barbara Plaza breezeway. He slipped on newspapers and empty bottles, but he quickly recovered.

But in his faltering, I had caught up. "Stop! Police!" I drew my Glock and followed him into the field of closed shops. Sirens whirred, and static crackled from the radio on my belt.

He ducked left into an alley.

I skidded to a stop and listened to my panting. Held my breath to listen to him creep. Gun pointed to the dirt, I slunk closer to the alley, my pulse racing and my heart beating so loud, he probably heard me coming.

Broken glass crunched to the right of me.

I spun to my right, gun up, my finger on the trigger.

Nothing.

I smelled him, though. Sweat, patchouli oil, fear . . .

I stepped forward.

A bead of sweat dropped into my eye, blinding me for a moment. I ignored the sting and crept deeper into the alley, my arms locked and on fire.

Ten yards ahead, I spotted Dude's backpack.

Sirens sounded closer.

"You hear that?" I shouted. "You ain't gettin' outta here."

He burst from a corner behind me.

I whirled around and chased him back out to the open square.

He slipped, cutting his elbows and knees on broken glass.

I caught up to him and trained my gun at his chest.

He threw up his bloody hands. His neck tat writhed from his heavy breathing and racing pulse. Tears ran down his sweaty face. "I ain't done nothin'."

A patrol car sped into the empty lot, sirens and wigwags going, tires kicking up dirt.

Colin had abandoned the car and was now running across the field and holding Dude's backpack. "You okay?" he asked once he reached me.

"Yeah." To the uniform, a guy named Corleto, I said, "Watch it. He's bleeding."

Officer Corleto cuffed Orange Hockey Jersey and sat him on the ground. Then, he took Dude's information. Afterward, Corleto retreated to his black-and-white to run the man's name through the computer.

I finally holstered my gun and stood over my suspect. "What the hell, dude? Why'd you run? We only wanted to ask you a few questions."

Colin lifted the heavy backpack. "Did you run cuz you got somethin' in here?"

Dude closed his bloodshot eyes.

Colin unzipped the bag and peered in. "You kidding me?" He pulled out two DVD cases with yellow stickies on their fronts. In black marker, someone had scribbled, *Bat Man, the dark night returns.*

"Bootleg DVDs?" I asked Dude. "I busted my ass chasing you cuz you think I'm interested in some . . . ? Where were you yesterday, about three in the morning?"

"I ain't got nothin' to say," Dude muttered, avoiding my eyes. "I want my lawyer."

I spun on my heel and stomped back toward the abandoned stores.

A minute later, Colin found me stewing in the front seat of Corleto's black-and-white, guzzling a bottle of water.

"So," he said, "TeShawn Shaw, twenty-two years old, last known address was some shithole on Nicolet. Last arrest was for trespassing on December tenth. He was in our own freakin' jail on the night of the fire. Can you believe that shit?"

I gulped from the water bottle, my nerves still jangled from the foot pursuit. "He may not be the one hanging around Don Mateo. There could be some other dread-head in an orange . . ."

"True."

"We'll go back up the hill," I said, screwing on the bottle cap. "We'll ask Nora the Realtor, show her a six-pack, and have her choose."

"Got it." Colin trudged back to our car and muttered, "This fuckin' case."

Yeah. No witnesses. No true motive.

Yeah. This case.

22

At almost five o'clock, the squad room had more customers than 7-Eleven on a Saturday night. Weeping witnesses were hunched over in chairs, clutching tissues or packs of cigarettes. Handcuffed suspects shuffled down hallways while exhausted detectives clutched the perps' elbows and guided them to the Box or to a jail cell. Except for those wearing steel bracelets, everyone cradled in their hands foam cups filled with coffee, water, or soda. Somewhere in the bowels of the building, a man shouted, "I ain't do it! I ain't do it!"

There's no place like home.

I collapsed at my desk, breathless, as though I had run there.

"What's next on the agenda?" Colin asked as he plopped into his chair.

Nora Galbreath had positively identified TeShawn Shaw as the Guy in the Orange Hockey Jersey. Ruby Emmett had also confirmed that she had witnessed Shaw roaming Don Mateo Drive.

"Check on our outstanding warrant requests," I told Colin now.

"Yep," he said, logging on to his computer.

Juliet Chatman's journal, found during the search of the converted garage and now stowed in evidence box 1, was waiting for me.

I flipped to another entry: November 20.

We had lunch today since she's back in town for the moment. We talked about our boring husbands. Well, for her, ex-husband. Weird, but I feel sorry for the insufferable twit. Mel can't help who she is. Born poor and thrown into high society and expected to miraculously have the manners of the Queen? She's like me. Ha ha. As usual, she had too much to drink and got vulgar. After lunch, I sent her a bouquet of lilies, as is custom when something dies. To be served divorce papers in the middle of Pilates was wicked. Ron is a mean bastard.

Had Ben Oliver been truthful—were they all just friends?

I flipped back to an entry dated April 11.

My life is one big pile of crap. I loathe him. Totally. Completely. And the kids. I love them but I'm tired of them, tired of their noise, tired of their constant need. Tired of Chloe eating all the time. Tired of Cody setting fires and beating kids up and flunking school and just being an asshole. If there is a God (and with all that's going on right now, I am doubtful), He should come back <u>now</u> or I will end it all because if He doesn't do it soon, I will end it for Him. And then, quiet at last. ☺

What did that mean? "I will end it for Him"?

CC is out in the back in the swing again. Upset. My fault. Of course. Because I made a crack about this precious house of ours (well, <u>his</u> house, don't I ever forget it). I kissed his precious little forehead and apologized for being a cruel monster. For fuck's sake!! Why can't he MAN UP? Always getting his feelings hurt. And when will he let them go??? They've been dead for years now. And it's perfectly normal for me to want a bigger house.

Colin rolled his chair over to mine and looked over my shoulder. "Whatcha reading?"

"Juliet's journal." I pushed away his face. "Your breath smells like bacon."

"That's a bad thing?"

Light-headed, I closed my eyes and tried to see nothing for a moment.

I will end it for Him.

Fail.

I opened my eyes. "The warrants?"

"Should be here any minute."

I watched him—thinking about nothing, just enjoying the break—until my telephone blipped. I grabbed the receiver and answered.

"Detective," the man said, "this is Christopher Chatman." He sounded thick-tongued.

I jerked as though God had lit my fuse, then snapped my fingers at Colin and mouthed, "Christopher Chatman." I fumbled for the phone's recording adapter, stuck the what's it into the thingamabob, and hit the speaker button. "Mr. Chatman," I said, "I was planning to call you."

"The hospital discharged me this morning," he said, "and I'm staying with my friend Ben for the moment. He said that you stopped by the hospital yesterday."

"Yes," I said. "But we didn't want to trouble you until it was absolutely necessary. You're recovering from a horrific ordeal."

"It has been very difficult for me."

"I'm so very sorry for your loss, Mr. Chatman."

Silence.

I crossed my eyes at Colin.

"How soon will you complete your investigation?" he asked. "And I must admit: I'm still unclear about what you're investigating. You are a homicide detective, correct?"

"I am, and I hope to be finished soon, sir. But I have several questions that still need answering."

"Questions? Like?"

"Like how your wife and children were killed."

He made a gurgling noise, then croaked, "*Killed?* I thought . . . The fire . . ."

"Yes, sir. The fire played a part in all of this, but just a part." My pulse banged at the spaces behind my eyebrows. I pulled the small silver hoops out of my earlobes. Too heavy.

He coughed, then cleared his throat. "I'll tell you everything you need to know, Detective. But tomorrow Ben's having people over. And if they see me talking to you . . . I don't want to have any visitors, having to explain and say over and over again, and with my head injury . . . Can you come over now? While I'm alone? While I can still think?"

I stifled a groan—Lena wouldn't *totally* kill me. She preferred that I flaked because of work and not because of what's-his-face. My husband. "Of course," I told Chatman.

"Ben and Sarah are out. Come through the side gate. See you soon."

I hung up, then slipped the silver hoops back into my ears. "So what should we ask?"

"Why were you at work so late, Mr. Chatman?" Colin said.

I added, "How come you were so broke that you needed to borrow money from Ben Oliver, Mr. Chatman?"

"What does Melissa Kemper have to do with any of this, Mr. Chatman?"

"We'll go easy on him," I said, grabbing my bag from the desk drawer. "Cuz he's injured and he's lost his family."

"You're so sweet," Colin said, pulling on his blazer.

I twirled car keys around my finger and smiled. "A real Mary Poppins, I am."

23

Ben and Sarah Oliver lived on Joaquin Way, in a salmon-colored Mediterranean with white window frames and a rust-colored, ceramic-tiled roof. Their Westchester Bluffs neighborhood overlooked the wetlands of Ballona Creek, the campus of Loyola Marymount University, and the Pacific Ocean, now lost in the blues and grays of dense winter fog. At half past six, all living rooms on Joaquin Way—except for the Olivers'—glowed with electronic entertainment. In the Oliver home, no light burned beyond the faux balconies hanging from each second-story window, and no cars were parked in the driveway.

Colin, driving his Dodge Charger, parked behind my Porsche, and we met at the curb. He took a deep breath and slowly exhaled. "Smells like my grandma up here." He pointed at bushes. "Wild rye. Sage. Lavender. Yep. Just like Grandma."

"So," I said, stepping closer to him, "I want this to go easy, all right? Like a slow dance at the prom. Don't wanna put my hand up his skirt too quickly cuz he'll shut us down."

Colin nodded. "Got it."

I squinted at him. "Do you really 'got it'? Cuz you've said that before and . . ."

"Yeah, Lou. I got it." Then, he winked at me.

We strolled through the side gate, unlocked as promised.

A white party canopy had been set up over the two-tiered backyard. Tall cocktail tables were set up underneath, as well as a scattering of chairs that waited for the asses of invited guests who'd soon hoist plates of cheese and baby lamb chops on their laps.

Colin and I quickly stepped across the slick flagstone pathway and descended steep steps that led to an ivy-covered guesthouse.

The arched wood door opened. "Evening." Christopher Chatman's gray Adidas tracksuit clung to his small frame. The purple scratches on his face zigzagged past bandages. White gauze covered both of his hands, and a sling supported his left arm. "Thank you for coming out so late in the day," he said. The novocaine effect had worn off, but his voice was still smoky and white-man-singing-"Ol' Man River"-deep. He coughed—sandpaper and mucus stirred together in a mixing bowl.

"It's no problem at all." I considered his bandaged hands and sling. "How are you?"

His red eyes still watered from soot and sorrow. "It's just a fractured radius. My head, however, is not a 'just.' I hit it when the firemen jumped me. And the bandages . . . I got pretty cut up from the wood and glass on the ground." He gazed at his sling. "Wasn't thinking. Just took off toward my house." His attempt to take a deep breath resulted in a coughing fit.

I moved closer to him, just in case he fainted.

He waved me off. "Just . . ." He coughed. "Not feeling well," he wheezed, trying to catch his breath. "May I please see your identification?"

I cocked my head. *Huh?*

"I'm sorry," he said. "If you're not comfortable showing me . . ."

"It's no problem." I reached into my pocket.

"Just so that I know for sure that you are who you say you are," Chatman explained. "There have been reporters . . ." He studied my identification card, handed it back to me, then took Colin's.

I peeked past him and into the guesthouse. The window in the small dining room overlooked the Olivers' canopied backyard. The kitchen sparkled with white tile and white older-model appliances. Spotless hardwood floors and a potbellied fireplace aglow with dying embers made me think of Adeline St. Lawrence's use of the word "hobbit."

"So reporters have been bothering you?" Colin asked.

"A few," Chatman said. "Usually Ben or Sarah protect me." He handed back Colin's card.

"Do we check out?" I asked.

Embarrassed, Chatman's face darkened. "I used to be the type to trust someone's word. Lately, though, I follow Euripides' thought: 'The day is for honest men, the night for thieves.'"

I bristled. "Says the banker who works wonky hours."

"Ha," he said with a good-natured grin. "It's all good. Didn't mean to make you feel weird about it." He turned on his heel and limped back into the living room. "Please have a seat."

Colin and I perched together on the couch since the only other option was an armchair.

Countless medicine vials and water glasses crowded the glass coffee table. The smell of burning wood mingled with those of thick mucus, cinnamon potpourri, and chicken broth.

My stomach loosened as nausea crept up my throat.

"Detective Norton, I googled you," Chatman said as he limped to the armchair. "As I read more about the fire, I was comforted to know that you've been successful in the past." He looked at Colin. "I found nothing about you on the Internet."

Colin cleared his throat. "Well, I'm . . . I . . ."

"If you're not googleable, then you must not exist." He grinned. "That was a joke. A bad one, I guess." To me, he said, "I was also happy to read that you recovered your sister's remains. The Darson case . . . What a nightmare. But some good came out of it."

"Yes." I offered him a smile tighter than a pair of size 6 shoes on size 9 feet.

"I'm afraid I can't talk long." He sat on the edge of the armchair. "The painkillers make me sleepy. A bit breathless. A little punchy. Maybe we can start now, and then you can come back again if you need to?"

"Sounds good," I said.

"I'm glad the pills do that," he continued. "Force me to sleep, I mean. When I *don't* take them—I'm terrified of becoming addicted, so I've skipped a dose here and there—but when I don't take them, I have nightmares." He paused, then said, "What would you like to know?"

"Are you currently employed with Vandervelde, Lansing, and Gray?" I asked.

"I am." He smiled. "That was an easy one."

"And your employment is in good standing?" I asked.

He started to stand from the armchair. "Would you like something to drink? I'm sorry I didn't ask earlier—"

"We're fine, thanks," Colin said.

"Harder question," I said. "Tell us about the night before the fire."

The man's smile dimmed as he eased back onto the armchair's edge. "Well . . . We ate dinner around seven, seven thirty."

"Who cooked?" I asked.

"My wife. I can make money, but I can't make a meat loaf to save my life. I made everyone strawberry shakes for dessert."

"Anything eventful before dinner?" I asked.

He shook his head. "Nothing strange. Okay, well. My wife . . ." He stopped speaking.

When he didn't continue, Colin asked, "Your wife what?"

Chatman flexed his free hand, then stared at the vials on the coffee table. "She drank a lot that night. Well, she had started to drink a lot every night. But on Monday evening, she was . . . I asked if she was okay. She nodded, but it looked like she was about to cry. I left it alone because my prodding would cause her to shut down even more."

"Sarah Oliver mentioned that she stopped by that evening," I said.

He nodded. "Zumba class. My wife didn't go."

"Okay," I said. "Tell me about dinner and Juliet's behavior on Monday night."

He shook his head. "She was very sharp with me. At one point, she told me to stop calling Chloe 'dumpling.' She said that I was passive-aggressively calling Chloe fat." He looked at me. "That's not what I meant, and that's what I've always called Chloe." He sniffed, then swiped at his nose. "After dinner, we all went to the den to watch *A Christmas Story*. My wife had another glass of wine—she fell asleep on the chaise in the first twenty minutes of the film. The kids lasted for about an hour."

"What time did you all go up to the bedrooms?" Colin asked.

"I woke everyone up around nine," he said. "Tucked the kids in, then hung out in the bedroom with my wife for a moment. Flipped through a few channels and found *Four Weddings and a Funeral*, one of our favorite movies. Watched it, and then we talked about paint. Talked about Chloe and soccer, about Christmas shopping, and . . ." He blinked, and a teardrop rolled slowly down his cheek. "Then, around eleven, she took a Valium, and I left to drive to the office."

"Juliet had a prescription?" I asked, knowing the answer.

"She took them for anxiety," he said. "I'm not comfortable with it, especially since she drinks so—" He gasped. "The wine. The Valium." His eyes bugged. "Did she overdose? Is that why she couldn't get up and save—?"

I held out a hand. "Mr. Chatman, all of that is still being—"

"No," he shouted. "No, no, no. Why didn't I . . . ?" He covered his mouth with his free hand. "It's my fault. I should've said something. I shouldn't have gone to the office."

"And why did you go in so late?" I asked.

In the dim light, his skin glistened with sweat. "Had to prepare for an early-morning teleconference with the team in Chicago. In my business, just like your business actually, hours are unpredictable. I left the office around 4:10, and when I got home . . . Fire trucks. My house . . . on fire. Everything on fire. The flames . . . They'd already swept through and stole my family. But the fire . . . it left me behind." He gritted his teeth and tapped the arm of his chair. "I want to talk to you, Detective Norton and Detective . . ." He squinted at Colin.

My partner blushed. "Taggert."

Christopher Chatman coughed and coughed, then plucked a tissue from the box on the coffee table, then coughed some more and spat what he had coughed into the tissue. "I haven't really talked to anyone about this. Not even Ben. Not an hour passes that I don't think about ending it. Taking what the fire denied me. I'm lost without them. And I just need to understand."

"Understand what, Mr. Chatman?" I shivered even though the room was warm.

"Why God is doing this to me." He dried his eyes on the bandages of his hand, then took a wheezy breath. "Let's move on, please." He used tissue to dab at his sweaty forehead. "Maybe another easy question."

"Would you like me to get you help?" I asked.

He cocked his head. "Help? Like . . . from a psychiatrist?"

I nodded.

He sighed. "Thought you were going to ask an easy question."

I offered an understanding smile. "You're a commodities broker, correct?"

"That's correct."

"Is that basically a stockbroker?" Colin asked.

"I don't trade in bonds or stocks," Chatman explained. "I trade grain, livestock, gold, silver . . . So it works like this: Some of my clients, for instance, think the price of gold will rise now that the dollar is uncertain. On the other hand, other clients think the price of gold will fall. I advise them, they place their orders with me, I buy or sell on their behalf."

"You get a commission regardless," I said.

He nodded.

"You don't seem like the banker type," Colin said. "You're not . . ."

"An asshole?" Chatman shrugged. "I'm good at numbers; I'm good at guessing. I'm interested in helping people live better lives. Happier people means the world is a better place. I compete against myself—do better, Christopher. Make people more money, Christopher. Learn from your mistakes, Christopher. Some see that as a weakness, but . . ." He shrugged again. His anguish about his family had passed, and he was talking to us as though we were potential clients.

"Any enemies at work?" Colin asked.

"No," he said.

"Juliet mention being frightened of anyone?" I asked, remembering that 911 call. "Had anyone threatened her? Any road rage incidents?"

"Are you saying that this fire . . . ?" He shook his head. "That it was deliberately set?"

"We aren't sure what caused the fire," I said. "We don't know if it was arson or truly an accident, so we need as much information as possible." I exhaled. "So I'll need you to think real hard on this. And I'll need you to make me a list of people who may have had the slightest problem with you. You may have dated their ex, used their coffee creamer without permission . . ."

His gaze dropped as he thought about that. "Okay."

"And put on that list any recent visitors or workers you've had at the house. You all were remodeling, and so . . ."

His eyes shimmered with tears. "There were a few contractors and day laborers, and . . . I thought nothing of it, how the guys leered at my wife sometimes. I figured, you know, Mexican men, that's what they do, gawk and stare, even though she wasn't at her prettiest."

"Because she was sick, right?" Colin said.

"She caught a virus," Chatman answered.

"Did she go see a doctor?" Colin asked.

The man shrugged. "I encouraged her to. If she did, she didn't tell me. Over the last year, she didn't tell me a lot of things. Once, she'd taken too many pills and she'd thrown up before I got home. She didn't say anything about it, and I didn't see any evidence of it. Just saw an empty wine bottle. It was Chloe who told me. Told me that Mommy had taken medicine and vomited. That was just last week, and I never brought it up to her. I wanted to think it was the paint fumes that had made her sick."

"About that," I said. "You were painting the upstairs bedrooms and bathrooms."

"Yes," Chatman responded.

"The windows were shut," I said. "Usually, when you paint, you crack open windows for ventilation. To get rid of some of the fumes."

He shifted in the armchair. "Usually."

I waited, then said, "But not in this case."

"We were burglarized a few years ago," he said. "The thief came in through a cracked window in the den. I still beat myself up about that happening. It could've ended differently—we all could've been killed. Anyway, you can't arm the security system with a cracked window, and since I was leaving for work so late . . . My wife and I didn't want to take that chance again."

"Investigators found lengths of PVC pipe in the window sliders," I said.

"All the windows had them." He swiped at the beads of sweat forming on his temples. "To keep someone on the outside from sliding open the windows."

"But it keeps people on the *inside* from escaping in an emergency," I said. "People forget when they're scared. They're not thinking clearly and forget about all the weird workarounds like PVC pipes in the windows."

"You're right," he admitted. "We were reacting from the burglary."

"Did you call Juliet early Tuesday morning?" I asked. "Like an, 'I'm leaving the office now' call right before you left the office to come back home?"

"Call her?" He peered at me as though I had asked him about the mechanics of wormholes and quantum tunneling. "I didn't want to wake her. She wasn't feeling well." With a shaky hand, he touched each bandage on his face. "Oh God . . . It's true."

"What's true?" I asked.

He twisted the gold wedding band on his finger. "Ben told me about your meeting at Ruby's. He told me, and I didn't believe him. In your eyes, I'm already guilty. I didn't believe Ben because I'm . . . I'm . . . I've never claimed to be the salt of the earth. But I work long, long days to provide for my family. I tithe ten percent. And I pray. Although not recently. God and I aren't on speaking terms right now."

"Your son," Colin said.

"Played with fire all the time," Chatman said. "And it's possible that he . . .

that he . . ." His eyelids fluttered. Dark sweat rings were forming in his jacket's underarms.

"Of all the people you know," I said, "why do you think it's possible that *he* could've set the fire?"

Chatman stared at his knees. "He hated me. And he was in this weird phase where he'd set fire to my things."

Colin and I exchanged glances.

Chatman offered us a tired smile. "Yes, I knew he was burning my clothes. He'd also burn my papers, my files—anything just to annoy me. I actually had to lock my office door because he'd sneak in and . . . The house. He knew how much it meant to me." He rubbed his face with his free hand and shook his head. "No. He didn't do this. He loved his mother, his sister. He wouldn't . . . I don't know. I don't know anything anymore."

"We should probably let you rest," I said.

"There are a few more people we need to talk to," Colin said.

Chatman flinched. "Like who? The hockey-jersey guy?"

"We don't know the answer to that question," I said, knowing that the hockey-jersey guy had been scratched out of the equation.

"Surveillance cameras," Chatman said. "We have a security system. You should be able to see someone coming or going, right?"

"Right," I said. "And we'll check those."

"Who are these people you need to talk to?" Chatman asked. "And what would anyone else have to offer besides gossip? Between this and the insurance company, I'm just . . . This is the worst moment of my life, but no one will let me grieve. Everyone is questioning my integrity, and I'm not used to that."

"People died, sir," I said. "We have to ask questions, including unpleasant ones."

"Especially since you increased your home policy to five hundred and fifty thousand dollars," Colin said.

I glared at my partner. *Damn it, Colin.*

"I had to replace everything that the burglar stole," Chatman shouted. "And we hadn't increased our policy since my son had been born. What's strange about that? Am I the only man in the world who has increased his policy?"

"Calm down, sir," I said, hands out. Then, I threw my partner another glare. *You got it? You got shit, dude.* "Detective Taggert, why don't you . . . ?"

"Yep." Colin stood from the love seat. "I'll go do that." He stomped out of the cottage and slammed the door.

Chatman gaped at me with wounded eyes. "It's just so hurtful. I mean, your partner just inferred . . . How would *he* react if some pencil pusher from the insurance company came looking for him just *hours* after his family died?"

"*You* called the insurance company, Mr. Chatman," I whispered. "Well, Mr. Oliver called on your behalf."

He blinked at me, and after a moment's reflection, he nodded. "My head is killing me."

"I'll let you rest now, sir," I said.

Christopher Chatman took a breath, but it caught in his throat. He threw out a congested rattle, then took another breath. "Really: I don't mean to sound so harsh. You're just doing your job. I'm not the guy who thinks he knows it all and deserves special treatment. I apologize, but I'm barely . . . here." He peered at me. "You know how it feels . . . to experience loss. Your sister . . . And to have the cops tell you that *you* are the reason why . . ."

Damn. The first time Detective Tommy Peet had interviewed my mother, he had done more than infer that we were to blame for Tori's disappearance.

At the front door, Christopher Chatman warned me to take care while navigating the slippery flagstones. "Before you go . . ." He leaned against the door frame. "My family. Were they . . . ? Will I be able to see them?" His eyes grew bright and his nostrils flared. "Are they . . . ?"

"They are recognizable, sir," I said. "But whether or not you'd want an open service is up to you."

He blinked rapidly. "They didn't suffer, then?"

If suffocating to death because your lungs were being twisted inside your chest wasn't suffering . . . "I can't answer that question, sir."

Chatman smiled. "Thank you for all that you're doing, Detective Norton."

I crept up those steep stairs and tiptoed over those slick flagstones, passing the cocktail tables and high chairs. Once I reached the side gate, I glanced back over my shoulder.

The commodities broker stood in the doorway of the guesthouse, a dark figure lit from behind. He looked smaller now, and his tracksuit hung loosely from his body like molten skin.

Talking to me had diminished him.

I wanted to apologize to him and prepare him for the future: Didn't matter if he killed his family or didn't kill his family. By the end of this investigation, Christopher Chatman would be nothing.

24

The air had gained twenty pounds of wet weight, making the scents of lavender and night-blooming jasmine stronger and muting the dog barks, heels clicking on pavement, and car doors whooshing open and closing with thuds.

Colin paced near my SUV. "Sorry 'bout that insurance remark. It just . . . popped out of my mouth."

I didn't speak to him until I leaned against the passenger door of the Porsche.

He stopped pacing and stood in front of me, his legs wide apart, his face tilted to the night sky. Heat rolled off his body in waves, and, like the jasmine and lavender, the foggy atmosphere had compounded the smell of his cologne.

Nothing is more dangerous than a hard man in soft air after a long day.

I dropped my gaze to the asphalt and stared at the toes of my shoes.

"Guy's a jerk," he said. "He just hides it well."

"You'd know."

"Whatcha thinkin'?"

"That maybe my next partner will be less of an asshole."

"I don't like him."

"The feeling was mutual."

"But he's fascinated by you."

I smirked. "I do that to all the mourning husbands, sociopaths, and video-game geeks. It's my wonder power."

"So what now?"

"Off to happy hour with the ladies. I need a drink after today's adventure. And you?"

His neck reddened as he shrugged. His blue-eyed gaze focused beyond the bluffs.

"See you in the morning, then?" I asked, meandering to the driver's side.

"Yep." He shoved his hands into the pockets of his 501s and moseyed back to his car. Seconds later, he zoomed past. He did not wave, nor did he blow his horn.

I slipped behind the steering wheel and texted Lena. *On my way.* I turned the key to start the engine but didn't immediately pull away from the curb.

Christopher Chatman had googled me. Strange but . . . not. He knew about my cases and my sister. But then anyone who had read the *Times* this past summer knew about my sister. And Chatman seemed both innocent and guilty. Sometimes, the husband did it—Jean-Claude Romand, the Frenchman who had lied to his family about everything possible, then killed them and burned down the house with them in it. And sometimes the husband *didn't* do it—the Connecticut doctor William Petit, who had been beaten with a bat by two psychopathic home invaders that had raped and killed his wife and two daughters and then burned down the house. While he was never a suspect and the murderers apprehended, some folks still wondered about Dr. Petit's quick recovery from the assault and about his successful escape from the flames.

Which husband was Christopher Chatman?

I glanced at my reflection in the rearview mirror. The dark circles and bags beneath my eyes were filled with worry and overstimulation.

Every cop—hell, every Angeleno—owned that same set of bags.

If you're just gonna sit there and stare into space," Syeeda said, tapping her boot on the ground, "me and Lena will hang out with the desperate housewives at the next table."

I snapped back to the here and now, and to my best friends. "Sorry. Just thinking about . . ." The cantina twinkled with crimson and turquoise lights, punctuated by the bright-white glints of cell phones and bleached-teeth grins. "This case . . ." I took a sip of sangria, my eyes on the giant bowl of *ceviche* in the middle of the table. The fumes from the cilantro and lime had already given me heartburn.

Syeeda gulped the rest of her wine—she knew what I was thinking. "Wanna get something off your chest?"

I smirked. "Why? So you can make it first-page news?"

"Homeboy in the hockey jersey—"

"Didn't do it. Off the record."

"Is he the only homeboy in LA with an orange hockey jersey, though? I'm thinkin'—"

I held up my hands. "Can we not talk shop right now? I'm not drinking enough as is."

With that, Syeeda grabbed the pitcher and refilled both our glasses. "One last thing and I'll shut up. As you go about your day filled with fingerprints and gene sequencing and arson reports, I just ask that you don't lose sight of the fact that two kids are dead and . . ."

I blinked at her. "I can never forget that."

"Let's move on, please," Lena said. "I have something for you two." She adjusted her torn-just-so sweatshirt, then rummaged through her giant Birkin bag, finally pulling out two envelopes. "One of these is ridiculous, and the other is totally awesome."

I pointed to the red envelope with the snowman stamp and Connecticut return address. "That's the awesome one."

"Guess again." She tossed the red envelope to me, then kicked off her fuchsia stilettos.

I tore open the flap.

"Can you believe this?" Lena spat.

"Can we open the envelope first?" Syeeda asked.

I pulled out the Christmas card. "Oh wow." All the pressure and anxiety and tingly limbs from the meeting with Christopher Chatman burst into a shower of pink glitter. And I laughed.

"Season's greetings *indeed*," Syeeda said, wide-eyed.

On the front of the card was Lena's ex-husband, Chauncey, wearing a red cable-knit sweater. He sat on a giant boulder beside his new husband, Brando, who wore a gray cable-knit sweater. Two Weimaraners, wearing black sweaters, lounged at the couple's feet.

I snickered. "It's very sweet that your ex-husband and his husband thought about you during this time of giving."

"Am I supposed to be *happy* for him?" Lena screeched over the roar of the crowd. "Just cuz it's Christmas? Am I supposed to hoist a rainbow flag even though this *asshole* dumped me for this *other* asshole?"

"Brando's eyes are very far apart," Syeeda noted.

"He looks like a hammerhead shark," I said, peering at the picture. "A hammerhead shark dressed in L.L.Bean."

"This ain't funny," Lena muttered.

"Oh, Lena." Syeeda picked up the unopened envelope. "It's the most wonderful time of the year. Parties and eggnog and holly and—" She slid out a slick pink card.

"Diamond Heavenlick" had been written in white italics across the card's top. In the picture beneath, Lena (I guess it was Lena) wore a black crop top, a way-up-to-there plaid schoolgirl's skirt, black spanky panties, and fuck-me pumps with transparent heels. She had wrapped most of herself around a silver pole.

"Okay," I said. "This is wrong."

"So wrong that it's right," Lena said. "Sy, turn it over."

Wiggle with Me.

And I laughed until I couldn't breathe.

Syeeda stared at the invite. "Who is Heaven . . . ? Huh?"

"It's my first pole-dance recital," Lena said, hopping in her chair. "Diamond Heavenlick: that's my stripper name."

Syeeda and I gawked at each other.

"I just ended my first three-month session," Lena said, "and I feel as though I've finally accomplished something." She touched my hand. "Sorry, Elouise. At Krav Maga, I only accomplished sleeping with Avarim, and to my great disappointment that was not worthy of a recital." She picked up her sangria glass and sipped through the straw. "I'm discovering a new part of me. I've found my secret sexy."

"We thought you were doing this for kicks," Syeeda said. "We didn't think . . . *recitals?*"

Lena giggled. "Lou, bring Taggert with you."

My face warmed. "Why?"

She gave a sly smile. "I'm tired of Russia and Israel. I need to see America again: the Rockies and purple mountain majesty and amber waves of grain. And since *you're* not being a patriot and hittin' it, *someone* should, especially in today's post-9/11 world." Her eyes met mine. "Unless you *are* hittin' it and you're not telling us."

"Well, now," Syeeda said, turning in her chair to face me.

"I'm not," I said, reaching for my drink.

"*Yet,*" Syeeda said.

"I'm not," I repeated and crunched ice cubes.

Lena spooned ceviche onto her plate. "You're an idiot, then."

"Fine."

"I commend you trying with Gregory," she said. "You want to be a part of something special. *Pour toujours et à jamais.*"

"We've talked about this, *Diamond*," Syeeda said, pouring sangria into our glasses.

"He's a chronic adulterer." Lena pointed the spoon at me. "And he will never, ever change, and you, *ma chérie*, must accept that unfortunate truth."

"Wait a minute," I said. "Your Russian boyfriend is—"

"Married," Lena completed. "And I'm fine with that. And *Olga* is fine with that."

"Until one of you *stops* being fine with that," Syeeda said.

Lena scoffed and plucked Chauncey's card from the bowl of tortilla chips. "After what this bastard in the sweater did to me, do you think that I'm ready for something *meaningful*?"

"You'll screw somebody else's husband," I said, "so that you won't have to deal with all those yucky emotions and gooey commitment?"

Lena grabbed her cell phone from the table and swiped her finger across its screen. "*À bon chat, bon rat.*"

"*Tit for tat?*" I asked. "Whose tit? And easier for whom? Not for the wife. Or do we not matter?"

Syeeda clapped her hands. "Okay, ladies. Let's all stay in our lanes."

Lena rolled her eyes. "Build a bridge and get over it, Elouise. I'm just doing me."

"There's a word or two for that," I groused, glass to my lips.

"Luckily, I don't give a shit," Lena spat.

A lie—I could hear the panicky quaver in her voice.

I sipped. "It's all fun and games until somebody gets shot."

"Tha *fuck*, Lou?" Lena said. "This is different from you and Greg. Olga knows."

"Did *she* tell you that?" I asked. "Or did you take *his* word for it? The word of the chronic adulterer?"

Lena folded her arms and dropped her chin to her chest.

Syeeda broke a tortilla chip into tiny pieces.

All around us, dishes clinked, women giggled, and men outshouted one another.

Syeeda tapped the recital invitation. "We'll come wiggle with you, Lena. Will there be strip-tinis and hors d'oeuvres? Shall I bring dollar bills, or is this an exhibition-type event?"

Lena tried to meet my eyes, but her gaze skittered back to the bowl of ceviche.

Under the table, Syeeda's knee nudged mine.

I didn't speak.

Syeeda kicked my calf.

"We'll come wiggle with you, Lena," I parroted.

Lena finally looked at me and forced a smile that didn't reach her dark, angry eyes.

I returned her smile with one of my own, one devoid of affection or forgiveness, one that lamented a friendship under siege.

Thursday, December 13

25

My mother's green Honda Accord was parked in the driveway of her Inglewood townhouse. Martin's Toyota Camry was not. She had probably kicked him out before my early-morning arrival. Sent him to pick up a bulb of elephant garlic at the farmer's market in a tiny Romanian village just to keep me from knowing that he had stayed the night.

But I was paid to spot little things: the single gray whisker in the bathroom sink that had not washed away with the others. The vial of Flomax in the medicine cabinet, prescribed for men with enlarged prostates. The bottle of Sam Adams on the fridge door (mom drank Chardonnay, never beer).

Two months ago, during one of our weekly breakfasts, I had told my mother that I was cool with Martin living there, cool with him sleeping in her bed.

Mom had blushed, then muttered into her cup, "Why do you say crazy things like that?"

Nervous, I had salted my eggs until they'd become inedible. "I just hope you're using protection. Yesterday, I read an article that said older people are getting bad cases of gonorrhea."

Mom's big brown eyes had turned the size of turkey platters. "You say the craziest things," she had grumbled. A week later, though, I spotted a grocery store receipt on the kitchen counter. I glimpsed Trojans Lubricated Condoms among A1 Steak Sauce and organic bananas. Left me satisfied. And horrified.

This morning, Georgia Starr greeted me at the front door with a broad smile. She pulled me into a hug scented with ylang-ylang, coconut, and vanilla. She wore one of her favorite caftans—pastel flowers outlined in thick browns and greens. "You have a key," she said as I followed her into the house. "Why did you ring the bell?"

I sat my bag on the foyer's tile. "Because if I walk in on you and Martin, I'll have to get a lobotomy, and with half a brain, I wouldn't be as great a cop as I am now."

She padded to the kitchen. "I like your pantsuit. I guess you're not chasing any thugs through the alleys in those high-heeled boots."

"No, that was yesterday." I pulled off those boots and left them in line with the other shoes there. Then, I futzed with the sharp crease in my gray slacks to avoid looking at the brass and sapphire cremation urn sitting on the fireplace mantel. I peered at the vase of pink stargazer lilies on the dining room table. "So sparkly, so gorgeous," I said, tapping a white-edged petal.

"Martin gave them to me," Mom said. "We just celebrated our one-year anniversary."

I joined her in the kitchen, warm from sweet rolls in the oven, fragrant from coffee dripping into the pot.

Mom's face glowed as she eased from the cabinets to the refrigerator, pulling cups, sugar, and cream from here and there. A small smile played on her lips—she probably didn't know that it was there. And her hair, a short bob now and completely gray, caught light from the kitchen overheads.

"What are you staring at?" she asked as she divided the rolls onto two plates.

I smiled. "So sparkly, so gorgeous."

She settled into the breakfast nook. "I feel blessed this morning."

It would have been a true Massengill moment between a mother and daughter, but I knew we would eventually discuss issues far more sensitive than feminine freshness. But we would, as is our custom, take the scenic route. And so beads of flop sweat pebbled on my neck as I sipped my coffee and waited.

One . . . two . . .

"How is Gregory?" she asked, her eyes burning into my forehead.

"Slammed at work—big game release in May."

He hadn't made it home in time for late-night dessert. At almost one o'clock, he had simply undressed and fallen into bed, snoring before I could count to ten.

"And how are you dealing with that?" Mom asked.

I shrugged. "With a job like mine, I can't complain about his."

"With the budget cuts, aren't they making you go home? No more over-time?"

I nodded.

She nibbled on a piece of roll. "Does that mean . . . ?"

That half-asked question made my heart, already skipping from caffeine, jump from skipping to full gallop. When she didn't continue, I said, "Does that mean what?"

She tore away another piece of roll. "I was just talking to Martin the other day and . . . I was thinking, you know . . . With the new year coming and . . ." She smiled to herself. "Wouldn't it be nice, next year this time, to have a little one runnin' around here?"

The coffee started to burn a hole into my chest. "Aren't you and Martin a little too old to have a baby?"

"Ha-ha, very funny," she said. "Fine. I'll change the subject." She sat up, back straight, and cradled the coffee mug between her palms. "Tori's ashes."

Dread gripped my insides and turned everything to ice. Maybe the con-versation about a baby would've been better.

The last talk between Mom and me about Tori's ashes had occurred in my living room. After finding Tori's remains in the basement of Crase Li-quor Emporium, after forensic anthropologists and the coroner confirmed that the bones were those of Victoria Starr, and after we had approved cre-mation, I had suggested to Mom that we divide the ashes between us.

Mom had gone wild-eyed. "Why would you want to separate her like that? And why does she need to be sprinkled or shoved into somebody's box? I just got her back. How could you be so cruel?"

Back and forth like that. Tears, accusations, and screaming.

Greg, returned from Japan for just a week, had been upstairs packing (I had kicked him out after he'd confessed to his two-timing). But after Mom stormed out of the house, he came downstairs to find me sobbing on the couch. Over the three days of Mom and me not speaking, he held me and assured me that I wasn't being cruel. And then he asked for another chance. Weak as I was, and feeling so very alone, I had said yes.

After Mom and I had drifted back into speaking again, I swore to my-self never to mention Tori's ashes to her again.

But now here we were.

Mom gazed at me with sad eyes. "How much will a small memorial service cost?"

I managed a one-shouldered shrug. "Don't worry about the price—I'll take care of that."

She gave a small nod, then stared into her cup. "She liked Griffith Park and the horses. Maybe we could have something near there. Remember how we would go all the time?"

"And then," I said, "after the horses, we'd go to the zoo, and Dad would . . ." Blood drained from my face, and I jammed my lips together—talking about Victor Starr could "poof" him into the kitchen à la Rumpelstiltskin. Worse, I didn't know whether I wanted that to happen or not.

Silence washed over the house. Then, birds in the backyard chirped. The neighbors' sprinklers *tcheted-tcheted-tcheted*.

"Do you think . . . ?" Mom inhaled, then slowly released that breath. "Would it be too soon to have the service on New Year's Eve?"

I blinked at her.

"As a celebration," she explained. "A letting go." Her hands fluttered in the air like butterflies until they finally settled on her chest. "And on the next day, January first, we all start the new year and . . ." She tugged at her earlobe. "She loved wearing those silly New Year's Eve party hats, remember?"

"If that's what you want to do, Mom." My voice sounded thirteen and small and uncertain—as though she was going to lose it again and then disappear for good and forever.

She let out another breath. "I'll make a guest list. Won't be too long. Maybe you can ask Lena to handle the catering? Maybe Syeeda could write something real nice for the obituary? Will you ask them?"

I reached for her hands. "Okay."

"And you'll say something?" Tears in her eyes shone like crushed diamonds. "And maybe you can . . ." She slid off the bench and headed to the drawer filled with Important Stuff. She pulled out a pink plastic sleeve and returned to the nook. "You can read this," she said, handing me the sleeve.

I plucked a doily from the plastic and immediately recognized my big sister's handwriting. The backward tilt of the *V* and the big dots over the lowercase *i*. It was a poem titled "I Love My Mom." The organ in my chest twisted—I was having a heart attack.

"I know it won't be Valentine's Day," Mom said, "but she wrote this back in third grade and she gave it to me and I kept it and so I thought . . ."

> *If I had to pick a Mom*
> *It would be you.*
> *If I could buy something for you for Valentine's Day*
> *I would be happy.*
> *But Mom you always say I got all I need . . . you.*
> *I just want to give you something*
> *So I give you love.*
> *Happy Valentine's.*
> *Love, Tori*

I wanted to swallow, but my constricted throat wouldn't let me.

Mom came to stand over me. She placed her hands on my shoulders and rested her chin atop my head. "You'll read it for me?" she asked, sounding strained.

A tear slipped down my cheek. "Yes."

She kissed the top of my head. "You're a good girl, Elouise." She slipped over to the sink and gazed out the window. "Next year this time . . . Wonder what we'll be talking about?" And she prattled on about the neighbor's new parakeet and the rising cost of gas.

I closed my eyes.

Ba-bump. Ba-bump.

My heart. It was still there. It was still working.

Why did it feel broken?

26

Adeline St. Lawrence lived in Corona, fifty miles east of Los Angeles, in a California-style, two-story behemoth with columns and arched windows. Her tract home resembled every other tract home in that cul-de-sac, only St. Lawrence's stucco exterior had been painted buckwheat instead of sandstone.

Before I rang the bell, a woman with café au lait skin and sea-green eyes opened the door with a cell phone trapped between her right shoulder and ear. A lit cigarette from the hard pack of Parliaments she clutched dangled between her fuchsia-painted lips. The calla-lily hair clip held a lock of long blond weave behind her left ear. Glitter sparkled in her eyeliner but paled in comparison to her bejeweled ankle boots and military-style studded jacket.

As I stood there with her, happiness chirped in my heart like a bluebird on the first day of spring.

She was Too Much of Everything.

"I'm on my way out," she told me, phone still to her ear. "I'm not buyin' nothing, I don't need you to paint my curb, and I already know Jesus, *thankyouverymuch.*" The three-carat diamond on her ring finger no longer twinkled—all that acid tongue and cigarette smoke.

I badged her.

The woman cocked an eyebrow, then yanked the cig from her mouth. "You the cop working on Juliet's case?"

I nodded. "You Adeline?"

She nodded. "We talkin' *today?*"

"Yes."

"Thought I said tomorrow."

"And tomorrow *is* today."

Adeline tossed the cigarette to the ground and smashed it with the toe of her boot. She slipped the phone into her jacket pocket and stomped back into the living room. Her hips and ass, clad in black satin leggings, were as wide as a mule deer's but not as firm.

My heart cartwheeled again.

Too. Much.

The house boasted nine-foot ceilings, a fireplace, and a series of covered patios. But there wasn't much furniture. A glass coffee table there, three floor plants there, there, and over there. A wobbly-looking dining room table with two matching chairs, as well as a mahogany sideboard. Sparse. Not out of style, but out of economics. Out of living one's dreams and still being unable to afford that dream's furniture.

Adeline plopped on the love seat.

I sat on the adjoining couch.

"Them boots is givin' me life," she said, eyeing my footwear. "Prada?"

"Jimmy Choo," I said. "And yours?"

"Custom-made. I own six boutiques. You should come in and let my girls dress you."

"Maybe I will. Thanks."

She lifted an eyebrow. "Well?"

Guess that was my cue that sartorial solidarity had ended. I pulled my notepad from my bag. "Anything you're able to tell me about Juliet and Christopher—"

"Including what I know about her money?" she asked.

"Well—"

"So her beneficiaries: the kids in one policy and her parents in the other. She wasn't gon' leave *him* shit. Fuck him—that's what she told *me*. But before we really get started, Detective, I wanna put somethin' out there." St. Lawrence grabbed a gold cigarette case from the coffee table and pulled a smoke from the five there. "Write *this* down in your little notebook: Christopher Chatman is a sociopathic son of a bitch who thinks he got everybody fooled. But he ain't got Addy St. Lawrence fooled. And if he thinks he's gon' get away with killing *her* best friend? He needs to think again. Quote. Unquote."

By now, I'm sure my mouth hung open. I shifted on the couch to grab control of my interview. "So how did you and Juliet—?"

"We all went to UCLA," Adeline interrupted. "Jules, Christopher, Benji, and yours truly. Jules and I were roommates all four years. Back then, she had this awful feathered haircut, and her clothes . . . Woo, woo, *woo*! That girl was tacky. So she and Christopher started goin' out, and at first she was like, why does he like me? Cuz homeboy was *caught up* with her. Obsessed, in my opinion. Back then, though, Jules thought I was bein' dramatic. *Hmph.* Guess who was right? Me, that's who."

Five minutes in and my underarms were already prickly with sweat.

Adeline hopped up and stepped over to the sideboard. She grabbed a photo album from the top shelf and returned to the couch. "Lemme show you somethin'." She flipped through pages that stuck together and smelled of cigarette smoke and old glue. She stopped at a picture and tapped it. "I took this on their first date. See how he's lookin' at her?"

In the photograph, Juliet was smiling, closed mouth, tiny and dowdy with that feathered hair and an ill-fitting ruffled blouse. Christopher Chatman, not as small, quietly handsome and big-eyed, did not look at the camera. Instead, he smiled down at her. Although I couldn't see his full face, I did see awe in his expression. He was, as St. Lawrence said, *caught up*.

"Dude was crazy, even back then," she said.

"Crazy in love, maybe," I said.

She smirked. "I see he got you fooled, too."

My cheeks warmed. "But I'm sure you'll straighten me out."

She tapped ashes into a Grand Canyon ashtray on the coffee table. "I was like her big sister. Took her to get her eyebrows waxed the first time. Took her to Vegas for her first legal drink. Told her the truth about men and sex—somebody had to since her momma wouldn't. I was the one who begged Juliet to slow down and to date other guys but . . ."

She took a drag, then peered at me through tendrils of smoke. "Christopher paid for everything. Juliet's books, her meal plans, sometimes some of her tuition. She thought he was bein' nice and generous. I thought he was being a control freak, makin' her dependent on him, buyin' her love." She turned a page in the album, touching every other picture of the Chatmans' Once Upon a Time. Pictures of Christopher and Juliet together were almost always the same—Juliet facing the camera, Christopher looking down at Juliet.

And I thought of other pictures I'd come across in the investigation—in almost every shot, Christopher was looking at Juliet. But she never looked at him.

"When did things get serious between them?" I asked.

Smoke curled from Adeline's nostrils. "He proposed to her in the middle of our junior year. She turned him down. Told him that they were too young to get married. *That* was true. Then, he asked her again at the start of senior year. She said, 'not yet, still too young.'" The woman dumped more ashes into the ashtray. "*That* wasn't true."

"Because?" I asked.

She smirked. "Juliet didn't wanna marry him cuz she was in love with somebody else. And she ended up in the other dude's bed, and he got turned out cuz I taught her every trick in the book."

My eyes bugged, and I almost forgot that I was working a case and not catching up on gossip with a college girlfriend. "So who was this other guy?"

Adeline smoked but said nothing.

"Everything you tell me is confidential," I said.

"For how long?"

"Until the court case. So when did Juliet finally accept Christopher's proposal?"

"On Valentine's Day, senior year. By now, the other guy had told her that he didn't feel that way about her, that it was just about sex. So Juliet, rejected, went back to Christopher, heartbroken. He took her to dinner at Monty's Steakhouse at the base of campus and gave her a sapphire and diamond engagement ring. She never took that ring off."

That ring now sat in a coroner's cabinet, in an envelope with her wedding band and diamond stud earrings.

"She *did* love Christopher," Adeline continued. "Hated him but loved him until the day she died." Mouth set into a frown, she studied the photograph she had snapped on her friend's engagement night.

"Did he ever cheat on her?" I asked.

She threw back her head and laughed. "Who'd want his scrawny, weak ass?"

"So Juliet never expressed concern about him and Melissa Kemper fooling around?"

"Jules woulda told me if she suspected that he was screwing around. Hell, he could barely get it up with *her*."

So another "no affair" in the Melissa Kemper column.

Adeline snorted. "Melissa Kemper. That woman was a hot. Ass. Mess. She was too busy tryin' to get up in Benji's bed. You meet Mr. Oliver yet?"

I nodded.

She lifted an eyebrow.

"Okay, yes, I have met him and yes . . . Yes. Did he and Melissa . . . ?"

She snorted again. "Not even in her dreams. And she sure as *hell* don't want Sarah comin' after her. Lady Lawyer got that man under lock and key."

Adeline continued to talk as she set out a plate of Lorna Doones and bottles of Snapple. She told me that everyone had graduated from college; that Juliet, a biology major, had failed to get into medical school and decided to become a pharmaceutical rep instead; that Christopher had been accepted to UCLA's Anderson School of Management; and that Juliet kept postponing their wedding. It had been Maris Weatherbee who had forced her daughter to pick a date and stick with it. "The thing with *that* . . ." St. Lawrence paused with the mouth of the Snapple bottle touching her lips.

When she didn't continue, I said, "The thing with . . . *what?*"

Adeline blinked, then sat back. "I just remembered somethin'." She waggled her head, and placed the bottle on the table.

"Is it something I should know?"

She let out a long sigh. "Jules was a drama queen."

Just like her best friend.

The woman shook her head again. "Nothin'. Never mind."

I leaned forward. "Addy, please tell me."

She stared at me, deciding whether or not to talk. "Jules didn't . . ." She poked her tongue against the inside of her cheek. "She, umm . . . She was unhappy, so she took a bunch of pills, but she didn't mean to kill herself. She was just . . ." Her lower lip quivered. "I swore to her that I'd never . . . It was all a mistake. Can we . . . ?" She took a deep breath, then held it.

"Juliet quit working," I said, taking a new direction.

"Right before Chloe was born," Adeline confirmed. "She wanted to be a stay-at-home mom. She was old-fashioned that way."

I cocked an eyebrow. "But?"

"But she got bored." Adeline sighed, gaining confidence again. "How many times can you do laundry and make macaroni and do playdates and play patty-cakes in a day? So she got pissed off a lot because *now* she had time to pay attention to her marriage and to that house."

"Did her dissatisfaction . . . lead her elsewhere?"

Adeline smirked. "Like to a motel?" She grabbed the bottle of iced tea, screwed off the top, and sipped.

I waited, but the woman didn't speak. "Did she have an affair?" I asked.

"Yes."

"With?"

Adeline shook her head.

"Why not?"

"Cuz shit gon' get twisted and that hobbit motherfucka will get to twist shit some more and Juliet ain't here to defend—"

"That's my job, Addy," I said, touching her wrist. "*I* will speak for her and for the kids. *I* will keep shit from twisting as much as I can. But *you* need to tell me shit straight. So who did she see?"

"Jules wouldn't tell me their real names," she admitted.

"Why not?"

Adeline shrugged. "Guess she enjoyed keeping some stuff to herself, this . . . secret life she led." She stared at the Snapple label as she thought. "Jules was unhappy. She was depressed, and she was ashamed that she'd gone outside her marriage. And she stayed that way, ashamed, even though she tried to hide it. But I saw it. We went to lunch last week, and I saw it. She thought she could hide it behind eye shadow and diamond earrings, but she had that cocaine confidence, 'cept it was wine and not blow." Adeline shrugged. "I saw just how . . . *messed up* she was. I didn't like it."

"Was Juliet . . . ? Did she ever attempt suicide again? Or even *talk* about being tired and just ending it? I ask because we found a strange letter that could be taken as a suicide note."

Adeline wedged the bottle between her knees.

"Was Juliet Chatman—?"

"I heard your question," she snapped, fire in her eyes.

"She was?"

Adeline shook her head.

"She wasn't?"

She shook her head again.

"So she marries Christopher," I said, pissed that I drove all the way to effin' Corona to be cock-blocked by a chick wearing a fake flower in her hair. "Were they happy for the most part?"

"At first," Adeline said, "but the last nine years she was always stressed about somethin'. The kids, the house, him. She found out . . . He was . . . This is all just . . ." Her jaw tightened, and the vein in her forehead bulged. *Boom!* A sob broke from her chest, and then another sob followed, and soon she was fully weeping into her hands.

My mind whirled as she bawled—*Juliet was stressed about* what? *She found out* what? *He was* what? *This is all just* what?

Juliet was a suicidal type. Juliet was an adulteress type. And *this* coming from her best friend, who was now whispering, "I'm so sorry," and, "Thought I was through crying," as she dabbed at her eyes with napkins until another wave of anguish knocked her down.

Five minutes later, and all cried out, Adeline took a deep breath and released it through pursed lips. She squared her shoulders, then said, "Okay. Okay. What . . . ?"

"We were discussing their marriage," I said. "And there's no need to rush."

"I just miss her so much," she whispered. "And I'm angry and I'm sad." She blew her nose into a napkin. "Jules tried to get over a lot of things she didn't like. Except for that damned house. Both of them drove each other crazy over that house."

She plucked the neglected cigarette from the ashtray and took a long drag, holding in the smoke as long as she could. Nicotine relaxed the tight muscles in her face, and she released the smoke into the air with a sigh. "Stress was startin' to change her, you know? She was losin' weight, always in pain." Fighting anxiety, Adeline hugged herself and started rocking on the couch. "She was throwin' up and crampin'. I forced her to get checked out."

"When did you talk to her last?"

"Friday." She twisted her mouth, then forced the Parliament between her lips.

"Did she ever talk about getting a divorce?" I asked.

She killed that cigarette in the ashtray and grabbed another from the gold case. "Uh-huh, but she wouldn't get one."

"Why not?"

"Raised Catholic. No divorce. I told her that she'd get paid—they'd been together for, what? Twenty years? *And* she'd get child support. That's one thing he had goin' for him: he worked his little hobbit ass off."

"So: he adored her." I held up one finger and then held up another. "He provided for her and the kids. He worked hard. Why was she so unhappy?"

The woman stared at the burning end of the long brown cigarette.

"Was she was in love with someone else?" I asked.

St. Lawrence didn't speak.

"Did Christopher abuse her?" I asked, my stomach twisting.

"Physically? No."

"He abused her psychologically?"

She bit her lip. "Yes."

"He have something on her?"

She didn't nod, nor did she shake her head.

"What is it, Addy?" I pled. "If I know, then I'll be able to figure out what happened in that house, and then arrest whoever is responsible. Juliet and Cody and Chloe: they need you to speak for them. No one else can do that right now. No one."

The cigarette shook between her fingers. "One of the last things Jules said to me on Friday . . ." She squeezed shut her eyes. "She said, 'I chose wrong, Addy. I chose wrong.'"

Sadness gripped my heart and swept through my body like damp fog.

Adeline covered her mouth with her hand and forced her breathing to slow.

I leaned forward and whispered, "What if I told you that we found suit-cases in the trunk of her SUV? Suitcases filled with clothes for her and the kids. But no suitcase for him."

Adeline kept rocking, kept smoking, kept fighting tears.

"What if I told you," I said, leaning forward so much that I was almost on my knees, "that we also found a gun in Juliet's hand? A gun that she'd just purchased for protection?"

Smoke wafted from Adeline's mouth.

"You have nothing to say?" I asked.

She tapped the cigarette against the ashtray. "Is Christopher Chatman still alive?"

"Yes, he is."

She drew on the cig, then let smoke curl from her nostrils. "If Christopher Chatman is still alive, then somethin' happened before Juliet could blow his fuckin' brains out."

27

Was Juliet Chatman planning to kill her husband?

As we stood on the front porch of her house, Adeline St. Lawrence had hinted at the possibility—blow his fuckin' brains out, quote, unquote—but had ended our interview without answering my very direct question. "Take me to court, then," she had sassed, hand on her hip. "It look like I give a fuck?"

"It does not look like you give a fuck."

She crossed her arms.

"Addy," I said, "please. Was she planning to kill him? If you don't care, why should anyone else?"

She glared at me, but that hard look softened. "Yes, she was planning . . . what you said."

Back behind the wheel of the car, I took a deep breath and then slowly exhaled. I smelled like an AA meeting. Away from nicotine-laced air for only a minute, I was shaky from withdrawal. With a trembling hand, I pulled my phone from my bag and checked for messages.

While I had been nibbling stale Lorna Doones with Adeline St. Lawrence, Dixie Shipman (Adeline's sista from another mista) had left me a voice mail. *Once you get back from Narnia or Wherever-the-Hell you are, gimme a call. I've been diggin' around some, and all I can say is, 'Mr. Chatman, Mr. Chatman, Lawd have mercy, Mr. Chatman.' I'll be at TCK for a mani-pedi. My treat, if you come down.*

I considered my fingernails. Working the Chatman case with all its soot and ashes made my hands look like I, too, had been digging around—in bogs and lumberyards for splinters and grubs. And since I had the cuticles of a hobo, I decided to take Dixie's offer for free nail help as well as her offer to share information about the case. Of course.

An overturned tomato truck on the 10 freeway west and the subsequent single available lane meant that it took almost two hours to drive back to Los Angeles. Five minutes before three o'clock, I found myself at the spa, melting into a massage chair with my slacks rolled up, one hand soaking in soapy water and one foot being massaged by Jun.

Dixie sat at the next booth with one foot hidden in a tub of bubbles and the other foot propped on a stool before Patsy, her regular aesthetician. "You cut 'em down too low last time," she shouted to Patsy over the Luther Vandross song blasting from the spa's speakers. "Don't do that or I'm a get somebody else." The ex-cop turned back to me. "Like I said, his people weren't the Gettys. Far from."

"So how did the Chatmans get their money?" I asked.

"So Virginia Oliver is tellin' me this, okay? And *she* says Ava and Henry Chatman were stingy as hell, *that's* how. They were born right before the Depression began."

"Chatman had old-people parents," I said.

"Yep. She was forty-three when she had him. Anyway, she and Henry grew up squeezin' pennies 'til they bled. They left Cleveland in fifty-two, came to California and bought the house on Don Mateo in fifty-three. They didn't open a bank account until sixty-three."

"When Christopher was born," I noted. "Guess the sunshine and oranges helped Henry's little swimmers."

"Guess so," Dixie said. "Henry Chatman put his paychecks into some tiny savings and loan. They bought the house on Don Mateo and installed a wall safe in the master bedroom. I don't know how much they stashed in there at first, but Mrs. Oliver said it was several thousand."

"Okay. Nothing sounds wacky yet, Dix."

Dixie switched feet to let Patsy scrub calluses on the other heel. "Be patient, damn. In ninety-eight, Momma Chatman started speakin' in tongues, started callin' Christopher 'Jimmy,' and couldn't remember which channel showed *Oprah*. So, after gettin' lost in the mall, and vacuumin' the house in the middle of the night, and not remembering her birth date, Ava was diagnosed with dementia and put into Ocean Breeze Estates in Camarillo by her beloved son, Jimmy aka Christopher."

"Sad." Then, I told Jun to paint my toenails a sassy toreador red. A wasteful act since I'd be slipping on boots again. Like dressing Naomi Campbell in a burqa.

"Ava goes bye-bye," Dixie continued, "and the next month, Henry slips on the porch and breaks his hip. He comes down with pneumonia and dies three days after Memorial Day. When he died, they had $237,000 cash in the bank. They also had pensions, a couple of savings bonds, and three insurance policies with MG Standard."

"So how much money is that?"

"A little over two mil," Dixie said, eyebrow cocked.

I admired my manicured hand with its smooth, buffed nails. "Lucky boy. All that money *and* the house is empty."

"Not for long, though," Dixie said. "Christopher and Juliet move in with baby Cody in 2001 and life's swell. Since Ava is still alive, they go up and visit her sometimes. But in 2002, during one of those visits, Ava died."

I shrugged.

Dixie smirked. "When the staff at the convalescent home asked Christopher what had happened, he told them, 'All of a sudden, she stopped breathing.' What did he mean, 'she stopped breathing'? And 'all of a sudden'? Ava hadn't been sick, not beyond the regular symptoms that come with dementia. So everybody at the home was kinda surprised. And they couldn't revive her cuz she had a DNR in place—and nobody remembers when she got *that*."

"Was there an autopsy?"

"Nope."

"Did someone see Christopher or Juliet do anything inappropriate that afternoon?"

"No."

"Feh."

"Girl, you trippin'."

"Ava Chatman was in her nineties, Dixie. She had dementia. She was old as hell. Eventually, she was supposed to stop breathing."

Dixie rolled her eyes. "C'mon now, Detective Elouise Norton. Christopher Chatman inherited almost three million dollars that afternoon."

"Interesting," I said. "That's all I got."

Two dead parents. Three million dollars.

Yeah. Very interesting.

28

Four o'clock, and I sauntered into the squad room, where the living was easy. I had avoided the station all day, and not much had changed. One person had killed another person. A dick had made an arrest. The alleged murderer, dull-eyed, high, blood crusted beneath his fingernails, protested. Dick rolled his eyes, wrote his report, produced a pair of steel bracelets. Another name written in red on the board. Another case to solve.

Colin sat at his desk with the Chatman murder book before him. His eyes darted back and forth between two pages. He didn't look up when I plopped into my seat.

"Miss me?" I asked, hanging my jacket on the back of the chair.

"Like I miss crabs and cold sores," he said, his attention still directed to the book.

I logged on to my computer. "Are they ever gone long enough for you to miss them?"

He flicked me a look. "Didn't think I'd see you today."

"Been busy, my friend. The Princess was in another castle." And I caught him up on my conversation with Adeline St. Lawrence and Dixie Shipman.

"Juliet Chatman was no vestal virgin, was she?" he said, narrowing his eyes.

I shrugged. "And what are you working on, sir?"

"The warrants came in, so Luke's working on the phones, and I'm pulling pictures off the cameras."

I sang, "It's beginning to look a lot like Christmas . . ."

"You're in a mood."

"Driving way the hell out to the Inland Empire on a Thursday will do that."

My iPhone rang, and a picture of python stilettos lit up the display.

I squinted at the phone, then answered. "Hey, Lena."

"Look," she said. "I didn't mean . . ."

"I know."

"This is a weird time in my life, no excuses, but . . . Sorry, okay?"

"It's cool," I said, then told her about breakfast with my mother and the memorial service for Tori. "Could you arrange the catering?"

"Of course," she trilled. "Ooh! The chef over at Budino's owes me a favor." And then she went on and on about crostini, truffles, and Viognier from Sonoma.

I thanked her, and we told each other, "I love you."

Colin dabbed at fake tears. "Wind beneath my wings."

I rolled my eyes. "What were we discussing?"

"Pictures from the Chatmans' camera." He rolled his chair to my desk with a stack of shots.

Chatmans at Disneyland . . . Chloe in a pink soccer uniform . . . Cody and Christopher in Dodgers caps at a game . . . Family picture in front of a church . . . No one smiling . . . Smile but forced . . . Monkey face . . . Photo bomb . . .

"How many pics are there?" I asked.

"On this card, three hundred and thirty-eight." Colin placed his elbows on my desk. "So what do you see?"

I picked up one contact sheet. "I see . . . a sad family."

Christopher and Juliet were sitting in the backyard, on opposite sides of the swing . . . Strained smiles . . . Crossed arms . . .

"I see two adults going through the motions." Sadness pulled at my limbs and slowed my sifting. "These pictures are killing my vibe."

Colin studied the shot of the couple on the swing. "I hate this invention."

I furrowed my brows. "You hate swings?"

He shook his head. "Digital cameras. They cheapen the moment. You can take as many pictures as you want. Awesome, right? Woo-freakin'-hoo. But unlimited pictures means, what? Lots of throwaway pieces of crap, one after the other. Fingers in shots, people blinking . . . How many cat pictures do you need?" He sat back in his chair and crossed his legs. "Old-school snapshots—the ones we grew up taking? Twelve shots. Twenty-four, if your folks had dough. Those pictures worked cuz the photographer chose *that specific moment* for one of twelve takes."

I glanced at him and then glanced back at the swing shot. "But then we'd never get to see pictures like this. Shots of people totally over it. People so dissatisfied that you're convinced that somebody's about to get pushed off this swing and bludgeoned to death with a sledgehammer."

"We live for those moments, don't we?" he asked.

I fluttered my eyelids. "Oh, Colin Taggert. You're so deep."

He rolled back to his desk. "Got somethin' else for you. Video from the Chatmans' security system. No sound. E-mailing you the file right now."

I logged in to my e-mail account and double-clicked on the file.

10:53 P.M., 12/10: The Chatmans' front porch.

10:57 P.M., 12/10: The same porch shot with the top of a man's head now visible. He turns away from the front door and strolls down the walkway.

"That Christopher Chatman?" I asked.

"Yeah," Colin said. "Leaving for work just like he said he did."

10:59 P.M., 12/10: A Jaguar backs out of the driveway, disappears from the frame.

11:00 P.M., 12/10: The Chatmans' front porch. No one standing there.

"Skip ahead to almost four o'clock," Colin instructed. "Nothin' happens until then."

3:51 A.M., 12/11: The responding officer runs onto the porch, bangs the door, looks up at the sky, bangs some more, yells into his shoulder mic.

4:00 A.M., 12/11: A fireman shouts and bangs on the front door. Another fireman with a blowtorch kneels before the iron door. Sparks fly. The recording blinks. Blank screen.

"And the rest is history," Colin said.

"So Chatman left the house," I said, eyes still on the monitor. "And he didn't return until well after the fire's start."

He nodded. "And I looked at the tape from the second camera bolted to the side of the house. Nobody's lurking around that side until the firemen come and knock it down."

"What about before this?"

Colin blinked. "Before what?"

"Any recordings before eleven?" I asked. "Say nine o'clock? Or during dinner?"

Colin scrolled through the recordings. "Cameras were off, I guess. They probably disarm them when they're up and walking around. I don't know."

"What if the evildoer was lurking around during dinner?" I asked.

"Peeping through windows while the family watched *A Christmas Story*? When everybody was passed out in a Valium haze?"

He cocked his head. "You're still saying that the threat could've been from the outside?"

"I'm saying . . ." I twisted in my chair. "I don't know what I'm saying."

No Christopher Chatman at the house.

No black dude wearing an orange hockey jersey at the house.

The fire had started *inside* the house.

And the only adult *inside* the house was the only individual with the Valium scrip, a newly purchased handgun, and a handwritten note threatening to end it all. An adult who'd had both suicidal and homicidal tendencies.

And that adult was Juliet Chatman.

Colin and I sifted through all 338 photos pulled from the Chatmans' digital camera. With each depressing or staged shot, my shoulders slumped and my torso caved. By the time Lieutenant Rodriguez charged into the squad room holding a pink box filled with Mexican pastries, my forehead hung just an inch from my desktop.

"Time for an update on the Chatman case," our boss said, dropping the box on Luke's desk. He grabbed a *cuernito* for him and another for me so that I wouldn't have to beat up the three men now swarming around the desserts. He handed me the coiled, sweet bread, then leaned against my desk.

Luke, Pepe, and Colin, each double-fisting pastries, sat back in their chairs.

I licked sugar and cinnamon from the tips of my fingers, then said, "I'm sorry to say that after working this for two days now, I have no suspect. I don't know who done it."

The men looked at me with tense smiles, waiting for the punch line.

I took a bite of *cuernito*.

Their smiles dropped.

"Stop jerking off, Lou," Lieutenant Rodriguez growled, his face dark.

"I'm not, sir."

"Well," Colin said, "we keep bein' pointed in Juliet's direction but . . ."

"But what?" Lieutenant Rodriguez snapped.

I squinted at Colin. "But I'm hoping to find more hard evidence before making statements like my partner just did."

To Pepe and Luke, Lieutenant Rodriguez said, "So what can you guys give Lou that ain't just supposition and circumstantial?"

"We talked to Baby Ted Bundy," Luke said.

"AKA Parker McMann, Cody's BFF." Pepe nodded to our wall of "Most Wanted." "He'll be up there in about six years."

"So," Luke said, flipping through his notepad, "Parker says, 'Hell yeah, Cody hated his dad, kinda hated his sister, but was a momma's boy through and through.'"

"He was plannin' to do something to the house," Pepe said, "but nothing like what happened. Just enough so they would have to move."

"All for Juliet," Luke continued. "He wanted to make her happy since his daddy couldn't."

"So the boy just burned his daddy's blazers in the meantime," Colin said.

"Practice," I said with a nod. "Anything else, guys?"

Pepe scanned his legal pad. "I'm looking at Juliet's e-mails right now, and as you can imagine, it's slow goin'." He passed around stapled copies of paper. "These are just a few of the most interesting so far. On Monday, December 10, around half past eleven in the morning, the office manager from the kids' school, a Mrs. Benewitz, e-mailed Juliet."

Sarah Oliver just retrieved Cody and will be taking him back to the doctor. Boys just never settle down, do they? After Thursday's accident, I thought Cody would give that skateboard a rest, but I guess not. I wanted to send you the attached anyway. It is the Emergency Form for this school year. Please fill it out and return it to me as soon as possible.

At 11:45 A.M., Juliet had responded:

I filled out the form back in September. Nothing's different. Thanks for your help and patience today.

In less than two minutes, Mrs. Benewitz had replied:

Hi, Mrs. Chatman. I consulted that form. But when we tried calling your husband's office number today after not being able to reach you, the operator at the firm said he was no longer in that office. Maybe the phone number has been changed? Thank you again for your attention to this.

"So Cody reinjured his arm on Monday," I said. "The school called his parents, no one answered, and they called Sarah Oliver, who picked the kid up."

"Where was Juliet on Monday?" Lieutenant Rodriguez asked.

"Getting a CT scan that she never showed up for," Colin said.

"So we don't know, in other words," Lieutenant Rodriguez retorted. "Lou?"

I looked up from the e-mails. "We don't, but when we get the financials, we'll figure out where she had coffee, what she ate for lunch, and everything else. When I called Christopher Chatman's office yesterday, the same thing happened—the operator said he was no longer working there. I didn't believe her, mostly because she sounded stupid."

Pepe nodded. "Juliet explains the office thing in the next message."

Oh yes. That's right. They're changing the phone systems and he has a new extension. The regular receptionist is out on sick leave and the new receptionist is a bit dim. She's probably working with old information. Sorry about that. I'll get the new number and correct the attached form. Thank you again.

"Did she e-mail Mrs. Benewitz the new number on the corrected form?" I asked.

Pepe shook his head.

I flipped to the next printout.

Weekly newsletter from the kids' school . . . Credit card payment confirmation . . . Free books alert . . . A message from My Google Voice, (454) 555-2342, on December 10 at 1:15 P.M.

I read the message aloud: "*I don't know what to tell you. Wish I did.*" I glanced at Pepe. "Ruh-roh."

Her original message had been sent seven minutes before:

I'm reaching out to you one more time. If you don't respond, I'll assume that we aren't going forward with this. My heart is broken. Didn't think I'd even have to ask you to respond after everything we've gone through. I shouldn't put this in e-mail—you always remind me of leaving behind digital footprints— but after today, it won't matter. I love you. There. I said it. Now what are you going to do?

"Any response from My Google Voice?" I asked. "And whose account is it?"

"No response," Pepe said. "And it's a Google anonymous account. To find the user, we'll need another court order."

"*Going forward* with what?" I wondered as I reread Juliet's message.

"*Everything we've gone through*," Colin said. "*Digital footprints?* Doesn't sound like she's talkin' to her hubby."

"Thank you, Captain Obvious," I said. "I'll want to see everything you pull, Pep. Bill payments, the spam folder, the megillah, all right? And find all of these My Google messages."

"Gomez," Lieutenant Rodriguez barked. "What about you?"

Luke wiped crumbs from his mustache. "So I've started on Chatman's cell phone."

"The one we found in the Jag?" Colin asked. "Or the legit one?"

"The legit one," Luke said, starting on his second *concha*. "So on December 10 at 11:06 A.M., Chatman receives a call from his wife's number. A minute long, which means he didn't answer. She left this message." He clicked a sound file on his computer.

Where the hell are you, Christopher? Juliet's voice was deep, smoky, and pissed. *Damn it, you are just . . . just . . . Fine. Call me. Immediately.* Hate and loathing stuck from those words like shards of glass dusted with ricin.

"At 11:27 A.M., Ben Oliver left him a message," Luke said. "Asking Chatman to call him back. Around noon, Melissa Kemper leaves the same innocuous request: 'Call me back.' Chatman calls Mercedes-Benz Financial around 12:30. That call lasted twelve minutes."

"I want that recorded conversation with Benz," I said.

Luke took a big bite of pastry. "Thought you'd say that. Chatman calls Melissa Kemper back after the call with Benz, and *they* talk for two minutes."

"He ever call Juliet back?" I asked.

Luke shook his head. "No more outgoing calls on that phone for the rest of the afternoon. But she does keep calling him every thirty minutes, one minute each. No messages left."

"Where the hell is he?" I asked. "Why didn't he pick up his injured kid from school? Why isn't he calling her back? A commodities broker without a cell to his ear? No way."

"Meetings," Colin said.

"Yeah, right," I snarked.

"Greg answers every time *you* call?" Colin asked. "Greg calls you back *immediately* every time you leave a message? And where was *she*? Why didn't *she* pick up her injured kid? We know she wasn't at the doctor's office. A housewife without a cell to her ear? No way."

My cheeks burned, and every man—except Colin—studied his fingernails.

Lieutenant Rodriguez cleared his throat. "Let's, umm . . ."

"Tread carefully, amigo," Luke advised Colin. "Unless you won't miss your balls."

"Just doin' my job," Colin said. "Just searchin' for the truth."

I tried to swallow my anger, but it stuck in my throat like a chunk of carrot. "What about the morning after the fire? Say nine, ten o'clock that Tuesday morning. Chatman use his legit phone at all?"

Luke said, "Nope."

"He was in the hospital by that time, remember?" Colin said.

"Any calls from his cell like an hour or so before the fire started?" I asked, scanning the call log. "Like, between two o'clock and three?"

Luke said, "Nope."

"He didn't use the phone to set off a device," Colin said. "If that's what you're thinkin'."

"He didn't use *this* phone," I pointed out. "There's the secret cell." To Luke, I said, "I want the calls off that second cell phone as soon as possible. Give me a list of everything: missed calls, contact lists, Web site downloads, how many times he played *Bejeweled*—I want it all." I tugged at my earring. "I bet y'all a bag of sour apple Jolly Ranchers that he did all of his sexy talk on that down-low cell phone."

The men said, "Eh."

"Why the 'eh'?" I asked, stunned. "Are you not entertained?"

"Say Chatman was having a 'thing' with what's-her-face in Vegas," Colin said. "He *still* wasn't there at the house when the fire started. You just saw the security tape. Not at the house."

"He didn't have to be there at the house to start the fire," I reminded Colin. "He still could've timed it either the old-fashioned way or by using that secret cell."

Colin brushed sugar off his chinos "Don't think so. The most popular timed device in arson is a cheap coffeepot. Leave the pot on, put a paper towel on or near the hot plate, let the pot burn 'til it's hot enough to catch the paper towel."

"The fire report didn't mention a coffeepot," Lieutenant Rodriguez said.

"Another popular way," Colin said. "Frying chicken. Just leave the burner on beneath the pan, and the grease in the pan catches fire."

"But this wasn't a grease fire," Pepe pointed out. "And it didn't start in the kitchen. Petroleum product in the bathroom."

"The Burning Man starts his fires with candles and lighter fluid," Colin said. "And the Chatman fire—"

"Started from the electrical outlet in the upstairs bathroom," I said. "I know, I know."

"Last fact," Colin said. "Women—*mothers*—are the usual suspects in fires that kill their children."

"Except those mothers usually survive," I pointed out. "Juliet Chatman died with her daughter in her arms. Or have you forgotten?"

"Elouise," Luke said, "we can probably all agree that this Chatman guy is an asshole—"

"'Asshole' is a pretty lenient term for someone who possibly poisoned and murdered Juliet and the kids," I spat.

"About that," Pepe said. "Isn't it possible that *Juliet* poisoned the kids? Say she did poison them, but then she changed her mind about it."

"Which is why she called 911," Colin added. "But by then, the kids were dead and it was too late."

Luke nodded. "She was waitin' for Chatman to come back home. She was holding that gun, ready to blow his ass to kingdom come. Her best friend told you she wanted to off him."

"But Chatman worked later than what she'd planned," Colin said. "So she starts the fire and dopes up on Valium, knowing that we're gonna look at *him* for all this."

"A mother would never do that to her children," I said, even though I had implied a similar scenario to Dr. Kulkanis just a day ago.

"Susan Smith," Colin said.

"Casey Anthony," Lieutenant Rodriguez added.

"Both of those bitches are still alive," I pointed out. "They had no intentions of dying."

"But why would Juliet wanna live?" Colin asked. "Her kids are dead. And *she's* dying—ovarian cancer, remember?"

"She didn't know she was dying," I said. "*Remember?* And the kids didn't die from the Valium—they died from carbon monoxide poisoning from the *fire*. And where the hell are her car keys?"

Lieutenant Rodriguez cocked his head. "Why do the keys matter?"

"She was trapped," I said. "Someone took the keys and—"

"Oh my Lord, *really?*" Colin said, rolling his eyes. "And *now* he's taken the keys? You're so freakin' stubborn."

"Christopher Chatman isn't innocent," I said. "My gut is telling me that."

"He may not be innocent," Colin said, "but that doesn't mean he's guilty."

After the team disbanded, after Lieutenant Rodriguez carried the box of remaining pastries to the coffeepot, Colin rolled his chair to my desk. "Just cuz we're partners—"

"Whatever, dude." I logged back on to my computer. "I'm done with you right now."

"Show me somethin' hard, Lou, and I'll go to the mat with you about Chatman. But from what I've seen so far—"

I swung around to face him. "No good mother would do that to her kids."

"No good *father* would do that to *his* kids."

"Who says he's a good father?"

"He was there, wasn't he? The kids had everything they wanted, and Juliet didn't have to work. So they argued about the house. So what? Greg cheated on you a thousand times, and even now you come in miserable because he said something crazy or went MIA for the day and so nobody can speak to you cuz he's fucked your head up with his *bullshit*. But I don't think he'd kill his kids cuz he was a jerk to *you*. Your father left—"

I kicked my waste can. "Say one more word."

Sensing danger, Colin rolled away. "Look: you're my partner, and I care about you." He waved his hand at our small group. "We *all* care about you. Hell, I got issues with my daddy, too. And I'm sure my mother has issues with her husband. None of this is strange, all right? We're *all* fucked up. But you're gettin' lost in this, and I'm worried cuz you're a kick-ass detective. Better than all of us in this building. So I'm just sayin' . . . You warned me about wanderin' off the beaten path, but here you are—"

"Here I am, working my case," I shouted. "Here I am, following a trail that will ultimately lead to Christopher Chatman because the first rule in a case like this is, 'No one wants to kill your wife and kids except you.'"

"I'm not sayin' there's no such thing as a killer husband," Colin shouted back.

"Then what *are* you saying?" I asked, standing from my chair. "That I'm so . . . so *dick-matized* by Greg that I can't do my job? That cuz my daddy abandoned me when I was a wittle-bitty girl—?"

"No," Colin said, also standing. "I'm sayin' that your judgment on this—"

"Oh, you're questioning my *judgment*?" I took a step closer to Colin.

All commotion in the room stopped.

"Oh shit," Pepe said, coming to stand with us. He touched Colin's shoulder. "Why don't we—"

"If you're about to get us jacked up in court," Colin snarled, "hell, yeah, I'm questioning your judgment."

Lieutenant Rodriguez had stormed out of his office and was now back in the squad room. "What the hell's going on?"

Colin knocked Pepe's hand off his shoulder and started to pace near his desk.

I ran my fingers through my hair, more yanking it than combing it. "Taggert's being an asshole, sir."

"Fuck you, Lou," Colin muttered.

"Taggert, shut it," Lieutenant Rodriguez snapped. He pointed to me, then pointed to the door. "Cool off. Be productive while you're at it." He pointed to Colin. "You're fuckin' up."

Colin gaped at the bigger man. "*I'm* fucking up? What did I—?"

"Always back your partner," Lieutenant Rodriguez said. "Especially if you have as much experience doin' this shit as a Girl Scout. Don't know how y'all worked in the mountains, but that's how we roll in my unit. Got it?"

"So I can't have an opinion?" Colin asked, arms spread.

"Opinions are like assholes," our boss said.

"And you're an asshole," I spat.

"Detective Norton," Lieutenant Rodriguez shouted. To Colin, he said, "She's senior."

"And she can still be wrong," Colin countered. "But I guess you folks don't mind takin' the hit—"

"You hear that?" I said to our superior. "*You folks?*" As I grabbed my bag and the Chatman case file, I eyed my boss with bemusement.

Lieutenant Rodriguez chuckled, then muttered, "*Dios mío.*"

Colin shook his head in awe. "What kind of thin-blue-line, fascist bullshit—?"

"Lou," Lieutenant Rodriguez growled. "My office. Now. *Please.*"

I stomped past him. "See you later, cowboy."

Always back your partner.

But if Colin wouldn't back me, then I would go it alone.

It wouldn't be the first time a man didn't have my back.

It wouldn't be the last time, either.

Lieutenant Rodriguez slammed his office door shut.

My arms spread wide as I opened my mouth to say, "All I'm—"

But my boss pointed at me with a single thick finger. "You're fucking up."

I gaped at him, then cocked my head. "*Excuse* me?"

He now pointed toward the detectives' bureau beyond his closed door. "I will back you out there in the midst of those assholes, *especially* Taggert, but in here—"

"What are you saying?"

"That's he right: you're letting outside shit—"

"No—"

"Hey," he shouted. "At ease, Detective."

Everything in me numbed, and weird prickling spread across my chest.

Lieutenant Rodriguez exhaled, then crossed his arms. "Next time you're in here with me means what?"

Pangs of anger exploded behind my eyes like little bombs. "Means I'm off the case."

He glared at me. "Anything else?"

"No, sir."

"Dismissed."

I gave him a short nod, then left him to whatever he did at his desk all day.

Everyone's gaze followed me as I stomped out of the station and into the frigid night, out to the parking garage and to the Crown Vic. I was nauseated and light-headed, and it felt like an alien was clawing in my belly, trying to burst through and spray the world with acid.

On every case, a detective decidedly depersonalizes all of it to stay sane. *The dead victim ain't my sister, the perp ain't my husband, and the murder didn't happen on my block.* Yes, a cop brings her own experiences to the squad room and to a murder scene. She filters bullshit through her prejudices and bigotry. Tells herself, same shit, different toilet. She pushes the rock up the hill even when she knows the fucker will roll down the other side. But she'll do anything for justice.

So to be told that I couldn't *see* because my boobs were blocking the view? That I couldn't think correctly because the little girl inside of me was sobbing on the living room couch, waiting for her deadbeat daddy to make her whole again?

I released a single primitive scream, and the alien pushed past my pancreas and lodged near my clavicles. Stuck.

Be productive.

That had been an order from my boss.

Fifteen minutes later, I had parked a block away from Ben Oliver's house. Just as I was about to leave the car, the Motorola blurped from the passenger seat.

"Lou, you there?" the man asked.

I smiled and grabbed the radio. "Now, you're a voice I haven't heard in a while."

"I tried you at the station," Zucca said, "but Taggert said you went out in a huff."

"Bitches be huffy," I said, glimpsing all of the activity on the Oliver property.

"The blood found in Christopher Chatman's Jaguar."

"What about it?"

"Belongs to Juliet Chatman . . . and to someone else."

My mouth opened, but no words came—someone else?

"You there?" the criminalist asked.

"Yeah," I said. "At this point, any news is good news. Any idea who 'someone else' is?"

"Nope."

"We need a sample from Chatman, don't we?"

"That would help, yes."

There could have been many reasons Juliet's blood had been found in her husband's car. Couldn't wait to hear those reasons from the man himself.

"PC?" Lieutenant Rodriguez barked over the radio, less convinced of the need for a warrant for Chatman's DNA.

"He's the husband and father of the deceased," I said. "He and Juliet were having financial and marital difficulties. She thought she was pregnant. We need his DNA to compare against what was found at the crime scene."

Lieutenant Rodriguez sighed. "Hit or miss. The judge likes 'em cleaner than this."

"If it's nothing, it's nothing. At least we know it's his blood. If it's not his blood, then we have a bigger problem. And we want to know if it's a bigger problem, right?"

"Yup. We'll send it over ASAP."

Case file in hand, I trekked back to the Oliver lawn. Two Hispanic valets wearing short red jackets were setting up a key cubby. A catering company truck had blocked the driveway, and two workers pushed silver carts down the truck's loading ramp.

The man of the house, dressed in a blue polo shirt and khakis, stood in the front door with his arms crossed. "An evening visit from Detective Elouise Norton," he called out, his dark eyes bright with amusement. "Must be my lucky day."

"Aye, it is," I said, hopping up onto the porch. "How are you?"

"Been better." We shook hands—firm, dry, a second longer than appropriate. "Nice seeing you again, Detective Norton."

"Is it really?" I asked, eyebrow cocked.

Ben laughed and his white teeth glistened. "Guess I should apologize for that."

"Are we talking about the mugging in Ruby Emmett's living room on Tuesday night?"

"Gimme a break, all right? My family had just died under suspicious circumstances. Can you honestly ding me for not trusting you? I'm protecting my friend, my brother, in a way. Christopher is far more important to me than MG Standard's bottom line or your caseload. I'm successful at my job because I'm not scared of lions. I must admit, though, you are certainly one of the pride's . . . finest."

I rolled my eyes, but my lips fell into a lopsided grin. "Flattery will get you almost everywhere. Especially on a day like today."

"Oh, the places I'll go, then," he said. "Or try to, at least." He smiled, then bit his lower lip. "Believe it or not, you and I have the same mission: making sure that those who need help get help. So with that said . . ." He offered me his hand again. "Truce?"

Why so friendly? Why no lobbing ten-dollar words at my head?

We shook again.

This time, he squeezed my hand.

"Party tonight?" I asked.

"Yep. How can I help you, Detective?"

"I'm here to talk with you about the case."

He smiled and tilted his head. "So this trip wasn't just to hang out? Should've known better—you don't seem like the 'pleasure trip' type."

"Shakespeare said, 'Every man has business and desire, even homicide detectives.'" I paused, then added, "I'm paraphrasing, of course."

"Of course," he said. "Let's go inside."

"I apologize for not going through your secretary for this meeting," I said, slipping off my blazer and not sorry at all. "I know you're a busy man."

He took my jacket and hung it on the coatrack. "I was actually sneaking in a couple of *X-Files* reruns before getting ready for tonight."

As we talked about aliens, Mulder and Scully, and the absence of good sci-fi on television, he led me down the hallway to the living room. A giant white-flocked noble fir, bright with tinsel and colorful ornaments, overwhelmed the room. Three red velvet stockings hung from the mantel above the roaring fireplace. The scent of cinnamon and peppermint wafted from an invisible plug-in air freshener.

He sat on the love seat as I studied the pictures on the mantel. In one shot, taken on a sailboat, the woman who resembled Lena Horne—Sarah Oliver—was embracing Ben as the wind whipped her long hair. In another photograph, Amelia, a ten-year-old version of Lena Horne wearing two long ponytails, smiled her snaggletoothed smile as she sat on a white sand beach. I glanced at Ben over my shoulder. "Your wife and daughter are beautiful."

The attorney tore his eyes away from my ass to meet my gaze. "They're out doing last-minute shopping. It's strange that we're still having the party tonight. I wanted to cancel, but Sarah insists on moving forward. She can't stop crying, though. And Amelia . . . she keeps asking if Coco is awake now, and . . . She loved . . ." He cleared his throat, then bumped his fist against his mouth.

I settled into the armchair across from him. From the case file, I pulled out a photo taken from the surveillance video camera. "First things first: could you please identify this person?"

Ben took the still, glanced at it, then handed it back to me. "That's Christopher standing on the front porch of his house. Why?"

"Just need to verify his alibi. This was taken four and a half hours before the fire started." I sat back in the chair. "I talked with your grandmother yesterday."

He smiled. "She thinks you're way too skinny. I told her that your weight seemed . . ." Embarrassed, he chuckled. "You look . . . great."

"You're being very complimentary today. And you're using small words for my benefit. How sweet."

"I don't have to put on with you. You see past it all anyway. So why bother?"

"Yep. Why bother? Your grandmother mentioned that Mr. Chatman experienced financial difficulties a year or so ago. That he asked you for a loan."

Ben shrugged, then crossed his legs.

"Would you say Mr. Chatman is good at his job?"

"Christopher's very busy. So busy that he has to turn away potential clients."

"If he's so flush with business, why then did he need to borrow money from you?"

Ben's eyes turned onyx, but almost immediately softened.

I held his gaze for a moment, then said, "Melissa Kemper had something explosive to tell Juliet. She says so in that note I found. What do you think that was?"

He rubbed his bottom lip. "Before I answer, may I ask *you* a question?"

I gave a small smile of assent.

"Why are you only focusing on Christopher?"

"Am I?"

He nodded. "Seems like you're ignoring evidence that doesn't fit your theory that he had something to do with this tragedy."

"Oh, really?" I leaned forward, interested. "What am I ignoring?"

He stared at me.

I lifted an eyebrow and waited.

The catering truck rumbled to life, and its gears grinded.

"Your wife, I hear, hated Cody," I said.

Ben's Adam's apple bobbed in his throat.

"What did *you* think of him?"

He rubbed his hands together as he thought. "He was a little . . ." He stopped, narrowed his eyes. "He was a little off."

"He hurt your daughter."

Ben nodded.

"And resented his sister."

His lips twisted into a crooked smile. "You trying to pin this on a kid now?"

I rolled my eyes. "You just told me that I'm focusing too much on—"

"But you think his *son* set the fire that *killed* his mother, his sister, *himself*? That little psychopath was far from suicidal." He covered his lips with a fist. His eyes shimmered with new tears.

"I'm sorry that we're having this conversation—"

He waved his hand. "It's . . . I just . . . I miss them. I can still hear Coco's laugh, and how her laugh sounded like Mimi's and . . ." He inhaled, then slowly, slowly released that breath.

"Melissa Kemper," I said.

"Was more than just Christopher's friend."

I froze. "You told me—no, you told *everyone* in Ruby Emmett's living room that she was only a friend, that she had nothing to do with this case. What's changed in two days?"

"Nothing's changed. She *doesn't* have anything to do with this case." He hopped up from the couch and ambled over to the wet bar near the bay window. He picked up a carafe and poured amber liquid into two glass mugs. Then, he returned to the couch and handed me a cup.

I sipped—my stomach warmed. *Rum.* The corners of my mouth lifted into a smile.

"Incredible," he said, amused. "You're enjoying it. You're . . . *human.*"

I sat the mug on the coffee table. "The city of Los Angeles requires that I act human at least once a day before six P.M."

He looked at his wristwatch. "You cut it close. It's ten minutes 'til."

"Anyway," I said, "wish I could finish this—it's delicious. Alas, I'm still on duty."

"Guess we'll have drinks, then, when you're off duty."

"Guess so."

His eyes flicked to my left hand. "I see an engagement ring but no wedding band."

I considered the princess-cut solitaire Greg had slipped on my finger so many years ago.

"Which is it?" he asked. "Engaged or soon-to-be divorced?"

"Limbo."

"Me, too. Soon to be divorced, I mean. Maybe." He squinted at me. "Sorry."

"Don't be."

"She thinks that I'm not. Did he screw up or did you?"

Sharpness twanged near my temples. It happened anytime I discussed my marriage. "You were saying about Melissa Kemper?"

He studied me for a few seconds. "I told you that she moved to Las Vegas with her kid."

"You did tell me that."

"Christopher called her two weeks later. Then he flew out there and they had dinner. They talked about his job, her new life in Vegas, regular stuff. Nothing . . . *romantic*. Just friends shooting the shit. But then their relationship changed. Juliet had no idea. She thought he was busy working, that he had no time for high jinks, especially with a woman like Melissa. Especially since Christopher is a good guy." He sighed, then placed his chin in his hand. "And I just gave a dog a bone."

"Pardon?"

"Because of my honesty, he really is a suspect to you now since he dicked around."

"My thinking is more sophisticated than that. 'Adulterer' is not synonymous with 'murderer.'"

"And you know that because . . . ?"

I didn't speak.

"Personal or professional experience?"

"Yes."

He chuckled. "Me, too."

"Was Melissa satisfied with their relationship?" I asked, voice tight. "Or did she turn on him and give him the ultimatum? You know: it's me or your family?"

"If she did, he chose Juliet and the kids. Which meant . . ."

"Melissa had been dumped again. And so she was pissed and wanted to tell Juliet what a creep her husband was. So she wrote that note I found."

He pointed at me. "And *that's* the story with Melissa. Like I said: she has nothing to do with the fire. Just good ole domestic drama."

"So why did he ask you for money?" I asked.

Ben traced the rim of his mug as he thought. "Back to that?"

"I have warrants for their finances, Ben. It will come out. All of it. You know this."

He twisted his mouth as he stared into his cider. "Bills. Taking from Peter to pay Paul as the cliché goes. Christopher could never catch up, and you could say that I owed him."

"But he had inherited close to three million dollars," I said.

He shrugged.

"How much you loan him?"

"Total? About twenty grand."

"Did he pay you back?"

He smiled, then cocked his head.

"If we could all have friends like you," I said, shaking my head. "Were you shocked that he was asking for money?"

Ben laughed. "*Shocked* doesn't even describe . . ." He rubbed his face and groaned. "I mean, here he was, asking *me* for money. And *I'm* confused because he was always out buying Louis Vuitton bags and shit, fancy cars and titanium watches."

He slumped in his chair, then rested his index finger on his forehead. "I lost a lot of money this year on tech investments and clients not paying. We've had to look over our budget and consider everything twice. Amelia's tuition, her health care—she has sickle-cell anemia. We've changed the type of bread we buy, switched cable plans, postponed a much-needed divorce—all to save money. Yet here's Christopher telling me this sob story about being broke while he's still buying crap from the Sharper Image."

"But what's all that fanciness out there?" I asked, pointing to the windows. "Parties aren't cheap."

"I'm paying for that on the firm's dime—clients and out-of-town partners. Our holiday parties are legendary. We couldn't cancel even though . . ." He sighed, then rubbed his temples. "Even though I'm barely here."

"So you gave Mr. Chatman money. Why didn't you tell him no?"

Ben left the couch and wandered over to the Christmas tree. He straightened an ornament hanging from a weak limb.

I slipped over to him. "Was there someone else? Were *you* having an affair?"

"No, it wasn't that."

"You *were* having an affair." I took a few steps closer. "And Christopher found out and threatened to tell your wife if you didn't fork over the money."

He turned to face me.

"If I'm wrong, then tell me, Ben."

We stood there, mere inches apart, both of us barely breathing.

Outside, a car door slammed. In the driveway, a little girl whined, "Mommy, the bag's too heavy." Keys jangled. The house's front door opened. An alarm sensor chimed. Footsteps thudded down the hallway.

The girl from the mantel picture ran into the living room's entryway. "Daddy!" She saw me standing by her father and froze.

Ben stooped and held out his arms. "Ladybug!"

Amelia tore her eyes away from me and smiled. "Daddy, guess what we bought?"

I moved back to the armchair.

The girl ran into her father's arms, those ponytails flapping, her sparkly sneakers blinking red with every step she took.

He swooped the girl into the air, hugged her, then kissed her cheeks.

Sarah Oliver filled the entryway her daughter had just abandoned. "Ben, those lazy-ass valets didn't—" She peered at me and then appraised her husband. That long hair, so free in that sailboat picture, had been pinned into a severe chignon. She wore all white—from her wedge-heeled Uggs and tight white leggings to her clingy turtleneck.

"Honey," Ben said to her, "this is Detective Lou Norton."

"We talked at the hospital," I said.

"Yes," Sarah said. "She cornered me in the bathroom."

I cocked my head as an icy smile crackled across my mouth. *This bitch . . .* To Ben, now being smothered with kisses from his daughter, I said, "Thank you for talking with me. I'm gonna pop out back to see if Mr. Chatman is up to talking with me again."

Ben nodded, then tugged his daughter's ponytail, causing a fit of giggles.

"You have a lovely home," I said to Sarah Oliver.

"Thank you." She gave me a look that shredded intestines and pulverized livers.

Fortunately, I wore Kevlar beneath my sweater.

I slipped past the woman of the house and made it to the front door.

She followed me in case I tried to steal something.

Or someone.

31

Christopher Chatman greeted me at the arched door of the ivy-covered guesthouse. His left arm was still in the sling, and he held a water glass in his free hand. His long-sleeved T-shirt clung to his slight muscles. He had the sleepy gaze of a man still waking from a nap—or recovering from a concussion. "Surprised to see you tonight. We had discussed talking later."

I fake apologized for not calling ahead of time. "With investigations like this, we often jump from one lead to another. That means showing up to a place unannounced."

The Motorola vibrated from my hip. I pulled it off my belt and glanced in the display. A text from Lieutenant Rodriguez. *Warrant for CC DNA signed.*

Chatman led me to the living room. The pill vials and water glasses had been replaced with a soup bowl and a paperback copy of *Blink*.

I settled on the love seat. "New developments since the last time we spoke."

He sat in the armchair. "We spoke only yesterday. Sorry that it's a little warm in here. With the fireplace, it heats up pretty quickly."

"No problem," I said. "Yesterday, I learned that Juliet was a pharma rep."

"And she was pretty good at it."

"But she left the field. Why?"

He shrugged. "She wanted to be home with the kids."

"Why didn't she go to medical school?"

His head fell back, and he stared at the shadows dancing on the ceiling. "Couldn't pass organic chemistry. She took it three times, and flunked it three times. So she went the pharma way. Medicine but not really. If she was a banker's wife, though, she'd still get the house, the car, the prestige."

"Some folks call that gold digging."

"It is what it is." He tugged at a loose string on his sling. "I kept her in expensive shoes and handbags, and she kept me focused."

"Any financial turmoil because of her not working?"

He wrapped the loose string around his middle finger until it looked like purple sausage. "No. I just worked harder and longer."

"No outstanding loans? No recent bankruptcies?"

"Regular month-to-month bills. Nothing that my year-end bonus couldn't handle."

"And the loan from Ben Oliver?"

His eyes widened with surprise. "He told you about that?"

"His grandmother brought it up first."

He released the string and his finger relaxed.

"So?"

"So it wasn't a big deal. We had just paid an ungodly amount in taxes, and the deposit for the kids' school was due. The bank froze my account like they do whenever large sums of money are being spent, so I couldn't pay the deposit. I asked Ben for it, which I hated to do but . . . He owed me." He met my eyes. "Just a friendly, informal loan from one best friend to another."

"Got it," I said. "I had to ask, okay?"

"Certainly," he said.

"So why commodities?"

"I like making money, but I also like predicting *what* will make money. I like tangible trading—items people use every day rather than numbers and theory. Feels more . . . *honest*. Back when I was getting started, I didn't care about buying yachts and fancy cars. I enjoyed learning about the world and predicting whether or not I was right in what I'd learned. Of course, I never admitted that to my parents. I told them that I wanted to go into finance to help churches and poor folks." He placed his bare feet on the coffee table. "You know: level the playing field for the Lord's people."

"A Christian Warren Buffett," I said.

"I'm not that bright. I simply invested my parents' money and tripled it in rice, wheat, and gold. Then, they'd tithe ten percent, put more into the plate for the church's building fund, and save the rest. Yeah: I made them a lot of money. To be completely honest, I'm shocked that I'm still doing it. I'm tired of it, frankly. Maybe I'm too old. And now, with tsunamis and superstorms and droughts, it's getting harder to predict with any accuracy.

More than that, I don't have that *hunger* anymore. I thought I'd be out of it by now, but what can I say? I love the game but hate the people."

"Ha. I can say the same."

He smiled. "Guess you could."

I narrowed my eyes. "If you hate it, why do you do it?"

"My wife." He gave a one-shouldered shrug. "And if *you* hate it, solving murders and dealing with the worst in society, why do *you* do it? I'm sure your husband isn't forcing you to risk life and limb every day."

I faked a grin—I didn't hate it. I loved it, and the promise of making someone's family whole rocked my boat. But when in Rome . . . "Correct: My husband isn't forcing me. He wanted me to be a lawyer. So did my mother. She didn't get over my decision. I thought he had, but . . ." I shrugged.

"My wife wanted me to be a broker more than *I* wanted to be a broker," Chatman said. "If I had quit, she would've gotten rid of me. I guess that will change. Unfortunately. I can quit anytime I want now. Didn't want to end it like this, though."

"Get rid of you," I said. "What do you mean by that?"

"It's a joke, Detective," he said with a grin. "I married up in some ways, and so I don't always think that I deserved her. My job was the only interesting thing about me. Without that, why would she stay?" His smile widened. "You've been married for how long?"

"Not as long as you," I said.

"With *your* job, though, I'm sure you two never run out of things to talk about. Your job is the stuff that makes TV and movies."

"You'd be surprised."

He rolled his eyes. "You're attractive and brave and good at what you do. I'm sure your husband thinks, How did I win the grand prize? Will she find out I'm a fraud, a fake? And when she does find out, will she leave me?"

My chest tightened—I no longer believed that to be true. "Things change."

"They do." He saw something in my expression, and he frowned.

I shifted in my seat—there had also been a flicker in his eye, and I saw my chance to open the door and peek into his failing marriage. "Little did I know back then . . . Life was supposed to be romantic dinners, roses, and vacations . . ." I shook my head. "Things change. I said that already, didn't I?"

He rubbed the bridge of his nose. "The last time my wife and . . . I know: TMI, but she'd just *lain* there, not moving, hating me for wanting her. Used to be that she couldn't go a day without touching me. Things change, as we've said three times now."

"It's like, don't they realize?" I said. "There are countless people who would trade spots with them just like that." I snapped my fingers.

"I wanted to tell her just once," he said, "'*You* need *me*. *You'd be lost without me.*' There can only be one flower, though. But that flower still needs a gardener to tend to it, to water it, to put it in sunlight. You could say that the gardener is God."

I covered my throat with my hand so he couldn't see my pulse pounding in my neck.

"I did everything I could to make her love me," he said as he stared at the last splash of salmon-colored soup in the bowl. "Even on Monday night. She'd made roast for dinner. Oh my *Lord*, I hated her roasts. She never flavored or basted the meat, and then she cooked it until it was so dry, it could tear out your teeth."

"Bet you never told *her* that," I said, forcing lightness into my tone.

He grinned. "Hell no. I ate it because that's what husbands—and wives—do. Eat shit like quinoa and eggplant and meat that defangs . . ." He jerked, suddenly aware of his candor.

I nodded to assure him. "But you pretend and eat and dance around the crevasse that's eating up your life a little bit each day."

"Amen."

"Amen," said the spider to the fly.

He hugged a small pillow to his chest, then rubbed his chin against the nubby fabric.

"Despite the obvious difficulties you and Juliet had," I said, "hell, that *any* married couple has—would you say that you otherwise had an open, honest relationship?"

He considered me with a lifted eyebrow.

I smirked. "Answer as best as you can."

He tossed the pillow to the ground. "Okay. Honest relationship?" Head back, he exhaled. "Well . . . Back when we were young, my wife trusted me and believed everything I told her. Naïveté, I guess. She was too young and too inexperienced to believe otherwise."

"To believe that you weren't always as forthcoming as you should be?"

"Good word: forthcoming." He flicked his hand. "Detective Norton, you know better than that. Everyone lies. Even you."

"They do," I said. "Even me. Earlier this evening, I got a call from our forensics investigator."

He slid his index finger alongside his thumb. "Oh?"

"Back on the morning of the fire, we found blood and needed to know whose it was."

"Blood? That's strange. No one was injured . . . *like that*. Right?"

I touched my forehead like Colombo always did. "Oh, yeah. I should mention that the blood wasn't found in the *house*. It was found in your *car*."

He bolted upright. "What? Why? How . . . ?"

"I'm hoping you can answer the what, why, and how."

Flummoxed, he blinked. "I . . . I have no idea whose blood it is. My son's? He was always bustin' himself up from skateboarding . . . My wife's? No. Can't be, since she never drove my car." His eyes darted this way and that as his mind turned over every pebble of possibility. "Although she did . . ." He sat still as the memory gelled. "Two weeks ago, we were going . . . somewhere and . . ." His voice trailed off, then he pinched his earlobe and squinted—the memory had been a mirage. "She could've had a bloody nose. She'd been having those recently."

"To help advance the case," I said, "we need your help with something. We would like a sample of your DNA to match against the blood we found."

He gaped at me.

"We won't ask you any questions as the tech takes the sample," I explained. "And if it makes you feel more comfortable, we can do it here whenever you want. You can even have Ben Oliver or another attorney with you."

He blinked several times until his brain screamed, "Found it!" and he pushed a smile onto his lips. "If you think it's important, sure, I'll do it. No problem, Detective. We'll figure out a good time."

That was easy. "A few more questions and I'll let you rest."

By now, dark circles had formed in the cloth beneath his armpits. His sweaty face relaxed some, but his left knee bounced.

"You have a storage unit in Culver City," I said.

Loathing—of me, of this unscheduled chat—gripped his face and clenched his jaw. "Yes, I do."

"When I receive the warrant to search it, what will I find in that unit?"

His face twitched, and he swallowed several times until those facial nerves had settled down. "Work-related items. Old files. Reference materials. Nothing strange. No bodies, if that's what you're wondering. I only rented it once Cody started burning anything that belonged to me." A chuckle erupted from his gut as anger smoldered in his eyes. "Why do you need to search my storage unit? How is it related to my family's . . . to the fire?"

Unblinking, I said, "I'm not at liberty to say."

There was a knock on the door.

Chatman and I stared at each other until he shouted, "Come in."

The door opened, and Sarah Oliver, still dressed in white, stepped across the threshold. And the once too-warm guesthouse grew as cold as Nunavut in January. "Excuse me for interrupting," she said, her tone a mix of silk and ice cubes. "But, Christopher, our first guests will be arriving soon and—"

"Right." To me, he said, "An old friend from UCLA is coming early. He's the only person I plan to see tonight."

"Before I forget," I said. "Do you know where your wife's car keys are? We've been looking but haven't found them."

He took a second before he shrugged. "Usually, she left them on the breakfast bar. I think I saw them there before I left the house Monday night."

I rose from the love seat. "I'll let you get to it, then."

"Maybe next time you'll call," Sarah Oliver said.

"Probably not," I replied.

She led me from behind up those slick steps and past the party canopy to the front of the house, all without saying a word. A marvelous trick—I was the Alaskan husky and she was the driver who didn't need to shout, "Mush!"

I wanted to stop in my step and ask, "What the hell is your deal?" But I didn't.

Once I reached the curb, though, pissiness trumped manners. So I placed my hands on my hips and turned around.

I was standing there alone.

Sarah Oliver had deserted me.

I hadn't even noticed.

A marvelous trick.

32

Christopher Chatman's storage unit was located in the industrial section of Culver City, behind a Sizzler steakhouse and a store that sold custom kitchen counters. As I drove into the complex, I spotted Pepe's silver Impala. Luke, in the passenger seat, was gnawing on a fried chicken drumstick. Pepe, behind the steering wheel, was smoking and texting on his cell phone. And Colin . . . was MIA.

"He's still coolin' off," Luke said, climbing out of the car.

Pepe took a final drag from his cigarette and tossed the butt to the concrete. "He's definitely on L.T.'s shit list right now."

"He can't help it," Luke said. "He's just a boy."

"He's twenty-eight years old," I snapped.

Luke grinned at me. "Then, it's something else. What could it be, *ese*, that's makin' the young detective loopy and stupid?"

I looked up to the sky—the moon was missing tonight, hidden by a silver marine layer. "To be honest? I've run out of fucks to give. Shall we, gentlemen?"

154 . . . 167 . . . 169 . . . Orange door after orange door. A graveyard for people's crap. A mecca for people's mess. I had searched units like these before and had found bikes, dinette sets, bloody knives, and the decapitated head of a hooker shoved into a kitchen trash bag.

Unit 173 looked just like the others. Dirt and dead leaves had piled at the bottom of the door, and no one had rolled up that door in a week or so.

As we waited for the manager of the storage facility, Pepe smoked as Luke picked chicken from his teeth. My mind was clogged with so much space junk that it threatened to blink out. I closed my eyes but couldn't send it all to my mind's black hole.

Finally, Sudanek Tomschik joined us. He was a squat man who smelled of cabbage and phlegm. "Please I see the paper once again?" His voice was Slavic and as jangled as keys in a can of nails.

Pepe handed Sudanek the search warrant.

The old man's gray caterpillar eyebrows lifted and dropped as he read. Then, he pushed out cabbage air from his diaphragm, and said, "*Spasibo*." He tapped the unit's combination into a digital keypad. Once a hidden mechanism clicked, he pulled up the metal door. Stale air washed over us.

I shone my flashlight into the darkness.

Box . . . Box . . . Six boxes total . . .

"There a light?" I asked Sudanek.

"*Dah*." He slapped the wall.

Boom!

Fluorescent light crackled from the grimy tubes running along the ceiling. Nothing changed. Boxes, but no cobwebs, no dinette sets, no bodies . . . yet.

Pepe walked Sudanek back toward the business office.

Luke and I pulled on blue latex gloves and stared at the space in silence.

My phone vibrated: Syeeda.

"Busy right now," I told her, "unless you have something I need."

She chuckled. "Ben Oliver was suspended by the bar ten years ago."

"For?"

"Withholding evidence."

I shrugged. "Not related."

"I've also been Facebooking."

"With whom?"

"A former colleague of Juliet Chatman's."

My throat closed, and I croaked, "Go on."

"Seems she didn't willingly leave pharma sales," Syeeda said. "Her expense account was audited in 2004. Many things came up, including two unauthorized stays at the Four Seasons Newport Beach. The colleague says Juliet went both times with someone *not* her husband. The firm didn't press charges, but she had to pay up and get the hell out. "

"But you're not gonna write that story," I said.

"Knowing this helps me and it helps you. Fills out the story."

"So will you also write that Cody regularly bullied little girls and set shit on fire all the time?"

Syeeda didn't speak.

"Let's hold off on character assassinations for the moment, okay? For what it's worth, everything you told me is good to know. And if you would kindly forward that ex-colleague's contact information, I'd appreciate it. Thanks, pal."

She sighed and hung up without saying good-bye.

An affair in 2004. This happened the year Chloe had been conceived. Did one thing relate to the other? Hell, did one thing *lead* to the other?

Once Pepe returned, I measured the room's dimensions, then asked him to take pictures of the exterior, interior, and the stack of boxes.

"What are we looking for again?" Luke asked.

I flexed my gloved right hand. "The official answer? We seek to obtain any financial records detailing malfeasance that may have led to the deaths of Juliet, Cody, and Chloe Chatman."

"So who gets what?" Pepe asked.

"I'll take . . . that one." I pointed to the box closest to us. Fingerprints had been left in the dust on the box top.

Pepe snapped pictures of those fingerprints.

I removed the box top.

Paper, paper everywhere. Prospectus prepared for . . . Prospectus prepared for . . . About thirty of them, and all prepared for clients of Vandervelde, Lansing & Gray.

"I got me some CDs and jump drives." Luke said, combing through another box.

"We want those." I scanned the last of the business statements. "Luke, put this box and the one you have in my trunk, please?"

"We shoulda brought some music," Luke said as he waddled over to retrieve the box. "And some chips and dip."

"Next time." I slipped the top off the next box—it looked like my mother's drawer of Important Stuff.

More paper. More folders. Matchbooks. Receipts.

I plucked out the first document: AT&T statement from October. "Found a phone bill."

Pepe looked over my shoulder. "This is the number for his secret cell phone. What else is in there?"

More phone bills . . . CD marked FLAG DAY 2011 . . . CD marked ALL SAINTS DAY 2012 . . . ST. PATRICK'S DAY 2010 . . . Lots of deposit slips, wire-transfer slips . . . Two passbooks . . .

"I want all of this." I found a deposit slip. "L.O.K.I. Consulting—"

Pop-pop! High-pitched gunshots cracked through the stillness.

We froze.

"Sounds close," Luke said. "Like, real close."

"That a .22?" I pulled my Glock from its shoulder holster.

"Yep," Pepe said, pulling out his Sig.

We inched to the unit's door and peeked out to see my Crown Vic and Pepe's Impala, both untouched.

Pepe and I darted out to the driveway and ran out into the night.

Luke, steps behind us, keyed his Motorola. "Shots fired," he said, then provided Dispatch with our location.

The reflection of green lights from the traffic signals, then yellow lights, then red lights glistened on the wet blacktop—the only illumination on this moonless night. The oniony, charred-meat aroma of *carnitas* wafted from the Del Taco across the street.

Pepe pointed to the ground. "Look."

My eyes dropped to the sidewalk and to crimson drops of blood leading to the ivy forest beneath the 405 freeway overpass.

Guns out, radios crackling from our hips, we followed the blood trail south. There were no lights beneath the freeway. Nothing but ivy and darkness and noise from speeding cars and the reek of piss from thousands of God's creatures sprayed into the dirt. Mangled wires . . . Torn newspaper . . . Ripped pillows the color of feces . . . Blankets lighter than air . . . Flies, lots of flies . . .

"Homeless camp," Luke said.

"Yep." Nausea worked its way from my stomach to the back of my throat. But my breathing remained steady. Guess my lungs didn't know I wanted to vomit.

An Olde English malt-liquor bottle rolled from a patch of ivy and onto the dirt path ten yards in front of us.

We stopped and raised our guns.

"Police," I shouted, barely audible over the commotion of the 405. "You hurt?"

No response.

I glanced at Pepe.

His eyes were trained on the ivy.

The leaves rustled.

I took a deep breath, then shouted, "Police. Are you hurt?"

The creature writhed beneath the filthy blankets.

Pepe stepped forward and deeper into the cloud of flies.

Luke took Pepe's place.

I stayed in my spot, legs steady and spread apart, gun trained on the blanket.

Seconds slammed into each other.

Pepe crept closer, then looked at me over his shoulder. He mouthed, "On three . . ."

One . . . two . . .

Pepe bent and grabbed the edge of the blanket.

Three!

He yanked.

The pit bull snarled.

Pepe reeled back and fell on his ass.

Luke shouted, "Shit!"

The dishwater-colored pit bull didn't lunge. No, it stayed in its spot. Blood gushed from its left flank. The dog bared its teeth, but didn't mean it.

"Someone shot a dog," I screeched, relief erupting from me.

Pepe, sweating and wild-eyed, stumbled to his feet.

The poor animal's head dropped back into the ivy.

"Just a graze," Luke said. "Poor baby."

"That son of a bitch was about to eat me," Pepe shouted.

"Oh, stop wettin' your panties, Peter." I dropped my arms but didn't holster my gun—a pit bull is still a pit bull. I radioed in for Animal Control to ferry the dog to a vet for stitches and kibble. "What kind of asshole shoots a dog?" I made a sad face at the pup. "You'll be okay, Bullet."

Luke smiled. "Bullet. I like that. I'll stay with her. She kinda reminds me of Lupita." He inched closer to the dog with his hand out for sniffing. "*Duérmete mi niño,*" he sang softly. "*Duérmete mi amor.*"

As Luke lullabied Bullet, Pepe and I trudged back to the storage unit, sweaty but enervated. As detectives, our hearts no longer pounded from the chase but pounded from all that had been left behind *after* the chase. Not tonight, though, and it felt good.

Pepe stepped back into the unit, and muttered, "Shit."

I stood beside him and saw it, too. And my knees weakened as though someone had punched me in the gut.

The space closest to the unit's door was empty. Problem was: that space had been occupied by two file-storage boxes filled with deposit slips and phone bills.

And now those boxes were gone.

33

The grainy black-and-white footage from the surveillance camera showed Pepe and me, guns drawn, tiptoeing out of Christopher Chatman's storage unit. Luke waited ten seconds, then followed us off camera, radio to his mouth.

Twenty seconds later, two individuals wearing dark hoodies crept on camera from the north to the storage unit. Suspect 1 stood at the doorway as lookout while suspect 2 entered the unit. The hoods kept their faces hidden in shadow—they knew that they were being recorded. Ten seconds later, suspect 2 returned to the door holding two stacked document boxes. Suspect 1 took the top box. They both looked south, to where we had been following the trail of blood. Then, they ran north and out of camera range.

Pepe and I had returned at the six-minute mark, smiles on our faces, minds already knitting together the story we'd tell at the station the next day. Pepe had entered the unit. My face was hidden but my shoulders had hunched to my ears.

Luke, Pepe, and I now stood in Sudanek's musty little office, our faces sweaty, our mouths agape as we watched the surveillance recording on the fifteen-inch television monitor.

Luke popped an antacid tablet and muttered, "*Carajo.*"

Sudanek shrugged. "Happen all times. People watch. People, they steal. What do you do?" He shrugged again and burped into the back of his hand. "They call you. They steal from *you*. What do *you* do?"

We couldn't answer—embarrassment had squeezed out all irate thoughts.

Luke waddled to the Impala to complete a stolen-property form. Pepe and I plodded north, in the direction the thieves had taken. My feet burned in the high-heeled boots, and my legs stayed rigid—I didn't deserve to walk with a spring in my step.

We passed Del Taco and approached an alleyway near the Dollar Store.

"What the hell happened?" Pepe wondered.

"They shot the dog, knew that we would hear the shots, knew that we would leave to investigate the shots, waited until we left, and grabbed what they could."

"Looking for what?"

"Pawnable things? I don't know."

"Chatman knew you were coming here?"

"Uh-huh."

Pepe paused, then asked, "Is it possible . . . ?"

"Certainly."

"So?"

I halted in my step. "What's that?"

Up ahead and deeper into the alley, two document boxes sat near a garbage bin.

Pepe sprinted toward the Dumpster as though the boxes would disappear at any moment.

Aching feet be damned, I raced behind him with the same horrid expectation. By the time I reached his side, Pepe had already taken off the box tops. I watched him shuffle through the boxes, shifting from foot to foot, pressure building in my bladder as though I had to pee.

Receipts . . . random pieces of paper . . . No CDs. No deposit slips.

"Not pawnable?" Pepe asked.

"Guess not."

"CDs and deposit slips, though—"

"Aren't pawnable, either."

"So?"

I closed my eyes and groaned.

Pepe rubbed his mouth. "As my Korean grandma says, *Jen-jang.*"

I shivered. "Does your grandma have a saying for 'our ass is grass'?"

"Yeah, but it loses a lot in translation." He stared at the boxes, then said, "If she saw me now, she'd call me a *byung-shin.*"

"Dumb ass?"

He nodded. "Will you tell L.T. or . . . ?"

I squeezed the Motorola so hard that it cracked. "I'll tell him, since it's my investigation. And then I'll have to tell Chatman. That is, if he doesn't already know."

34

On the way home, I stopped at Target for a bottle of sangria and a big bag of Doritos. On impulse, I also threw into the shopping cart three Christmas candles and an Anita Baker Christmas CD.

Ho, ho, ho. Fa, la, la.

Syeeda called again as I pushed my basket through Pain Relief. "Sorry for rushing you off the phone earlier," I told her. "And right now, I don't feel much for talking."

"Bad day at the office, kitten?" she cooed.

"I just pulled the economy-sized tub of ibuprofen off the shelf and dropped it in a cart filled with wine and Doritos, so you know how my day has gone."

"Damn," she said. "That's pretty bad. Lena told me that you guys made up? And that you're planning Tori's memorial?"

"Yep. Can you write a nice obit?"

"Anything for you. And something else for you: Christopher Chatman."

I pushed my cart toward checkout. "What about him?"

"I'm sure you're gonna look into his work history, but I called his firm today and told the receptionist that I was writing a story about the house fire. She said he didn't work there."

"Same thing happened to me," I said, grabbing a tabloid from the magazine rack.

"I pressed her a bit, and she said that he's on leave. It's all very hush-hush and weird."

"Could be something, could—"

"Be nothing. Right. You always say that."

I smiled. "Cuz it always works."

. . .

As I pulled into my garage, Colin left his third voice-mail message. I would not listen to it—this message would sound no different than the previous two. *You take shit the wrong way. Am I supposed to keep quiet cuz I'm new here? When will I be here long enough to have an opinion? I'm sorry if you're offended* blahblahblah.

Not that I wanted to talk to him—I had already confessed to Lieutenant Rodriguez that possibly important documents had been stolen and their boxes abandoned in an alleyway. My boss had then inflicted upon me a tongue-lashing that would make DMX and Pepe's grandmother blush. But he didn't take me off the case. Yet. Or worse: ask for my badge and gun. Yet. So, yeah, I didn't feel like hearing a Tic-Tac-crunchin', cowboy-boot-wearin', spoiled-brat bastard tell me that it had been stupid for all three of us to leave an unlocked storage unit.

Byung-shin.

Aiden, my next-door neighbor, was now exercising in his garage—Eminem's "Lose Yourself" blasted from his stereo as his leg press went *clank-bang.*

The condo was cold and dark, and after the crap day I'd had, I vowed to change that. I sat one candle in the middle of the dining room table, then lit it with a fireplace match. I arranged the two remaining candles on the living room mantel, then lit those. The walls flickered with gold and grays, and the smell of synthetic gingerbread wafted as the wax melted. In the garage, I found the purple plastic storage bin full of ornaments. I carried the bin back into the house and dropped it next to the tree. I slipped the CD into the stereo—Anita's smooth alto launched into "I'll Be Home for Christmas."

Part of me wanted to join Aiden for an hour's worth of exercise. But I had a Christmas tree to decorate. After that, I had to snuggle with Greg on the couch and watch Ernest Borgnine and Shelley Winters in *The Poseidon Adventure* while eating the last pieces of cold fried chicken in the fridge I had bought back on Monday. And also chug from the new bottle of sangria.

Ho, ho, ho. Fa, la, la.

The landline rang from the coffee table. Caller ID announced that Greg was calling.

I grabbed the phone and fell back on the couch. "I'm dead from the brain down, so don't ask me any difficult questions."

"Why do kamikaze pilots wear helmets?" Greg asked in his wonderfully husky voice.

"Because their mothers make them. What's up, and why aren't you home?"

"About to do a sync up with Creative cuz stupid shit is starting to happen and I'm stuck in my own bog and so I need to check in."

"Sounds like a day full of suck."

"But nothing's worse than dead people. That was your day, right?"

I told him all that had happened since we'd last seen each other, including Christopher Chatman's property being stolen and my argument with Colin.

"He's an asshole," Greg growled. "He's nothing like Bruno."

Correct: Bruno Abbiati, my partner before Colin, and now retired, was 260 pounds, saggy-jowled, and twenty years my senior.

"Colin's okay," I said, suddenly protective of my new partner. "He just has to get with the program and shut his mouth."

"Why can't you get a female partner, anyway?"

"Cuz there are only so many female detectives on the force."

"Why can't Pepe—?"

"Cuz he's Luke's partner." And gay. Also perfect for me.

"It just puts you in an awkward position," Greg explained.

"News flash," I said. "Men and women can work together without sleeping together."

He snorted. "Okay."

That single word had yanked something inside me, and I sat up on the couch. "Men and women *can't* work together without sleeping with each other?"

"Sure, they can."

My hand gripped the receiver tighter. "You have what's-her-face on your team right now. The one who wears the tight *Star Wars* T-shirts. You gettin' down with her?"

He groaned. "I didn't mean—let's not start. I was calling to let you know that I'm gonna be home late."

"Cuz you're bangin' the chick in the tight *Star Wars* T-shirt."

"Lou. Stop. I know you'd never sleep with Colin."

"I wouldn't?"

"Nope." He laughed. "Cuz you have the best at home."

Was this a *dare*? Did he really know what I would and wouldn't do?

"You always see drama where there ain't none," he said. "You can't let a day pass without poking at shit."

Shots fired. Officer down.

After picking my teeth off the carpet, I bade him good night. The ornaments stayed in the purple bin. The tree remained naked, and the candles were snuffed. I replaced the sounds of Anita Baker's CD with the frantic screams of passengers drowning aboard the SS *Poseidon*.

I didn't plan to eat all three chicken breasts. Nor did I plan to finish the bag of Doritos. I had set out to drink one glass of sangria, but that glass had turned into a tumbler. Then, three tumblers.

At seven minutes to eleven, I still lay on the couch, still nibbling chicken crust from the bottom of the deli bag, still watching Gene Hackman lead a scrappy group of cruise-ship survivors to safety.

The doorbell rang.

I lay there, greasy, still pretending not to be home.

The doorbell rang again.

I sat up.

The den shifted once, shifted twice, then spun all the way around.

I stumbled to the foyer. Part of me knew that I'd had too much to drink. The rest of me didn't believe that since my feet still worked. I squinted through the peephole.

No one stood there. Just an empty porch.

My inner gyroscope cracked, and my forehead banged against the door.

I muttered, "Ouch," then stumbled back to the couch.

A knock on the door.

I stared at that door.

The knob twisted.

I squinted.

The doorknob twisted slowly left, slowly right.

I whispered, "What the . . . ?"

Bile, chicken, and tortilla chips bubbled in my stomach, and I fought the urge to vomit.

That happened. I saw that happen . . . Right?

I crept back to the foyer, uncertain that the twisting had been real.

But the doorknob slowly twisted right and left again.

"Hello?" I croaked.

No answer.

I placed my ear against the door's cool wood.

Couldn't hear a thing.

I squinted through the peephole again.

Empty porch.

On weak legs, I hurried up the stairs and to my bedroom closet. I opened the Glock's case, plucked the gun from the foam, and crept back down the stairs to the foyer. I took a deep breath and yanked open the door.

Night air swept over me, and I sobered up a click. For the second time that night, I slipped into the darkness with a gun in my hand.

Blades of grass wet my bare feet, and my toes grew numb from the cold.

Around the corner . . .

Television light glowed from Aiden's downstairs windows.

In the little park across the street, a small group of people hung out at the marble water fountain. Even though the fountain had been turned off, even though there were no exterior lights, they were all smoking—their lit cigarettes bobbed in the darkness like fireflies. One of the men glanced in my direction. Then, his buddies turned to look at me.

Nothing to see here, folks. Just a drunk, barefoot, off-duty cop patrolling her home with a Glock in hand.

The man and his buddies agreed, and they returned to their smokes and jokes.

I moved on . . . toes squelching wet earth and grass . . . pulse racing beneath the grip of the gun . . .

"There's nothing out here," I mumbled.

I stopped at the base of Greg's office window and looked down to my feet.

Shoe prints left in moist earth.

Buzzing filled my ears as I stared at those boot treads.

It's Thursday. The gardener came—those are probably his prints, and you're drunk.

I stared at the ground a moment more, feeling my body lean forward as I listened to that buzzing . . .

Lou!

I snapped upright, awake now, then crept back around the corner. The scent of gingerbread rode atop the smells of marshland and burned popcorn and guided me home.

"You always see drama where there ain't none," I said.

I slammed the door and locked it. Then, I sat on the bottom step of the staircase, feet muddied, gun still in my hand. And I didn't move from that step until the DVD player shut off. And as I stumbled up the stairs at midnight, washed off, placed the gun on my nightstand, then climbed into bed, I told myself that the entire day had been just a dream. A terrible, neverending dream.

Friday, December 14

35

I clomped into the station at a little past eight in the morning. And even though I wore my favorite pantsuit, the tan one with the flared leg, along with cranberry-colored Michael Kors heels that cost as much as a black-market liver, I still felt like stir-fried shit.

Luke sat at his desk, his eyes trained on a report or a form or maybe nothing at all. Pepe stood at the watercooler, a thick manila envelope tucked beneath his left arm, his gaze trained on the red letters that spelled AR-ROWHEAD.

Colin was also seated at his desk. Dark circles hung beneath his blood-shot eyes, and his fingers looked as though mice had been gnawing on his nails. He hadn't slept, and he now watched me like a kicked golden retriever watching a lion. When I didn't speak, he cleared his throat. "Syeeda's article came out."

I dropped my bag into the bottom drawer of my desk. "Oh boy."

He handed me the section of the *Times*.

The lede: TRAGEDY IN THE HILLS. Above it, beautiful pictures of Cody and Chloe at a sunset luau. My heart raced, scared what her words were about to do to me.

> They were just kids, and they were murdered in what was supposed to be the safest place in the world. Cody Chatman, 12, was found in his bed, his favorite Gameboy clutched to his chest. And Chloe Chatman, 8, called "Coco" by so many who loved her, perished in her mother's arms . . .

Syeeda had interviewed the kids' teachers and friends, church members and neighbors. She ended the piece with a call for justice and a plea for information with my name and the tip line listed.

I had finished reading the piece but couldn't take my eyes off the Chatman kids.

"The warrants came back for the family's financials," Colin said, "and I found a few things."

I handed him the newspaper and plopped into my chair. "Wonderful."

A stuffed envelope with my name printed in thick black ink sat beneath my desktop Christmas tree.

I tossed Colin a hollow smile. "You heard what happened?"

"Yeah. About twenty minutes ago, L.T. went buck wild on the dynamic duo over there."

That explained Luke and Pepe's catatonia. PTSD provided by Lieutenant Zak Rodriguez.

"Where is he now?" I asked.

"With the captain."

I licked my dry lips. *Will I have a job at the end of that meeting?* Stupid mistake, all of us leaving that storage unit. A mistake that had jeopardized the case and, possibly, the successful prosecution of the murderer. And those two thoughts—stupid mistake, murderer free—thrashed about my mind, bucking broncos on speed in a china shop.

I needed to solve the case *now*, before there was no china shop left.

"Lou?" Colin said.

"Colin?" I logged on to my computer.

He hesitated, then said, "I . . . umm . . ."

My fingers stopped tapping at the keyboard. "Yeah?"

He inhaled, then slowly exhaled. "Sorry."

I gave him a short nod—didn't want to fight or demand or anything. Just work my case.

After checking e-mails, I looked over to my partner. "Find anything good?"

He brightened, as kicked golden retrievers do once shown some positive attention, and he rolled his chair over to my desk. "Their credit reports show four different accounts with Bank of America, one checking, two savings, one credit. But Christopher Chatman had a separate account at Pacific Western Bank in Thousand Oaks."

"Juliet wasn't on it?"

"Nope." He turned the page. "The Chatmans have racked up $753,610 in debt. They owe *everybody*, including three credit-card companies,

Jaguar, and Mercedes-Benz Financial—and both of those loans are in arrears—a mall's worth of department stores, and, finally, the architectural firm that did the remodel for the house and the garage. As for the mortgage statement: the house was paid off back in 1989."

I squinted at him. "Why are they in so much debt when the biggest bill no longer exists? And, again, how do you spend three million dollars in ten years? I know I grew up like Thelma Evans, but that's a lot of money. Especially if he's this hotshot money man."

"Collecting Beanie Babies?" He held up a finger. "Wait. There's more." Then, he pulled out the statements from Pacific Western Bank, with some entries highlighted yellow—specifically, a $5,000 deposit in April, a $12,500 deposit in July, and another $5,000 deposit in September.

I tapped the desktop. "Yesterday, Ben Oliver told me that he had loaned Chatman about twenty thousand dollars. I asked Chatman about the money, and he said it was to cover a large deposit for the kids' school."

"You believe him?" Colin asked.

"Eh." I found the next highlighted transaction: in August, one hundred thousand dollars had been deposited into the account at Pacific Western Bank.

"Who gave him a hundred K?" I asked.

"Don't know yet," Colin said. "Still working on it."

"You've been busy."

"Had some time to myself."

"I should ignore you more." I rolled over to my file cabinet and unlocked it. I grabbed an envelope Pepe had stuffed with plastic baggies of evidence taken from Chatman's Jaguar on the first day of the investigation. I grabbed a pair of latex gloves from my desk drawer, tugged them on, opened the flap, and dipped my hand into the pocket. "Let's see . . ."

Bank statement from an account used by Juliet and Christopher Chatman for Monday, December 10.

Check card SW Diner – 12.63	Check 2202 – 60.00
Check card Rite Aid – 28.49	La Brea Gas – 72.00
Withdrawal – 60.00	Check card CVS – 19.19

"Two drugstores on one day." I sat the statement down, then reached into the envelope again. "Nothing remarkable in her last days. Breakfast—one of my favorite places to eat. Gas—she filled up the truck. She got some money out and went to two drugstores. Or she *didn't* go to two drugstores—the card used could be his."

A CVS receipt was stapled to the pharmacist's instructions for taking diazepam, aka Valium. The prescription had been written for Juliet Chatman.

I placed that receipt on my desk but paused before reaching into the envelope again.

Valium for Juliet Chatman. Monday, December 10, 5:13 P.M. The prescription had been purchased on the last full day of Juliet's life.

But Juliet had stopped taking Valium back in the summer. According to Dr. Kulkanis, Juliet had been too fatigued to continue taking the drug.

Had she been planning to drug the kids just as Colin suggested?

I stared at the slip until I *saw*. "Give me the checking-account banking statements from this past August on."

Colin shuffled through a stack of papers, then handed them to me.

I found *August 10: CVS.* I flipped to the next month's statement. *September 9: CVS. October 10: CVS. November 11: CVS.* "I need to know if Juliet's debit card was used for these purchases."

Colin compared the last four digits shown on the CVS receipts to the full account numbers from Bank of America and Pacific Western Bank. "This is his Pacific Western card. Why is that important?"

I picked up the receipt again and looked at the other items Christopher Chatman had purchased: *Prescription, 4 Slim Jim, Self magazine, Smucker's Strawberry Toppings.*

My telephone rang—a 702 area code. I hit the speaker button, and before I could finish saying, "Lou Norton," the caller shouted, "You and your goons need to stop it." She sounded pissed—the heat of her anger spiked through the speaker.

"Excuse me," I said, frowning. "Who is this?"

"This is Melissa Kemper speaking, that's who."

Colin and I gaped at each other. And then, we both grabbed notepads.

"Good morning, Ms. Kemper." I snapped the recording device onto the phone.

"For the last twenty-four hours," Melissa Kemper shouted, "you sons of bitches have been calling my house and hanging up. My tires were slashed this morning, and my trash cans were turned over last night and my bank just called because one of you sons of whores wanted my personal financial information."

Colin shook his head—*wasn't me.*

"Ms. Kemper," I said, "no one from our division has called your bank. I *am* investigating a homicide involving family friends of yours, and I was planning to call you today to discuss—"

"I gave Christopher *money*," she shouted. "It was a *gift*. Is that against the law?"

I scribbled on my pad and then turned the pad to Colin. *Is she that mystery $100K?*

"And it's no one's business anyway," the woman continued. "And Ben Oliver is a sneaky motherfucker, and he's done some awful, *awful* shit, and you need to be harassing *him* and poking around in *his* private business." Then, she wept into the phone.

I offered lots of, "Ms. Kemper, please" and "Please, calm down."

Finally, she took several deep breaths, sniffled, and hiccupped.

"Ms. Kemper," I said.

"I have nothing else to say to you, *bitch*."

And then dial tone—she had hung up on me.

"So?" I sat the receiver back into the cradle.

"I'll book us a flight to Vegas later today," Colin said, tapping on his keyboard, "and an economy sedan."

"Perfect. Now, what number am I thinking?"

"Thirty."

"Sixty-three." I grabbed the phone and scanned a tacked-up list of my favorite ex-LAPD police officers.

"Who you callin'?" Colin asked.

"Gus Lebo," I said. "Left us for Vegas a few months before you came."

No answer.

"Hey, Gus. It's Lou Norton. I'm working a case that's leading me into your new territory. Me and my partner will fly in later today to talk to her. Name is Melissa Kemper. We're just talkin', but I wanted to give you a courtesy call cuz I'm courteous. Hope you're well."

I clicked into the public records database and typed "Melissa Kemper." "She's such a pleasant woman. Like a delicate orchid perched upon a single strand of silk." Her driver's license picture filled my computer screen.

The joker in drag (as Nora Galbreath had nicknamed Kemper so long ago, or so it seemed) lived in North Las Vegas, on 4821 Wisp o' Willow Way, in a four-bedroom, two-bathroom house. She had no felonies, but she did have three outstanding parking tickets. Most important: no guns had been registered in her name.

"You think she'll freak out on us?" Colin asked.

I stared at the woman's driver's license photograph. "If she does, then we'll have friends who know we're there."

36

My desk phone chirped again.

Colin covered his face with his hands. "The harpy's back."

"Nope. A plain, ole 323 area code." I grabbed the receiver. "Lou Norton."

"Sounds like your horse came through," the male caller said.

"Mr. Benjamin Oliver," I said. "So nice to hear your voice this morning."

"Likewise. I'm down in the lobby, here for my formal interview where you make me sign forms and lock me into a story. May I come up?"

As we waited for the attorney, I took Colin's elbow. "Do not mention the stolen boxes, understand? You mention those boxes, and that's it for us."

"I won't, Lou."

I held his gaze a moment more, then released him.

Three minutes later, Ben Oliver stood over my desk holding two coffee cups. He wore a frosted-gray suit tailored by Italian gods and black wing-tips cobbled by Italian virgin she-elves.

"Hope one of those coffees is for me," Colin said.

Ben regarded Colin as though he were a fallen leaf from a common tree. Then, he turned back to me. "I didn't know if you took cream and sugar." He offered me the cup in his right hand. "So, I said, 'screw it,' and told the girl to give me one of those caramel machi-whatever those are."

I smiled at him. "You Irish this up like you did yesterday's cider?"

Colin lifted an eyebrow. "Yesterday's cider?"

Ben gasped, faking shock. "What type of man do you think I am?"

I knew what kind of man he was, and knowing that made me want to run my caramel macchiato through tox screening. Twice. "Shall we?"

Ben grinned. "Let's."

I headed down the hallway to interview room 3.

Ben turned to see that Colin was trailing us.

"Next time," Colin fake whispered, "choose Italian. She likes shrimp scampi and Lambrusco."

Interview room 3 smelled like stale popcorn and two-day-old mac and cheese left in a pot on a hot summer day. A rose garden compared with the stinks haunting the other two rooms.

"So," Colin said, "what's shakin', Counselor?"

"Despite Detective Taggert's inference," Ben said to me, "I'm here on business. Juliet's parents are flying in from Mississippi sometime today, and I wanted to talk with you both before they came . . . And before heading to arbitration proceedings with lawyers from MG Standard."

I squinted at him.

He shook his head. "Unrelated to the Chatman case. I talked with Christopher before coming here. He believes he may have come off as a jerk last night."

"These are extraordinary circumstances," I said.

Ben tapped the lid of his cup. "Guess there's no right way to act in situations such as this."

Colin chuckled. "The hell there is."

I gave my partner the eye. *Not now.* Because there *were* correct ways and less correct ways to act. But I wouldn't share that knowledge with Ben or anyone under investigation.

The attorney stared at Colin, curious about those mysterious ways. Then, he tore his eyes away from my partner to meet mine. "Did Christopher answer all of your questions?"

Colin placed his hands behind his head. "In other words, are we finished investigating him?"

Ben waited for my response.

I cocked my head but didn't speak.

Ben sighed. "Don't do that, Elouise."

I gaped at him. "Don't do what, Benjamin?"

"Act as though my question is more than what it is. If you were an auto mechanic and I were your customer, and I asked if my car was ready, that doesn't mean that I thought you were being indolent on the job. Sometimes a lollipop is just a lollipop."

"Sometimes, it is," I conceded. "And to answer your 'just a question,' no, we're not finished talking to Mr. Chatman. We have a few more items to cross off the list."

"Like finding out whose blood that is in his car?" Ben asked.

"For instance," I said.

"Seems a little . . . plethoric, wouldn't you say? To serve a warrant on a man who just lost his family to a fire? Asking him for spit? Blood? *Pubic hair? Really?*"

"And when would be the right time?" Colin asked. "A month from now? A year?"

Ben kept his gaze trained on me. "We've had this discussion, haven't we?"

I gave him a one-shouldered shrug. "And by me having DNA from Mr. Chatman, we may find out that the blood does *not* belong to him, and *that* knowledge may point me in the direction of someone else, thus further expanding my list of suspects. Correct?" I leaned forward in my chair. "Why don't you want him to cooperate with my very simple request?"

"Very simple . . . ?" He shook his head in disbelief. "First, I didn't tell him to not cooperate. He'll do what you've asked of him. Second, do you want to know why I'm about to have this meeting with three jackasses from MG Standard?"

"I'm sure you'll tell us," Colin said, smirking.

"Last year," Ben continued, "my client's son—a twenty-four-year-old private in the U.S. Army—was killed by a car bomb in Afghanistan. A week later, his mother, my client, received a letter from MG Standard saying that William's insurance-policy payout had been put into an interest-bearing account. They included a checkbook that was linked to that account. But my client didn't touch the money right then—she'd just lost her son, and she couldn't even think about spending what he had left her.

"Last month, she finally decided to spend from the account, and she sent a check to Macy's to pay off a credit card. She wrote a check from her dead son's so-called interest-bearing account, and guess what? The check *bounced*."

The smirk on Colin's face vanished.

"William's four-hundred-thousand-dollar payout wasn't sitting in the bank," Ben explained. "His four hundred thousand was sitting in MG Standard's corporate account, earning interest for the *company* but not for the family of Private First Class and now deceased William Ramos. And the money still isn't in the kid's account. Where the hell is that money, and why hasn't the family received it yet?"

Colin cleared his throat, then said, "We can't speak to that. I mean, we don't know—"

"The protean schemes of insurance companies," Ben completed with a nod. "And I don't expect you to—that's *my* job. I'm only sharing this with you both so that next time, when I ask about the status of the investigation involving this perfidious insurance company, you don't regard *me* as the villain. I'm more of the guard dog."

"But again," I said, "*you* called MG Standard on the morning of the fire. We didn't."

"Indeed," Ben said with a nod. "Again: I know how they treat their customers. Better to do it when the situation's just happened."

"So what are you gettin' out of this?" Colin asked. "Being the guard dog?"

"Nothing," Ben said, glancing at his wristwatch. "I am not engaging in sleight of hand. I'm not a beneficiary on the home policy, nor am I on Juliet's life policies."

"You know about Juliet's policies?" Colin asked.

"I helped her select them."

"We're only going where the evidence points us," I said.

"You sure about that?" Ben tossed his empty cup into the wastebasket in the corner of the room. "I have no dog in this fight, Detective Norton. It is axiomatic that I want my friend to heal *and* to have access to resources that will help him do that. It is also axiomatic that we need your help for him to receive those resources."

"So when will Mr. Chatman be available for DNA?" I asked. "As I told him, we can come to him, anytime."

Ben shrugged. "I'll talk with him today. Don't worry—you'll get your precious swab of spit." Then, he rubbed his hands together. "Now, should I give a formal statement of what I know about this unfortunate situation?"

Colin waved. "You'll be working with me on that."

Ben's smile didn't reach his eyes. "Exciting for you." Then, he turned to me and his smile broadened and his eyes crinkled. He offered me his hand. "Detective Norton, always a pleasure."

I took his hand into my smaller one.

He squeezed my hand. "Thanks for taking time out to talk."

"And thanks again for the coffee," I said, even though I had yet to take a sip.

He ran his thumb across my thumb. "No problem." He squeezed again and let me go.

37

Sometimes *a lollipop is just a lollipop.*

You always see drama where there ain't none.

Sure, sometimes I needed to mute the voices in my head and ignore my tingling Spidey senses. Those times, however, were few and far between. I had a job to do—uncovering the truth, even if that kept Christopher Chatman from "moving on" with his precious "resources."

Colin wandered back to the squad room and found me at my desk. "So he came all this way to bring you coffee and sign a form?"

"Scalawags and insurance attorneys kiss the ground I walk on."

The red voice-mail light on my phone was blinking. Gus Lebo's deep voice—southern minister meets numbers runner—boomed over my speaker. A lot of "honey," "pleased," and "crazy-ass broads" in his "thanks for givin' me a head's up" message.

I kept the phone to my ear and dialed Greg's cell.

He picked up on the third ring. "Didn't think I'd hear from you today," he shouted over the clatter of kitchen sounds.

"Phones work both ways," I said. "It's loud in your world. Where are you?"

"Grabbing food for everybody," he said. "Long day."

A female giggled in the background.

The hair on my body bristled. "So I have to fly to Vegas."

Silence. Then: "When?"

"This afternoon, but we will—"

"*We?*"

"*We* will be back after we finish the interview."

Silence. Then: "Hunh."

"What does 'hunh' mean?"

"Friday night in Vegas," he said. "Convenient."

I closed my eyes. "It's a Friday *afternoon* in *North* Las Vegas. Big difference."

"Whatever, Lou. So you'll be back tonight—unless Taggert has another bright idea to interview this person tomorrow morning?"

"Of course," I snapped. "Lena's recital is tonight, and I can't miss it. So good-bye, and tell whoever the hell is with you to stop laughing so much. She sounds like a hyena."

Back to work.

I grabbed the manila envelope that had been left beneath my Christmas tree and emptied it onto my desk. Copies of checks . . . more copies of checks . . . a crumpled wire-transfer receipt with the print almost faded.

The first check copy came from the account of Vandervelde, Lansing & Gray. Dated April 9, the check had been made payable to Peggy Tanner for $10,103.96. It had been endorsed by Ms. Tanner and then deposited into Pacific Western Bank in Thousand Oaks.

Peggy Tanner . . .

I rolled my chair over to the filing cabinet and pulled off the top of a box marked CC HOME OFFICE. After a few seconds of browsing through the contents, I found that prospectus prepared by Christopher Chatman for Peggy Tanner.

Dot connected.

The warmth of satisfaction rolled over me, but I didn't linger in it.

Back to the Christmas-gift envelope.

The next check copy, dated July 12, had also come from Vandervelde, Lansing & Gray. Payable to Sol Y. Hirsch for $7,997.41. Endorsed by Sol Hirsch in big loopy letters and deposited into Pacific Western Bank.

Pacific Western . . . Christopher Chatman had an account at Pacific Western.

Another dot.

I picked up a wire-transfer receipt and peered at ghost print. *Banco . . . Central de . . . Venezuela.* A transfer of $107,500 from L.O.K.I. Consulting Services on September 20.

"Hey," I said, calling out to Colin, "these docs you pulled. Where'd you find all of this? In the boxes we grabbed from the storage unit?"

Colin blinked at me. "Guh?"

I leaned back in my chair and stretched. "Where did you find this? I didn't see check copies from his clients last night."

"I didn't find any copies of checks," Colin said.

My turn to say, "Guh?"

Colin shook his head. "Nuh."

I squinted at him. "You left an envelope on my desk, remember? It was right under my Christmas tree when I got in this . . ."

"I didn't leave anything under your tree," he said, staring at the pile. "Luke!"

Luke stood at the whiteboard with Rocky, a night-shift dick who had caught a fatal stabbing at a strip club. Conversational key words: "Hennessy," "glitter," "serrated blade," "bad tipper," "crotch," "bled out."

I held up the empty manila envelope. "You leave this for me?"

Luke said, "Nope," then turned back to Rocky and his killer-stripper story.

"So I did some surfing on Christopher Chatman," Colin said. "He doesn't have a Facebook page. Juliet did, but she hadn't posted on it since Easter. A lot of 'Rest in Peace' messages on there now. Cody has a page. In his photo albums, there's not one shot of his dad."

"Is that a teenage-boy thing?"

Colin shrugged. "You're askin' a guy with a tattoo of his dad's favorite snack."

"Yours is the first Cracker Jack tat I've ever seen."

"I *did* find this." Colin rolled over to my desk and handed me several pieces of paper. "Printouts from Internet forums Cody visited. A site called Sk8B8. Originally created by skaters. Now a domain for angry little bastards with too much time and technology and not enough homework."

One of Cody's posts, dated December 8, had been titled, "Going away now."

. . . tired of this. Tired of them. They'll get what they been asking 4. Me gone.

Another post two days before Thanksgiving: "Don't understand."

How can 2 ppl stay 2gether & hate other. THEY WANT THE WORLD 2 THINK THEY R PERFECT. How am I like this? Why I have bad thought? Don't love them. They keep hurting me w there lies. Blame me 4 everything. I cant chill out anymore. Cant act like it all ok anymore. They need 2 WAKEUP. I will make them wakeup.

And another, posted on October 30:

basterdbumbumbumallof you. Hahahaha.

I sighed. "This kid was . . ."

"Fucked up in the head?" Colin asked.

"Yeah."

"Do you think . . . ?"

"Possibly."

"But . . . ?"

"Not really. You?"

Colin shrugged.

I turned back to the pile of paper on my desk. Why had someone put this envelope beneath my Christmas tree? *Who* had left this envelope beneath my Christmas tree? What connections was I supposed to make?

The check copies had been sent to clients of Vandervelde, Lansing & Gray. The clients were all Christopher Chatman's. He had made them a lot of money.

So . . . ?

I shoved the check copies back into the envelope. "How about a side quest before we fly to Vegas?"

Colin stood from his chair and pulled on his blazer. "To Oz?"

"To Oz."

38

The mid-afternoon drive over the hill and into the valley was one fender bender and two stalled cars long. Even in sixty-degree weather, brown haze hung over the basin. As Colin drove, I read Juliet's diary. A mile before our exit, Pepe texted me that Adeline St. Lawrence had arrived at the station to complete a witness statement. I had also reached the last entry in the diary with hollowness in my chest.

Thursday, December 6: I made the mistake of looking in the mirror this morning. My skin is pea green. There are hollow circles beneath my eyes. I have lots of zits. Cody told me that I looked like warmed-over zombie shit. I have no energy to tell him to stop cursing, especially since he's right. I do look like zombie shit.

No wonder CC's now ashamed of me. No wonder he won't respond to me or even look me in the eyes. I was gorgeous once upon a time. He says he's overwhelmed. That being sick has slowed him down.

I wish our marriage would've...not worked (?) since technically it is working, but then how can it be working if I now have a fucking gun in my trunk? Is marriage, is life supposed to hurt like this?? Maybe if I had been brave, maybe if I had listened to Addy, this BULLSHIT would've ended a long time ago.

Vanity of vanities, all is vanity. Christopher's mother would say that all the time, usually talking about me. I write it now, yes, in reference to me but also to this life he and I have led together. He doesn't trust me, I don't trust him, after all these years married. So what was the point? Why keep going? I know it's taken twenty years but someone now has to make a decision. Guess that someone is me.

And so my decision is this: I WILL NOT DIE HERE.

The office building at 10113 Thousand Oaks Boulevard was a smoked glass, fourteen-story high-rise, the tallest in an uninteresting office park that had planned gardens and walking paths and boringness.

The Stepford wifeness of it all ended at the sixth floor. Colin and I marched out of the elevator and into the fancy-pants lobby of Vandervelde, Lansing & Gray. This was not the lobby of your grandpa's commodities firm. It had sharp lines and angles, crimson-cream-brown furniture, and splashes and blocks of art trapped in modern frames. Flat-screen monitors hung on the walls showing videos of handsome young people as diverse as a bag of Skittles smiling and opening glass doors for one another. An impressive glass and bronze staircase spiraled from the sixth floor up to the seventh.

"Ooh la la, Sassoon," I said to Colin, eyebrows lifted.

"Shoulda wore my Louis Vuitton handcuffs," he said.

"The ones with the mink lining?"

He winked at me. "Your favorites."

During the drive over, I had clicked onto the firm's Web site and learned that they traded everything—from grains and rendering products to silver and oil futures. With more than two hundred brokers in five offices across the country, including Thousand Oaks, it would be easy for a receptionist to lose track of names.

And we found that receptionist seated at the circular front desk, its gold nameplate reading TIFFANI LANE.

"She's kinda cute," Colin said, straightening his tie, fire burning in his eyes.

"If you like young, blond, and bosomy."

As a detective, I knew things. And I knew that the woman seated here no way, no how resembled the desktop framed pictures of the chunky brunette hugging the fattest cat in the world. I also knew that the chick seated here, the one synthesized by Merck, Johnson & Johnson, and Victoria's Secret, had not collected the six hundred troll dolls lining the desk's edge.

"May I help you?" she asked, her baby-blue eyes big and bright.

"I know your voice," I said with a worried smile. "You're Stacy." The one who couldn't connect me to Christopher Chatman's office, I wanted to add but didn't.

Stacy grinned. "Awww. You remember me."

Colin badged her first and then told her that, oh yeah, I was his partner. "We're wondering if you could help us out," he said.

She leaned forward, her bountiful bosoms boosted for his benefit. "Anything to help, Detective Friendly."

"We need to talk to the head guy," he said. "The one who recruits all your brokers."

"That would be Mr. Meiselman," she said. "Do you have an appointment?"

"We do not have an appointment," he said, his eyes lingering on her magnificence. "But I promise not to take too much of his time."

"Cross your heart?" Stacy asked.

"Only if you cross yours," Colin said, doing his blue-steel-squinty-eyed thing.

Stacy crossed the heart spot on her lilac-colored sweater.

Colin crossed the heart spot on his tan corduroy blazer.

Stacy giggled.

Colin winked.

I threw up a little in my mouth.

Three minutes later, Colin and I were seated in an office that smelled of sweet tobacco and peppermint. The lightness of the bamboo, teak, and aluminum furniture spoke more of an architectural firm than a place of math and bankers. Framed maps of Los Angeles hung from the walls, and acrylic trophies from every nonprofit in Southern California sat on a credenza.

At six foot five and more than 250 pounds, the managing partner seated behind the desk did not match his furniture. He had a meaty, pockmarked nose and olive skin that belonged more to a wise guy named Tony Giamatti than a banker named Myron Meiselman.

After offering Pellegrino and Diet Coke, Colin and I declining each, Meiselman leaned back in his big leather chair. "So how can I help you?"

I offered him a business card and told him, very *la-la-la*, that we were investigating a case, that I needed information about one of his brokers, nothing special, *la-la-la*.

"Certainly," he said. "There are fifteen brokers in this branch, and I hired each of them. I can assure you that we only bring on the best and the brightest. Now, I didn't catch the name. Who were you asking about?"

"Christopher Chatman," I said.

An almost-imperceptible shock wave raced from his forehead down to his chin. "Oh. Yes. Chatman." He chewed on the stem of his silver-framed spectacles. "Very smart. Very talented. Incredibly perceptive."

"Incredibly trustworthy?" I asked, my head cocked.

An icy smile formed on his lips.

"Can you confirm that Mr. Chatman still works as a broker with your firm?"

Meiselman tapped the stem against his teeth, then slipped the glasses on the desk. "Yes. He is still an employee."

"Has he ever been involved in—?"

"I won't be able to answer that question, Detective Norton."

"I haven't finished asking it, sir."

Meiselman's smile widened. "I apologize," he said. "Go ahead, please."

"Has Mr. Chatman ever been disciplined for inappropriate dealings or whatnot?"

Meiselman shook his head. "Like I said, I won't be able to answer that question."

Colin reached into the case file for the copy of Peggy Tanner's check. "Is she one of the firm's clients?"

Meiselman studied the document with cold, hard eyes. "It is a check from our account. And Mrs. Tanner is a client."

"And is Mr. Chatman in charge of Ms. Tanner's account?" Colin asked.

Meiselman rubbed his jaw. "I'm afraid I can't discuss this account or any other accounts with you." His nostrils flared as he handed the copy back to Colin.

"At least not without a subpoena," I said.

Meiselman nodded, then slowly exhaled.

"Can you tell me the last time Mr. Chatman was in the office?" I asked.

"Hours are very fluid here," Meiselman explained. "So no, I can't."

"According to Mr. Chatman," Colin said, "he was here Monday night around eleven to Tuesday morning until about three thirty."

The big man squinted at me. "Really?"

I nodded. "That's what he told me. Are those hours unusual?"

"Our clients are worldwide," he said. "While you're sleeping and dreaming about winning the lottery, China is going full steam, which means my brokers are going full steam."

"Homicide detectives never sleep, nor do we dream," I said with a tight smile. "As William Burroughs said, 'Nobody owns life, but anyone who can pick up a frying pan owns death.' And last time I checked, sir, there are a lot of frying pans in this city."

Meiselman nodded. "Of course. I apologize."

"Are you aware," I said, "that Mr. Chatman's family died in a house fire early Tuesday morning? That we are investigating that fire as suspicious? That my partner and I are homicide detectives?"

Meiselman's eyes darkened, and he whispered, "Yes, I am aware of those things."

"Do you think—?"

His desk phone chirped, and relief washed over his face. "I'm sorry, but I need to take this, Detectives. It's my colleague in Chicago—I've been waiting all day for him to call."

Colin and I stood from our chairs.

Meiselman stayed seated but offered his hand. "Sorry I couldn't be of much help."

"Thank you for taking time to talk with us," I said, taking his hand.

"No problem. Be careful." Then, he grabbed the receiver and said, "Meiselman here."

Be careful.

What a weird thing to say. Not "good-bye" or "have a nice day."

But *"be careful."*

Of what?

39

To Colin's immense pleasure, Stacy had not flitted away to the copier or to the mail room. She still sat at the reception desk, holding down the fort for the chubby, cat-lovin', troll-collectin' Tiffani Lane. "Detective Friendly is back," she twittered.

Colin winked at her. "Wouldn't leave without sayin' good-bye, darlin'."

"Also, there's only one exit." I pointed to the elevator lobby. "That one over there."

"Ha-ha, Detective Friendly's partner." She opened a tube of lip gloss.

The sticky aroma of strawberries and vanilla made my stomach queasy, and I pitied the schmo required to kiss her. But then I wasn't in the demographic, so maybe that scent was akin to queen-bee pheromones and dog whistles.

Colin examined a pink-haired troll doll, then sat it back in its space. "Question for you, pretty lady. What's up with this dude Christopher Chatman?"

She bit her shiny bottom lip. "Between me and you?"

"Between me, you, and my partner here. I share everything with her."

She flicked a look at me, then slid her eyes back to Colin. "Everything?"

"Everything," Colin said, unblinking.

My whole body went cold because what the *hell*? But I didn't move. I clenched my jaw and ignored the tingling in my left arm. Any verbing, even an ill-timed heart attack, would startle the blond bunny rabbit into her hidey-hole, along with the answers to our many questions.

"Does he still work here?" Colin asked.

Stacy stroked her throat. "Yeah, but not for long."

"He's on his way out?"

She motioned for him to come closer. "You didn't hear this from me, but the only reason he's still working here is because he's sick and they can't fire him because he threatened to sue."

"Sick?" Colin asked. "With what?"

"Don't know. But last time he was in he gave me these crazy-looking flowers. They were probably expensive, but they looked totally gross." She rolled her eyes. "He's *so* not my type."

"But he's rich," Colin pointed out.

"Uh-huh, but I like men who . . ." She leaned forward and whispered in his ear.

He smiled but didn't blush.

She backed away from him with a Cheshire grin.

"So why are they trying to get rid of him?" Colin asked.

Stacy shrugged. "I've heard so many rumors. All I know is they took his keys and he can't go back into his office anymore and that I should call security if he gets rowdy."

"And why can't he go back into his office?" he asked.

The tip of her tongue licked the side of her mouth. "You're gonna have to pound that answer out of me, Detective Friendly."

Back in the oak-paneled austerity of the elevator car, I gaped at my partner.

"What?" he asked. "You use your alleged hotness all the time to advance the cause."

"Dude, my hotness has been confirmed by popular vote *and* papal conclave."

"Well, you sucked today." He dumped Tic Tacs into his mouth and crunched.

"What did she whisper to you?"

"Let's just say that I've done more than that at Sunday school."

"Yeah," I said. "You didn't look impressed. So I want Chatman's work computer. And also: he's sick? Juliet wrote a line about him being sick, but, other than that, anybody else mention him being sick?"

"Nope," Colin said. "And if he can no longer go into his office, where was he really on the morning of the fire? He couldn't have been getting ready for that conference call with Chicago."

We stopped at the security office and found Titus Otter, a short old black man wearing Lennon glasses and a cheap black suit two sizes too big. He sat behind a console and peered at nine security-surveillance monitors. In another life, Titus Otter had wandered the sandy beaches of the Galápagos Islands.

I told him that I needed his help in unraveling a great big mystery, then mentioned that my favorite uncle's name was Titus, and, finally, played up the connection between security guards and the police force.

The old man's chest inflated like a zeppelin's, and he nodded his tapered head. "Who do you wanna know about?" Although he resembled the tortoise, his light, springy voice belonged to the hare. "I've been at this desk now for ten years. Seen people come. Helped people go."

"Christopher Chatman," Colin said. "Works on the sixth floor."

"The brother?" Titus asked me, his eyebrows raised. "Of course I know him. Nice fella. Fancy dresser. Brings me coffee every morning. Talks to me like I'm somebody. Ain't but a handful of us around here, but he ain't one of them . . ." He glanced at Colin, then back at me.

Uncle Toms. That's what Titus wanted to say.

I nodded.

"We need to confirm something Christopher told us," I said.

Titus's smooth brow furrowed. "He gives me advice about my retirement and all that, and he don't charge me a nickel. Hope that ain't caused him no trouble."

"We hope not, either," I said. "You heard anything about him recently? Him getting into trouble with his bosses or being blackballed by his co-workers?"

"Nope," Titus said. "But he tendin' to go off by himself more and more. He don't seem troubled, though. He comes back smiling, just like he was going."

"When was the last time you saw him?" I asked.

Titus's rheumy eyes looked up to the ceiling, and his bottom lip folded beneath the top. "I say . . . two weeks ago. A Friday, it was."

"He say anything to you that day?" I asked.

"He mentioned bein' sick," Titus said. "But he didn't elaborate, and I didn't ask. I tol' him that I'd pray for him and encouraged him to stay strong. That we need him here. He smiled, shook my hand, and went on upstairs. He's a good boy. Hope they ain't tryna run him out of there." He nodded to the floors above us.

"We need to see some old tape," I said. "From this past Monday, December tenth, around eleven thirty P.M. to Tuesday, December eleventh, around four A.M. From the ground floor and up to the firm's lobby."

Titus pushed a button, and the main monitor scrambled. He rewound and fast-forwarded until a white time stamp on the bottom right-hand corner said *12/10, 11:37 P.M.*

Christopher Chatman, dressed in the blue Adidas tracksuit, entered the ground-floor lobby with a postal-style bag slung over his shoulder and a coffee cup in his hand.

My heart pounded—I hadn't expected him to be telling the truth.

Chatman walked to the elevator bank and stepped into the third car.

Titus hit another button.

We were now looking at the stylish and empty lobby of Vandervelde, Lansing & Gray. The elevator door opened, and at 11:41 P.M., Chatman stepped out of the car. He approached the glass doors of the firm and looked in—but he didn't reach for the handle. Instead, he looked at his watch, then sat on the couch.

"What's he doing?" Colin asked.

"Waiting for somebody?" I wondered.

Chatman pulled out a stack of magazines and a newspaper from his bag.

"Fast-forward," Colin told Titus.

In quick time, we watched Chatman sit, sip, sit, read, and sit some more. Sometimes, he did not read, and instead he just sat there, staring at his knees.

At ten minutes after four o'clock, Chatman looked at his watch again. Then, he stuffed his reading materials back into his satchel. He walked back to the elevator and stepped into the waiting car. Seconds later, he stepped out from that car and into the ground-floor lobby. He strolled to the exit of the building. Thirty minutes later, he would witness his house burning and his wife and children and life as he knew it gone forever.

40

So he lied. There was no early-morning conference call with Chicago. He had no office. He barely had a job. Still, he had not used his cell phone as he sat in the firm's lobby.

Damn that man.

"So what now?" Colin asked as he pulled into the airport's short-term parking lot.

"Don't know," I said. "He lies, though. And he lies big. At least we know that's true."

Neither Colin nor I had packed a bag—we wouldn't stay overnight in Sin City. Personally? I didn't want to stay long—staying long meant taking that soggy trip down Memory Lane with its "remember the time when" weeds and its "we used to" cracks.

Remember the time when Greg and I stayed at the Luxor for our third anniversary?

Remember the time when we hit the jackpot at a Caesars Palace slot machine right before the Cher concert?

We used to stumble up and down Las Vegas Boulevard, beautiful and free.

We used to be in love and so happy. So very, very happy.

Nope. Today's trip would be a sterile in-and-out visit.

Reminiscence-free.

Memories were for suckas.

Colin and I didn't talk much during the fifty-four-minute flight. Too much brain hurt and not enough sleep. He netted two bags of roasted peanuts, though, and I caught a catnap in which I dreamed vividly of making out with Ben Oliver in a Ferris-wheel car spinning over the Atlantic Ocean.

My limbs stayed limp, and my strange dream lingered as Colin and I wove past passengers in McCarran Airport and hopped on the monorail that whisked us to the airport's main terminal. By the time we reached the

Hertz rental counter, I had regained strength in my weakened knees and had shaken off most of that fantasy of Ben and me. And as Colin tried to persuade the pug-faced rental diva behind the counter, my spine had stiffened again and all sexy thoughts involving that insurance attorney, what's-his-name, were tucked away for the flight back home.

"Got any Mustangs or Camaros or something sporty left?" Colin asked the woman.

"You should've upgraded when you called," she sniffed.

He did the squinty-eyed trick that had worked so well with Stacy just a couple of hours before. "Wanna check your little computer again?"

She blinked at him and her head swiveled on her neck. "No, I do not."

A minute later, Colin and I reached slot 7 and the red Kia Spectra.

"Guess you're fresh out of pimp juice," I said.

"Maybe you should drive," he said.

"Sorry, I'm dead." I slipped into the passenger seat, troll-big in the tiny Korean car.

"This sucks major ass," Colin muttered, his knees to the windshield. "Where we goin'?"

"Head north on the fifteen."

It was a little after three and the sun still sat high in the sky. Vegas vamps lined the interstate highway.

COMEDIAN GEORGE WALLACE VOTED THE BEST 10:00 P.M. SHOW!

BEAUTIFUL BABES AT LAX NIGHTCLUB!

PAY ONE PRICE AND EAT ALL DAY AT EXCALIBUR'S BUFFET!

The devil was busy.

I kept my eyes trained north to the Sheep Range Mountains and the tract homes and the towering construction cranes now paused indefinitely over half-built high-rise condos that no one had the ends to buy.

Seven miles north from the Strip, Colin exited the freeway. He made a left turn here, a right turn there, traffic light, stop sign, and we reached Desert Sun Villas.

"Damn," I said, peering at the security gate. "Looks like we need a key code to enter."

We parked a half block away, rolled down the car windows, and waited. We didn't listen to the radio and didn't talk on the phone. Just sat in the quiet for about five minutes until . . .

"What did you do last night?" I asked.

His right leg bounced up and down, then stopped. "Dakota drove up from the O.C."

I lifted my eyebrows. "Really?"

"Really."

An old woman behind the wheel of a Corolla pulled up to the entrance of Desert Sun Villas.

The entry gates slowly creaked open.

Colin followed the car.

"We're looking for 4821 Wisp o' Willow Way," I said.

And we found it: a two-story, adobe-colored house with Christmas lights on the eaves and a wicker snowman on the stony, succulent-filled front yard.

"Ain't she Jewish?" Colin asked.

"News flash," I said. "We took the 'Christ' out of 'Christmas.'"

Colin busted a U-turn and parked in the direction of the exit.

"From Orange County," I said. "That's a helluva drive. She stay overnight?"

"She did."

I grabbed the case file from the backseat. "You two reconcile?"

"Not in the least."

"Then, why?"

"Biology."

"Gets you every time. Ready?"

"Always."

41

We marched up the walkway of 4821 Wisp o' Willow Way, to the little patio area beside the front door. A potted fern sat between two white plastic chairs that needed to be washed. A pair of ancient flip-flops sat at the foot of one of those chairs. The Willkommen mat's borders were edged with wiener dogs and marionettes wearing lederhosen.

Colin rang the doorbell.

A small dog yapped.

"Shit," he muttered.

"But it's a tiny dog," I said, shifting the file to my left arm.

Somewhere in the house, a woman shouted, "Down, Snowy. Bad girl. *Bad.*"

The door opened, and a swift current of tobacco, dog and lunch-meat smells washed over us.

Melissa Kemper had not aged since she'd posed in that *Los Angeles Confidential* picture. In fact, less skin sagged around her cheeks—a postdivorce nip and tuck. A few gray strands stuck out from her natural red hair, demanding to be Clairoled. Her eyes, though . . . They were the color of mint and the Arctic Sea. The Dachshund in her arms licked her jowls and left behind patches of pink skin in a sea of toast-colored foundation.

The Chanel T-shirt (and the G cups straining against it), the Chanel signature sandals, and the tight Juicy Couture sweats told me that she had done well dropping the two hundred pounds of man.

"Yeah?" Melissa Kemper's lovely green eyes drilled into me.

We showed her our badges, and I made the introductions.

Flared nostrils, rapid blinking, cocked chin, flared nostrils again, and, finally, closed eyes—all in two seconds—flashed across Melissa's face. "What chutzpah you have, showing up here," she spat. "I don't have to talk to you. This is America. I have rights."

"You do have rights," Colin said with an easy smile. "But stonewalling us will look bad to the jury deciding who to fry for the deaths of Juliet, Cody, and Chloe Chatman."

Those words—"deaths" and "fry"—made Melissa let out a long sigh. "Fine."

We were led into a small living room with dog-paw-printed cream carpet and tall stacks of unopened boxes from Louis Vuitton, Target, and Walmart. Game controllers and DVD cases lay scattered on the floor alongside socks, Diet Coke cans, and rubber dog toys. Used paper plates, crumpled napkins, and filled ashtrays covered the coffee table. *Divorce Court* played on the big-screen television that sat right next to another big-screen television that still wore its SALE! tag.

"Let's get this over with," Melissa said, plopping onto a dingy-white love seat.

"Yes. Let's." My muscles tightened as I sat on the filthy couch, two butt prints away from a worrisome stain that reeked of old urine.

Colin took a long moment before sitting in the matching armchair.

Pictures hung all around us, the used-to-be Melissa Kemper giving good face and showing off her liposuctioned ass. Boudoir shots that you'd see in a man's *boudoir* and not in his living room.

I pulled a notepad and pen from my bag. "We're here because of your relationship with Christopher Chatman."

Melissa tugged at a chin hair and kept her hypnotic eyes on me.

"But first," I said, "how did you hear about the fires?"

"My ex called me," Melissa said, crossing her arms. "I had nothing to do with the fire. You ask anyone. *Anyone!* And they'll tell you, all of them, that Melissa Kemper is a *mensch*. She would never hurt a fly."

Colin opened his mouth to respond.

"I know what you're thinking," Melissa continued, "but it wasn't like I was in *love* with Christopher. I never pulled any of that 'if I can't have him, you can't have him either' bullshit. My hands are clean." And she washed her hands with imaginary soap and showed them to us. Clean, except for the schmutz on her left thumb.

"Ms. Kemper," I said, "we—"

"You gotta understand," she continued, "I had just moved here with my kid. I didn't know my neighbors. I didn't know anybody. I was lonely and a little depressed and not thinking right. And I thought Christopher could introduce me to some important people here so that—"

"How would he be able to do that?" I asked. "Introduce you to people, I mean."

"Because of his position at the university."

"His *position*?" Colin asked.

"Over at UNLV. He's a visiting economics professor. I thought by being with *him*, I'd get to schmooze with some nice bankers or attorneys."

Melissa searched my expression for some judgmental gesture, like a smirk or a cocked eyebrow. But she only found a poker-faced pro. "It was nothing," she explained. "I'm talking about the relationship with Christopher and me. There wasn't anything romantic. I wanted something more, and he knew better, and . . . I took care of him. Bought him suits and shoes. It was nice taking care of a man again, even if he didn't want me in *that* way. I didn't need another future ex-husband. And Christopher knew that. Besides, he loved Juliet."

She shook her head. "And Juliet. Talk about *difficult*, and I'm being *very* nice when I say that. *Very* nice. She was incredibly demanding and stuck up and . . . She acted like she wasn't from Mississippi."

"If you weren't having an affair, why did you send her this?" I handed her the PDF of her note to Juliet. *Dear Juliet, you need to know some things. I don't want to bring it up in a letter—you've ignored my other ones so far—so please stop ignoring me and pick up the phone and CALL ME. It's a matter of life and death!!!*

"That?" Melissa said. "Acting like a yenta. But she never called me back."

"What were you planning to do if she'd called back?"

She shrugged. "Yank her out of the freakin' Matrix."

"The neighbors say that Juliet and Christopher were happy together," Colin said.

"And Mr. Chatman has only spoken positively of his wife," I added.

Melissa rolled her eyes. "He's saying good things *now* because she's *dead*. Everybody's a saint when they're *dead*. The woman was cheating on him, but now she's Mother Teresa? Are you *kidding* me?"

"Who was Juliet cheating with?" Colin asked with more calm than I could've mustered.

Melissa waggled her head. "What's-his-face, her personal trainer, the guido with the Jersey Shore eyebrows. And if I'm called on the stand, I'll *prove* that Saint Juliet was boppin' everybody except her husband, even when said husband was undergoing chemo."

"*Chemo?*" I said.

"Oh, so your little investigation hasn't turned that up?" Melissa scoffed. "Christopher was diagnosed with cancer back in August and just finished treatment a few weeks ago."

On my notepad, I scribbled, "cancer, wtf?" next to "professor at unlv, wtf?" And was this the reason his bosses at the firm couldn't fire him? "Did he say where he got treatment?" I asked.

"I think he said . . ." She narrowed her eyes as she tried to remember. "He said MSK. Don't know what that means, though."

I recalled hospitals in Southern California. None were abbreviated MSK, and I jotted, "What is MSK?" on my to-do list.

"She was planning to leave him," Melissa claimed. "But he got sick, and so she couldn't."

"I don't understand," I said. "Are you saying that Juliet was planning to leave Christopher so she could be with Jersey Shore Eyebrows?"

"I don't know *what* she was planning to do," Melissa said. "She stopped talking to me and started confiding in Ben, who is such a dog, and I hope his *dick* falls off. And I hope you're questioning him like this."

"We are," Colin said, throwing me a glance.

"Because Ben, that son of a bitch, thinks he's above it all," Melissa ranted. "He thinks that no one knows who he really is. But I know him. Asshole."

"And who is he?" I asked.

She turned her head in defiance, and the cords in her neck stood out.

"I can wait," I said. "The trial will be an incredible time for sharing and discovering."

But she couldn't stand my feigned indifference—she knew so effin' much. "He's a liar and a cheat. Got kicked out of the state bar once and . . . and . . . Just ask him about the paralegal and about Martha's Vineyard 2003. Shady asshole through and through. *Anyway*, Juliet thought Christopher was a schmuck. Can you believe that? This smart, accomplished man a *schmuck*? We'd go to lunch together, Juliet and me, and she'd always complain: Christopher's touching me, Christopher's talking to me, Christopher's *whine-whine-whining* me. Honey, you want some cheese with that whine?"

The Dachshund darted to the dining room, stuck its butt near the wine rack, and took a dump.

"Snowy, I'm gonna spank your little tuches." Melissa made a face, but she didn't move to clean up Snowy's poop.

And now the stink of dog crap rode atop the tobacco and fried-bologna fumes.

"When did Christopher pull back from your friendship?" I asked, *this close* to vomiting.

"About a month ago," she said. "He told me that he wasn't ready for a relationship, that *I* wasn't ready for a relationship. My ex has totally made me crazy. I mean, *look* at me. Look at all these stupid boxes of crap I don't need. Look at this *house*." She motioned to the air. "Ron has totally destroyed me. Ruined my life. Sapped me of my strength."

I'd never let Greg destroy so much of my motivation that I'd let dog shit stay on the carpet. I was *not* a member of *that* Traveling Pants Sisterhood.

"Christopher was totally heartbroken over Juliet's betrayal. He pleaded with her on the phone right out there." She pointed to the front door. "And he told her that he needed her, that being with her would help him survive the worst moment of his life."

The smile on her face faded. "I was so pissed off because *look* at him. The man's a living god. And after she rejected him yet again, he drove back to the Bellagio and swallowed a handful of pills."

Ice filled my veins. "Pills? Like to . . . *kill* himself?"

Melissa nodded solemnly and whispered, "He wrote a note and everything."

"You see the note?" Colin asked.

"No, I didn't see the note," Melissa spat, all *how could you ask such a thing?*

"Who told you there was a note?" he said.

"Christopher did," she said. "And obviously it didn't take. The suicide, I mean. He said it was fate, that he was meant to live. He told me how he never wanted to leave his wife and kids. I hate to talk bad about the dead, but Juliet was such a *dragon*."

I turned a page in the notebook. "Let's talk about the money. On the phone this morning, you claimed it was a gift."

Melissa offered a sheepish grin. "Not exactly."

"Okay. *How* exactly?"

She scratched her freckled forearm. "I came into some money through an investment made by Ron and me. We're partners in a sports bar that kept opening and closing. Permit issues. Anyway, it took four years for the bar to make a profit—by then, Ron had forgotten about it. So when Shamrock's got in the black, we finally got a check from our business manager. Ron and I, we were going through the divorce at the time, and I didn't want him to know about the money because he'd want half. So I gave the money to Christopher, and he set up an account that didn't have my name attached to it."

"How much are we talking about?" Colin asked.

"About a hundred thousand dollars," Melissa said.

The deposit Colin had discovered while reviewing the Chatmans' banking records: $100,000.

"It's my play money," Melissa continued, dabbing at her glistening forehead. "And it would come in handy right now. The plumbing in this piece-of-shit house is atrocious. The roof leaks. The garage floods when it rains and—"

"You haven't bugged Mr. Chatman for the money?" I asked.

"Yes, I've asked him," she said. "I'm not scared of him, not that he's that type anyway. I've left him a million messages since last week. At first, he wouldn't call me back, but I told him I would come to LA and ask for it in person if he kept ignoring me."

"I'm bettin' he called you back," Colin said.

She nodded. "On Monday. And then the fire happened, and I haven't had a chance to bring it up again. The man's family just died, you know?"

"When on Monday did you two talk?" I asked.

"Around noon. I recorded part of our conversation."

Colin and I glanced at each other.

She blinked rapidly. "Perfectly legal. There's an app for that."

"Why did you record the call?" I asked.

Those green eyes of hers darkened. "In case I needed . . . backup. You wanna hear it?"

Colin and I nodded.

She reached beneath the nest of napkins on the coffee table and produced a cell phone. She scrolled through something on the screen, then set the phone back among the trash. Her recorded, nasally voice filled the room.

Melissa: *"I need about fifty thousand dollars. My toilets won't flush."*
Christoper Chatman: *"When do you need it by?"*
Melissa: *"Sooner rather than later. I've been calling you and calling you."*
Christopher Chatman: *"I know, and I'm sorry for not getting back to you."*
Melissa: *"Where have you been?"*

Christopher Chatman: *"At the hospital, trying to get healthy."*

Melissa: *"Back east?"*

Christopher Chatman: *"Yeah."*

Melissa: *[gasp] "The cancer's back? Oh no."*

Christopher Chatman: *[chuckle] "No, it's not back. Just one last checkup. And I forgot my phone at home, and when I got back to LA, I couldn't find it." [chuckle] "Cody put it in the microwave."*

Melissa: *[sigh] "I'm sorry."*

Christopher Chatman: *"No, I'm sorry. About everything."*

Melissa: *"If I were insecure, I'd think you were tryin' to avoid me."*

Christopher Chatman: *"Never. You mean too much to me."*

Melissa: *"Go away with me. Just for a few days. We won't have to do anything. We'll just . . . be. I still have the cabin in Tahoe."*

Christopher Chatman: *"My sick leave is ending, and I'm supposed to go back to work the first week in January. Hey, let me call you back."*

Dial tone—he had ended the call.

"And the rest is history," Melissa said with a sad shake of her head.

"What did you do about the plumbing?" Colin asked.

"Had Ron pay for it," Melissa said. "Is he okay? Christopher, I mean."

"He's managing," I said, my voice hard. "What, with his family dead and everything."

"So let's talk about *this*." Colin slipped a witness statement on the coffee table.

Melissa glanced at the form and her shoulders slumped. "Should I attend the funeral? Does that seem kosher? Mourning the wife of the man I . . . ?" Her bloodshot eyes begged for an answer, for direction.

I pointed to the form. "We'd really appreciate it if you could fill this out."

She blinked at me, and a teardrop tumbled down her rouged cheek.

Hard for me to feel sorry for her. In my own life, there had been too many Melissa Kempers driving up to virtual Tahoe with my husband, women who thought that I was a dragon, frigid and angry and not to be mourned.

Screw 'em.

And screw Melissa Kemper.

42

Once Melissa had signed her witness statement, Colin and I rushed out of that crap-trap and into the fresh, dry air with its normal city-desert smells of dust, pig farms, and spilled beer. I wanted to shower and then change into a fresh set of clothes. Colin wanted to wander off the road a bit and onto the Strip to play a few hands of blackjack, then grab a prime-rib dinner and a burlesque show at the Tropicana.

"I can enjoy the ladies," he said, slipping behind the Kia's steering wheel, "and you can holler at those Australian strippers."

"Thunder from Down Under?" I checked my phone: two text messages.

Greg: *Umm. We supposed to go to dinner before Lena's thing?*

Lena: *Where RU????? U still coming????*

I tapped my response to Greg: *Just finished. Will be home soon.* To Lena, I sent a simple *yep*.

"Well?" Colin asked, bright-eyed.

"As tempting as gorging myself on meat and men sounds, we need to get back to LA. We have festivities tonight, or have you forgotten?"

"Never been to a pole-dancing recital," Colin said as he drove toward the entry gates.

I punched the air-conditioner button all the way to "roar." "Won't be as memorable as our meeting with Melissa Kemper. Suicide attempt at the Bellagio? And I guess cancer is the illness Stacy the receptionist was talking about?"

"But what about the teaching gig at UNL—?" He tapped the car's brakes. "Hey—"

"Good idea," I said. "Head south on the fifteen."

So we wandered off the road. Twenty minutes later, Colin and I crowded the frigid office of Moses Sokolski, the dean of the economics department at the University of Nevada, Las Vegas.

Sokolski, a white-haired goblin of a man, had more pressing matters at hand, and as he spoke *at* us, he did not look away from his computer monitor. "There are no Christopher Chatmans in this program. Visiting, adjunct, or tenured. I should know: I've taught here for twenty years."

Colin and I returned to the car. For a long time, we didn't speak.

College boys hurtled past the car on bikes and skateboards. Pods of young women in shorts and tank tops wandered back and forth, talking to each other while simultaneously texting or gabbing on their cell phones.

"Men lie to women all the time," Colin explained. "And women believe the lies men tell all the time. It's like flowers and sunshine. It's a symbiotic relationship."

"First of all," I said, "the sun doesn't need flowers to exist, so, no, it's not symbiotic but very one-way. And, second, when you lie to Dakota, do you think she actually believes that you still truly love her and that's why she flew all the way from Colorado Springs and drove up from Orange County? Because you wanted to talk to her about getting back together? And do you actually believe that *she* believes that you aren't as shallow as she thought? That you aren't screwing her simply because of biology and not because she doesn't have cold sores and won't steal shit from your wallet when you fall asleep afterward? You think she actually *believes* your bull?"

He started the car. "Look: I'm not gonna ding Chatman for lying to Melissa Kemper. You're supposed to lie to your hoe."

I pulled my phone from my bag. "You're so full of shit that it's now falling out of your mouth."

"Who you callin'?" he asked.

"Dixie don't need no stinkin' warrant to do what I'm about to ask her to do."

"Think she'll help?"

"If that means MG Standard not having to pay out Christopher Chatman's claim, hell yeah, she'll be happy to help."

"You got ten minutes," Dixie grumbled, not sounding happy at all. "I'm meetin' Marcus at El Torito."

"Which one is Marcus?"

"Desk sergeant over at Hollywood."

"Dark-skinned? Thick-necked? Does MMA on his time off?"

"Hallelujah. You got nine minutes now—what do you want?"

"I'm in Vegas working the Chatman case. What's a hospital with the initials MSK?"

"Ain't nothing here in Los Angeles," she said. "But in New York, it's Memorial Sloan Kettering."

"Well, could you call Memorial Sloan Kettering and see if Christopher Chatman received cancer treatment there?"

It took less than five minutes for Dixie to learn that Christopher Chatman, Social Security number ending in 9717, born on June 21, 1963, had never been a patient at Memorial Sloan Kettering.

"Keep going since I still have four minutes," I told her, even though blood was now in the water and she needed no further encouragement from me. "Who is their health insurance company?"

"Blue Cross," Dixie said. "Let me make a few more calls."

En route to the airport, Colin pulled into a Sonic drive-in for a quick preflight meal.

Before I took a bite from my chili dog, Dixie called back. "UCLA, no Christopher Chatman. No Christopher Chatman at USC, Stanford, or Fred Hutch. City of Hope had a Christopher Chatman, but he died from leukemia back in nineteen eighty-seven."

My stomach growled, and I stuck a piece of bun into my mouth. "What about community hospitals, university hospitals, cancer specialty places, shamans . . . ?"

"Okay, so you trippin' now," Dixie said. "I can't call every hospital in the world, and I *ain't* callin' every hospital in the world. Especially on a Friday night, with a fine-ass kickboxin' cop and a strawberry margarita waitin' for me. We friends but not like that, boo."

"So?"

She sighed. "*So* you need more people."

After finishing half of my hot dog, I called Syeeda.

She gasped. "You're actually asking—?"

"Are we gonna do this or not?"

"Let's."

"You still have your person in the insurance world?"

"Yep. Who do you want info on?"

"First," I said, "this is so off the record . . ." I squeezed the bridge of my nose. "Sy, I can't have even a *suggestion* of this printed until two years from now when I give you an exclusive."

"I vow on our friendship," she said solemnly.

I gave her Christopher Chatman's name and Social Security number.

"I'll call you back," she said.

I pointed at Colin. "You didn't hear that."

"Hear what?"

"When?"

He smiled and winked.

I finished the second half of my hot dog in time to take Syeeda's call.

"Blue Cross hasn't paid any cancer-care costs for the Chatman family. Looks like Maria Kulkanis, M.D., billed them for a diagnostic ultrasound on December sixth, but that's it."

"Is their policy up-to-date?"

"Yeah, and the premium is paid to the end of this year. They're still listed as primary."

"Maybe his secondary paid?"

"My girl didn't see a notation that there is a secondary health insurance policy. Juliet Chatman went to Dr. Kulkanis on December sixth, last week. And Christopher Chatman went to Los Angeles Orthopaedic Hospital back in August for his back."

Surprise spiked my heart. "His *back*? But not for cancer?"

"Nope."

"Can you call her back?" I asked. "Juliet had been prescribed Valium by Dr. Kulkanis. Ask her if Blue Cross was billed for that prescription after July."

Two minutes later, Syeeda called back. "No scrip filled in June or July. But she filled it in August, September, October, November, and December."

"Thanks, friend o' mine."

"See you tonight?"

"Yep."

After I had ended the call, Colin asked, "What did she say?"

"Someone was getting Valium," I said.

His face blanched. "It's still possible that Juliet started popping pills again."

"True," I said. "Sy also said that there are no cancer treatments in Christopher Chatman's Blue Cross records. No cancer diagnoses, either." I cocked an eyebrow. "Acceptable lies to his hoe, or is Christopher Chatman crazy with an extra side of crazy?"

Colin tapped the steering wheel but didn't respond.

"At this rate, I bet that suicide attempt was fiction, too."

"Okay," Colin said, "he's a pathological liar. But who started the fire?"

I slumped as much as I could in that tiny front seat.

My partner's gaze fixed on a distant point within Sonic.

Who started the fire?

I shook my head and whispered, "I don't know."

43

Colin and I climbed aboard our airplane at ten minutes to six o'clock. I longed to close my eyes and take a quick catnap, and maybe lose myself in a dream like the one I'd had on the flight to Vegas. But my conscious mind refused to relax, leaving me rigid in the middle seat, eyes wide, mind pinging between the Chatman case and Greg's pissy text message.

Colin slept, mouth open, head occasionally falling to rest on my shoulder.

Annoyed, I pushed him away a few times and growled, "Get off of me. You're snoring."

He muttered something, then leaned in the opposite direction.

A little after seven o'clock, the plane landed at LAX. As we taxied to the gate, I turned on my phone: Dixie had left a voice-mail message. "Girl! That motha-clucka canceled on me. He thinks I'm stupid. That I didn't hear his babymomma in the background shoutin' at one of them nappy-headed kids. I'm so pissed off right now that I'm still at work. Call me."

I rushed off the plane with the phone to my ear.

Colin, still trying to wake up, shambled behind me through the crowded terminal as though his legs and feet had been dipped in peanut butter.

"Now which babymomma is this?" I asked Dixie. "He got three."

"The Filipino chick, the one in Dispatch."

"I heard she got that nasty woman's disease," I said. "Which means Marcus does, too. Which means you dodged a bullet and three weeks of penicillin."

After trying to determine if Christopher Chatman had received cancer care and not finding any evidence that he had, Dixie had reviewed his medical history—lower back pain, therapy, anxiety disorder . . .

"When did he see the shrink?" I asked.

"September 2005."

"For how long?"

"Just that month. You think that means anything?"

He had just become a father for the second time—Chloe had been born that July. Two kids, a wife, and one income—if anything made you anxious . . .

"Could mean something," I said to Dixie. "Could mean nothing."

Colin dropped me at home and I tossed him a "see you soon" while racing up the walkway to the front door. I had forty minutes before Greg turned into a fully realized asshole, brimming with barbed words and moody glances.

I showered for ten minutes, took another five to flat-iron my hair, spent a minute on makeup and several seconds wrangling my never-been-worn, block-print Diane von Furstenberg wrap dress.

The dress fit, glory, glory.

My hair obeyed.

My toes still shone with toreador-red nail polish.

Power without a Glock.

In the Porsche, I zoomed through the slick streets of Culver City, heart pounding in my chest as my phone vibrated with passive-aggressive texts from my husband.

If you have something better to do . . .

I could be at work right now.

U there? R U busy?

I didn't respond. Against the law to text and drive.

Five minutes after eight o'clock, I pulled in front of the new French bistro and left the car keys with the valet.

Greg, dressed in a cashmere sweater and jeans, stood in the lit-bead-draped bar. He was chatting with a leather-clad, beauty-shop blonde (he never chatted with men, not ever). Seeing me enter, Greg said something to the blonde, laughed as she laughed, then sauntered over to meet me. "Wow," he said, looking at his wristwatch. "Only six minutes late."

My smile froze as I stared at him. "And you look very handsome as well."

"I get to be pissed off," he growled.

"I wasn't in Vegas for the buffets," I whispered as pressure pushed behind my eyes. "You know I'm working a case. And that case took me out of town for a moment."

"Out of town with Colin Taggert."

"Absolutely. He's also a homicide detective assigned to this case that required travel."

"Sounds good on paper," he snarked.

Panic whirled through me. "I apologize for being six minutes late. Won't happen again. And we don't have to do this"—I waved to the restaurant—"if you're not feeling it."

He clenched his jaw, then forced himself to smile. "Hell, we're here now." He glanced down at my dress and lifted an eyebrow. "You look incredible. But you know that, don't you?"

"Always nice to hear."

He touched the small of my back, then dropped his hand to my ass.

The ice around my heart cracked and started to thaw.

The restaurant's front-desk host, a man as thin as a Communion wafer and just as pale, led us to a table with a view of the restaurant's small lavender and herb garden.

Greg's whiskey-colored eyes skirted over the menu, then found my cleavage. His gaze narrowed and lingered there for a moment until he'd had enough and focused again on the food.

My skin tingled under his attention. I wanted to move my shoe up and down his calf, but something kept that foot tied to the ground.

Over glasses of Napa Cabernet, he told me that he didn't feel like talking about the zombie game. "The stupid mistakes I'm finding . . . None of it makes sense, and I'm startin' to think somebody's trying to sabotage me. There was an article on IGN's Web site today, all about my failure being imminent, that I haven't fucked up yet but odds are that I will, and that schadenfreude bullshit. If I have to program this son of a bitch myself and do all the voices and sell it from the back of a U-Haul, I'll do it."

"Sounds like you're never coming home," I said.

He refilled his wineglass. "If that's what it's gonna take."

But me being six minutes late because I'd been trying to solve the murder of three, real-life human beings? Oh, the *horror*!

The waitress slipped the tomato tarte tatin between us while Greg showed me on his phone a new sketch of my video-game doppelgänger now dressed in a tight, low-cut police uniform. "I see that I got the boobs right," he said, his eyes flitting back to my dress.

I jerked as though a knife had jabbed my spine. Had his ogling my breasts happened for simply artistic reasons and not because he wanted to free them from La Perla and cover them with millions of kisses?

Over steak au poivre for him and *poulet roti* for me, I told him about the

Chatmans' weird medical shenanigans. And as I told him about the Valium prescription, he picked at his potato gratin and haricot vert. As I talked about Melissa Kemper, he glanced at his watch. When I brought up the visit to Christopher Chatman's commodities firm, he yawned, then peeked at the striking brunette with extreme eyelashes sitting two tables away.

Dessert came: chocolate fondant with homemade vanilla *crème glacée*.

The brunette and her eyelashes left the table and headed for the restroom.

I counted in my head. *One . . . two . . . three . . .*

Greg wiped his mouth with a napkin, then said, "I need to make a call."

Five seconds.

I nodded. "Yep."

He left the table.

My mouth, full of melting chocolate, mixed with unfallen, salty tears.

Alone now, my mind raced, and thoughts tumbled as my eyes searched the moonlit garden for answers.

Stay.

Go.

He's making a call.

No, he's not.

Finish the fondant first.

Finally, the strongest thought wound through the fray and reached my mind's door.

I pushed away from the table, my feet numb but my legs strong, and stomped in the direction my husband and the woman had taken.

This isn't happening . . . This isn't happening . . .

I held my breath and peeked around the corner into the corridor . . .

Ah.

Okay.

There he was. There *she* was. Talking. Together. Her hand on his shoulder. His smile, the brightest I've seen since . . .

Trembling and sweaty, I thanked the ghost-faced host as I strode out of the restaurant. With a shaky hand, I gave ten dollars and the parking ticket for my car to the valet. Weak-kneed, I slipped behind the wheel of my "please, baby, please" Porsche and sped away from the clatter of plates and the chatter of laughter.

At the first stoplight, I nearly rammed into the back of a Miata.

Pinballs clanged from my purse.

Greg was calling.

And the phone kept clanging as I pulled into the parking lot between the HoneyBaked Store and the Secret Pole Dance Studio, a squat concrete building that looked more like a sewing-machine shop than a place where women learned to writhe around a silver stick. I parked and sat, aware that right over there, down the block, was the storage facility where Chatman's boxes had been stolen.

Shit. Another failure.

The rumble started in my toes, twisted past my intestines, and burned my throat. The tears came, and I wept, unable to stop, unable to breathe, helpless against my body's spasms.

In ten minutes, I was all cried out. My head fell back against the headrest as control draped over me. There was a heaviness in my limbs, but it was not a sinking kind of heaviness; instead, it was being tethered to something that would not let me float away into the lonely, vast universe.

The next time the pinballs clanged, I answered. "Yes?"

"What the hell's wrong with you?" Greg shouted.

"Nothing's wrong with me," I said, calm and over it. "Did you ever go to the doctor?"

He paused. "What?"

"The doctor. Back on Tuesday, you told me you'd go. Did you go yet?"

"I haven't had a chance . . . I don't wanna talk to you on a phone. Where are you?"

And as he shouted questions at me, I sat there, tethered to whatever was holding me.

After he had run out of breath and had apologized for the obvious and tried to explain that he knew the brunette from college, he fell silent. "Lou," he whispered, "say something."

No tangled thoughts. No fear. I heard his breathing. I pictured his hand over his eyes. I felt his anxiety pulse through the phone. And all of me went clammy and cold.

"Lou. Baby, say something."

And so, I did.

"I want a divorce."

44

Maybe Greg *had* been telling the truth. Maybe he *did* know the pretty brunette from college. At this point in our marriage, though, at this point in
my *life*, my mind's fingers had grown raw from sifting lies from the truth.
"That's it. I'm done." I shifted in the Porsche's seat and watched people gather
near the entrance to the pole-dancing studio.

Syeeda sat beside me, her doe eyes wide with worry. She took my hand
and squeezed. "Are you sure? Maybe you should sleep on it. You can crash
at my house again, if you want. Stay as long as you need. We'll make s'mores."

"I'm sure that we're over," I said. "So over that I'm calling Lena's divorce
attorney on Monday morning. Really: why keep going? It's not like we have
kids. We don't have to stay married for anyone other than ourselves, and I
don't wanna do that anymore." I shook my head. "And he's the one staying
away, but thanks for the offer of shelter and s'mores."

She ruffled my hair.

I took her hand. "Forgot to tell you that the article today . . . really good.
Very touching."

She squeezed my hand. "Just doin' my job, Detective."

Colin's red Dodge Charger roared into the parking lot.

Syeeda checked her makeup in the visor. "Lena is determined to sleep
with that man by the end of the year." She glanced at me. "Is Colin interested?"

My partner left his car, and as he walked, he tugged at his black V-neck
sweater.

I shrugged. "I'm not sure what he wants."

At the entrance, Colin's gaze started at my face, then drifted down to
my cleavage and exposed feet before buoying back up to my boobs.

I rolled my eyes. "Take a picture. It'll last longer."

He blushed. "I forget sometimes that you're a girl."

I smirked. "I forget sometimes what that even means."

"Where's your hubby?"

I shrugged, then took a deep breath and tried to smile.

Colin tapped my arm. "What do you sistas say about doing bad by yourself?"

Syeeda laughed. "Did he just say 'sistas'?"

I shook my head and chuckled. "Shut up, Colin."

Half of the studio was walled with mirrors, and all of it had been decorated with rhinestones and velvet cutout silhouettes of women in different pole positions. The aromas of baby powder and vanilla wafted from candles and sticks of burning incense. Friends and family sat in a semicircle of white folding chairs around a silver pole reflecting light from a spinning disco ball. Silver light flecked our faces as we all drank sweet, pink libations laced with vodka.

Against my will, I nodded to the beat of Lil' Kim and 50 Cent bragging about magic sticks and magic . . . boxes.

Colin gaped at me as I grooved and rapped with Syeeda. And his eyes bugged as I shouted the X-rated lyrics.

"*Really?*" he said. "Is this the cop who always wears the white hat now rapping about *head*?"

I waved one hand in the air and used the other to chug from my cup. Tonight, I didn't give a shit, a fuck, or even a rat's ass—it had been a helluva week.

The first three student "pieces" involved feather boas, a leather whip, and a giant lollipop. Makin' it rain, droppin' it low, and shakin' it fast. In between each set, a studio staff member wiped down the pole with enough alcohol to sanitize a hepatitis ward.

A break gave us all time to refresh our cups of Pink Panties. As we waited, Lil' Kim returned, raunchier than ever.

"Do you know all the lyrics to her songs?" Colin asked, his eyes on my wriggling hips.

I nodded, snapped my fingers, and bumped him with my hip.

The lights dimmed—Diamond Heavenlick's turn. She wore a blue-and-green-plaid naughty schoolgirl's uniform with patent-leather platform Mary Janes. She writhed before us as R. Kelly explained that he saw nothing wrong with a little bump and grind.

In six minutes, Lena did the Cleopatra, the Dark Pixie, and reverse-grabs, all of which required athleticism and a bikini wax unlike any other. Not since college had I seen Lena do more than a wiggle here and a shimmy there. But tonight she was flying around a pole with her short legs nearly horizontal.

"Damn," Colin said, wide-eyed. "She's better than a lot of strippers I've seen. And she don't have any bullet wounds or scars and shit."

As a finale, Lena leapt up to the top of the pole and spun down until she landed into the splits.

We all stood and clapped as Lil Wayne bragged that his girl licked him like a lollipop.

Twenty minutes later, we stumbled out to the parking lot, which smelled of fried dough and confectioners' sugar. Lena and Colin lingered near the entrance while Syeeda wandered over to the donut shop.

My phone rang. Not pinballs—not Greg.

"Detective Norton, good evening," the man said. "It's Ben Oliver."

I stopped in my step—his voice sounded like the chocolate fondant I had abandoned earlier at the French bistro. "Ben. Hello. What a surprise."

"A pleasant surprise, I hope."

"Depends on why you're calling. And on a Friday night, it better be intriguing." The pink drinks had boosted my swagger.

He chuckled. "I just ended a meeting, and it went really well for my client and me. Also, it's a beautiful, crisp night out and I'm in a great mood. So I wanna buy you a fancy drink in a fancy bar somewhere in this fancy town."

The asphalt shook beneath my feet, moved past my calves, and drilled into my stomach. Was he trying to play me? Did he know that I was trying to play him? Was I one hundred percent certain that I was trying to play him, because if I was, why—?

"Hello?" he said. "You there?"

"I'm here," I said. "I like fancy drinks in fancy bars. But if I agree, I'll need to ask a few work-related questions."

"Ask me whatever you want. How about the bar at the Ritz-Carlton, Marina del Rey?"

I agreed, then ended the call.

Colin was ambling toward me.

"What happened?" I called out to him. "No lust connection between you and Lena?"

He shrugged, then glanced back at Lena standing at the studio doors with Syeeda. "She's cute and rich and everything but . . ."

"But her ego is bigger than yours."

"Remarkable, right? Heading home?"

I grimaced and shook my head.

"So tell me what happened. Y'all fight?"

"Oh, it's far worse than that."

Colin crossed his arms. He thought to himself for a moment, then took a step closer to me. "I know I'm supposed to say that I'm sorry because of black love and whatnot . . ."

"Oh, quiet, you."

He stroked my cheek with his forefinger.

"You did not just do that," I said, squinting at him.

He smiled. The pink drinks had boosted his swagger, too.

"You're my kinda friend, Colin," I said, not flinching from his touch. "More importantly, you're my partner. And I'm your senior."

"I'm not askin' you to marry me, Lou. We're off duty, and it's obvious that we're attracted to each other."

"*Obvious?*" I asked. "To whom?"

He smiled. "C'mon. Everybody's doin' it. Vernell and Kent in the Gang Unit hook up all the time. And Montez and Felicia in Robbery . . ."

"And if everybody blah-blah-blahed, would you do that, too?"

"Hell yeah, I would. Twice. Three times if I worked out that day." His finger slid to the dip between my clavicles and rested lightly on my pulse point.

My breathing quickened—I hadn't had sex in six months, and that was really starting to piss me off.

And Colin was a big, brave man who wrestled murderers and blasted shotguns and gushed testosterone like the *Titanic* had gushed seawater. Right now, though, he didn't have to do much to take me over the rainbow.

"You're thinkin' about it," he said. "Anything I can do to persuade you?"

Heat rippled off of me and off of him. Every inch of skin on my body waxed toward him, all of me wanting so badly to be touched and kissed. Biology. But I took a step back. "We have a long day tomorrow, *partner.*"

His face flushed and his hand dropped to his side. "Yep."

"And we'll forget this happened, yes?"

"Yep."

Colin and I stood there, in the Secret Pole Dance Studio parking lot, still contemplating it, knowing that it happened all the time between men and women on the police force, knowing that sex changed *everything*—for good but most times for bad, but, damn, in times like these . . .

He started toward his car. But then he stopped and turned back. "You think too damned much about things. Sometimes, humans just . . . *fuck*. That's what we do. Lollipops just bein' lollipops." He sighed, then saluted me. "Have a good one."

45

The Ritz-Carlton overlooked the marina, a floating parking lot for catamarans, sailboats, and small yachts. People gathered around the circular bar, leaned against the railing, or squeezed onto white divans separated by small, tabletop fire pits. The driving bass line of an old Lady Gaga song made the wooden floor planks vibrate.

Ben Oliver was still dressed in a suit but wore no tie. He had snagged a divan farthest from the crowd. It was loud, and we sat close, mouth to ear, to shout above the noise. *Hello, I'm fine, you look great, you look great, too.* I ordered sangria and he ordered single-malt Scotch. I warmed beneath his appreciative gaze but quickly launched into the cop act. "Let's get business out of the way," I said, tapping his knee. "And then we can find more interesting topics to discuss. Religion and politics, for example."

His eyes twinkled. "Or which is better: *Alien* or *Aliens?*"

I pointed at him. "Easy question. *Alien.* John Hurt, Ian Holm, Tom Skerritt, Sigourney Weaver, and Yaphet 'Cool Ass' Kotto." I shifted in my seat. "I flew to Vegas this afternoon. To talk with Melissa Kemper. She said lots of interesting things."

Ben considered the amber-colored liquid in his glass. "I'm sure she did."

"She told me to ask you about the paralegal."

His index finger rubbed the glass's rim.

I nudged him with my shoulder. "So who is the paralegal?"

He laughed, then shook his head. "The paralegal is unrelated to your investigation. And it happened a long time ago. It didn't mean anything."

"Never does."

Over in a corner, a couple groped each other in the dark. The man, silver-haired and wedding-banded, unhinged his jaw like an anaconda and bent to kiss the blond woman, sixty years his junior. She pushed him away and giggled.

I tore my eyes away from that couple and focused on Ben. "She also told me to ask you about Martha's Vineyard."

His head snapped back as though I had popped him in the nose. "What the *hell* is her problem?" He took a deep breath. "Every year, Christopher's family joins my family at our vacation home in Martha's Vineyard. Back in 2003, Melissa wanted to come, but I refused to invite her. You've spent time with her, so you know that she's loud, obnoxious, and a slob. But she and her son popped up anyway, and Juliet and Sarah were pissed. Of course, that time of year, the inns were all booked, and Melissa expected me to put her up in the house."

"Did you?"

"Hell no. Does that answer your question?"

There had to be more, but I gave a one-shouldered shrug anyway. "People have mentioned Mr. Chatman being sick, and I've been trying to confirm his condition. But our server's down at the station." I lied. "So no cybersleuthing for me at the moment."

He tossed the booze down his throat, then winced. "Technology is a fickle bitch."

"Indeed. When did his treatment start?"

"August."

"And *how* was he treated?"

"Surgery."

"Why Memorial Sloan Kettering?"

Ben sat his glass on the table. "He didn't want people to know he was sick, nor did he want the kids to worry. I offered to go with him, but he tends to go it alone."

Easier to live a lie that way.

"The guys at the firm were already being jerks," Ben continued, "and they smelled blood in the water. They started poaching his clients, and Christopher . . . Desperate times, desperate measures. And it backfired on him."

"That's an understatement," I muttered, uncertain of what he meant by "desperate times, desperate measures."

Ben smirked. "Securities fraud. A serious wobbler—hard to prove in court. He'll get a slap on the wrist, pay a fine, and then be sent home to write an essay on why his actions were bad."

The hair raised on the back of my neck. *Securities fraud?*

"Anyway," he continued, "I think he went to New York because he wanted to get away from all of that. Who knows? I've never had a life-threatening disease, nor have I had to fight to keep my job while being sick. I'm not gonna second-guess his thinking."

"Fair enough," I said, my mind still reeling from Ben's securities-fraud disclosure.

His finger poked the small of my back.

I smiled. "What was *that* for?"

He poked me again, slower this time.

I grabbed his finger. "Is that poke indicating business or pleasure?"

Our finger hold slipped into a handhold.

"That's where his tumor was," he said. "Only two centimeters, but it's cancer. You want that shit cut out of you. He thought about waiting until it got bigger, but I convinced him to get it over with. Told him that if he waited, he risked it spreading to his liver and lungs."

"So he flies back east and then . . . ?" I asked.

"He stays with a cousin who lives in the Bronx," Ben explained. "Two weeks later, he's back at home with a bloody bandage and stitches."

"Did you see his wound?"

Ben made a face and pulled his hand out of mine. "Of course I saw it. When Juliet wasn't around to change his dressing, I changed it. What kind of question was that?"

All feeling left my face—I was losing him. "I have to ask."

He crossed his arms. "Do you? *Really?*"

I took both of his hands in mine. "Relax before you pop a blood vessel."

"Are we close to the fun part of this visit?"

"It's the next exit. Did he return to work?"

He took in a long breath before he pulled away from me again. "Between the pain and the meds, he was out of it. But two weeks before the fire, he started going into the office a couple of times a week. He was scared that if he waited, he'd have no clients."

But according to Stacy the receptionist, Chatman wasn't allowed into his office.

I picked up my glass of sangria. "The securities-fraud investigation—"

"A mere formality," Ben said with a dismissive flick of his hand. "He did nothing wrong. But the powers that be can't *not* look into it."

"And who is this cousin living in the Bronx?" I asked, then sipped my drink.

Ben squinted at me. "My blood pressure skyrockets when we're together, you know that? You're suspicious of everything, of everyone."

I slipped my arm around his waist. "You forget: we aren't friends. Despite my charms and good looks, I am still conducting a murder investigation."

He pulled me closer to him. "I haven't forgotten, Detective Norton."

"He got sick," I said. "How did that affect Juliet?"

"She had been planning to leave him, but now she couldn't abandon him. That's what she told me. He needed her, and so she stayed."

"She confided in you a lot."

His hand brushed my hair from my face. "I keep everyone's secrets."

"That seems exhausting," I said, placing my hand atop his knee. "Did Mr. Chatman know that his wife wanted a divorce?"

Ben nodded. "I think we passed that exit two miles back."

"You're so eager to go off-roading," I whispered.

"An incredibly sexy woman is practically sitting in my lap."

"So tell me about Christopher's professorship at UNLV."

"His . . . *what*?"

"His professorship at UNLV."

He didn't speak, and his eyebrows furrowed.

"What about L.O.K.I. Consulting Services?" I dipped into my glass for a piece of nectarine, then offered it to him.

He snagged the fruit with his teeth and chewed. "Who are they? What do they do?"

I shrugged, then offered him more fruit. He took it, then watched me lick my sticky fingertips.

"You'll be wrong if you take this SEC angle," he said, his gaze on my lips. "Christopher's an ass, but he's not a thief. You haven't told me anything that would be grounds for MG Standard to deny his claim nor for you to charge him with something as horrendous as murdering his family."

"Arguing the case already?" I asked.

He rubbed my knee. "Well, *yeah*."

"You're gonna lose and I'm gonna win," I taunted.

"Oh, yeah?" His hand slipped up to my bare thigh.

"Yeah." I bit my lip, then said, "Guess where we are."

"Where I've wanted to be ever since we met."

"And now that we're here . . ." I pressed my breasts against his arm. "What do you want to talk about?"

He squeezed my thigh. "First, why are you sitting here with me and not with some hotshot cop? Or at home cuddling with a hotshot husband?"

"I don't do cops. And my husband . . . will soon be my *ex*-husband."

"I'm sorry about that." He lifted my hand and kissed it. "But only a little sorry."

My skin smoldered as his warm breath writhed up my wrist. "Why are you here, Benjamin Oliver? You hate cops. I'm a cop."

"Not happy at home."

"The standard reply."

"She checked out a long time ago. Started living a separate life. And now I find out about shit way after the fact. She doesn't want me to touch her, and she refuses to look at me. What am I supposed to do? Stop living?"

"Divorce."

He placed my palm across his cheek. "Can't do that."

"Why not? This is America, land of the free, home of the . . ." My free hand inched toward the danger zone—and from what I could tell, Ben's danger zone had a very wide range.

But his cell phone whistled from the inside of his jacket.

We froze, our faces less than an inch apart.

His phone whistled again.

I nuzzled my nose against his. "Special ringtone for a special someone."

He slowly moved away from me. "Sorry." He reached into his pocket and glanced at the text message in the phone's display. His body stiffened.

"Everything okay?" I asked.

"No. It's Sarah. Amelia's throwing up, and her blood pressure's too high. Damn."

"Sickle-cell anemia, right?"

"Yeah. I have to go to the emergency room. Sorry."

I waded back into shallow waters. "Don't apologize. Go be with your little girl. I hope she's okay."

He sighed. "I wish circumstances . . . I wish *everything* . . . were different."

"Me, too. Alas . . ." I shrugged.

"Alas . . ." He kissed my cheek.

I closed my eyes as his lips brushed against my earlobe.

"Good night, Elouise."

"Good night, Benjamin," I said, reclaiming my hands.

And I watched him weave through the crowd, uncertain now who was being played.

46

Greg was not home, and the house was cold and dark. I shivered—my hands and face were strangely cold—as I rushed from lamp to light switch, throwing light into the shadow. After punching up the thermostat to seventy-six degrees and hearing the *click-whoosh* of the heater, I returned to the dining room. Greg had stopped by—today's mail sat on the kitchen counter and the flip-flops he kept near the laundry-room door were gone.

I did not climb the dark staircase to my bedroom—that space now meant nothing and everything to me. With the house warmer now, I flopped onto the living room couch and grabbed a steno pad and pen from the coffee table to scribble down all that I had learned at the Ritz-Carlton.

Cancer treatment: *Something* had happened to Christopher Chatman's back. Ben had seen the wound and had tended to his friend's recovery. Dixie had mentioned Chatman's back problems and treatment at Orthopaedic Hospital. Had he undergone surgery and passed *that* wound off as tumor-related?

UNLV: Ben's silence had been strange, and his expression—clueless. Had Chatman kept that lie solely for Melissa Kemper?

And the biggest WTF moment: Christopher Chatman was being investigated for securities fraud. *That's* why Myron Meiselman over at Vandervelde, Lansing & Gray couldn't answer my questions—a federal investigation was taking place. But what had Chatman done exactly? And did it relate to that mysterious envelope of checks and deposit slips left beneath my desktop Christmas tree?

And would any of that lead Chatman to burn down his house and kill his family?

Ben didn't seem to think so, but then he was the man's best friend and wanted to think the best of him. Hell: no one wants to be homies with a sociopath.

"Ben Oliver," I said as my mind slipped through images of our evening.

Remembering made my head swirl. The kind of swirling you experience at county fairs—cones of cotton candy and corn dogs, rides on the Tilt-a-Whirl, the Charlie Daniels Band playing "Devil Went Down to Georgia" one more time. Giddy. Nauseated. Confused. Nauseated again. Screaming, "One more time!" for the band to play even though you hate country music, but today . . .

Because, wow. Banter? At the dinner table with Greg, we couldn't banter and we couldn't flirt, but just minutes ago I had bantered and flirted and touched with another man. And it was . . . *nice*. Benjamin Oliver, the married-jerk insurance attorney who was homies with a sociopath and probably a sociopath *himself*, had given me something I had not had in a very long time, sensations that I enjoyed and missed. *Craved*.

I had not sought Ben's attention—"faithful" had been my middle name and blood type for eleven years, and that fidelity had been discounted by the man I loved.

My face burned—remorse, anger, desire, and confusion all dumped into one pot.

Next door at Aiden's place, the stereo blasted Katy Perry. California girls *were* undeniable. A mile away, a helicopter *thump-thump-thumped* over the 405 freeway. Across the street at the park, a small jazz combo played "My Favorite Things."

I hummed a few bars, then spotted the bin of Christmas ornaments still near the tree.

I plucked off my snakeskin stilettos and wiggled my tortured toes. I padded to the laundry room, the bones in my toes clicking, and found yoga pants and a matching tank top in the dryer.

I unwrapped myself from the Diane von Furstenberg dress and pulled on the new set of clothes.

Don't you need to take off a few more things?

I considered my platinum engagement ring.

Greg had proposed to me during a gondola ride through the canals in Long Beach. The princess-cut diamond had cost the required two paychecks of someone who was not a low-level designer like Greg had been at the time.

I tugged off the ring, unclasped the cross necklace, and then placed both on the kitchen counter. My finger beveled where the ring had lived for so long.

Later, I would drop both the ring and pendant into my mahogany jewelry box, the one filled with honor society pins from junior high and high school, a 1984 Sam the Eagle Olympics pin, and my first pair of silver hoop earrings from Claire's. Talismans that had meant so much once upon a time.

I grabbed a remote control from the fireplace mantel, and with one push of a button Anita Baker's voice poured from the stereo. I lit the gingerbread candles, and soon the aromas of sugar and spices wafted from the melting wax.

"Icicle lights first," I said, lifting the top off the bin. And then the jewel-colored balls. No special ornaments this year, ornaments that had been chosen by Greg and me over our eleven years together. The Eiffel Tower from Paris. The red-lacquer temple from Japan. Mario and Luigi . . .

The telephone rang, and Caller ID announced, "*Out of area, Out of area.*"

I ignored the call as I continued to futz with strings of blue and white tree lights.

The phone kept ringing. "*Out of area, out of area.*"

I grabbed the receiver from the couch. "Hello?"

The caller didn't speak.

I aimed the remote control at the stereo, muting Anita Baker midnote. "Hello?"

In the background, espresso machines hissed and metal blades whirred.

"Greg?"

Just hissing and whirring.

Anger—at me for hoping that Greg was calling—flared in my chest, and I punched the END CALL button.

I tossed the phone on the couch and gaped at my Christmas tree: it was beautiful. Smiling broadly, I spread my arms wide and shouted, "*Fa, la, la, la, la.*"

And then I smelled it. Not gingerbread. Not melting wax. But burning wood and burning . . . something. Thick smoke. Nearby.

I stood still.

God frying bacon.

That's how Virginia Oliver had described that early-morning fire at the Chatman house.

And that's what I was hearing right now.

Fire.

At *my* house.

God frying bacon.

Damn.

She was right.

47

Somewhere on my property, a fire burned.

I bolted to the foyer and threw open the front door.

A thick curtain of black smoke bellowed from the south side of my house.

"Oh *shit*!" I raced back to the kitchen and grabbed the fire extinguisher from beneath the sink. I ran outside and toward the side of my house, the wet grass slick beneath my feet. I rounded the corner. The change in the air—hot, thick, burning—made me falter in my step.

Flames and black smoke had engulfed my side yard and now rolled up the side of my house and splashed into the sky.

My neighbor Ira slid open his second-story window. "What the hell's burning?"

"I don't know," I shouted back.

His wife stood behind him and cried, "Fire!"

Ira shouted, "Call 911."

Heart in my throat, I aimed the fire extinguisher at the base of the blaze.

Leaves and ashes shot into the air as water and foam tried to smother black smoke.

My lungs tightened as they filled with burning debris. Heat poured from the blaze and stung my eyes, pushing me back until I could only squint at the fiery blossom that refused to die.

A fire-engine siren wailed. Neighbors shouted over the murmur of televisions. The jazz band still played standards in the park.

"Move back, Lou," my neighbor Aiden commanded as he pulled me away.

Big men in yellow jackets pushed past me with a hose that blasted torrents of water.

"You okay?" Aiden asked me. His red face was flecked with ashes, and his gray eyes were bloodshot. "You okay?"

I nodded, even though, no, I was not okay.

"Greg here?"

"No." I scanned the crowd, searching for Greg's face, hoping that he had somehow heard the sirens.

Near the curbside, I found one face not like the others. One face that didn't belong.

And the face that didn't belong, the one looking at the fire with a camera phone, noticed my staring at him, and his smile dropped. He glanced at the fire, then glanced back at me—he was making a choice. He took a step back.

I took a step forward.

He took two steps back.

I took another step forward.

He blinked, swallowed . . . *Bam!* He sprinted west.

I tore after him, barefooted and without a gun.

He jammed up Bluff Creek Drive, then darted left to cut through Aiden's side yard.

I ran in the same direction, anger fueling my speed.

He hopped over the short perimeter fence, but the cuff of his cargo shorts caught. He stumbled and slid down the slope.

I swung my legs over the fence and dove after him.

Together, we tumbled through sharp twigs and bark and dropped to the sidewalk.

He tried to stand while swinging his fist.

I tried to duck—too slow.

His knuckles glanced my left cheekbone.

I saw stars but recovered to strike him in the face with a single palm-heel hit.

He grabbed his nose and crumpled back onto the sidewalk.

"What the hell is wrong with you?" I shouted at him. "Why did you run from me?"

Eli Moss growled at me as blood from his nostrils gushed between his fingers.

"Answer me," I said, raising my hand again, "before I beat your fucking face—"

Someone caught my fist before it met Moss's nose.

"Relax, Lou," Aiden yelled, breathing hard, clenching my fist. "It's okay."

I tried to pull free from the muscled man, but his grip held me like a vise.

Aiden nodded but tightened his grip. "It's okay."

Seven minutes later, Eli Moss, restrained by handcuffs, was shoved into the backseat of a police cruiser.

I glimpsed down at my bloody feet—from Moss's nose and from sharp twigs and rock. Pain zigzagged from the bottom of my body to the top. I clenched to will it away.

No good.

My knees buckled, and I sank to the wet grass.

A damp breeze from the ocean washed over me, and I lay there, too calm, too cold.

This was all a dream.

I closed my eyes against the swirling blue and red lights of cop cars and fire trucks, closed my eyes and waited to burst through vivid slumber into the waking world.

48

Friday nights at the Pacific Division were no different than Friday nights at Southwest. Drunks, wife beaters, gangbangers, babymommas with toddlers on hips and pink bail slips in free hands, terrified high school kids huddled on benches as they waited for their parents to arrive. And tonight, an arsonist.

Through the one-way glass, I watched Adonis Thistle, the stocky black detective from the Arson Unit, interrogate Eli Moss.

Greg placed a pair of socks and sneakers at my feet, then stepped back to the doorway.

I winced while slipping on the anklets and the shoes. Other than a tender cheek, a fiery headache, and cut-up feet, I felt like crap dunked in bile and blood, then twisted dry—and then frozen, thawed, and reheated, but only halfway.

"Why were you at Detective Norton's home this evening?" Thistle demanded as he leaned forward with his knuckles on the metal table.

Eli Moss, swollen-nosed and red-faced, shouted, "That *bitch* hit me."

"I should go in there and beat him down," Greg mumbled.

I killed my third bottle of water and kept my eyes on the scene in the box.

"Why did you have a bag of leaves in the back of your SUV?" Thistle asked.

Moss crossed his arms, then tucked his chin into his chest. "Why was I assaulted by a cop?"

"Why were there candles, lighters, and kerosene in the back of your SUV? Why were you recording the fire?"

"This is America," Moss shouted back. "I can carry whatever the fuck I want in the back of my SUV and record whatever the fuck I wanna record."

Thistle banged his palm on the table.

Moss jumped in his seat, his bruised face darkening even more. "I don't even know what this is about. I don't even know why I'm here. She chased me down like a dog, then assaulted me for no reason."

Thistle gaped at him. "You kiddin' me with that bullshit, ain't you?"

"I have no idea what you're talking about. You don't, either."

"I know that you swung at her first—there were people on the scene who will testify to that." Thistle pointed at him with a crooked finger. "It's over, son. You fucked up real good, you know that? Tryin' to burn down a cop's house? *That's* what this is about."

Moss found interest in his scraped knuckles. But his jiggling knee betrayed his feigned indifference.

"He's not gonna talk," Greg declared. "He's gonna just sit there and ask for a lawyer, who'll say that his client was gardening and the candles belong to his wife, and the cop beat him down for no good reason, and he's gonna sue us for everything we got."

Dread filled my gut as I considered Greg's prediction.

"Lou," Greg whispered. "Baby."

I grunted: I knew that "Lou" and I knew that "Baby"—apple pie, testosterone, and silver mulled into a salve.

He poured it on every time he wanted to be forgiven.

I glanced at him. "Not now, Gregory."

He sighed: he knew that "Gregory"—razor blades, arsenic, and lemons.

Sammy Khan, Thistle's partner, joined us. "So he the one who started the Chatman house fire, too?"

Greg gawked at Khan. "The Chatman . . . ?" Then, he gawked at me. "That *asshole* in there is connected to one of your *cases*?"

I started to speak, but my tongue lay in my mouth like a stomped-on slug.

Sammy Khan took a step back. "Maybe I should let you two—"

"Your *job* almost burned down my house and got you killed?" Greg bellowed.

I crossed my arms. "You don't need an excuse anymore, remember?"

Greg gaped at me, and then his shoulders slumped. He peered at the ceiling and chuckled. "You're right. I don't. I'm out of here."

I waved my hand at the door. "Be out, then." I turned my back to him and directed my gaze to Detective Thistle and Eli Moss.

Greg stomped to the exit.

My chest tightened, and something there expanded, tightened, and then—*pop*.

Heartbreak. Again.

Saturday, December 15

49

At almost three o'clock on a Saturday morning, I should have been home hitting another round of REM sleep. But I didn't want to go home, not after the fire, not after the fight—with Greg and with Eli Moss. Going home meant seeing ribbons of yellow police tape blocking off my destroyed yard. Going home meant smelling ashes and wet earth and the exhaust of fire trucks and firemen. So I asked Adonis Thistle to drive me to my station seven miles away.

Two miles in, he looked over to me. "Want me to turn back so you can kick Moss's ass some more?"

I zipped up my jacket with an aching hand and muttered, "No. I'm . . ." I could barely form words now—my face had stiffened from the arsonist's punch.

In my mind, I saw Eli Moss sitting in the interview room, blood-pressure cuff around his right arm and pneumographs on his chest. I saw Officer Lipsky peering at his laptop, then asking Moss question after question.

Do you intend to answer the polygraph questions truthfully?

Did you participate in any way in causing the death of Juliet Chatman?

Do you know who caused the death of Chloe Chatman?

Did you start the fire at the Chatman house?

Then, Lipsky had left Moss in the box to tell me that the suspect had passed the exam. "He's an arsonist, but right now he ain't lookin' like a murderer."

I had crossed my arms—I didn't believe that Moss needed to be dismissed so quickly. He had set the other fires around the neighborhood, and he had filmed the Chatman house fire. Of course he would come after me and burn down my house—I was investigating the murders of three people *he* had killed.

And polygraphs? Not hard science. Unreliable. Inadmissible in court. Usually.

Moss had also claimed to have an alibi. At work at the airport. Hell, *everybody's* at work when they burn shit down and kill people.

Before leaving Pacific, Sammy Khan had patted my shoulder. "We'll check out his alibi, Lou. Do some more digging around. We ain't lettin' this go, all right? If he has anything to do with the Chatman fire, we'll let you know ASAP."

Now, Thistle pulled up to the front of Southwest Division, then touched my arm. "We protect our own—you know we're gonna get that bastard. Don't worry 'bout that."

I gave him a weak but grateful smile. "I've always told myself: if my house ever burns down, I want Adonis Thistle to work it."

"Bullshit."

"The truth."

"And if truth was a whore," he said, "I'd buy her a drink and ask her where the hell she's been all my life."

The lobby was unusually quiet for an early Saturday morning. Swope, the pasty-faced desk sergeant, gawked at me—first, for limping through the glass doors at that time of night, and second, for, well . . . my face. "You get run over by a Sherman tank?"

"Thought I'd switch up my look this evening," I said, limping past him.

"You need one of them spa days you chicks like. Bathe in the mud and put them zucchinis on your eyes. And a sirloin on your cheek."

"*Cucumbers* go on your eyes." I stopped at the elevator. "Anything going on?"

He shook his head. "Pretty quiet up there. No one got dead tonight. But then we got four hours to go. Plenty of time to ruin a pleasant evening with some ass-clown totin' an Uzi."

There was no one in the women's locker room. I pulled jeans and an LAPD T-shirt from my gym bag, then stood beneath the jets of shower water as pounds of blood, dirt, and anxiety washed off my body and into the drain. After toweling off, I dabbed Neosporin over every cut place. Clean and feeling lighter inside and out, I retreated to the squad room and to my desk and to the growing stacks of reports, photographs, and diagrams—all connected to the Chatman case. Only two dicks worked the phones, and as I trudged past them, neither looked away from their own oceans of case-work.

I collapsed into my chair, my mind empty and full at the same time.

By now, Colin was probably spooning with Dakota. The same with Pepe and his rocket scientist. And Luke—he was either sleeping next to Lupita or next to one of his badge bunnies. And here I was, fresh from my attempt to have a "personal life," with tonight's adventures featuring pink drinks, pole dancing, insurance attorneys, fights with husbands and arsonists, and declarations of divorce.

Viewer discretion advised. Do not attempt this at home.

I studied Colin's and my handwriting on the whiteboard propped on the file cabinet.

COUSIN FOR RECOVERY SARCOMA—MSK / PROFESSOR—UNLV / CH FIRM—DOES HE STILL WORK THERE? / KEMPER $$$ JULIET—DIVORCE / CANCER, SUICIDE—BELLAGIO / SIGNIFICANCE OF VLG CHKS???

Then, I added, SECURITIES FRAUD (!!), 2 CM TUMOR.

"What am I missing?" I whispered. *These are all trees. I need the forest. Now.*

I grabbed the murder book from Colin's desk, hoping that the quiet of the squad room would help me see something in the report, something in the statements and pictures I had studied since catching the case back on Tuesday. The fifth day of this investigation, and I had learned about a not-mistress and bad loans and Valium. But who set the fire? Without hard (or even medium-well) evidence that Chatman had started the blaze, directly or indirectly, I only had a liar and a thief. But not a murderer.

Eli Moss—he was a professional liar and a serial pyro. He had attempted to destroy my house. But he had passed the murder parts of his lie-detector test. He was at work the night of the Chatman fire. Of course he was.

So what?

Maybe Moss had passed the murder parts of the poly because *maybe* he had not truly and sincerely intended to kill the Chatmans. Just . . . burn down their house. *Maybe?*

Nothing was certain in this case—not even "up is down" and "down is up." With the Chatman case, "up" was "strawberry," and "down" was "washing machine."

I ran my tongue across the inside of my cut lip, then closed the big binder. My eyes found those words again on the whiteboard. Suicide, cancer . . . And then it overpowered me—exhaustion, and lots of it. Even as I started to snore and drift off to sleep, the Chatman case kept at me. At first, a mosquito's quiet buzz, but then a beehive on steroids. But the buzzing softened . . . shushed . . . *ssh* . . .

"L.T. brought donuts!"

Colin's voice pulled me from sleep.

Where am I?

My body creaked as I lifted my head off the desk.

At work. Still.

Pepe ambled toward my cubicle. "Hey, Lou! You better—" His eyes swept over me. "What the *hell?*"

Colin and Luke, standing at the coffeepot, heard Pepe's half question and turned in our direction.

Luke said, "Oh *shit*."

Colin rushed over to me, anger sparking off of him, his face the color of cranberries and grape jam. "Did Greg—?"

"No," I said, holding up my hand.

"You said you two were fighting."

"Colin," I said. "Relax."

He crouched before me. "You protectin' that son of a bitch?"

"Last night," I said, "Eli Moss thought he was Tyson and I was Givens."

"Moss?" Luke asked. "The white guy who lives across the street from the Chatmans?"

I nodded, then launched into the story about the beautiful young detective decorating her Christmas tree, then discovering that her house was on fire. She had brawled in the streets with the Burning Man, who had passed his polygraph test and had provided an unconfirmed alibi that took him out of the running for starting the fatal Chatman house fire.

"But you don't believe that," Colin said.

I shook my head, then shrugged.

"But why did he target you?" Luke asked.

"Because she's investigating the Chatman case," Pepe said.

"If Moss didn't burn down the Chatman house and if he didn't kill them,"

I said, "why would he care what *I* did? Why me?" I touched my swollen, tender cheek. "I look like a piece of shit now. Just like you guys, but with better . . . everything."

Pepe and Luke tried to laugh. Colin's hands tightened into fists.

"Luke," I said, "can you and Pep check on warrants we have out with Judge Keener?"

"No problem." He and Pepe wandered back to the box of donuts.

Colin came out of his crouch to tower over me. "Why didn't you call me?"

"It was late, and I had already—"

"Sent me away?"

"It's not your job to take care of me."

"Where was your husband?"

"I wouldn't let him take care of me, either. And nowadays he's the kind of caretaker that puts you in a playpen, scatters a few Cheerios on the cushions, and turns the TV on before he leaves. And I hate Cheerios."

"Not funny," he grumbled.

I nudged his calf with my foot. "I'm sorry, Colin. Next time an arsonist tries to burn down my house and beat me up, I'll text you. Then you can watch me kick his ass in person."

Colin tried to smile, but only one side of his mouth lifted. He took a deep breath and then slowly exhaled. "Can I do anything for you now?"

"You can get me something better than that swill over there." I pointed to the goop bubbling in the coffeepot.

"Sure. Be right back."

I watched him leave the room.

And the world righted itself.

But then my desk phone rang.

"Yo, yo, Lou Norton." It was Gus Lebo from Vegas Homicide.

"What's up, my friend?" I asked, smiling.

"Any other time, I would describe to you in explicit detail what is indeed up whenever I call."

"But not today," I said. "Cuz something or somebody has jacked up your vibe."

"Melissa Kemper."

"Delightful lady. Likes little dogs and other people's husbands."

"Well, other people ain't gotta worry about her and their husbands no more."

According to Gus, at 9:04 A.M. that morning, a truck driver, Earl Littleton, had lost control of his rig (one of those trucks that advertise strip joints) and plowed into the backs and fronts of three cars. Including the late-model Jag driven by Melissa Kemper.

"Had to use the spreaders and rams to get folks out," Gus Lebo said. "I'm sending you some pics of the scene."

"She dead?" I whispered.

"Elvis is more alive than she is."

Six JPEGs popped into my mailbox: Melissa Kemper on the Clark County coroner's steel table, her glazed, green eyes fixed, her purple running shorts and Paramount Studios T-shirt dark with drying blood.

"Oh shit," I said, feeling a quick lick of nausea in my gut.

"When you talked to her, was she helpful at all?"

"Yeah," I said, closing the last picture. "She confirmed that my suspect is a big, fat liar and all-around jerk-wad." After I gave him the Twitter version of my interview with Melissa Kemper, I sat back in my chair and said, "Wow. Didn't see *this* coming."

"If I wasn't such a cynic," he said, "and this wasn't Vegas, I'd say that some type of fuckery is goin' on. But . . ."

I heard the shrug in his voice. "Alas . . ."

"Where's the husband?" Gus asked.

"Her ex-husband or my dead vic's husband?"

"Dead vic's."

"I could say that he's here in Los Angeles." I regarded the whiteboard full of lies. "But I wouldn't put five on it."

Damn.

Melissa Kemper. Dead.

I knew the world couldn't stay right.

50

The Southwest Division's forensic-tech department, located in the darkest corner of the second floor, consisted of one large cubicle that sat four. Only one member of the team had clocked in today. His momma called him Neil, but we called him Bang-Bang because that's all he did every day—go *bang-bang* on computer keyboards. Neil was a John Smith–looking white guy with nothing offensive or interesting about his appearance, especially now that he'd had the mole on his cheek removed. He was sipping a glass of water as numbers and letters scrolled across his computer screen.

"Bang-Bang, you're here." I switched the heavy Chatman case file to my other arm.

He rolled his eyes, pretending that he hated his nickname. "Hello."

Just like that. Hello.

No mention of my bruised face.

No inquiry about my mental state.

Just "hello," in a tone that had less spice than vanilla and egg whites.

I pointed at the Chatmans' scorched laptop sitting on the desk. "I'm here about that—you were helping me cuz there were all those crazy passwords and minefields and cosmic dust and shit keeping me from getting a look-see and such."

"Yes." He sat down his water glass. "Fire and water damaged a few things, but it's up for the most part. We can look at the CPU on my screen for a better view." He pulled over an empty chair. "Where do you want to start?"

"How about his search history. Cookies and browsers and search terms, oh my."

Neil clicked here and there in the Firefox browser. "The most recent searches."

Fraud, sentencing, extradition, Bernie Madoff, Vandervelde Lansing, ischemia, suffocation, sarcoma, DNA paternity.

"How recent?" I asked.

"Last one—*extradition*—on December tenth."

"Just a few days ago. The Monday before the fire." I tapped the pen against my lip. None of the terms related to fire deaths. Maybe "suffocation." And "ischemia"? That came from constricting blood vessels, like suffocation. Juliet and the kids hadn't died that way. And what the hell was up with "DNA paternity"? "Click on that one, please," I asked Neil.

A fussily designed Web page loaded on the screen. The DNA Doctors. A pretty woman peered into a microscope. A dad smiled with a girl—guess he *was* the father. A toll-free number and a page of FAQs.

Why would Chatman visit this site?

I wrote down the DNA Doctor's contact information. "Let's look at e-mail," I instructed Neil. "The Gmail in-box here would show any e-mails he's sent from his phone, right?"

"Yes, it would."

Chatman's in-box appeared on Neil's screen. His last e-mail string, created just yesterday, had been between him and Adeline St. Lawrence, Juliet's best friend.

> *Hey, Addy. Just checking in on you to see if you're okay. I know this is rough— we have to stick together no matter what, for Juliet's sake. We have to preserve her memory and protect her honor throughout everything that's about to happen. People are asking a lot of questions and I just want to talk to you about that. Hang in there. CC.*

Six minutes later, Adeline had responded.

> *HOW DARE YOU EMAIL ME!!! YOU DID THIS TO HER! YOU TOLD HER THAT YOU WOULD GET HER BACK! IT TOOK YOU NINE YEARS BUT I GUESS YOU KEPT YOUR PROMISE. HER HONOR??? YOU ARE THE ONE WHO IS ASHAMED! YOU ARE THE ONE WHO REFUSED TO MOVE PAST HER MISTAKE! YOU ARE SELFISH AND HATEFUL AND AFTER THE STATE OF CALIFORNIA FRIES YOU, I HOPE YOU BURN IN HELL FOREVER!! FUCK YOU!!!*

Neil's face twitched and reddened. "She's a little angry."

"They're not friends," I said.

Hours after his e-mail to St. Lawrence, Chatman had e-mailed Randall and Maris Weatherbee, Juliet's parents.

Hi, Mother and Dad. Thank you for coming to see me today. Please under-stand that my lawyer has told me not to talk about all that's happening, not even with you, and that breaks my heart. You are the only family I have and I feel so alone now. I know you have so many questions. They will be answered soon. I am not avoiding you and I don't understand why you are accusing me of that. My phone was misplaced in all of the madness, and the landline at the house is down, of course. I have not hurt anyone, like you are accusing me of doing, and I would never harm my wife and children. The investigation at my job has NOTHING to do with ANYTHING. Please don't let strangers influence you. I am constantly being bombarded by the police and I haven't had time to grieve. I pray for your love and patience.

"Do me a favor?" I asked Neil. "Give this a good scouring. Pull instant messages, e-mails, financial transactions, folder names, log-ins—everything. Basically, kill a tree."

"Found you." Colin held a Coffee Bean & Tea Leaf coffee cup in one hand and a file folder in the other.

I took the cup. "We're looking through Chatman's laptop. First, though . . ." I caught him up on my call from Vegas and Melissa Kemper's demise.

He gaped at me.

I said, "Yep," then pointed at the folder in his hand. "What you got?"

He pulled from the larger case file those check copies for Peggy Tanner, Sol Hirsch, and another client named Bill Levy. He placed the checks next to each other, endorsement side up. "Look at the signatures."

I looked. "Wait. That." I pointed to the *l* in Sol. "That looks like those." I pointed to the two *l*s in Bill. "And the *y* in Peggy," I said, "looks like the *y* in Levy."

"Uh-huh." He sat at an empty workstation, then logged in to public rec-ords. "Okay, there are 513 Peggy Tanners in the database, with 110 in California, five in LA, and one in San Fernando Valley."

"Let's try the Peggy in the valley." I pointed to Neil's desk phone. "May we?"

Neil's eyes glittered—he was in on the action. "Please."

A woman answered, and she sounded as old as the creaking branches of a hundred-year-old oak tree.

I identified myself as an LAPD detective. "May I ask you a few questions?"

She confirmed that she was Peggy Tanner, that she had an account with Vandervelde, Lansing & Gray, and that, yes, Christopher Chatman was her broker.

"Have you asked Mr. Chatman about your account recently?" I asked.

"No," she said, "but he sends me statements every quarter."

"When was the last statement you received?"

"October, I believe."

"Any check come with that?"

"Afraid not. The economy is just terrible right now."

"Has your experience with the firm been satisfactory?"

"He can be hard to reach sometimes, but overall yes. He's a lovely man. Just hope he makes me some money soon," she said with a chuckle.

Sol Hirsch sounded older than Peggy Tanner—the oak tree's pappy. Almost deaf, he shouted the similar responses—Chatman was a nice man, he sent quarterly statements, was hard to reach, no return on investment—gosh darn that Obama.

Just last week, Bill Levy had been placed in hospice and was unable to communicate. Another stroke. His son, Bill Junior, had seen no recent checks in the mail from Christopher Chatman or the commodities firm.

"They're all seniors," Neil noted. "And no one's been paid out yet."

I tapped the checks. "But those say Tanner got just over ten thousand dollars, and Hirsch got almost eight grand just months ago. Let's add up all three check amounts."

Neil blinked and scribbled on his pad: $26,901.37.

I narrowed my eyes. "I remember seeing deposit slips from Pacific Western . . . Oh." The bank boxes stolen from the storage unit—that's where I'd seen deposit slips.

"Still," Colin said, "I think you're right. He stole their money. Twice. The initial investment he took from them, and then the money he made in the market and kept for himself. Money his clients are still waiting for."

"Hence, the SEC investigation," I said, nodding.

"*Extradition, fraud, sentencing,*" Neil said. "Those were his last search terms, remember?"

Colin squinted at me. "That's great for the feds, but what about us? How does this prove he had something to do with the fire?"

I swallowed my smile and gathered the file. "Can't say. But I'm gonna have to force Mr. Chatman to get off the ride."

51

The polite bird in me thought of calling Christopher Chatman and requesting time to speak with him again. The rude-bitch cop in me, the one who hated liars, cheaters, and murderers, said, "Screw that. Catch his ass off guard."

"Door number two," Colin hollered from his desk, two fingers in the air.

I grabbed my bag and the case file. "Two it is." I paused, then said, "We'll have to be very careful with him."

"He poisonous or something?" Colin kidded.

"No. He's . . . he's too . . . *something*." I shrugged. "Just don't wander off the path with him, okay? We'll find ourselves in Oz with the Cheshire Cat and the Jolly Green Giant."

Colin waved a hand. "Stop bein' a girl. We've handled worse."

In this city, there were always villains to chase. And some villains were more perverted and obvious than the others. But those bad guys, the obvious ones, didn't scare me.

The quiet ones, the secret sorcerers, the ones who whisked you away to no-man's-land and beyond doing twisted shit to minds and bodies and souls en route. And you, the cop with the commendations and the impressive clearance rate and the stainless-steel reputation, if you were lucky enough to find your way back from no-man's-land and beyond, you were not whole and not good for anything, especially anything requiring a gun, and so you became the cautionary tale, the "Did you hear what happened to . . . ?" in the department.

I had been a cop for thirteen years—that cop would not be me. I would not be the captured or the conquered.

Not over my dead body.

. . .

Christopher Chatman's already-googly eyes googled more seeing Colin and me standing on the cottage's front porch. He looked fuller in his tracksuit than he had just two days ago. The bandages on his face and the back of his head had been peeled away, and his scratches had lightened. The arm sling remained, but the gauze on his hands had been replaced by lesser bandages. He smelled of soap and freshly ground coffee beans.

Just another banker on a regular Saturday morn.

"Did Eli do that to you?" he inquired, although my injuries didn't surprise him as much as my standing in front of him without warning.

"So you heard?" I asked.

He nodded. "And I also heard that he passed the lie-detector test for murdering my family."

"Correct," I said.

Chatman placed his hand on his hip. "Surely you don't believe that Eli's *innocent*. Surely you're not relying on his *word*."

I forced myself to smile. "So we were in the neighborhood, and we need to talk to you about some recent developments."

Chatman stepped forward, closing the door behind him. "I was just about to take a walk around the block—tired of being inside, and I need vitamin D. The party tents are gone—mind if we sit in the backyard?"

Colin and I followed him to a patio that boasted rattan couches and chairs with lime-green cushions, glass side tables, and a bamboo area rug. All of it overlooked a blue and white mosaic-tiled pool, a redwood jungle gym, and a lush green lawn bordered by rosebushes.

"Nice out here," Colin drawled as he slipped on his aviators and plopped onto the couch.

"Very peaceful," I added, sitting next to him. "Are the Olivers home?"

"They're at the hospital," Chatman said. "Amelia's sick. They've been there all night."

"Hope she's okay," I said.

"She's much better—well enough that Sarah came home to shower, then headed back."

"Oh, I thought I saw her car."

"They're using Ben's," Chatman clarified. "He stayed with Amelia— hasn't left her side since getting there. He'd been at some important meeting last night when Sarah called. He came right away—he's incredibly devoted to that little girl. She will always come first."

My face burned, and at the moment I was glad to be a darker hue.

"What's on your minds, Detectives?" Chatman asked.

"Melissa Kemper," I said.

Chatman offered us a sad smile. "You're aware . . . ?"

"Of?" I asked.

"The accident." He jammed his lips together and took a deep breath. "She's . . . she . . ." He shook his head, then closed his eyes. "Too much is happening. Everyone who matters to me is dying."

"Guess you have that effect on people," Colin cracked.

Chatman frowned. "You really think this is funny? One of my dearest friends is now gone because of some jackass in a big rig, and you feel it necessary to make a *joke?*"

Colin smirked. "So you *don't* have that effect—?"

"We had an extensive conversation with Melissa yesterday," I interrupted.

Chatman didn't blink. "Oh?"

"Oh?" Colin parroted. "That's all you have to say?"

Chatman cocked his head as a smile crept across his face. "Am I under arrest because I contemplated having an affair? Is there an almost-adultery statute in California's penal code that I don't know about?"

Asshole. I gritted my teeth and exhaled through my nose.

"She told us a lot before that truck rammed into her," Colin said. "Like how you tried to kill yourself after Juliet rejected you."

Chatman startled but quickly recovered with a chuckle. "Stupid, right? Detective Taggert, I'm sure you've done absurd things in the name of love. Men do those sorts of things."

"Tell us what happened that night at the Bellagio," Colin said, ignoring the bro moment.

Chatman's Adam's apple bobbed in his throat. "Private medical matter, and no how related to this case."

"Tell us anyway," I said. "Please."

Chatman released a heavy sigh. "I recalled my Shakespeare that night. On hotel stationery, I wrote to my wife, 'Darling, my love for you shall never die. Before I shuffle off this mortal coil—"

"*Hamlet,*" I said.

"Yes," he said. "I felt . . . dramatic. My marriage was essentially over, and there I was, alone in my room, alone with my thoughts. Years ago, my wife had cheated on me, and *now* Melissa hated me because I was still in love with my wife. I couldn't handle it anymore."

"Who had Juliet been with?" Colin asked.

"Doesn't matter."

"This other man, though. He could be a suspect," Colin pointed out.

"You already have the killer in custody," Chatman said. "Eli Moss: he murdered my family."

"Strange," Colin said. "Both women resented you, and now both women are dead. And you say you were nowhere near them at the times of their deaths. That's quite a magic trick."

Chatman's eyes flashed with anger. "Are you seriously accusing—?"

"So the night at the Bellagio," I said, "you wrote the note, and then?"

Chatman glared at Colin, then lifted his face to the sun. "I went to the sundries store in the hotel lobby. Bought some Advil and a bottle of raspberry-flavored vodka. Returned to the room and set about killing myself. Obviously, I'm awful at suicide."

From the corner of my eye, I glimpsed a flutter from the gauzy white curtain in the guesthouse's living room window.

Maybe.

"Mr. Chatman," I said, eyes on the window, "are we alone back here?"

"Of course. Why?"

"I thought I . . ." I shook my head. "So did you tell Juliet what you had done?"

"I told her that I had a bout of food poisoning from the buffet," Chatman explained. "I told her that I stayed overnight at the hospital but that I was better—no need to worry."

I squinted at him. "But why lie? Juliet didn't have to know that you had taken pills. The hospital wouldn't have called her if you didn't want them to. Why did you feel the need to make up a story like that?"

Chatman gaped at me as though I had just asked him a question in Klingon.

"And you never confessed to Juliet about Melissa?" Colin asked.

The banker touched his forehead. "Why would I do that? Melissa and I never happened in *that* way. Why would I destroy my marriage and break up my family over . . . nothing?"

"Melissa Kemper gave you a hundred thousand dollars," I pointed out.

288 | RACHEL HOWZELL HALL

"Yes." He gazed at a ladybug that had landed on his thigh. The vein in the middle of his forehead banged beneath the skin. "And I invested that money. Cows."

"She needed it more than the cows did," Colin said. "Plumbing."

"And I'll make sure her son gets everything I owed her." He flicked the ladybug off his leg, then ran his fingers across his scalp. "It's the least I can do."

"Now," I said, "about your cancer diagnosis and treatment at Memorial—"

Chatman cocked his head. "I've never told you that I had cancer."

"Ben and Melissa Kemper both—"

"I've had back problems that required surgery. And I was prescribed Vicodin for the pain." He scrunched his eyebrows. "Is that what you're asking about?"

"According to Ben," I said, "you were treated at Memorial Sloan Kettering for sarcoma in your back. And during your treatment, you stayed with a cousin in New York."

"I had *a* surgery," he corrected, "but not at Memorial Sloan Kettering and not in New York. And my cousin who lives in the Bronx *works* at that hospital." He offered a small smile. "Wouldn't a cancer diagnosis be in my medical and insurance records? Don't you homicide detectives know all and see all?"

I took a deep breath. "Have you received your family's autopsy reports?"

He swallowed. "I'm not ready to read them. Who would want to read about his kids' . . . ? I'm not ready."

"Are you at least aware of your wife's condition?" I asked.

He frowned. "What condition?"

"She had ovarian cancer," Colin said. "Terminal. She was dying."

The banker paled, all smirk and smart-ass gone the way of the dodo.

"You didn't know," Colin said.

Chatman's dark brown eyes hardened.

"Do you need a moment?" I asked.

"I'm fine," he spat. "You're making this investigation longer and more painful than it needs to be. My son . . . Chloe, they're *dead*. Someone ended their lives, and I'll never see them again. No more soccer games or X Games or . . . or . . ." His eyes filled with tears, and he scowled at us. "But then that's what you people do, correct? The insurance companies, too. You all bullshit around until the person dies from their disease or the survivor shoots himself in the head. You don't care—not about my wife, not about my *son*. You just want to thin the herd. And you sit here judging *me*. Excuse the metaphor, but that's like Hitler judging pedophiles."

"I understand why you're upset," Colin said, unable to control his smile. "If you had waited just four or five more months, you wouldn't have had to kill your wife. She would've died on her own. And your kids—I don't know why you—"

"How the *hell* could I kill my family in a fire," Chatman growled, "when I was forty miles away—?"

"About what you do at that office forty miles away." I pulled the mystery envelope from the expandable file and plucked out the Peggy Tanner check copy. "You recognize this name?"

Chatman blanched as he reached for the copy.

I let him look for ten seconds before grabbing it and slipping it back into the envelope.

"Where did you get that?" he demanded.

"Why is this check important?" I asked.

He didn't speak as he stared at the case file.

"If I were to call Ms. Tanner about her account with your firm," I said, "what would she tell me?"

Chatman squared his shoulders. "She'd tell you that I've made her a shitload of money."

"A shitload," I said. "That's, like, a lot, right? Another question: how did you spend your inheritance?"

"My . . . ? Are you referring to—?"

"The millions you inherited once your parents died." I lifted an eyebrow. "It may not be a lot of money to you, but to us poor folk raised on Top Ramen and hamburger . . . Three million in ten years. How did you do it?"

He cocked his head. "You've become acquainted with my wife since her death. She spent it trying to be people we weren't."

"So it's her fault," I said.

"I'd do anything to keep her happy. She and the kids mattered more to me than our budget."

"Okeydokey," I said. "Why haven't you let us take your DNA sample?"

"I'm not canceling my doctors' appointments just to convenience the LAPD," Chatman explained. "You said that you all would work around *my* schedule, not vice versa."

"When is the best time, then?" Colin asked. "You give us a date. Hell, we can do it right now. I got a kit in the car. A swipe here, a swipe there, and we're done."

Spit gathered at the corners of Chatman's mouth, ready to be swabbed and analyzed. "I'll look at my schedule."

"What do you do all day anyway?" Colin asked.

"I don't understand what you're asking me," the banker said.

"You visited the botanical gardens on the day before your family was killed," Colin said. "You go there often in the middle of the day?"

"I do."

"Why?" Colin asked. "Especially on *that* day? Shit gettin' you down at . . . *work*?"

The widower glared at him but didn't answer. He turned his attention to me. "Have any more questions for me, Elouise?"

"You callin' this veteran detective by her first name now?" Colin asked. "You two close like that?"

"*Detective Norton*," Chatman said, slower, "do you have anything else?"

"Yes, I do," I said. "Your wife made a 911 call the morning of the fire."

Chatman paled. "She did?"

"In it, she says something about someone trying to kill her. Who do you think—?"

"I did not kill my wife," he shouted. "I did not kill my family."

"What was she scared of?" I asked, refusing to shout. "*Who* was she scared of?"

He took a breath, then slowly released it. Calmer now, he said, "They had nothing to fear."

"Juliet bought a gun," I countered. "She had packed the kids up and filled the Benz's gas tank."

He opened his mouth to respond, then closed it.

I continued. "She had that gun with her when she and your daughter were trapped in your bedroom. Chloe died in her arms."

Chatman remained silent.

"No comment?" I asked.

We sat there, our eyes locked on each other. Finally, he said, "Any other questions?"

"Not at the moment."

"Am I free to go?"

"Certainly," Colin said.

He stood and scowled at us. "Then I will end this interview. I have my family's autopsy reports to read, since you so politely and delicately told me that my wife was dying from a horrible disease."

Chatman started toward the cottage but whirled back to face us. "When all of this is over, I'm having a long conversation with a friend of mine who works for the *Los Angeles Times*. Then, I'll ring up a friend who works for the mayor. So let me congratulate you now—your names will soon be in print. If you're lucky, you'll get to work as security guards at IHOP." Then, he stomped to the guesthouse, opened the door, and slammed it.

The sound echoed, and for a moment even the birds had been stunned into silence.

Colin stretched and yawned. "He forgot to validate our parking ticket."

I gathered my bag and stood from the couch. "I actually *like* IHOP. The Rooty Tooty Fresh 'N Fruity? Dude, that's art."

We started to the stone walkway, and I threw a last glance at the cottage and its ivy-covered walls.

That curtain *had* moved. I *know* it had.

So who moved it?

And who was in there hiding from me?

52

I wanted to throw Christopher Chatman down to the grass, yank his hands behind him, and cuff his wrists with a pair of steel bracelets. Then, I wanted to drive him downtown to Men's Central Jail. But first I needed an arrest warrant explaining why he needed to be abandoned in the dankest prison cell in hell, the one with the broken toilet and weevils in the oatmeal. Unfortunately, there was no "*Nobody wants to kill your wife and kids except you*" box to check on a warrant-request form.

Colin and I huffed back to the Crown Vic.

"He did it," Colin declared as though he had found the God particle in his container of Tic Tacs. "I didn't believe it at first, but he did it."

"Told you." I pulled away from the curb. "You see his face when I mentioned Juliet's cancer? Looked like he was gonna vomit all over my shoes."

"Suicide attempt at the Bellagio?" Colin said. "Really?"

"The scary thing is," I said, "is that he's drinking his own Kool-Aid. By now, him trying to kill himself *is* the truth. He's a sick fucker."

"What now?"

"You wanted to know what he does all day? Let's find out." I pulled two blocks away from the Oliver house and parked.

"Criminals are stupid," Colin stated.

"And we will catch him," I said, "*because* he is stupid."

Mantras for homicide detectives.

And we held fast to those thoughts, clutching them like fat kids clutching cupcakes.

"But *how* did he do it?" Colin wondered. "How did he start the fire?"

My phone rang, and I answered without checking the caller.

"I don't have a long time to talk." It was Adeline St. Lawrence. "I'm at the mortuary with Momma and Daddy Weatherbee."

"No problem, Addy. I'm just—"

"Did you get my package?"

"What package?"

She sighed with irritation. "I hired a messenger to bring you a manila envelope the other day. It was filled with copies of checks and a banking deposit slip."

Sharpness, like thousands of tiny razor blades, traveled up my left arm. "Peggy Tanner, Sol Hirsch—"

"Mm-hmm," she said. "Juliet gave them to me a few weeks ago. She wanted me to keep them just in case Christopher did something to her. And I guess he has."

Sarah Oliver's gray Infiniti SUV pulled out of the driveway. Christopher Chatman sat behind the steering wheel. He turned right, away from me.

I waited until he made a left at the end of the block, then started my tail. We wound our way down the hill, passing brown nannies pushing pink babies in high-end strollers. At the bottom of the hill, Chatman made a left, away from the airport. At Jefferson Boulevard, he made a right. He drove for a mile, then turned left onto the 405 freeway heading north.

Seconds later, I also zoomed onto the 405.

Miracle of miracles, the busiest freeway in the world wasn't packed with cars and trucks.

Good for Chatman.

Not so good for me—I could now be spotted. So I hung back and hid behind a UPS van in the middle lane.

And we drove. Past the 10 freeway interchange, past the exits for UCLA and the Getty museum. Over the hill we went, into the valley, less brown today because of the cold, the breeze, and its being Saturday.

The gray Infiniti drifted to the right lane.

"He's getting on the 101," Colin said.

Ten minutes later, Christopher Chatman exited Rancho Road and turned right onto Thousand Oaks Boulevard.

We passed a cigar shop, an optometrist, and a sushi bar. As we neared a shopping mall, he turned left into the lot of an EZ-Mail office store.

I passed the business and parked on the street.

Colin snapped pictures with his phone.

Chatman lumbered into the store. He had changed out of his tracksuit and now wore tan chinos and a blue Oxford shirt, his injured arm still trapped in that sling.

We sat and waited.

Chatman returned to the SUV with two stationery boxes in his good arm. He slipped the boxes onto the passenger seat, then returned to the store. In less than a minute, he was back at the car with envelopes in his hand.

I grabbed the case file from the backseat and peeked at Peggy Tanner's prospectus: PO Box 8181, Thousand Oaks.

Chatman climbed behind the steering wheel. He pulled back onto Thousand Oaks Boulevard, continuing east.

I left my spot and also headed east.

At Fairview Road, less than a mile away, Chatman made a right into another lot, this one belonging to Pacific Western Bank.

Colin took more pictures of Chatman entering the building.

Fifteen minutes later, the banker sped back to Thousand Oaks Boulevard, heading west and toward the freeway to Los Angeles.

"I'm going back to the mailbox place," I said, and made a U-turn on a side street.

The postal store sold envelopes, packing items, and scrapbooking materials. Gray metal mailboxes took up the entire east wall. A tiny clerk with stiff chocolate curls and a silver nose ring manned the counter. Her name tag said *Tressa*, and she couldn't take her eyes off Colin.

Colin pushed his aviators to the top of his golden head. He smiled, badged her, and crinkled those baby blues at her. "Hey, Tressa. How ya doin' today, darlin'?"

Tressa's eyes filled with cartoon hearts. "Okay, I guess."

I wandered over to the bin of tape guns.

Colin leaned on the counter. "I'm lookin' for a PO box, and maybe you can tell me if it's here." His eyes dipped to the slice of pale skin at the neck of her EZ-Mail polo shirt.

"Uh-huh," she said, barely breathing.

He gave her the mailbox number listed on the prospectus.

As the brunette tapped at her computer, Colin winked at me.

I held up a mini tape dispenser. "It's the most precious thing ever, right?"

"Okay," Tressa said. "That box is right over"—she pointed to the mailboxes near the rubber stamps and stamp pads—"it's over there."

"One more question," Colin said. "Does it belong to a guy named Chris Chatman?"

She glanced at the monitor. "Uh-huh. L.O.K.I. Consulting Services."

"Thanks, beautiful. I lied: I have one more question."

Tressa's eyelids fluttered. "Yeah?"

"Your daddy a thief?"

She blinked, confused by the question. "Is my . . . huh?"

Colin smiled. "Is your daddy a thief? Cuz he stole the sparkle from the stars and put 'em in your eyes."

I groaned and dropped the tape dispenser back into the basket.

Tressa gulped, and those heart-filled eyes of hers shimmered.

He tapped the clerk's hand. "Thanks for your help, beautiful." He gave her one last wink and strode toward the door.

53

After squeezing into one lane with three hundred other cars to pass an over-turned big rig and then slowing to a crawl as those same three hundred cars braked ever . . . so . . . *slightly* . . . to read the Amber Alert on the highway's digital message board, Colin and I reached the station at almost four o'clock.

Pepe greeted us with a box of cold Double-Doubles, even colder french fries, and warm Cokes. "You got visitors."

"Who?" I asked, my mouth filled with hamburger and potatoes.

"Juliet Chatman's parents."

I paused in midchew, then swallowed. The burger lodged in my esoph-agus, then landed in my stomach with a thud.

Colin stuffed fifteen fries into his mouth. "They been waitin' long?"

Pepe plucked a french fry from my box. "About an hour. They insisted on staying."

I sighed, then took another bite from my burger.

Colin wiped his mouth with a napkin. "Ready to have a nice little sit-down?"

"They only wanna talk to Lou," Pepe indicated.

Colin's eyebrows lifted, and his cheeks colored.

I slurped Coke for a few seconds, then sighed again. My face still ached, and my cheek was especially tight and puffy. I opened my desk drawer and found the tub of facial wipes. After removing a day's worth of dirt and sweat from my face, I grabbed a travel-sized packet of tissues and the case file, then headed to interview room 3.

The lanky old man held a black fedora in his brown hands. Neat and trim in his cocoa-colored suit, he stood as I entered. One of the two sandal-wood colognes in the air belonged to him. The woman, not as brown, but tiny as a mustard seed and put together in her tweed church skirt and pink silk blouse, remained seated. She clutched a pink rosary—Juliet's.

"We're so sorry for droppin' in unannounced," he Mississippi-drawled. His eyes flit around my face—bruised cheekbone, cut lip, tired eyes—and he frowned. "We been wantin' to talk with y'all right when we landed." He held out his large paw and we shook. "Randall Weatherbee, and this is my wife, Maris."

I took Maris's hand in mine. "I am so very sorry for your loss."

Juliet had inherited her mother's slanted eyes and sharp cheekbones.

Randall twisted the brim of his hat. "We been so . . . *confused* since all this started." His voice sounded thick and crisp like peanut brittle. "Since Ben called us that morning."

"And we was so angry," Maris spat, making anger sound like fluffed pillows scented with lavender satchels. "Cuz a whole day had gone by—"

"Wait," I said, holding up a hand. "The fire happened early Tuesday morning."

Maris lifted her chin. "And we ain't found out 'til Wednesday. I was madder than a wet hen that so much time had gone by."

"I am so sorry about that," I said, my gut twisting. "Juliet's next of kin is listed as her husband, and I thought that either he or Ben Oliver would have told you right away."

The woman rested her warm hand on my wrist. "And you're right. Christopher shoulda called us. I don't care if he was in the hospital or having dinner with the president. He shoulda called. I know that's his wife and kids, but that's our daughter and grandchildren."

"Where y'all at in the investigation?" Randall asked.

"Benji told us that y'all caught the man who burned down the house?" Maris said, twisting the rosary around her fist.

"We can't say anything about that yet," I said.

"But he the one, ain't he?" Randall asked, his eyes filled with hope. "The one who murdered . . . ?"

"We haven't made an arrest yet," I said, "but when we do, I will personally let you know. Have you talked lately with your son-in-law?"

"He says he can't say much cuz of y'all's investigation," Maris said.

"We visited with him yesterday," Randall continued, "after going to view . . ." A far-off look clouded his eyes. "He seemed . . . *flat*. No . . . emotion. Shock, probably. Sadness."

Maris gazed at her husband. "Randy's kinder than me. When we flew in from Gulfport, we drove right over to Benji's house and visited with

Christopher in that little cottage out back. We brought along some pictures of Juji and our grandbabies."

"Juji?" I asked.

Randall smiled. "That's what we call Juliet. It's silly, but . . ."

"It's cute." I smiled—my father had called me Lulu.

"We brought some lovely pictures," Maris said, "that we wanted to share with him and maybe use for the memorial." She took her husband's hand and squeezed. "This one picture I got, it's my li'l Coco, and she's in the living room and all her broken-up dolls are lined up on the couch and against the wall—"

"And we standing there in the doorway," Randall said, smiling, "lookin' at her holding a spoon to the dolls' mouths. And I say to her, 'Coco, you need some new baby-dolls.'"

"And Coco frowned and shook her head," Maris continued, "and she said, 'Poppa, just because you're sick and broken-up, you shouldn't be thrown away. Jesus wants us to heal the sick.'"

"And I just . . ." Fat tears tumbled down Randall's cheeks.

Maris rubbed his shoulder. "Randy took pictures of our little nurse, and so we thought . . . we thought we'd talk and cry with Christopher and pray and miss them and mourn them, together, like family, like . . ." She flapped her hands at her face and rocked in her seat.

"And we sittin' there," Randall said, "cryin' and rememberin', but Christopher, he really wasn't *lookin'* at the pictures. He put his eyes on 'em, but there was nothin' *there*. The engine was runnin' but nobody was driving."

"We told him that we planned to speak with you today," Maris said.

"*That's* when some life sprang into his eyes," Randall said. "He tol' us to call him afterward."

"Did he say why?" I asked.

"No," Maris said, "and that just about stirred my stew. Here we are, cryin' and carryin' on, and he care more about what we tell *you*."

"Before this week," I said, "when had been the last time you spoke with him?"

"Juji called us on Daddy's birthday," Maris recalled, "back on Thanksgiving. Then, Juji put the kids on. Cody ain't said much, but Coco read Daddy a poem she wrote. Sweet girl. After that, Christopher came on the line and we all chatted nicely. Everybody seemed so happy. But butter never did melt in that boy's mouth, bless his heart."

Randall cleared his throat. "We know that everything y'all find out will affect how Juji's insurance policies pay out."

"That's correct," I said.

"He ain't gettin' rich off my family's death," Randall muttered. "Not while I'm livin'."

I lifted an eyebrow. "You think money is what he cares about?"

Randall opened his mouth to speak but no words came.

"So do you like Christopher?" I asked.

"Years ago," Randall said, "we liked him plenty. But we didn't know him."

"Past tense," I said. "When did you *stop* liking him?"

"It wasn't like one big . . . *moment*," Randall explained. "It was like . . . it was like mold growin'. You ain't even know it's there 'til it's all over the place."

"And Juji started complaining more and more," Maris added. "And she started doin' things that wasn't healthy. All cuz of him."

"Not healthy? Like what?"

"Well, she's drinks now, for one," the woman explained. "And she stopped cooking meals for the babies, and you *know* I taught that girl how to cook. But now, McDonald's all the time. And she stopped goin' to church, and that truly worries me. Them kids, especially Cody, need to be at church."

"When was the last time you spoke to your daughter?" I asked.

"Back on Sunday," Maris answered. "She told me that she was planning to take the kids on a quick vacation, that they all needed a break, and that I wouldn't be able to reach her for a week or two. She promised to call when she got back."

"Do you know where she was going?" I asked.

The couple shook their heads.

"How did she sound when you talked with her? Did she seem upset? Had she and Christopher been arguing?"

"She sounded tired," Maris said. "I asked if he was goin' on the trip, and she laughed and told me no. She didn't say that they had been arguin', but they ain't really *argued*. No loud shoutin' or pushin'. Just this quiet . . . *hate*. Regular people, strangers, ain't able to tell when they actin' ugly to each other. Course we can. Her voice changes or she just ignores our callin'. That way, she ain't gotta pretend that everything is peachy keen."

"Our daughter is a proud woman," Randall explained.

"Did you encourage her to leave him?" I asked.

Randall dropped his head.

Maris held out her hands. "Why would we? All we saw was our daughter and our grandbabies bein' taken care of."

"Livin' in a nice house," he added. "Wearin' nice clothes and driving nice cars . . ."

"No marriage is perfect," she said.

"We thought that she loved him."

"Cuz he kept his promises—"

"And he gave her everything she ever wanted."

"*Almost* everything," Maris whispered. "Juji never felt . . . *whole*. That's what she told me." The woman squinted at the padded wall behind me. "I asked her to tell me what that meant, feeling *whole*. Sounds like some New Age voodoo to me. *Wholeness*. Even she can't put her finger on it. But she insists that she's just . . . *not whole* with him."

"And what did you say to her?" I asked.

"The last time she mentioned it, I told her to turn off *Dr. Phil* and get her behind back in a church pew. I told her that nothin' was wrong, that all wives lacked *somethin'* in their marriage. That what she was feelin' was normal. After Eve ate that apple, this became our lot in life."

I tapped my pen against my knee, ignoring that familiar internal burn that usually ignited during meals with my mother. "In other words, she needed to get over it."

Maris squared her shoulders as criticized mothers do. "Truly."

Annoyed, I leaned forward in my chair. "Tell me: what did you think of—?"

"*Him?*" Randall asked, his lip curled into a sneer.

"No," I said. "Your daughter."

Wide-eyed, Maris tried to formulate an answer but couldn't.

Randall patted his wife's knee. "Juliet's very bright."

That answer jump-started Maris. "She's talented. She coulda been a doctor if she had tried harder."

"She's very charitable. Will give the shirt off her back."

"She's prayerful. Devout."

My hands clenched tighter with each adjective. I didn't know their daughter personally, but what I did know . . . Bullshit, more bullshit, and hell no to everything they'd just said about her. There were no receipts that backed up those sweet-sounding declarations. "Mr. and Mrs. Weatherbee, I need the entire truth. The good and the not so good."

We sat in silence as the couple mulled this over.

Maris slumped inward. "She can start an argument in an empty house."

"Hard to please," Randall said as he fiddled with his hat's brim.

I nodded, envious that Juliet had had a father who had loved her and knew her and had stuck around to know that she was hard to please. A father who now mourned her death.

"Juji can be . . . *difficult*," Maris admitted. "She still supports Christopher and sticks by him. When he was flying back and forth to Las Vegas, she took care of the kids and the house without complaint. When he was buying new suits and shoes for himself, she never fussed. She always says, 'As long as the lights are on and my children have food, he can do what he'—" A sob broke from the old woman's chest. "I'm talkin' about her as though she's sitting in the next room."

Randall quickly wrapped his arm around her shoulders.

And the old woman cried until she shouted, "Could he have killed her? Did he do this? Cuz he ain't had to. She was dyin'. My baby was dyin'."

I offered the tissue packet I had brought along to the old man.

Randall handed several sheets to his wife, then pulled her back into a hug. "It's just that he ain't said those things he supposed to say, Detective Norton. He ain't said, 'I had nothing to do with this, Pop.' Or, 'I loved them and could never hurt them, Pop.' Not 'til he e-mailed me did he write those things. But he ain't *said* them yet to my face. If he innocent, why can't he *say* those things to us?"

Maris dried her tears. "But we ain't gon' ask him none of this, and we gon' keep being there for him, cuz he may just open up to us and tell us *something*. But we know him, what type of man he is. He thinks he knows how to act and what to say, but we can tell yesterday, when we was sittin' there with him, that there's somethin' *off* with him."

Her chin dipped. "She was so unhappy, and we told her to pray over it and not to divorce him. He ain't ever hit her and he ain't had different women all over the place and . . . My baby's dead. And my li'l Coco, and my Cody, my babies . . ." She hid her face in the crook of her elbow to weep.

"I ain't gon' lie to you, Detective," Randall said, fighting his own tears. "We seen the autopsy reports, and we read about Juliet having drugs in her system and that there were drugs in the babies' systems, too. We know that Juliet may have wanted to die—she was in so much pain, physically and mentally. She may have wanted to burn down that house—she truly hated that house. But her babies—" More tears rolled down his cheeks. "She would have never . . . never . . . Oh, Father God, help me." He joined in the weeping, no longer able to speak.

But I knew what he couldn't say.

Juliet would kill herself. She would even kill Christopher. But she would never murder her children.

54

Randall and Maris Weatherbee hugged me as though I were their cousin or next-door neighbor—not the cop investigating the murders of their daughter and grandchildren.

I promised to call them as soon as we made an arrest, then watched them trudge down the corridor. My heart ached for the old couple, and I wanted to ease their suffering right then, wanted to march into Lieutenant Rodriguez's office and demand an arrest warrant for Christopher Chatman. But I couldn't—I needed more. Just a little bit more.

Colin and Pepe had abandoned their desks for the evening, leaving me alone with night-shift dicks who had better things to do than sing my song of woe.

My cell phone was stuffed with voice-mail messages. Mom making sure we were still meeting at the funeral home. Syeeda and Lena offering me a bed to sleep in and martinis to drown my sorrows. The fire chief working my home fire—a guy named Kendricks—asking me to call him back. Adonis Thistle telling me that Eli Moss's alibi had checked out—his supervisor at the airport had confirmed that he had reported to work on the night before the Chatman fire and had not left until well into late Tuesday morning.

Moss didn't do it.

I texted Mom—*on my way*—then lumbered to the garage and to the Crown Vic.

It was dark out. Freed men hung around the station, trapped in clouds of cigarette smoke and the pull of jail. Across the street, the coin-op Laundromat's machines were all tumbling—fluff and fold on a Saturday night.

The Inglewood Mortuary was busier than the Laundromat. In the largest parlor, a little Hispanic boy nicknamed Junior lay in a white coffin. Eight days ago, the seven-year-old had caught an Avenues bullet in his chest as he played in his front yard. And tonight it looked like the entire neighborhood had come to the boy's viewing—from other little buzz-cut boys, also nicknamed Junior, to teens with tattooed wrists and drawn-on eyebrows to bosom-heavy *abuelitas* in rayon dresses and rosary-draped wrists.

I found my mother in the mortuary director's office. Landscapes, as well as aging shots of Los Angeles in the eighties, the era of Mayor Tom Bradley and Earvin "Magic" Johnson, hung on the walls. Mom stood at a white plaster pedestal, elegant in a poinsettia-colored sweater dress and high-heeled boots. She looked tight as she flipped through a large binder of memorial-book templates. One little tremor from a carelessly slammed door would shatter her and leave her as fine as her daughter's cremated remains.

I kissed her cool cheek. "You didn't have to come here."

She reached to stroke my face but her hand stopped short. "Gregory called me this afternoon, and he told me that . . ." Tears shimmered in her eyes as she studied my face without touching it. "You feel you have to do this *now*? Divorce him *now*?"

If she had been anyone else, I would've said, "Yes, right now. It's my life, it's my marriage, it's my timetable, I'm an adult, I do what I think is best." But she was my mother, and I backed away from her and into a chair, crumpling myself before my knees crumpled for me. "Mom," I said, sounding closer to seven years old than thirty-seven. My pulse raced as my gaze flitted from the pedestal to the funeral director's desk to the heavy drapes.

"You could've died today," she scolded. "Twice. From the fire and from that psychopath. You could've died, and yet you kick out the one other person in your life who cares enough to stick around."

"*Cares*? Did Greg tell you—?"

The office door opened.

A petite woman with honey-brown skin and lilac-colored hair wafted into the office on a scented cloud of magnolias and spearmint gum. She introduced herself as Bobbie Wallerstein, the director of the mortuary. She took a seat behind the desk and said, "The memorial service for Victoria . . . I believe you asked about New Year's Eve, eleven in the morning. Correct?"

I nodded and said, "Yes."

Then, Mom answered the remaining questions:

Yes, the service will take place here at the on-site chapel.

Yes, we will take the urn with us.

Yes, we will sprinkle Victoria's ashes at various locations around the city.

I wrote the check and handed it to Bobbie Wallerstein, wondering if my bank would call because that handwriting on the check . . . whose handwriting was that? *Mrs. Norton, someone just wrote a check payable to Inglewood Mortuary. We placed a hold on it and our Fraudulent Activity department will be contacting you soon.*

I would explain to that customer-service rep that an ice queen and a fairy with purple hair had watched me write, that I was just weeks away from memorializing my dead sister, days away from watching her ashes ride the wind and drift away from me, forever this time.

And then we were done, and my mother and I walked to the parking lot in silence.

A kiss on my cheek, a "call me in the morning," and Mom climbed into her Honda.

Once I could no longer see the Accord's brake lights, I wandered back to my car.

Don't know why I drove to the Chatman house.

Don't know why I approached the man who was already standing there.

Christopher Chatman had changed back into his blue tracksuit. He stood on the curb, his gaze trained on the destroyed house.

After five days of sadness, Christmas had returned to Don Mateo Drive. Jewel-colored and decorated Christmas trees twinkled in almost every living room window. But not in the Moss house. And not at the Chatman house, either.

On a Saturday just a week ago, a girl in a soccer uniform had played with her American Girl doll on that porch. A boy, angry and hormonal, sat in the living room with his laptop, typing messages of hate on Internet forums. A woman had opened windows, perhaps to thin out the smell of burned meat from the kitchen. And a man, her husband, their father, had pretended to be . . . normal.

"They're tearing it all down," Chatman marveled. "The only home I've ever had."

"Mr. Chatman," I said. "I spoke with—"

"I didn't come here to talk to you. I would prefer to be alone as I mourn, but since we are standing on a public curb . . ." His nostrils flared. "Since the day you walked into my life, I haven't slept. I haven't eaten. I've listened to Ben go on and on about how bright you are. If I didn't know any better, I'd think that you two had something going on."

I flinched. "A murder investigation—that's what's going on."

"Your rings are gone, Detective," he said with a smirk. "I noticed that earlier today, but thought it rude to mention in front of Detective Taggert. What happened? And did my friend have something to do with it?"

I kept my eyes on the house.

"He hasn't called you, has he? To apologize for cutting out on you last night?"

I didn't respond. But no, he had not.

"Marriage is a bitch," he lamented. "How did yours turn into such a pile of shit?"

I crossed my arms. "My personal life is not—"

"Oh, but it *is* a part of this investigation." He turned to face me. "Let me guess: All of your life, men have been nothing but dogs to you. Mean, snarling dogs who piss all over your leg and call it love. And now you can no longer separate the personal from the professional. Your bigotry—"

"*Bigotry?*"

"Yes. Your *bigotry* against me, against my maleness, is nauseating and offensive. And to be honest I'm a little disappointed. Because Ben is right— you *are* smart. I thought you would see beyond the obvious, ignore the low-hanging fruits of this tragedy, but I guess not." He shoved his hands in his pockets. "Don't think he'll throw it all away for you."

"Don't think you'll win in the end," I warned. "That you'll slip away into the night and live forever in beautiful Venezuela, living off the money you've stolen from your clients."

He shook his head. "There you go again. I tried to *save* my family that night. I literally had to be tackled to keep from possibly killing myself to save them. I even called you as soon as I could. Did I hire a defense attorney? No, I didn't. Do I regret some things? Of course. I especially regret leaving my family that night. And I wish I could've given you more names of people who had issues with me, with my wife or my son, but I honestly can't think of anyone. I did my best, Detective."

I chuckled. "Once more, but try a Russian accent this time. Even *you* don't believe you anymore."

"I talked to your boss, Lieutenant Rodriguez, just a few minutes ago. I made an appointment for tomorrow to give my DNA. Lieutenant Rodriguez will oversee the entire process tomorrow at Benjamin's house."

"I guess that's fantastic," I said. "Five days after your family died."

"You think you know everything," he spat, stepping closer to me. "That I'm nothing but one great lie. Is this a lie?" He lifted his shirt.

I stepped back, my hand on my Glock.

"Relax." He pointed to the scar on his lower back, near his right kidney. "My surgery happened. Not a lie." He dropped his shirt. "You wanna know who lied? Benjamin Oliver."

"Yeah?"

"And my wife. Wanna know what they lied about?"

"Please. Tell me."

"You're smart," he said, glaring at me. "Maybe I should let you figure it out. Or maybe I should just say that I loved Chloe just as I would had she come from me."

Something inside of me cracked, and light zigzagged through that breech. "Chloe." The only one he called by name. Never "my daughter." Not once.

A sad smile found Chatman's lips. "Want to know why I've been dragging my feet on having my DNA taken? It's because I didn't want the world to know that Chloe doesn't have my DNA. It's because I don't want the world to know that my wife was a *whore*. Oh, but then you know all of this already, don't you, *Detective*?"

He turned back to the house. "A few years ago, Chloe started looking more and more like Amelia—her eyes, the hair—and less like my son. If you don't believe me, you will have my DNA tomorrow. Compare it against Chloe's and you'll see."

He swiped his nose. "Another question: Do you know why Ben loaned me that money? Wanna take a guess?"

I gave my head the slightest shake.

He gasped. "You don't know that *either*? Well, then, I'll tell you. After keeping it a secret for so long, this year my wife started threatening Ben, and she told him that she would tell Sarah about them. And her threats worked for a while, and Ben would sneak us money to help take care of *his* daughter. We called it a loan so Sarah wouldn't know the truth. But my wife got tired of lying, and Ben . . . Well, Ben got tired of my wife. And he was truly tired of Melissa because she knew, too—she's the one who walked in on them back in 2003."

He exhaled. "One more question for you: do you really think that Sarah and my wife got along? You're a female; you know how it is between women. The whole . . . *frenemies* thing. I'll answer: they didn't get along. Sarah was sensing something between Ben and my wife, so she started following her. So if my wife had anyone to fear, it wouldn't be me. It would be Sarah Oliver."

"What are you saying?" I asked. "That the Olivers killed . . . ?"

"I'm saying: Do. Your. Job. Because, as you can see, five days in, you still know *nothing*."

55

Christopher Chatman. African American male. Born June 21, 1963. Banker. Widower. Liar. Some of what he had just told me had been lies—because that's what he did. Bees buzzed. Bears growled. Chatman lied. The rest of it was truths as thin as the twisted wisps of fog now clutching the ruined Chatman house like a child clutching her doll.

Long after Chatman had stomped away to Sarah Oliver's SUV, I stared at the house and wondered what secrets would be exposed—or not—during the trial. Finally, I shook my head. "Guess you're going in there now. Guess you wanna make sure . . ."

Make sure what?

That I'd seen and discovered and nosed about, touching everything, putting periods at the end of sentences, being a damn-good, busybody murder police woefully aware that time was not my friend.

"Detective Norton?"

The woman's voice pulled me from my cloud.

Nora Galbreath, dressed in a sequined-owl nightshirt and gray satin pajama bottoms, stood in her front doorway. She hugged herself and gazed nervously up the street. "I have something you should see."

A moment later, I stood in her den, in front of a wall of security monitors. Her husband, Micah, stood beside me, remote control in his hand. "I thought the fire destroyed your cameras," I said.

He shook his head. "The one closest to the Chatmans' is gone. This one's on the northern side, which is why what I'm about to show you may not be helpful." He stopped the video.

2:43 A.M., 12/11: A black-and-white shot of Don Mateo Drive.

2:45 A.M., 12/11: An Infiniti SUV parks in front of the Galbreaths' home.

My eyes widened—I couldn't see the driver, but I knew that Sarah Oliver drove a similar car.

The driver remained behind the wheel of the car, sitting . . . sitting . . .

Micah pressed FAST FORWARD and said, "Whoever it is just sits until . . ."

3:01 A.M., 12/11: Light flickers off the SUV's passenger-side window.

"The fire's started," I whispered.

3:04 A.M., 12/11: The SUV pulls away from the curb.

Face numb, I thanked the couple and accepted a disk of the video.

In tears, Nora walked me to the door. "I don't know what this means, but . . ." She covered her mouth with her hand, holding back a sob.

I hugged her—hell, I didn't know what it meant. That the Olivers started the fire, just as Christopher Chatman had implied minutes ago?

But why would they do that? And how could they set the fire—in the footage, no one had left the SUV?

As I walked back over to the Chatman property, I pulled my cell phone from my pocket to talk to someone other than myself. "I'm about to hit the Chatman place one last time, and I need you."

Colin grumbled about just getting on the freeway and going the opposite direction.

Pepe whined about just sitting down to dinner.

Luke couldn't wait to leave his house and Lupita and quickly agreed to handle another request warrant to search the Chatmans' property a second time.

Since my last visit here, something had nagged at my mind. A popcorn kernel stuck in a tooth. Couldn't figure out what that was, though. After talking with Christopher Chatman during that first interview, that mysterious thing had gained mass. My mind had continued to poke at it but couldn't push or pry it out.

Ordinary Monday night . . .

Juliet's awful cooking . . .

Strawberry milk shakes . . .

Milk shakes . . .

I called Colin again.

"Geez, Elouise," he snapped, "I can't freakin' fly there."

"When we searched the house the other day," I said, "did we ever find the vials left from Juliet's Valium prescription?"

"Don't remember loggin' in any vials."

The porch lights from Virginia Oliver's home popped on. The living room curtains fluttered. Virginia Oliver was peeking out at me with the telephone to her ear.

Who is she talking to?

Next, I called Fire Marshal Quigley about the vials.

"Right," he said, "the vics had Valium in their systems."

"We didn't find any vials in our initial search," I said. "What about you guys?"

"Nope. But if they were left in the upstairs rooms, a fire that hot would've melted them into nothing distinguishable. Just more burned-up trash."

I poked at that for a moment.

Trash.

On my phone, I scrolled through the pictures I had taken with the digital camera upon my first arrival to Don Mateo Drive.

Three trash receptacles sat at the curb of every house. In front of the Chatman house . . . no trash cans. Only fire and police vehicles.

I remembered mentioning the bins to Colin as we searched that day but . . . "We didn't search *those*." Had we even noticed the Chatmans' tubs that day? I closed my eyes and wandered the halls and bedrooms, the den, home office, and kitchen. No—I didn't see them.

I glanced down the street. *Where is Colin?*

My phone chimed.

A text from Luke. *I got the warrant signed. Sending to your car.*

I hustled back to the Crown Vic and grabbed a flashlight, latex gloves, and evidence baggies, then slunk back to the house.

I waited for Colin a few minutes more, then said, "To hell with it."

Warrant tucked into my jacket, I crept up the driveway. Glass and cockroaches crunched beneath my sneakers.

I threw a cone of light against the broken kitchen window.

Toppled-over pots of cacti. A cookbook stand. No trash cans on the service porch.

I tiptoed to the backyard, praying that a squatter—man or raccoon—had not made a home on the damp patio furniture.

Heaps of burned wooden slats. Piles of black plaster. A tower of twisted rebar.

Glass and cockroaches crunched.

But I hadn't moved from my spot.

I'm not alone.

I yanked my gun from my holster and spun around.

"Relax, it's me," Colin said, his face illuminated by my flashlight, his arms held up because he didn't want to get shot. "Watch where you're pointing that thing."

I stowed the Glock. "I'm looking for their trash cans."

He shuffled past me. "How was the funeral home?"

"Kinda dead." Then, I told him about the Galbreath's gift to the case. Colin ruffled his hair. "So . . . ?"

I shrugged. "We need to talk to Sarah and Ben Oliver."

"Maybe it was someone else's SUV."

"We won't bring up that possibility when we talk to them, *Detective*."

"Right." Then, he clicked on his flashlight and tossed light from the patio to the side of the garage. There, on the left side of Juliet's Away Place, sat three giant bins, each filled with a week's worth of grass clippings, trash, and recyclables.

"And now, we look." My skin crawled, and I covered my nose with the crook of my elbow. "They don't show *this* shit on TV."

Colin's eyes watered. "I'm gettin' cholera just lookin' at it."

"The cholera will probably clear up the syphilis."

"One can only hope."

I pointed to the stuffed black bin. "Let's try that guy first." I plucked the pair of latex gloves from my Windbreaker pocket, then lifted the top. Stink embraced me like a drunken uncle.

Colin pulled out the first trash bag and dropped it in front of me. "For you, darlin'."

"You give me the nicest things."

Rotten string beans . . . empty tub of strawberry ice cream . . . supermarket circulars . . . sticky red and white drinking straws . . .

"It's like picking through a tomb," Colin said as he scavenged through his own bag.

I plucked the straws from the refuse. "What if Chatman didn't drink a shake that night, like Juliet and the kids did? I see only three straws. What if these straws were the Valium delivery system?"

"Grind up the drug . . ."

I pointed to the empty tub of strawberry ice cream. "Put the ground-up drug in the sweetest shit known to man."

"They didn't taste it," Colin said. "With full stomachs, the drug absorbed well. Combine that with watching *A Christmas Story* for the 179th time, and, hell yeah, they'd be sleepy."

"Who made the shakes?" I asked.

"Chatman."

"We'll test the straws," I said, dropping them into a baggie. "And let's take the ice-cream tub, too."

Back to digging.

Balls of aluminum foil . . . orange juice containers . . . Lean Cuisine dinner cartons . . .

"Yahtzee," Colin called, pointing inside his trash bag.

Three orange pill vials.

The labels read "diazepam," the generic name for Valium. Each vial had been prescribed to Juliet Chatman.

Colin dropped each vial into its own bag. "We finished here?"

"Not yet," I said. "Lemme make sure that there's nothing else in here."

Empty butter tub . . . toilet paper rolls . . . small jar of petroleum jelly . . .

My stomach clenched. "Vaseline."

I opened the jar—half-empty. My hand shook as I held out the Vaseline tub.

Colin looked into the container, then gaped at me.

Yahtzee.

56

Back at Southwest, I perched at my desk while Colin paced. It was going on ten o'clock, and the room stank of puke left by a drunk driver. The noise from the sounds of police belts, handcuffs, and "I ain't done nothing wrong" threatened to make me scream and then curl into a tight ball. I was far from sleep, but my burning eyes and heavy limbs told me that I was just as far from being totally awake.

Fire Marshal Denton Quigley charged into the bureau dressed in blue jeans and a fire-department hoodie. He clutched a thick accordion file in one hand and a battered rucksack in the other. "Sure didn't expect to be here tonight," he said.

Colin pointed at me. "If it hadn't been for that nosy kid . . ."

Lieutenant Rodriguez left his office and came to stand over me with his arms crossed.

I had pulled him from poker night—he had been up a hundred dollars and had not been pleased to receive my phone call.

"Did Khan or Thistle call you?" Quigley asked me.

I shook my head. "What's up?"

"Eli Moss pled out," he said. "Admitted to setting your fire and the other fires."

"He's Burning Man?" Colin asked.

"Yup." Quigley watched me express no emotion. "Thought you'd be thrilled to hear that."

My limbs grew heavier, and I sighed.

"If that's the best you can do, then all right." He sat his file and bag on my worktable. "So why did you ask me to bring—?"

I held out the evidence bag containing the Vaseline jar. "Lint and glitter."

His eyebrow cocked.

"Back on Tuesday," I said, "we peeked in the Chatmans' dryer."

"And all this glitter shit came out," Colin said. "Like a unicorn had died in there."

"From Chloe Chatman," I added. "Girls that age wear clothes with lots of glitter on them. Anyway, I lifted the lint tray, but the lint trap was clean, even though the last load of clothes was still there."

Quigley nodded. "There shoulda been lint and glitter in the trap."

"Somebody cleaned it out," Lieutenant Rodriguez said.

"Somebody cleaned it out," I said, "and then somebody used it."

Colin blinked. "I don't get it."

"Lint burns longer than paper," Quigley explained. "There's cotton, and fiber, polyester, nylon, everything in a fluff of lint. And all of that makes a fire start easier."

"Which is why I asked you to bring some lint with you," I said with a smile. "Show Colin what we're talking about."

Quigley reached into his sack and pulled out a bag of lint. He cleared a spot on the worktable and then lit a piece of fluff with a gold lighter.

The lint quickly ignited and, just as quickly, disappeared.

"That's untreated. Now, watch this." He pulled out a small tube of petroleum jelly and squeezed a glob over a new fluff of lint. He lit the treated lint, and the Vaseline started to melt from the heat.

"The petroleum jelly helps start the fire and also lets it smolder some," Quigley explained. "Add more lint and more Vaseline, and the flame lasts longer. Put all of it in an electrical outlet, and the lint and Vaseline will catch a spark and smolder until the flames grow."

"Which means," I said, "when the wife and kids were knocked out, Chatman probably made a trailer."

"A what?" Colin asked me.

"A trail of lint. And it probably led from that bathroom outlet in between the paint cans to the hallways with all the still-wet thinner on the walls."

"And we found the vials," I told Quigley. "In the bins out back."

"What's the big deal with that?" Lieutenant Rodriguez asked me. "Of course, there'd be medicine vials in their trash. They were prescribed to one of the occupants. I bet if I went to *your* house, I'd find a vial with *your* name on it."

"And you'd find *one* vial per drug." I held up one finger. "One prescription a month. And I'd toss out the empty vial as soon as I brought home the new one. In *this* instance, the old ones weren't tossed. Why? Besides that, Juliet's doctor said she'd stopped taking the drugs back in the summer. And yet Juliet and the kids had crazy amounts of Valium in their systems."

Lieutenant Rodriguez leaned on the edge of my desk. "So?"

"*So* any fingerprints on Juliet's vials should either belong to her or to the pharmacist who initially filled the order."

"And if the fingerprints don't belong to Juliet or the pharmacist?" he asked.

"Then someone else drugged her and the kids. Which also means we've just eliminated one of our primary suspects: Juliet Chatman. It's no different than if we had found his prints on her gun. These pills were just another type of weapon."

"Chatman could've picked up the meds for her," Lieutenant Rodriguez said. "So his prints could be on the vials."

"And he handed her a pill each day without her ever touching a vial?" I asked, eyebrow cocked. "Even if he picked up her prescription as a favor, her prints should be on one of those vials, right?"

My boss nodded. "Fine. I'll put a rush on the prints."

"The prints on the Vaseline tub, too?"

"And the prints on the Vaseline tub, too."

"And process the straws?"

"And process the straws." He tapped my shoulder. "You doin' okay?"

I paused, then said, "Uh-huh."

His gray eyes searched mine. "I know what's going on."

"Yeah?"

"His Ducati. That's a beautiful bike. Art."

I squinted at him. "I won't take a tire iron to it."

"Promise?"

"Cross my heart, hope to die, and so on and so forth."

Satisfied with my promise, he and Quigley wandered back to his office and closed the door.

"So what is Chatman lookin' at?" Colin asked me.

"Arson," I said. "Three counts of murder. And if the SEC investigation is related, then murder for financial gain."

"Sounds like he's getting the needle."

"He will if California still does that kind of thing."

He glanced at his watch. "Think we'll get a print hit tonight?"

My desk phone rang. "Maybe this is them."

The caller didn't speak at first. After I said, "hello," twice, the caller said, "This is Sarah Oliver. Ben's wife."

My body went cold. "Hi."

"Hope I'm not catching you at a bad time. I know you're probably very busy right now. Although, looking at my husband's last phone calls, it seems you've been in constant contact with him beyond normal work hours."

Stunned, I paused before grabbing the recorder adapter and jamming it onto the phone. "I talked with Mr. Chatman this evening, and he told me many interesting things, some of which involves your family."

She laughed without humor. "I guess it all comes out now. I knew about Ben and Juliet."

Chatman had told the truth.

"Did you confront her about it?" I asked.

"No. But I confronted my husband. He asked for a divorce. I told him no."

"So Chloe—?"

"He showed interest in Chloe," she said. "But I told him no about that, too."

"What was there to tell him no about?"

"The girl had a father—Christopher. My money, our resources, would not be taken from Amelia just because he fucked around and got caught."

"And Juliet?"

"Was hopelessly in love with my husband," she said matter-of-factly. "And I have the e-mails to back that up. Perhaps I'll send them to you."

My heart jumped in my chest. Would they come from that mysterious Google account we'd found?

"Funny: Ben has that effect on women, where they just completely lose their way. You know this is true."

"But you never confronted her," I said, ignoring her observation.

She laughed that nasty, bitter laugh of hers. "Juliet wanted him, but she couldn't have him. She knew that. Therefore, there was nothing for she and I to discuss. Well, that's not true. That evil spawn of the devil she bore."

"No love lost on Cody Chatman, then."

"He tortured my daughter," she spat. "And now he's back in hell, where he belongs."

"Wow."

"You *obviously* are not a mother. If you were, and a teenaged boy had abused *your* daughter, you'd do anything to protect her, to punish him."

My stomach lurched. *Protect her. Punish him.* "You were pissed off at three of the four Chatmans, then." I held up one finger, even though she couldn't see it. "Juliet, for sleeping with your husband. Chloe, for being the product of that affair. And Cody, for bullying Amelia, your sick daughter." When she said nothing, I added, "Your rage is certainly understandable."

"I don't need your pity," she whispered.

I leaned forward on my desk. "You said you visited the Chatmans on the night of the fire. Right before Zumba."

Sarah said nothing for several seconds. "I did visit them, yes."

"Just that one time? Or did you come back later that night? After class?"

Silence again.

"And you took Juliet's keys that first visit," I said. "So that you could enter the house on your own. Am I right?"

I glanced at Colin, then walked onto the ledge. "I'm asking because a witness told me that you *did* return to the Chatman house that evening. The witness also told me that you were very upset with Juliet, that Cody had done something else to Amelia, and that both Juliet and Cody had reasons to fear you."

"If you're implying that I've committed a crime," Sarah said carefully, "if that's what you're doing, Detective Norton, then we have a problem."

"Did you return to the Chatman house before the fire?"

No response.

"Did you visit the upstairs bathroom when you stopped by to see if Juliet wanted to go to Zumba with you?"

Sarah Oliver snorted. "Ridiculous questions, one after the other."

Had Juliet peeked out her bedroom window that night? Had she glimpsed Sarah Oliver's SUV parked out front and so she grabbed the gun? Because she knew that Sarah had wanted to kill her?

My bladder pressed against my waistband. "I'd like you to come down to the station for a formal interview, for more ridiculous questions."

"My daughter is sick—Cody's fault. He harassed her every time she visited, and it just wore her down. Did you know that he locked Mimi and Coco out of the house last week? And he thought it was funny. She's not a regular little girl, Detective Norton. She can't handle stress like other children can."

"I understand—"

"I don't think you do," she snapped. "You wouldn't be asking me to come see you if you understood. I wasn't there last week when Cody Chatman was bullying her, but I'm here now. I will not leave her, not while she's vulnerable."

"Ben can watch her while you're here," I offered, not budging. "Shall I send a car to come get you?"

"Are you accusing me of murder?" she asked. "If so, I should call my lawyer before talking anymore to you."

"Who you should call first is your business."

She snorted. "Fine. See you soon, Detective Norton."

Sunday, December 16

57

When Lieutenant Rodriguez paged me, I was catching a nap in the cot room for much-needed slumber. Colin had been hunkered in the break room, weary-eyed and too tired to eat his breakfast burrito. Together, we plodded back to our desks. Colin dropped into his chair, and I sank into mine.

Lieutenant Rodriguez glided out of his office as though it were three in the afternoon and not three in the morning. He smiled broadly at us and waved a single sheet of paper in his hand. "Prints came back."

That yanked me awake. "And?"

He handed me the results.

Colin rolled his chair next to mine and peeked over my shoulder.

My hand flew to my heart as I studied the magnified whirls, ridges, and little pink dots. "On all three vials?"

"On all three vials," Lieutenant Rodriguez confirmed.

"Holy shit," Colin muttered. "Good job, partner. I doubted you."

"And the petroleum jelly?" I asked.

My boss sighed. "Sarah Oliver's prints are in the system from her days as a lawyer."

Chatman and Sarah had worked together to murder his family. What the *hell?*

The requests for arrest warrants took twenty minutes to complete.

A judge approving the warrants took another hour and a half.

The drive to Westchester by Colin, Lieutenant Rodriguez, and me, along with seven giants from our Violent Criminal Apprehension Team (including my favorites, Gino Walston and Ro "Samoan Ro" Matua), took only fifteen minutes.

At dawn, our convoy of Crown Vics and blacked-out Suburbans rolled silently up the hill and through twisty, tree-lined streets to arrest Christopher Chatman and Sarah Oliver for three counts of capital murder. The eastern rim of the world, edged in purples, oranges, and reds, promised a ray of sunshine before clouds rushed in to remind us that it was December 16th. We parked, careful not to slam car doors and awaken the man we had come to apprehend.

After Gino divided us into two teams—one team to apprehend Sarah Oliver, and another for Chatman—I tugged at the straps of my ballistics vest, then checked my Glock. I slowly inhaled, and my nerves loosened from their bundles.

"Ready, Lou?" Gino asked.

"Yep," I told him. "Make my dreams come true."

Gino and I led the Chatman team to the south side of Ben Oliver's house, while Samoan Ro and Lieutenant Rodriguez led the second team to the main house.

We crept past the wrought-iron gate and reached the backyard.

The early birds, mostly sparrows, were getting the worms and hopping on wet grass. A stray cat lounged near Amelia's abandoned scooter, licking its paws and washing its face.

We descended the slick flagstone steps to the cottage.

I banged on the door. "Police! Open up!"

No response.

Lieutenant Rodriguez, up at the main house, also banged on the door. "Police! Open up!"

My heart pounded as I banged the door three more times. "Police! Open up!"

Silence.

Gino twisted the doorknob.

Locked.

On a three count, my foot flew at the door's sweet spot, and the wood crunched and splintered. One more kick, and the door flew open. Gun drawn, I moved aside and let the big guys roll in.

"Anybody in there?" I shouted.

"Found him," Gino shouted back.

We rushed in and found Christopher Chatman's limp body draped across the couch. Colin and I huddled over the big cop, who was now moving Chatman to the floor.

"Looks like he tried to off himself," I said, eyeing the empty vial of Vicodin and near-empty bottle of vodka.

Samoan Ro and Lieutenant Rodriguez had run from the main house and now rushed into the cottage. "Ain't nobody in there," Samoan Ro shouted. "We checked every room. Empty."

I muttered, "Shit," then keyed the mic on my radio and called for EMT.

Chatman lay on the carpet, still not moving.

Gino pinched Chatman's nose and started CPR.

Colin took a team and canvassed the Olivers' property.

The rumble of fire trucks made lights in the houses on either side of us pop on.

Firemen hollered for us cops to leave the cottage as two red-faced EMTs shoved an endotracheal tube down Christopher Chatman's throat. They turned Chatman onto his left side, then gently slipped another tube into his mouth and down his esophagus to reach his stomach to start pumping out poison.

Once the EMTs had lifted Chatman onto a stretcher, I followed them as they rolled the man out to the front of the house.

Colin and Lieutenant Rodriguez came to stand beside me as Chatman was being loaded into the ambulance.

"It's a mess in that little house," Colin said. "Vicodin, vodka bottles, a handgun, a loaf of bread, wads of cash . . . I don't know what he was planning, if he was staying or going or throwing a party."

"I'm gonna ride with him," I told my boss and partner. "We need to find Sarah Oliver, and Chatman will wake up and he'll tell us. She may be at the hospital with her daughter, though I doubt it."

Lieutenant Rodriguez grabbed his radio and called in another crew to process the scene. Then, he called Luke and Pepe to join Samoan Ro and Gino to search for Sarah Oliver.

Before I climbed into the back of the rig, I glanced over to the Oliver house and stared at the dark first level to the upstairs bedrooms and bathroom windows. No life, nowhere.

Where were they?

58

Two one-way tickets to Caracas, Venezuela, for Sarah and Amelia Oliver," Colin said over the phone. "Their plane left at three fifty-seven this morning."

"Shit," I growled.

"And guess what else we found in the cottage?"

"Aurora Borealis."

"Close. Juliet Chatman's car keys."

I hung up and considered the jail ward at County Hospital. Injured bad guys, some wearing orange jumpsuits, others still wearing civilian clothes, sitting in plastic chairs, each suffering from a bloody condition. All were shackled to metal bars welded to the floor as they awaited stitches, bandages, and rides to jail.

"Detective Norton." An ER doc, his thick black hair in a ponytail, his last name possessing too many consonants for me to pronounce correctly on a first attempt so early in the day, came to my side. "Mr. Chatman's awake now."

"And lucid?"

"I'd say more lucid than ninety percent of the folks here," Dr. Chattopadhyay said. "We gave him charcoal to absorb the rest of the drug. And we'll keep him under observation for at least twenty-four hours. He's in five."

I strode down to exam room 5, also shackled—to wires and a tiny microphone to record the most important conversation I would have since catching this case.

Christopher Chatman lay wide awake in bed. His lips were black from the charcoal, his left hand was captured in another cast and taped up with life-saving interventions, and his right hand was handcuffed to the lift bar on the hospital bed.

I read him the Miranda, then said, "You know, I was just on my way to arrest you and Sarah Oliver this morning. For the murders of your family. But then this happened. Best-laid plans and whatnot."

Tears filled his eyes, even though his mouth lifted into a smile. "Did you arrest Sarah?"

"Your partner in crime? Nope. That's one smart lady. She's in Venezuela and you're . . . *here*. With me."

"The fire was her idea," he said. "She wanted to be sure. I would have never burned . . ."

"Down something you loved more than your family?" I cocked my head. "Which is why you chose your wife's pills."

He looked away from me.

I tsk-tsked him. "I guess this is custom for you. Women one-upping you, being cleverer than you. And so much smarter. Juliet sleeps with your best friend right under your nose. Gets pregnant. Passes Chloe off as yours for how many years?

"And then Sarah. She's pissed that her husband and your wife had this great love affair. She's pissed that Cody Chatman, *your* son, bullies her daughter. She harnesses the power of your possessive, sociopathic nuttiness to get you to help her kill your family. And *then*! I'm guessing that she steals the money you'd stolen from your clients. Talk about girl power."

He glared at me. "I'm no one's helper."

"Again: you're here and she's in South America eating empanadas." I folded my arms. "Pills. And pills that won't even kill somebody, not really. But Sarah goes hard and handles big shit like fire. I thought *I* was badass."

His eyebrows furrowed. "So you're parsing murder techniques now? One way is better than another?"

"No. Some are just wack and pointless. *Valium? Really?* Let me tell you: us cops sit around sometimes after a case, and we tell each other stories. And the way Sarah Oliver did it? And how she manipulated you? We'll be talking about her forever."

He closed his eyes and took several deep breaths.

"Tell me," I said. "What happened that night? What did Sarah do, and what did you do? Did she put the lint in the electrical outlet that night?"

"Are you really peppering me, a man just waking up from almost dying, with questions?"

"I don't need your confession."

He licked his stained lips. "Of course you do."

"Why kill Juliet, though? Why not divorce—?"

"So you're still asking questions?"

"I'm just interested in how a man can hurt an innocent—"

"Not innocent," he hissed. "My wife wronged me. And then she lied to me. Tried to humiliate me. Tried to force me to accept this girl who—"

"Tried to?" I gaped at him. "She didn't *try* to. She *did*. And that's why you're pissed and decided to play God." I cocked my head. "But why kill the kids?"

He rolled his eyes.

"Bored now?" I asked.

"Boring question."

I gave him a sad smile. "Everyone wants to be loved. But if you can't be loved, you'll be feared, right? You went Old Testament on them."

He grunted.

"So here Juliet is, thinking that Sarah has forgiven her, now they're BFFs and doing Zumba. But in reality Sarah's working with *you* to one day kill Juliet and the two children she resents."

"Your intellect *astounds* me."

I smiled. "I hear that a lot. Are you aware that Juliet knew you were stealing from your clients? Peggy Tanner. Sol Hirsch. Bill Levy. Those checks and deposit slips? Guess who gave them to me? Addy St. Lawrence. Guess who gave them to *her*?"

He blinked at me.

"Juliet knew, and so when the feds get this they'll know that Juliet knew. And they'll know that you've lied your way around Southern California for years and it all was crumbling around you. And they'll know that you and your lover—"

"Sarah isn't my lover."

"Wow. She didn't even have to *fuck* you to screw you? *And* she ends up with all of your ill-gotten gains."

"I'm many things, but stupid is not one of them." He laughed. "Last month, I took out almost all the money from that L.O.K.I. account in Venezuela."

"I have deposit slips—"

"One slip. Where are the others? In that Bankers Box you lost track of?"

The veins behind my eyeballs throbbed.

He frowned. "My private information stolen from right under your nose. How grossly irresponsible you are. All for a dog."

"How did you know about the dog?" I asked. "Were you there? Did you and Sarah . . . ?" I clamped my lips shut because I knew the answer. Of course they took the boxes.

"I can't steal something that belongs to me," he said with a lopsided smile. "So you still have . . . *nothing*."

I wanted to tell him that I had seen the tape from Vandervelde, Lansing & Gray on the morning of the fire. I wanted to tell him about the fingerprints found on the Valium vials and so much more. And I still had questions. What happened that resulted in Juliet's blood getting in his car? Was Juliet telling the 911 operator that Sarah Oliver had planned to kill her?

Chatman had a faraway look in his eyes. "Wish I was there to see Sarah walk up to the teller and try to make a withdrawal." He giggled. "I'm not totally cruel—I left her a buck seventy-five."

"And the rest?"

"The rest is buried under the big W," he said, grinning. "I also left her a note: 'If you want the remaining six million, you'll have to come back to the States.'"

I narrowed my eyes. "She may say, 'Forget the money.'"

He smirked. "You obviously don't know Sarah Oliver. Also, you're forgetting that there's something even more important to her than money. Amelia is a sickly child. Sickle-cell anemia. Sure, there are doctors over in South America, but right now their health-care system is as messed up as ours. Mimi needs care over here, so Sarah will eventually bring her back."

Chatman smiled. "If it makes you feel better, Ben didn't know—he's a brilliant attorney but refused to acknowledge that his wife and best friend hated his very existence." He shrugged. "She's probably slit his throat by now, dumped him off a bridge somewhere. Don't care. Anyway, by the time Sarah tries to sneak back into the U.S., I'll be long gone."

My face numbed. Ben was dead: somehow, I knew that. "Where will you be?" I forced myself to ask.

His smile dimmed. "It's an unspoken rule of all magicians not to reveal their secrets."

"How do I know that everything you told me is the truth? That you're the mastermind, that you left a dollar seventy-five, that a doctor and not you made that scar on your back? Hell, that your name is Christopher Chatman? How do I know?"

"Have a merry Christmas, Elouise." He sighed. "That was a lie, but you're smart—you probably know that I hope you have the most splendidly fucked-up Christmas in the history of the holiday. I'm done now. Please leave."

He wouldn't talk to me, no matter how long I stood over him, no matter how many questions I asked. Despite my jabs, he kept his face turned and his eyes closed.

For a long time, I stood in the doorway of his hospital room, letting the tape roll even in the silence, watching him sleep, a tense, wary part of me not believing that he was sleeping but believing that the handcuffs would somehow melt and then he would be free.

"Cody," he whispered.

I froze. Didn't speak and silently watched a single tear roll down his cheek.

"He wasn't supposed to . . . he was my boy." He squeezed shut his eyes and wept.

Sarah Oliver had done what Chatman had refused to do—kill his son, his blood. Which was why, according to Brooks's toxicology tests, Cody had less Valium in his system than Chloe.

And Sarah Oliver also did what Juliet couldn't do—destroy the house that Juliet had hated for so long.

As I stood there, I wished that Juliet had tried to flee that house with her children sooner. And I wished that Randall and Maris Weatherbee had pushed tradition aside to force their daughter to act. Alas, none of this happened.

The fire was burning—for twenty years, it had been burning. But Juliet didn't smell the smoke until it was too late.

It happens to many of us. For a few of us, that failure to act, that failure to *end it*, costs our lives.

It was almost eleven o'clock when I drove back to the station. I still could not figure it out, and a part of me feared that I would never completely understand the lies, the money, the murders. I knew that Christopher Chatman had been truly shocked as he'd pulled up to see his house on fire. That he *did* try to break past the barriers and the firemen to save his son—and *only* his son. Other than that, though, I feared that the Chatman case would remain a monstrous ball of string and that I would keep pulling the string but never reach the end of that spool.

As a child, I had been introduced early to the devils within men. Friends had been raped. My father had abandoned my mother, sister, and me on a Sunday morning. And my sister had been kidnapped and murdered. So when I joined the police force, I thought I had been prepared to meet the worst.

But I soon learned that no one is prepared to find the mummified remains of a forgotten aunt collapsed on the living room floor. No one is prepared to discover a bloody tub filled with a teenage girl's decapitated body parts. No one is prepared to stand over a man as he takes credit for murdering his family in spectacular fashion.

Someone has to stand there, though. Rough men, George Orwell said, who stand ready in the night to visit violence on those who would do us harm. To survive in the murder game, you had to dip your heart in molten steel. You had to pray to whoever answers prayers, and you had to believe unrelentingly in Better.

Or else . . .

A few minutes before noon, I pulled into my home garage.

Greg's Ducati was parked in its spot.

My stomach churned with dread.

He was home.

I took cautious steps inside.

The kitchen and living room were dark. A fire report completed by that arson investigator Kendricks sat on the dining room table. Christmas presents that hadn't been there before today sat beneath the tree.

I sniffed.

The scent of Friday night's fire remained.

I climbed the stairs, one by one.

In the bathroom, water pounded against the shower tiles.

I stepped into the bathroom and over a pair of jeans, a T-shirt, and size 13 Jordans.

Through the clear shower curtain, Greg's muscular figure was silhouetted in the water vapor. Soapy, white lather slipped down his body.

Arms crossed, heart pounding, I leaned against the sink. "Hey."

He stopped scrubbing and turned to face me. "Hey."

We stared at each other with nothing but the curtain between us.

In five seconds, my sneakers were off.

In ten seconds, my pants and shirt also lay in a heap on the tile.

In twenty seconds, I stood with him, naked in the shower, my mouth on his, his hands clenching my ass, my hair soaked with hot water.

He carried me from the shower and back out to the sink.

Wild breathing, trembling, clammy sweat, months and months gone by . . .

He held me tighter and tighter . . . His knees locked.

We waited until the shakes passed, and then our eyes locked.

He wiped away tears I didn't know I had cried.

Throat tight, I whispered, "Good-bye."

He kissed me. "I'll love you forever."

"I know."

He backed away from me, then slipped out the door.

I stayed on the bathroom sink, knees drawn to my chest.

His footsteps grew lighter, fainter.

The front door's alarm sensor chimed.

He was gone.

Wearing only a towel, I tiptoed down to the guest room to peek out the window.

Andrew, my brother-in-law, stood on the curb as Greg loaded suitcases into the Mazda SUV.

I retreated to the living room and lay on the couch. Still dressed in the towel, I stared at the dark television screen, seeing nothing and feeling even less. I reached for the remote controls. Turned on the television. Pressed PLAY on the DVD's remote. The title sequence of *The Poseidon Adventure*— big cruise ship, sun glinting off the ocean—filled the screen.

Right as the big wave washed over the boat, the doorbell rang.

Had Greg changed his mind?

Had *I* changed my mind?

Breathless, I hopped off the couch, ran to the foyer, and threw open the door.

The tall gentleman standing there had salt-and-pepper hair, a matching mustache and beard, and a sharp nose. His eyes dropped to my towel, and his caramel-colored skin flushed. His gaze quickly returned to my face. "Elouise?"

The lit fuse in my chest died, and I gave him a slight nod.

Those eyes . . . I knew those eyes.

He took a deep breath, then smiled wide. "Elouise . . . Lulu. It's Daddy."

About the Author

Rachel Howzell Hall is a writer/assistant development director at City of Hope, a national leader in cancer research and treatment. She lives in Los Angeles.